An Armada Three-in-One

Three Great
Hardy Boys® Mysteries

Rupert

906

if found,
please return

Junior House
Amplefoßth College
York.

Hardy Boys® Mysteries in Armada

* For contractual reasons, Armada has been obliged to publish from No. 57 onwards before publishing Nos. 40-56. These missing numbers will be published as soon as possible.

IMPRIMÉ EN FRANCE

And Whale
Adventure

The Hardy Boys® in
57 Night of the Werewolf
58 The Mystery of the Samurai Sword
59 The Pentagon Spy

Franklin W. Dixon

Armada

This Armada *Hardy Boys*® *Three-in-One* was
first published in the U.K. in Armada in 1985
by Fontana Paperbacks,
8 Grafton Street, London W1X 3LA.

Armada is an imprint of Fontana Paperbacks,
a division of the Collins Publishing Group.

Published pursuant to agreement with Simon & Schuster Inc.

Printed in Great Britain by
William Collins Sons & Co. Ltd., Glasgow.

CONDITIONS OF SALE
This book is sold subject to the condition
that is shall not, by way of trade or otherwise,
be lent, re-sold, hired out or otherwise circulated
without the publisher's prior consent in any form of
binding or cover other than that in which it is
published and without a similar condition
including this condition being imposed
on the subsequent purchaser.

1
Night of the
Werewolf

The Hardy Boys® in
Night of the Werewolf

Night of the Werewolf
was first published in the U.K. in a single volume
in hardback in 1980 by Angus & Robertson Ltd.,
and in Armada in 1981
by Fontana Paperbacks,
8 Grafton Street, London W1X 3LA.

© 1979 Stratemeyer Syndicate.

Contents

1

The Glowing Beast

"Oh, oh! Look who's here," said Frank Hardy. "Mountain Man himself."

"Man Mountain, you mean," quipped his brother, Joe.

It was Saturday evening, and the Hardys were munching pizzas in the Bayport Diner with their dates, Callie Shaw and Iola Morton. Iola's tubby brother Chet and lanky Biff Hooper had just walked in and came to their table.

"Boy, you've got to see that scene where Lobo Jack fights a bear on the edge of a cliff!" Chet exclaimed, his moonface alight with excitement.

"Don't tell me you saw that movie about the Rocky Mountain trappers again!" Joe groaned and the girls giggled. "What is this, the tenth time?"

11

Before Chet could bore them with more breathless scenes, the Hardys paid their bill and the group left. They were halfway across the parking lot when Iola gasped in fear.

"Good grief! What's that?"

The Bayport Diner lay on the edge of town and was bordered by a patch of woods. Iola pointed to a weird-looking creature bounding out from among the trees. *It was a snarling, wolflike beast whose fur glowed in the dark!*

"Watch out!" Frank cried. "That critter means business!"

Callie screamed in alarm as she saw the animal charging straight toward them, its fangs bared ferociously. The beast would be upon them before they could either reach the safety of the Hardys' car or retreat into the diner!

"Get behind us!" Joe shouted to the girls; then he and Frank thrust out their arms to fend off the expected attack.

Luckily Callie's scream had been heard and their plight seen from inside the diner. Chet, Biff, and several others dashed out to help.

"Beat it, you!" Biff bellowed, and the others joined in the outcry, yelling and waving their arms.

The glowing wolf-creature stopped short with a deep-throated growl, evidently startled by the noisy outburst from the young people. Then it turned and ran back into the woods.

"Wow! My legs were ready to give way," Iola confessed, clinging to Joe's arm. She and Callie were both pale with fright.

"What *was* that thing?" Chet asked as he hurried up to them.

"I've no idea," said Frank, "but I sure intend to find out."

He and Joe picked up flashlights from their car and were about to head into the woods when Callie called out anxiously, "Wait! Where are you going?"

"That brute could be dangerous!" a man from the diner added.

"Don't worry, we'll keep our distance," Joe replied. "We just want to see where it came from."

Blond, seventeen-year-old Joe Hardy and his dark-haired older brother, Frank, were the sons of famed private detective Fenton Hardy, who had once been a crack investigator on the New York City police force.

The two young sleuths never could resist a mystery, and the weird creature who had come streaking out of the darkness at them posed too great a challenge to pass up. Their father had taught them never to take foolish chances, but they felt the glare of their flashlight beams away from the diner would dazzle their quarry enough to keep it from attacking.

The phantom beast had disappeared among the trees and underbrush. Cautiously, the Hardys pressed forward, moving their flashlights to and fro and keeping their eyes peeled for a glimpse of its glowing fur.

14

"Maybe it veered off in a different direction," Joe conjectured.

"No, it went this way," Frank said. "Look at this freshly broken shrubbery. The stalks are still moist."

"But how could it vanish so fast? That fur alone would give it away at quite a distance."

"I know. I can't figure it out, either. If we found any of its hairs that brushed off on trees around here, we could take them back to the lab and examine them under a microscope."

"That's an idea! It might give us a clue to—," Joe broke off as his brother raised a hand for silence.

"Sounds like Chet calling us," said the older Hardy boy. The two listened.

Sure enough, their friend's yell from the parking lot was repeated. "Come back here, Frank and Joe!"

The Hardys retreated through the woods in the direction of the diner. Chet was leaning against their car with Biff and the girls standing next to him.

"What's up?" Frank asked.

"You got a radio call." Chet pointed to a red light blinking on the dashboard.

Frank opened the door and slipped behind the wheel. He flicked a switch on the specially licensed radio transceiver mounted under their instrument panel.

"H-1 here," he spoke into the hand mike. "Come in, please."

"G calling," crackled a voice from the speaker. "Do you read me?"

"Loud and clear, Aunt Gertrude. Anything wrong?"

"Yes. Customer's here and no one's minding the store."

"Customer? You mean a client?"

"Do I have to spell it out?" his aunt replied tartly.

"Must be a new case for Dad," murmured Joe, who was standing at the car door, listening in.

"Who is it, Aunt Gertrude?" Frank inquired into the mike. "Any idea what the problem is?"

"Come home and find out," was the withering response. "I know better than to discuss cases over the air, and so should you!"

"Right you are, Aunty." Frank chuckled wryly.

"As always," Joe muttered with a grin.

"We'll start back as soon as we take the girls home," Frank added and signed off.

"We can drop Callie off if it's something urgent," Chet offered.

"Of course they can, and don't worry about it," Iola said with an understanding smile as Joe started to apologize for ending the evening so abruptly.

Both the cute, pixie-faced girl and blonde, brown-eyed Callie Shaw, who was Frank's date, said good-by to the Hardys and walked off with Biff and Chet.

"Something should be done about that wolf-dog, or whatever it was," Frank said with a worried frown before starting the car.

Nick Pappadopolos, the shirt-sleeved proprietor of the diner, who had been talking to several people in

16

the parking lot, walked up to the group and overheard the remark.

"I'll take care of it," he promised. "I'll call the pound and tell 'em there's a dangerous animal loose. Who knows, it may even be rabid!"

"Thanks, Nick." Frank waved and backed out of the lot.

They were almost home when Joe said, "Frank, you forgot your jacket in the diner."

"I thought I left it in the back seat."

Joe squirmed around to look. "It's not there. You must have forgotten it."

Frank hesitated for a moment. Should he drive back and get his coat? He decided it was more important to meet the client who was waiting for them. "I'll pick it up tomorrow," he said and drove straight home.

A small red station wagon was parked in front of their white frame house on Elm Street. The boys scrutinized it quickly on their way to the garage.

Somewhat to their surprise, the unknown client turned out to be an attractive, though rather plump, teenage girl named Alena Tabor. She had curly brown hair and a fresh, apple-cheeked face.

"I didn't mean to call at such a late hour," she explained, "but I had car trouble on the way to Bayport."

"That's a shame," said Joe. "Can we help?"

"Thanks, it's fixed now. Just a broken fan belt, but it took hours getting road service."

"And now that you're here, Dad's away. I'm sorry about that," Frank said politely. "Is there anything we can do? Joe and I sometimes assist him on his cases."

"I know, and you also investigate mysteries on your own, which is why I'm here." Alena smiled. "Actually, you two are the ones I came to see. I'm the daughter of Karel Tabor."

"The architect!" Joe exclaimed, recognizing the name. "I believe Dad interviewed him recently."

Alena nodded. "Yes, in connection with that case Mr. Hardy's working on for the insurance underwriters. So we knew he would be busy. But my father thought you might help us with our problem."

"We'll sure try," Frank said. "What *is* your problem?"

"Werewolves."

The Hardys were startled. They stared at her, wide-eyed, as if not quite sure they had heard her correctly.

"You did say werewolves, didn't you?" Joe inquired.

Alena smiled. "I know, you probably think I'm crazy. But it so happens there's a tradition of werewolves in our family."

"Tell us about it," Frank said.

Alena related that the Tabors were descended from a Bohemian soldier—a native of what is now Czechoslovakia—who had come to the United States in Revolutionary War days. He had deserted from King George's hired Hessian troops, joined Washington's army, and later settled in the Mohawk Valley in northern New York.

"We still live up that way," Alena added, "in the Adirondack Mountains near Hawk River."

Joe looked puzzled. "From what Dad said, I thought your father's office was in New York City."

"It is. He commutes there every day by helicopter," Alena explained.

She said that her twenty-four-year-old brother John was also an architect and had recently graduated from college. A brilliant student, his building designs had won prizes in several competitions, and he expected to join their father's firm.

"But then he suffered a nervous breakdown from overwork," Alena went on unhappily, "and now we're wondering if he's going out of his mind."

Frank frowned. "What gave you that idea?"

"The family legend. It says that every seventh generation, some member of the Tabor family becomes a werewolf." She glanced nervously at the Hardys. "You know what a werewolf is, of course?"

"According to superstition, it's a human being who turns into a wolf, usually during the full moon every month," Joe said.

"That's right," Alena said. "And my brother and I are the seventh generation since the last reported werewolf in the Tabor family."

"You don't believe such yarns, do you?" Frank asked.

Alena shivered. "I don't know what to believe! Lately John has been behaving very strangely. And now there are stories about some awful creature

19

attacking people and livestock around Hawk River during the full moon—supposedly a werewolf with luminous fur that glows in the dark!"

"Fiddlesticks!" said Aunt Gertrude, who had been hovering in the living room after serving the young people cocoa. "Some local busybodies have probably heard of your family legend, dear."

Alena shook her head. "That's just it, they *haven't* heard it yet. We never talked about it in public. But Father mentioned it once to a magazine writer who was interviewing him. Now we're afraid someone may dig up that story."

"What exactly do you want us to do?" Joe asked.

Alena said her family owned a small cottage near Hawk River. She suggested that the Hardys drive up to the Adirondacks on Monday, bringing friends if they liked, and stay there during the ensuing full-moon period. By posing as vacationers, they could keep an eye on the situation without attracting attention or causing any gossip.

"Sounds like a great idea. We'll enjoy it," Frank said, and Joe agreed.

Just as Alena was leaving, weird howls echoed outside the house. Frank saw a look of fear pass over the girl's face. He told her to wait in the hall while he and Joe searched the area with flashlights.

Soon the boys returned. "Don't worry, no lurking werewolves," Joe reported. "Come on, we'll walk you to your car."

Alena smiled with relief. A few minutes later, she drove off and the boys returned to the house. Frank switched on the electronic alarm system before everyone settled down for the night.

"What do you make of this werewolf story?" he asked his brother later in their room.

"Don't know," Joe replied, pulling off his T-shirt. "Funny coincidence, that glowing wolf-dog turning up at the diner. But I think it's just as wise we didn't mention it to Alena, or to Aunt Gertrude or Mother, for that matter."

"Check," Frank agreed.

Some time later, the boys awoke with a start from the sound of a gunshot. It was followed instantly by a heavy thud at the front of their house!

2

A Silver Clue

Frank and Joe were out of bed in a jiffy, hastily flinging on clothes.

"Where'd that loud thump come from?" Joe asked excitedly, tugging on his jeans.

"Our front door, I think!" Frank replied.

They were met in the hallway by their mother and Aunt Gertrude, both in night robes, their aunt with her hair pinned up in curlers.

"One of you call the police, please!" Frank suggested as he and Joe hurried downstairs.

"What about you two?" Mrs. Hardy asked as the women followed anxiously.

"Don't be foolish!" Gertrude Hardy scolded her nephews. "If you go out the front door, you may be making targets of yourselves."

"Smart thinking, Aunty," Joe agreed. "We'll use a window instead."

He and Frank squirmed out a side window in case either the front or back door was being covered by the unknown enemy. Splitting up, they searched the grounds cautiously, only to meet again ten minutes later. Neither had sighted any intruder.

Just then they heard the front door open, and their aunt, who had been watching them through the window, called out, "The phone's dead!"

"No wonder, the line's been cut," Joe reported after picking out the dangling wire with his flashlight.

"I'll go find a police car or a public phone booth," Frank said. "You stay with Mom and Aunt Gertrude, Joe."

He quickly backed their car out of the garage and headed for the nearest storefront street. After beaming out a call over the police waveband, he soon sighted a responding prowl car and guided the officers to the Hardy house.

When they arrived, Joe was busy with a knife at the front door. "You were right, Frank," he reported. "Look what I dug out of the wood!" He held up a small, gleaming lump of metal.

"That looks like silver," exclaimed one of the policemen. He stared at the Hardys. "You mean this was fired into your front door?"

Frank nodded.

"Seems as if you have a new enemy," the other officer added.

23

Frank shrugged. "Or an old one. Who knows?"

The two patrolmen promised to cruise around the area, keeping a sharp lookout for suspicious characters. Later they would take the bullet to the police lab for ballistic examination.

As they drove off, Joe glanced at his brother. "A silver bullet! You know what that means?"

"You bet I do! According to superstition, that's the only kind that will kill a werewolf!"

"Boy, I wouldn't believe this if I heard it on the news," said Joe. "Do you suppose it means someone in town really thinks a werewolf is haunting Bayport?"

"Could be," Frank mused. "It could also mean that someone's warning us not to meddle in the Tabor case."

Even though the next day was Sunday, the telephone company sent out a special repairman to reconnect the Hardys' line. Meanwhile, Frank and Joe went to church with their mother and aunt. Afterwards they drove to the Morton farm, where they found Chet building a birchbark canoe.

The stout youth was stripped to the waist and perspiring freely in the hot August sunshine. He struggled to shape a huge strip of bark to a framework of cedar ribs and gunwales fitted around maple thwarts.

"Hey, not bad," Joe said admiringly.

"Except for one thing," Frank pointed out.

Chet shot him a peevish glance. "What's that?"

"You're supposed to shape the skin first and fit the ribs inside it. At least that was the Indian way."

"Listen! I know what I'm doing," said Chet, puffing and grunting.

"You'd better." Joe grinned. "You might just have to demonstrate that thing to us on a chilly mountain river before long."

"What do you mean?"

"We're going to a cottage in the Adirondacks for a week or two and you're invited to tag along," Frank replied. "Want to come?"

A dazzling smile burst over Chet's chubby face. "Wow! Do I!" he exclaimed, releasing his pressure on the birchbark.

Next moment he toppled over backwards as the tough, curling bark flapped back, knocking him galley-west. Roaring with laughter at Chet's surprised look, Frank and Joe helped him wrestle the birchbark back in place and secure it temporarily with clamps.

"I've been soaking that stuff since breakfast," their roly-poly pal complained, "but it dries out faster than I get it on."

Chet's usual good humor soon returned as he thought about their upcoming trip to the Adirondacks. "How soon do we leave?" he asked.

"Tomorrow morning," Frank responded. "Can you be ready by then?"

"You bet! This'll really give me a chance to show you how those old mountain men used to live out in the wilderness!"

"I can hardly wait." Joe chuckled.

"Don't worry, you'll see," Chet boasted. "Which reminds me. I've got something that belongs to one of you."

He trotted off to the front porch of the Morton farmhouse and returned with a lightweight jacket, which he tossed to Frank.

"That's the one I left at the diner last night," Frank said. "How'd you find it?"

"I didn't," Chet replied. "Someone else did."

"Who was it?"

"Search me. He never mentioned his name. I tried to call you last night but couldn't get through."

"Someone cut our phone line," Joe explained.

"No kidding!" Chet said that he had received a late call from a man who supposedly also failed to reach the Hardys by telephone. "The guy spotted your name tag in the jacket, Frank. When he couldn't get you, Nick Pappadopolos remembered seeing us all at the diner together and suggested he call me."

"What happened then?" Frank asked.

"I told him I knew you, so he said he'd drop off the jacket."

"Mighty nice of him," Joe remarked.

"Sure was. And this must belong to him," said Frank, picking up a key which had fallen out of a pocket when Chet tossed the jacket to him.

"How come?" his stout chum asked.

"It's not mine, and I'm sure it wasn't in my pocket last night."

"He must've stuck it in there absentmindedly," said Joe. "Tough break. He may be looking all over for that key. We ought to give it back to him. What'd the guy look like, Chet?"

"I don't know. He never rang our bell, so I didn't meet him. Probably came by late and didn't want to disturb us. I found the jacket lying on the porch this morning."

Frank, wanting to return the favor, decided to drive to the diner and see if Nick Pappadopolos knew the man who had found his jacket. To the Hardys' surprise, Nick had no idea what Frank was talking about.

"Nobody was in here last night asking about you," the proprietor declared, "and I never told anyone Chet Morton was a buddy of yours."

Frank and Joe looked at each other with puzzled frowns.

"Oh, Nick, sorry we bothered you," Frank said. Then the Hardys returned to the parking lot and climbed in their car.

"How do you figure it, Frank?" Joe asked. "Do you suppose Chet got the story wrong?"

Frank shook his head. "I doubt it. But there's something fishy somewhere."

"Like the way your jacket turned up on Chet's front porch, for instance."

The older Hardy boy nodded. "Maybe the guy didn't want to be seen."

"Let's have another look at that key, Frank." Joe took

27

it from his brother and examined it. The key was small and flat, with one serrated edge, and was stamped with the number 27.

"Looks like the kind that might open an airport locker," Joe suggested.

"Yes, except that airports don't usually have rental lockers anymore," Frank pointed out. "Too easy for terrorists to stash bombs in them."

"Wait a minute! The Bayport bus station still has lockers!"

"Right. Want to check them out?"

"Why not?"

On their way, Frank braked for a traffic light and pulled alongside a pickup truck belonging to the Prito Construction Company. Their pal, Tony Prito, was at the wheel with Biff Hooper beside him.

"What's up?" the muscular, dark-haired youth inquired through the open window.

The Hardys told them about their trip to the Adirondacks and invited their friends to come along.

"Boy, I wish I could," Tony said wistfully. "But Dad's keeping me too busy."

"Same here," said Biff. "I've been working at that construction site on Ridge Road."

"If the job gets done fast enough, we could come up for a day or two later on," Tony added.

"What's cooking with you Hardys?" Biff asked. "Another mystery?"

"Sort of, but just a small one right now." Frank

showed them the key and related the odd way in which his jacket had turned up on the Mortons' front porch after the stranger's call to Chet.

"But why would the guy give Chet a phony story?" Biff inquired.

"That's what we'd like to know," Joe replied. "If we can get a lead on who he is, maybe we can find out."

Tony and Biff were in no hurry. They had been checking the Ridge Road construction site to make sure no vandalism was taking place over the weekend. So they decided to accompany the Hardys to the bus station.

Joe's hunch was borne out when the key proved to fit locker number 27. Frank opened the door. A wrapped package lay inside.

"Any name or address on it?" Joe asked eagerly.

"Let's see." Frank lifted out the package to examine it. Suddenly he held it toward his ear as if to listen. "It's ticking!" he announced tensely.

"Leaping lizards!" Joe gasped. "It must be a bomb!"

3

Weird Lore

The youths stared at each other with stunned expressions. The package in Frank's hands might be laden with death and destruction!

"Better call the police!" Tony croaked.

"No time," said Frank. "When I moved this out of the locker, I may have armed the detonator and started the ticking." He glanced frantically at the Sunday travelers milling about the station.

"At least get it outside!" urged Joe.

"Right!" said Frank, who was already hurrying toward the entrance. "The problem is where to dump it!"

As the four dashed out to the street, Tony had an idea. "There's an old brick warehouse in the next block that's ready for the wrecker's ball!" he suggested.

"Just the place!" Frank agreed.

The boys ran desperately toward the warehouse, aware that with every passing second the package in Frank's hands might be ticking closer to disaster. As they reached the building, Frank gave a mighty heave and hurled the package into the fenced-off loading dock area.

Ka-booom! It hit the ground and exploded in a cloud of smoke and small flying debris. The blast was loud, but the concussion was not great. When the smoke cleared, there was no visible sign of damage to the building. Passersby paused in alarm and looked at the boys suspiciously, then hurried on about their business.

All four youths were pale and perspiring, but their faces now wore relieved smiles.

"Wow!" said Biff in a small voice. "The jolt when it hit the ground must have set off the bomb!"

"Thank goodness it was just a small one," Tony declared.

"It still wouldn't have done Frank any good if he'd been holding it," Joe pointed out. "Or the rest of us, either."

The next morning Frank and Joe stopped at the Morton farmhouse to pick up Chet. When they got underway again half an hour later, the car was loaded down with luggage and assorted gear, including their pal's handcrafted bow and a quiverful of arrows. In addition, his unfinished canoe was strapped to the car roof.

"For crying out loud, Chet," Joe complained, "we're only going to a cottage for a week, not on a full-scale wilderness expedition!"

"Listen, when you head into rugged country like the Adirondacks, you have to be ready for anything," retorted their stout chum, who was wedged into the car's narrow back seat. "I aim to be prepared!"

Their route from the Morton farm led back through Bayport. On the way, Joe suggested stopping at the library to see if they could find a book dealing with the subject of werewolves.

"What do you want that for?" Chet asked curiously.

"That's why we're going up to the Adirondacks. To hunt down a werewolf!" Joe explained.

"A *werewolf!*" Chet exclaimed, bug-eyed. "Are you serious?"

"Sure, it's a new case we're on," said Joe. "Didn't we mention that?"

"No, you didn't! If I'd known you were going to be tangling with some bloodthirsty wolfman nut, I'd have thought twice about coming!"

"What's to be scared of?" Frank teased. "If you run into him, the worst he can do is sink his fangs into your throat."

"Very funny," Chet said sourly. "Har-de-har-har with the Hardy boys."

"That's the spirit." Frank chuckled. "If the werewolf gets you, at least you'll die laughing!"

At the library, the Hardys consulted Miss Shannon at

the reference desk. She went straight to a bookshelf of new editions and brought back a volume with a colorful wrapper.

"This may be just what you're looking for," she advised. "It's a recent best-seller by a writer named Desmond Quorn. He's compiled all sorts of folklore and superstitions about werewolves, and he describes a number of alleged cases from old records."

"Sounds perfect," Frank said. "Thanks a lot."

After checking out the book, the Hardys rejoined their roly-poly chum, who was waiting sulkily in the car.

"Cheer up, Chet," said Joe. "Just one more stop."

"Now where?"

"Police headquarters."

"Oh, no!" Chet groaned. "Don't tell me there's even more trouble ahead, besides werewolves?"

"Nothing serious," Joe replied, suppressing a grin. "Just want to see about a bullet I dug out of our front door Saturday night."

"I knew it! That means there's a gunman after you guys, probably some mobster on the FBI's Most Wanted List!"

"Why do you suppose we brought *you* along?" Joe said with a straight face. "If there's a car chase and the bullets start flying, we'll have a shield of blubber protecting us in the back seat!"

Even Frank could not help laughing as he saw Chet's expression in the rearview mirror. But despite Joe's teasing, both Hardys knew there was no better friend in a tight spot than Chet Morton.

At headquarters they spoke to Chief Collig, a long-time acquaintance of their father's. He had a technician bring the bullet to his office from the ballistics lab.

"What can you tell us?" Frank inquired.

"It's definitely silver," the lab officer said. "Hand cast in a mold, I imagine."

"Enough marks to identify the gun?"

"No way. It's too mashed up. But my guess, judging from the weight of the slug, would be that it was fired from a .22."

"Probably some nut heard about the spooky dog you fellows sighted at the diner the other night," Chief Collig suggested. "So he got the wild notion there was a werewolf haunting Bayport and figured he might scare it off with a silver bullet."

"Could be," Frank murmured doubtfully.

"Anyhow, we'll keep an eye out for any local mental cases or oddballs on the loose with a gun," the chief promised.

"Thanks. By the way, Joe and I are going away for a few days. If you could have the scout car in our neighborhood check our house now and again at night, we'd appreciate it."

"Will do!"

The Hardys drove out of town and by eleven o'clock were on the New York State Thruway, heading north to the Adirondacks.

"My stomach's hollow," Chet complained. "Couldn't we stop for a bite to eat?"

"Too early for lunch," Joe objected.

"I don't mean a full meal. Just a quick snack to keep going, like a couple of burgers and fries."

"Okay." Frank grinned, veering off the road toward a diner. "This place looks decent."

Joe took the library book on werewolves inside and looked at it while they were in a booth waiting to be served. A picture of the author, Desmond Quorn, was on the back flap of the jacket.

"It says he lives near Kingston, New York," Joe remarked. "We'll be going right by there!"

"Hm, that's a thought," Frank agreed. "He might be able to give us some useful information."

The Hardys decided to call the author from the phone booth in the diner. Frank soon found his number by dialing information. Quorn immediately recognized the Hardys by name and invited them and their friend to have lunch with him.

"Thanks, we'll be happy to, sir," Frank said.

He and Joe had nothing but root beer and let Chet polish off the hamburgers they had ordered. But by the time they reached Kingston, Chet assured them that the snack had in no way spoiled his appetite for lunch.

The author's home proved to be a lovely old Dutch Colonial farmhouse. Desmond Quorn himself was a tall, thin man with graying blond hair and horn-rimmed glasses. An interesting talker with a fund of occult lore,

35

he fascinated the boys throughout lunch with yarns and legends about vampires and werewolves.

"What's your opinion, Mr. Quorn?" Chet asked uneasily between mouthfuls of apple pie. "Are there really such things as werewolves?"

Quorn shrugged and smiled. "I neither believe nor disbelieve. It just happens to be my hobby to collect all the folklore on the subject. But werewolves have certainly been reported in many countries, and a lot of people did believe in them in olden days."

"There's a scientific word for the belief that people can turn into wolves, isn't there?" said Frank.

"Yes, the word is *lycanthropy*. There's also a disease called *porphyria*, which may lead to mental disturbance. It can cause hair to grow on the skin and even make a person so sensitive to light that he prefers to stay in the dark and go out only at night. Possibly some so-called werewolf cases were just people suffering from *porphyria*."

"Where do you dig up reports on werewolf cases?"

"In old records of European court trials, to name one source," the author explained. "You see, in the Middle Ages, werewolves were supposed to be possessed by the Devil, or to have made a pact with him. The judges who condemned people to be burned at the stake as witches sometimes had so-called werewolves put to death, too. The name werewolf, by the way, comes from Anglo-Saxon words meaning 'man-wolf'."

Desmond Quorn added that there are also a number

of old books and writings on the subject, besides the stories handed down from one generation to another. He said he had many cases in his files, collected from all these sources.

"Would you by any chance have a record of a Bohemian werewolf named Tabor?" Joe asked as they all rose from the lunch table.

Quorn flashed him a curious glance. "Of course. And how odd you should ask. It so happens that twice recently I've had occasion to look up that case."

He led the boys into his study and pulled out a file drawer. The next moment he turned around with a startled expression on his face.

"What's wrong, sir?" Frank asked.

"My data on the Tabor case!" Quorn exclaimed. "It's been stolen!"

4

Telltale Limp

The Hardys were as startled as their host. They could not help wondering if the theft had anything to do with their own investigation.

"What makes you so sure the information was stolen?" Frank asked.

"Because the papers were right here in this folder last Friday," Quorn replied. "And I haven't consulted the file since then!"

"Any idea who might have taken them?"

"Indeed I do," the author replied angrily. "I had a visitor on Friday named Julien Sorel, who also inquired about the Tabor case. He must have snitched the records from the file folder when I left the room for a few moments."

"Know anything about him?"

"Nothing, except that he spoke with a French accent. He phoned and said he had read and enjoyed my book, and asked if he could stop in to get my autograph. Then when he was here, he brought up the Tabor case."

Frank said, "Did he mention where he was from?"

Quorn hesitated. "No, but from things he said, I got the impression that he had just arrived in this country recently, perhaps as a tourist."

Their host soon recovered from his annoyance and was able to tell the Hardys the main facts of the case in question, since he had checked and discussed it only a few days earlier.

"According to legend, the Tabors bore a curse," he related. "The family was said to spawn a werewolf every seventh generation, which was roughly every two hundred years. The last case occurred in the eighteenth century, somewhere around 1760. But there are records of two previous ancestors being condemned as werewolves in the fourteenth and sixteenth centuries."

"What happened to the last one?" Joe asked.

"His name was Jan Tabor. The story goes that he was shot in the leg by a huntsman with a silver bullet one night while he was prowling about in the form of a wolf. The next morning he turned into a human again, but the huntsman spotted him because he was limping from the bullet. So his vengeful neighbors dragged him off to the town square to be tried as a werewolf."

"Wow!" Chet shuddered. "That kind of stuff gives me the creeps!"

"In those days," Quorn continued, "it was dangerous to be thought different from other people, or to get your neighbors mad at you."

"You mentioned there were two times recently when you had occasion to look up your files on the Tabors," Frank said.

Desmond Quorn nodded. "Yes, another reader called three or four months ago to inquire about them, when my book first came out. I don't think he gave me any name, or if he did, I don't remember."

After thanking their host for the pleasant lunch, the Hardys and Chet continued their journey. All three were thrilled by the magnificent scenery of the Adirondack region, a land of rugged mountains, swift rivers, sweet-smelling deep green forests and still blue lakes.

They telephoned Alena Tabor before reaching Hawk River and found her waiting for them when they arrived later that afternoon. The cottage, built of hewn logs, stood on a bank of the river. Alena came out to greet them as they pulled up in front.

"I'm so glad you could make it," she said after the Hardys had introduced Chet. "You're just in time for a party!"

"Sounds great." Joe grinned. "What sort of party?"

"A barbecue at our house. It starts at seven o'clock this evening." She gave the boys directions for getting there and added, "You'll have a chance to meet my father and brother, too."

"You said your brother's name was John, didn't you?" Frank asked.

"That's right."

"Which would be the same as the Czech name, Jan, wouldn't it?"

Alena nodded, her expression immediately turning serious. "Yes, and by a strange coincidence, that was the name of the last alleged werewolf in the Tabor family. Jan Tabor was the father of the Hessian mercenary who came to America."

She told the boys that her mother had died several years ago, and that the woman who now kept house for the Tabors was half Mohawk Indian.

"We call her Pocahontas, or just Pokey." Alena smiled. "She looks a bit stern and overpowering, but don't let her bulldoze you when you meet her. Incidentally, I'll introduce you as chums of my girlfriend in Oakville. You can pretend you're renting the cottage. That way, neither my brother nor anyone else will be suspicious of you."

"Suits us," Joe said.

The cottage was comfortably furnished with dishes and bedding, and even had a telephone. But Chet paid no attention to any of it. Instead, he looked out the window as Alena drove off in her car.

"Wow! What a knockout!" he murmured. Judging by the bashful admiration he had bestowed on her when introduced, it was apparent to the Hardys that Chet had fallen hard for the rosy-cheeked girl.

"It's her plumpness he likes," Joe whispered loudly behind his hand to Frank.

"What do you mean, plumpness?" Chet retorted. "Her dimensions are perfect!"

A red sunset was blazing behind the tall pine trees and an appetizing smell of steak was wafting from the barbecue pit when the three Bayporters arrived at the Tabor home. It was a handsome house of gray fieldstone that seemed to fit perfectly in its wilderness setting. Adjoining the house was a patio and enclosed swimming pool on one side, and a hangar for Karel Tabor's private helicopter on the other.

"What a beautiful home you have!" Frank told Alena after she had shown them around.

"My father designed it himself," she said proudly.

Mr. Tabor was a broad-shouldered man of about fifty. The boys could see that his daughter took after him in features, but unlike her, he looked rather pale and gaunt. At the moment, he was welcoming guests and keeping an eye on the sizzling beef, but as soon as everyone was served, he made it a point to draw up a camp chair near the Hardys, Alena, and Chet.

"Your father came to my office in New York not long ago, in connection with an insurance investigation," Karel Tabor told Frank and Joe, "and from all I hear, you two seem to have inherited his knack for detection."

"We've learned a lot from watching Dad and working with him," said Frank.

"Well, I certainly hope you can shed some light on this mystery that's—," the architect broke off and his expression changed to a somewhat forced smile as a slender, wiry-looking young man in a plaid flannel shirt and jeans approached. "This is my son, John," Mr. Tabor said to the Hardys and Chet.

John had the same curly brown hair and features as his father and sister, but also a tense, nervous manner. He barely seemed to register the boys' names as they were introduced and shook hands.

"You fellows must be new in these parts," he said, obviously trying to make polite conversation.

"They're friends of Magda's down in Oakville," Alena put in hastily. "They're renting our river cottage for a week or so."

"Hope you enjoy yourselves," John commented, his glance roving over the other guests and the flickering flames from the barbecue pit.

Alena urged her brother to try some of the steak and barbecue sauce. But he shrugged her suggestion aside, saying he was not hungry, and soon excused himself to wander off restlessly.

Mr. Tabor sighed and shook his head. "I wish we knew what was troubling him," he murmured as soon as John was out of earshot.

"Alena tells us he's an architect, too," Frank remarked.

The elder Tabor nodded. "Yes, and a highly gifted one, if I do say so. At any rate, he's done some apprentice work for our company during his last two years of study, and it certainly shows great promise, not to mention the prizes he's won."

"What's the name of your firm?" Joe asked.

"Chelsea Builders. It's actually a corporation with stockholders and a board of directors. I'm just the president. I didn't mean to imply that I own the firm."

"How did your son's trouble start?" said Frank.

"When he was studying for his licensing exam," Mr. Tabor replied, "he worked too hard. I'm afraid that brought on his breakdown. After a while he began to show signs of nervous exhaustion. That's when he began harking back to this old family legend about werewolves. So I persuaded him to go to a mental sanatorium for treatment, the Pine Manor Rest Home in the Catskills."

"Did that help?"

Mr. Tabor shook his head. "Frankly, no. He left the sanatorium on his own accord, and I made no objection since he showed no sign of improvement. In fact, in some ways he seemed worse. By then the fear seemed to be preying on him that he himself might be turning into a werewolf. I thought it might be better to keep his mind occupied, so I agreed that he should come home and resume his studies."

"How about the local werewolf scare, around Hawk River?" Joe put in. "When did all that start?"

"About the same time John returned. And to make matters worse, he's developed a habit of slipping out of the house at night during the full moon—at least he did during the last full-moon period. Then, when he shows up again, he can't remember where he's been or what he's been doing."

As if by common impulse, both Hardys found their glances straying upward. Darkness had fallen, and the moon shone in the black-blue sky like a round copper coin.

"I know what you're thinking, and that's exactly what I'm afraid of too—that John may start acting strangely again," Mr. Tabor said gloomily. "But I'm also afraid of saying anything or mentioning these local werewolf stories for fear of upsetting him or maybe making his delusions worse."

"But why should John expect the curse to fall on *him?*" Frank inquired. "There must be lots of other members of the Tabor family still in Europe."

"No, actually there aren't," said the architect. "The last alleged werewolf, Jan Tabor, had only one other son besides my ancestor who came to this country. Most of his descendants in the old country were wiped out during World War II. So far as I know, our only relative who still bears the family name is a distant cousin. He escaped from behind the Iron Curtain just before Czechoslovakia fell under Communist rule after the war."

The conversation seemed to have left Mr. Tabor

looking rather haggard and depressed. He plucked a bottle of pills from his pocket and excused himself to get a glass of water.

"Dad has a weak heart," Alena explained to the boys in a low, concerned voice. "This worry about John is an added strain on him."

She looked up nervously as a series of weird, comical howls split the darkness.

Arrooo-o-o—Arrooo-o-o!

"What on earth was that?" Alena exclaimed.

A figure wearing a rubber Halloween wolfman mask over his head emerged from among the trees into the circle of firelight and the glow of the patio lamps. He hobbled rapidly across the lawn and disappeared into the woods on the other side of the house.

The weird-looking intruder touched off a wave of nervous laughter among the guests, while Frank and Joe darted off in pursuit.

"Which way did he go? Can you see him?" Joe called out to his brother as they probed about in the darkness.

"Nope, not a glimpse. We should've brought flashlights. I guess we're out of luck."

As the Hardys returned to the barbecue party, Chet came to meet them, looking surprised. "What did you two get so excited about? That goofy wolfman act was just a joke."

"Like fun it was," Frank retorted. "That was an intentional dirty trick, and whoever pulled it knew all about the Tabor werewolf legend."

5

A Frightening Phantom

"What do you mean?" Chet asked with a puzzled frown.

"Didn't you notice the way the guy was limping?" said Frank.

"Not only that, he had a big reddish stain on his trouser leg," Joe put in, "as if he might have been bleeding from a gunshot wound, just like the last accused werewolf, Jan Tabor, in the 1700s!"

Chet stared at the Hardys uneasily for a moment. Then he flashed a nervous grin and tried to scoff the matter aside. "Aw, don't tell me you take that stuff seriously?"

"Of course not," Frank said. "Jan Tabor was probably just an innocent victim of hysteria, same as those poor women who were condemned in the Salem witchcraft trials in colonial days. The point is, Alena told us no one around here knew about that old legend and their family curse. But that wise guy in the wolf-man mask sure did, and he was deliberately trying to upset the Tabors!"

The boys glanced at Alena and her father, who were both shaken by the unpleasant prank.

"Where's John?" muttered Joe.

"Over there," Chet said, pointing discreetly to the refreshment table. From the expression on young Tabor's face, he seemed more nervous and keyed-up than ever.

Frank and Joe could overhear other guests nearby chattering about what had happened.

"I wish I could believe that thing that was prowling around Hawk River last month was just some joker in a rubber mask!" said one voice.

"Whatever it was that scared our dog and broke into the Barnett's henhouse had more than rubber fangs!" said another.

"And just think, it may show up again tonight! There's another full moon out!"

"How soon do you start back to school?" Joe asked Alena loudly to distract her from paying any attention to the remarks.

"Right after Labor Day," she replied.

"What school do you attend?" Chet inquired.

"A boarding school in eastern New York."

"Hi you! John!" shouted a bellowing but evidently female voice suddenly. "Phone call!"

The boys were startled, as much by the sight of the speaker as by the sheer booming volume of her voice. She was a huge woman, with black braids hanging down on each side of her coppery-skinned face, and was clad in a shapeless brown sweater pulled over a bright red-and-yellow gingham housedress.

"That's Pocahontas." Alena giggled, seeing the Hardys' and Chet's stunned expressions. "She's our cook and housekeeper, not to say general boss lady of the establishment; at least she would be if we gave her half a chance!"

John Tabor followed her meekly into the house. When he came out again a few minutes later, Frank and Joe noticed that he seemed strangely silent and withdrawn. He did not even reply when one of the guests spoke to him.

The party broke up around ten o'clock.

"Did you see how John was acting after he got that phone call?" Frank remarked to his brother as the boys drove back to the cottage.

"I'll say I did! He was walking around like a zombie."

Chet was ready to change into pajamas and flop down on his bunk, to recuperate from their exhausting trip from Bayport, followed by the open-air barbecue.

But Joe stopped him. "Hey! Where do you think you're going?"

"To bed, where else?"

"Guess again, pal. Our evening hasn't even started yet."

Chet stared in heavy-lidded, open-mouthed dismay. "What do you mean, it hasn't even started? I'm ready to hit the hay. Aren't you?"

"Tell him, Frank."

The older Hardy slapped Chet on the shoulder. "We could use some shut-eye, all right. But we've got other plans and we need your help."

"How?"

"You saw that full moon," Frank replied. "Which means the werewolf could be out again tonight. Joe and I'll scout around the village, but we'd like you to keep watch outside the Tabors' house. If John doesn't come out, but the werewolf still appears, it proves John isn't the nut who's terrorizing Hawk River."

Chet's face fell, but with his usual good nature and stout-hearted gumption he agreed to the Hardys' plan.

Just then a weird, wailing sound was heard.

Chet gulped. "What was that?"

The sound came again faintly.

"Seemed like a wolf howl!" exclaimed Joe.

He and Frank dashed out of the cabin, followed less enthusiastically by Chet, but the boys could see nothing in the moonlit darkness. Nor was the sound repeated.

"Maybe it was just the wind," Frank concluded.

Shortly before eleven o'clock, the boys put on warm lumberjackets and climbed into the Hardys' car. With Joe at the wheel, they took the river road and headed toward the Tabor estate.

Parking their car in a grove of trees some distance from the drive, they approached the house on foot. The windows were not yet dark, and from time to time they could glimpse moving figures inside, one of whom was recognizable as John Tabor.

"Good. So we know he's home," Frank murmured. One by one the lights went out, and presently the whole household seemed to be wrapped in slumbering darkness.

"Okay, get settled, you brawny North Woodsman!" Joe said to Chet.

The Hardys lent their shoulders and hands to their stout chum to help him clamber up into the crotch of a tree, where he managed to prop himself firmly against the trunk. From this point he had a full view of the house.

"If John Tabor sticks his nose out, you follow him," Frank instructed Chet.

"Right. Leave him to me, fellows! If he thinks he's going to flash his fangs around Hawk River tonight without being spotted, he has another thing coming!"

Waving good-by to their friend, the Hardys started out toward the village on foot, leaving their car where it was. A breeze had sprung up, bringing a chilly hint of the crisp fall weather to come. The boys were glad they had their lumberjackets and caps as they trudged along. The mountain scenery loomed all around them, looking more magnificent than ever in the daylight.

The village of Hawk River consisted of one main business street, which ran parallel to the water, with

several side streets and unpaved dirt lanes crossing it. Beyond them the houses straggled off toward outlying farms and orchards.

Frank and Joe roved about quietly, seeing no one. They had brought flashlights, but had little need of them due to the bright full moon. Soon they heard the town-hall clock chime midnight.

"The witching hour!" Joe chuckled.

They reached the end of one of the side streets and decided to continue into more open country. Minutes later both boys stiffened as a distant howl echoed through the night, then another!

"Come on!" cried Frank. "That must be the real thing!"

They ran in the direction of the sounds and presently saw a figure dashing toward them out of the darkness. It proved to be a boy their own age, obviously scared out of his wits!

"What's the matter?" Frank called out as the youth came closer.

"I just saw a wolf back there!" the boy panted. "It came right at me, and the thing glowed in the dark!"

6

The Missing Suspect

Having seen such a beast themselves, the Hardys were not inclined to laugh at the youth's fantastic story. He was so terrified that he would have kept on running had they not each taken him by an arm and calmed him.

"Look, no werewolf's going to get you," Joe assured him. "Not if we stick together. Whatever the thing is, it'll think twice before tackling all of us!"

To back up his promise, he broke off some thick branches from a windfallen tree nearby. Keeping one as a club to protect himself, he passed out the other two to his brother and the frightened teenager, who said his name was Bob Renaud.

When no wolf creature appeared, Bob plucked up his courage and accompanied the Hardys in search of the glowing phantom. But the boys found no sign of the beast.

"It must have gone that way," Bob surmised, pointing to a fork in the road. "I dodged through the trees when I got this far, trying to shake it off, so it may have missed my trail."

"Tell us how you first sighted it," Frank asked.

"Well, I was out on a date with my girlfriend. I dropped her off at her house just after eleven-thirty and started driving home, when all of a sudden *bang!* I got a flat tire." Bob related that after pulling off the road, he had gotten out and jacked up the car in order to change the wheel.

"Then I heard a bloodcurdling wolf howl," he went on. "I looked around and saw this snarling thing coming at me, all glowing like a ghost! Boy, I'm telling you, I dropped everything and took off!" Bob shook his head, still a bit jittery at the recollection. "I hope you don't think I'm making all this up."

"Don't worry, we believe you," Frank assured him.

He and Joe escorted Bob to his car. By now, the boy had recovered his nerve, and he finished changing his tire. Then he waved good-by to the Hardys, who hurried back in the direction Bob had indicated.

"By now that critter could be a mile away," Joe mumbled.

"Maybe so, but let's keep looking," Frank urged. "It might howl again and give us an idea which way it's gone."

The words were barely out of his mouth when the breezy nighttime silence was shattered by an echoing shotgun blast. It was immediately followed by another as the unseen gunner let go his second barrel!

A startled look flashed between the Hardys. Without a word, they speeded up their pace, sprinting around a bend in the road just ahead.

A farmhouse loomed in the moonlight not far away. As Frank and Joe approached it, an angry-looking farmer burst out of the driveway gate, clutching a shotgun in one hand. He wore an old coat flung over a pair of long underwear, and rubber boots. Evidently he had pulled on the first thing that came to hand before charging out of his house.

"What happened?" Frank called out.

"That doggone werewolf!" the farmer fumed. "I heard it attacking my livestock in the barn, so I grabbed my gun and went after it!"

"You actually saw the creature?"

"You bet I did! It musta heard me comin'! Went boundin' outa the barn just as I ran through the back door toward the yard. I gave it both barrels, but the thing got away!"

"What did it look like?" Joe asked.

"Big wolf-dog! And its fur glowed fiery white. I'm not jokin', boys!"

Frank nodded. "We believe you. We just met another guy who saw it before it came here!"

"Which way did it go?" put in the younger Hardy.

"It leaped clear over this gate and went into them woods." The farmer pointed across the road.

Frank and Joe accompanied him as he probed about among the trees, lending their flashlights to the search. But the ghostly beast had disappeared. They finally said good night to the farmer and headed back to town.

A number of people in Hawk River had been wakened by the distant wolf howls. None of them, however, had glimpsed the prowling creature itself.

"I've a hunch that farmer was the last one to see it tonight," Frank remarked to his brother.

"Same here," Joe agreed. "Let's go and find out what Chet has to report."

As they approached the driveway of the Tabor estate, their ears were assailed by a strange, grating noise.

"Are you thinking what I'm thinking?" Joe asked.

"I'm afraid so," Frank replied. "But let's hope we're wrong."

Unfortunately they were not. The sound they had heard proved to be low, rumbling snores. Chet was slumped sound asleep in his snug tree perch, with his chin on his chest.

"Wake up, Strongheart!" said Joe, reaching up to tug the stout boy's ankle.

Chet twitched nervously and awoke with a violent start that almost sent him tumbling out of the tree into the arms of the Hardy boys.

"Wh-what happened?" he stuttered, clutching at the branch for support.

"Don't panic, the battle's over." Frank grinned. He and Joe related the night's sensational events.

"I don't suppose you'd know whether John Tabor sneaked out of the house?" Joe inquired.

"We-e-ell, actually no, I don't," Chet confessed shamefacedly. "But I sure didn't see any sign of him before I dozed off."

"Which was probably seconds after we left," said Frank. "I think we'd better wake up the Tabors."

Chet swung himself out of the tree and accompanied his pals up to the front door of the house. Frank decided not to ring the bell, hoping a knock or two might be less alarming.

Soon Karel Tabor himself appeared at the door. "Come in, boys," he said. "Is anything wrong?"

"The werewolf's on the prowl again, Mr. Tabor," Frank explained. "I hope you won't misunderstand our reason for coming here, but it might be a good idea to check if John's home in bed."

"Good thinking," the architect nodded. "I'm glad you came. Assuming John is upstairs, sound asleep, you fellows will be able to bear witness that he has nothing to do with this werewolf scare!"

Despite his words, the boys could tell from Mr. Tabor's expression and voice that he was far from confident that this was the case. He invited the Hardys and Chet to sit down while he went up to look in his son's room.

When he returned a few moments later, the young detectives knew at a glance that the news was bad.

"John's bed hasn't been slept in," the architect announced in a husky voice.

"That still doesn't prove he's the werewolf," Frank said, hoping to provide some comfort. "Have you any idea where he might have gone?"

"None." Mr. Tabor shook his head gloomily, not trusting himself to say any more for fear his voice might tremble.

"In that case, I'd like to wait here with Joe and Chet till he shows up," Frank suggested. "If our presence in the house won't bother you?"

"Not at all! Do stay, by all means. I'll be glad of any help you can give us."

Mr. Tabor asked Pocahontas to make coffee, and she went off with a glowering expression, shaking her head and mumbling to herself in Mohawk.

Presently Alena came down in her robe and slippers, having heard her father and the boys chatting in low voices.

"Is something wrong?" she inquired anxiously. An alarming thought flashed through her mind. "Dad," she added, "Has anything happened to John?"

Karel Tabor took his daughter's hand into his own. "He seems to have gone off somewhere, my dear," he said, "and the so-called werewolf just paid another visit to Hawk River."

"Oh, no!" Alena's face showed her distresss. "Isn't there anything we can do?"

"Nothing, except wait for John to come home."

"We don't mean to intrude," Frank said uncomfortably, "but we'd like to be on hand to question your brother when he does return."

"Of course, please stay!" Alena replied. "Dad and I appreciate having you here to help."

The atmosphere eased somewhat when Pocahontas brought in the coffee. The group chatted as well as they could under the circumstances, and the Hardys reported what had happened during their nocturnal expedition in and beyond the village.

As their vigil lengthened and time dragged by, everyone's spirits drooped. The boys found it hard to keep their eyes open. However, they snapped wide awake when, soon after three o'clock, footsteps were heard outside and the front door opened.

"It's John!" Alena cried in relief. She sprang up from her chair and hurled herself into her brother's arms.

If she expected an equally cordial response, she was doomed to disappointment. Instead of greeting his sister with a smiling remark, John merely stared at her, his face blank and expressionless. He did not return the embrace, either.

"Where on earth have you been, Son?" his father demanded.

"Where have I been?" John echoed. Dull-eyed, he raised one hand and scratched his head slowly. "Search me. I haven't the faintest idea. In fact, I don't even know where I am now."

7

Forest Castle

"John! Don't you recognize your own home?" Alena shook her brother impatiently. "Why did you go out tonight? Tell us where you've been!"

The young architect did not reply. He shrugged off her questions in silence and started toward the stairway leading up to the second floor. But Alena grabbed him by the arm.

"Dad, something's wrong with him!" she cried. "He's acting so weirdly. Oughtn't we call a doctor?"

Karel Tabor hesitated before replying. "No, I don't think so. Whatever's wrong with John, he'll probably sleep it off. Calling a doctor would only provoke scandal and gossip. Don't you think so, boys?"

"I'm afraid you're right." Frank nodded. "It might

even lead to accusations that your son was responsible for tonight's werewolf scare, if the news ever leaked out."

"John is awfully drowsy and heavy-lidded," Joe pointed out. He had risen from the sofa with his brother to examine young Tabor more closely. "I'll bet he'll drop off to sleep and tomorrow he won't even remember all this."

"Probably not," Frank agreed, opening John's eyelids more widely with his thumb and forefinger in order to check his pupils. "From what Dad's told us about such things, I don't think he's been drugged, but he looks as if he's in a trance!"

John stood limply now, staring off into the distance, utterly indifferent to, or not even aware of, what was going on around him.

The Hardys helped his father lead him upstairs and put him to bed.

Next morning at their cabin, Frank and Joe were awakened by a radio call. They had taken a special transceiver with them to ensure communications with Bayport and their father in case of an emergency. Now a red light was flashing on the set, and a repeated buzz was coming from the loudspeaker.

Joe leaped out of bed and switched on the mike and scrambler. The tuning dial had already been set to the agreed-on frequency.

"H-2 here. Come in please. Do you read me?"

"Loud and clear. F-H calling."

"Hi, Dad. What's up?"

Fenton Hardy replied that he had returned to Bayport the previous night, only to find the boys gone. "I was interested to hear about your werewolf case," he went on.

Joe filled him in quickly and added, "Mr. Tabor says he's met you at his company office."

"That's right," the famous detective replied. "I'm investigating a case for Federal Insurance Underwriters. It involves three buildings that were designed by Karel Tabor, with the actual construction work supervised by his firm, Chelsea Builders. All three have suffered recent disasters."

"Wow! That's pretty unusual, isn't it?"

"So the insurance underwriters think. They feel it stretches coincidences a bit far."

"Exactly what sort of disasters were they?"

"A fire, a gas explosion, and an apparent structural collapse."

"Hm, interesting." Joe frowned thoughtfully. "Still, all three occurrences *could* be due to accidents, couldn't they, Dad?"

"Maybe, or to poor design or sabotage, or even a plain old jinx. It's my job to find out."

"Any leads yet?"

"Nothing sufficient to act on. But while you fellows are up in the Adirondacks region, there's something you can do for me."

"Sure, Dad. Just name it."

Mr. Hardy explained that Karel Tabor was known to be working on two new projects at the moment. One was the design of a Manhattan skyscraper. The other was the restoration of an historic timbered mansion not far from Hawk River, dating back to Revolutionary days.

The private investigator gave the exact location and continued, "I'd like you and Frank to drive there and look around. See if you can spot any clues or signs of possible trouble. If anything's about to go wrong, the insurance company would like to know beforehand, not after it's too late."

"We'll check it out," Joe promised.

"Good," Mr. Hardy replied. "Incidentally, don't mention any of this to Karel Tabor."

"Understood, Dad. We won't say a word." The younger Hardy boy hesitated a moment before asking, "If there *is* anything crooked about those three building disasters, do you really think Mr. Tabor could be mixed up in it?"

"Too early to tell, Joe. At this moment I wouldn't even speculate as to why an architect or builder might want to damage his own work. But until we know more, I guess my answer would have to be yes. Tabor is under a certain amount of suspicion."

So far, the Hardys and Chet had tended to sympathize with Mr. Tabor's werewolf trouble and his son's seeming involvement in the weird mystery. The possibility that the architect might be implicated in anything unethical or criminal shocked all three boys.

As soon as breakfast was over, Frank and Joe started out in their car, leaving Chet behind to hold down the fort. After stopping for gas at Hawk River, they drove north on Route 30.

The old timbered mansion of which their father had spoken was perched on a steep, wooded hill overlooking Indian Lake. Hardhatted workmen were busy restoring it, while a number of tourists and local people stood by, watching idly.

Frank pulled off the road into a convenient parking spot. Then he and Joe got out and approached the work site.

"What a huge mansion up here in the wilderness!" Joe muttered.

"Sure is," Frank agreed. "Looks as if it's been mouldering away for a while, too. I bet they'll have quite a job restoring it."

The immense, weatherbeaten house was constructed of hand-hewn timbers, some of them visibly rotted. But the structure had obviously been built by an oldtime master craftsman.

As the boys clambered up the slope for a closer view, someone suddenly yelled in alarm. "Look out!" The Hardys turned just in time to see a long crane arm swinging overhead. A heavy balk of timber which it had been carrying was slipping out of its sling!

The next instant something struck them from behind, and both boys pitched headlong on the ground. A split second later the timber balk crashed to earth, almost on the very spot where they had been standing!

The Hardys picked themselves up breathlessly. When Joe saw what a narrow escape they had had, he let out a faint gasp.

The man who had pushed them out of the way, a tall young construction worker, was standing on the other side of the fallen timber. "You two all right?" he called.

"Yes, we're okay," said Frank, dusting himself off. "Thanks for the shove." The thought flashed through his mind that what happened might have been no accident. Perhaps one of the workmen had recognized them, or someone had found out beforehand that Fenton Hardy was sending them to the site. But Frank quickly discarded the idea of an attempt on their lives when he saw the crew's obvious concern over the matter and realized that the young workman had risked his own life to save them.

"Sorry if we got in the way," Frank apologized.

"Wasn't your fault," the man replied. "That crane sling was improperly secured. Besides, the crew should have roped off this area to keep spectators out of danger."

He signaled the crane arm back into position and helped his mates put the balk of timber into its sling again. Then, after the load had been secured, it was hoisted over to the house to replace one of the rotted structural beams.

Joe noticed the muscular young fellow's bronzed hawklike features and long dark hair, tucked up under his steel hardhat. "Are you an Indian?" he asked curiously.

"That's right." The workman grinned. "I'm Mohawk, and proud of it."

"You must be one of those 'high-steel Mohawks' we've read about," said Frank.

"Right again." The Indian explained that he and many of his fellow tribesmen had been employed on numerous construction jobs in the New York area. Experience had shown they were especially well fitted for work on skyscrapers and bridges because their superb natural sense of balance enabled them to keep their footing on high girders.

Thrusting out his hand, the Indian added, "My name's Eagle, by the way, Hank Eagle."

"I'm Frank Hardy," Frank said, returning the handshake. "And this is my brother Joe."

Hank Eagle's face took on a pleasantly surprised expression. "Hey, don't tell me you're those two detectives, the sons of Fenton Hardy?"

The boys nodded. "We are."

"Your father was at our company office not long ago, talking to my boss."

"You work for Chelsea Builders?" Joe asked.

"Sure do," said Hank. "Usually in New York City, but today I was sent out here to report on the progress of this job. Mr. Tabor knows this is my neck of the woods, and—well, I'm hoping to be an architect myself someday, if I can ever get my degree. But that takes a lot of night courses."

"Good for you," Frank said. "Stick with it."

"You fellows doing any detective work right now?" the Mohawk inquired, giving them a shrewd glance.

"Oh, in a way," Joe replied cautiously, remembering his father's admonition and trying to sound casual. "We were up here in the Adirondacks on vacation, and Dad's been investigating those disasters that happened to three other architectural projects of Mr. Tabor's, so he asked us to drop up to Indian Lake to look for any signs of trouble."

"Confidentially," Hank said, "that's why my boss sent *me* here, too. I'm sure glad to know I've got a couple of smart guys like you backing me up."

He offered to show the boys the interior of the mansion, and Frank and Joe gladly accepted. The huge building had a high balcony jutting out from the upper floor. Its original wooden supports had rotted away, so it had been propped up with temporary piling until they could be replaced. The balcony offered a breathtaking view of the green forested hillside and the vast, crystal-blue lake spread out below.

"Really beautiful!" Frank murmured, enjoying the scenery and inhaling the tangy mountain air. "Who ever built this place?"

"A British Indian agent, some time before the Revolutionary War," their Mohawk friend replied.

"Over two hundred years ago!" Joe exclaimed.

"Right." Hank nodded. "He was King George's personal envoy to the Indians in this part of America. He put up the mansion as his castle in the forest and got very buddy-buddy with all the Iroquois nations, including the Mohawks. In fact, he married a Mohawk squaw, whose brother was—well, the Iroquois nations didn't really have chiefs, but her brother was one of their tribal leaders or wise men, only younger than most. His Mohawk name, translated into English, meant 'Dark Eagle,' and he was one of my ancestors," Hank said proudly.

"No kidding!" Frank was impressed.

"Yup, my great-great-great grandfather, or something like that."

"That means the British agent who was King George's personal rep was your great-great-great granduncle."

"Which may connect you to British nobility," Joe pointed out.

Hank Eagle burst out laughing. "You can't prove it by me, but in a way you're not so far off. You see, like most of the Iroquois, the Mohawks were close allies of the British, who had helped them fight the French. So when the American Revolution came along, they sided with their old pals, the Redcoats, against the Yankee settlers. And the British were anxious to keep it that way, so they invited Dark Eagle over to London and gave him the big hello. He actually met the King and hobnobbed with all the nobility at court. According to the history books, he was good-looking and his brother-in-law, the British agent, had had him well educated, so they made quite a fuss over him."

Frank said, "But he still helped the Redcoats against our side, I presume."

"Yup, he did," Hank admitted. "He even led some of the Tory-Indian scalping raids on the American settlements. But you have to remember, those were pretty bloody times."

After the war, Hank related, Dark Eagle made peace with his Yankee enemies and inherited his brother-in-law's timber castle, which he renamed Eagle's Nest. Years later, it lapsed into ruin. Now the wooden mansion had been purchased by a wealthy buyer, who had hired the architect Karel Tabor to restore it.

"Were you raised around here?" Joe asked as the boys walked outside again.

"Sure was, in a Mohawk village near Hawk River. You'll have to visit me there sometime. My uncle's the medicine man."

Frank noticed a man watching them closely. He was elderly and wizened-looking, with dark glasses and long gray hair. When he realized he had been noticed, the stranger turned suddenly and hurried away.

"Wait a minute!" Frank called and went after him. But before he could overtake the eavesdropper, his quarry leaped into a green foreign-made car and sped off!

8

A Sinking Feeling

The man gunned his engine hard. When he took off, his rear wheels churned up a cloud of dust, and the car's back end slewed around sharply as he swung onto the paved highway. As a result, Frank was not able to spot the license number.

Disgusted, the Hardy boy returned to his brother and their Mohawk friend, Hank Eagle.

"What happened?" Joe asked.

"That fellow was eavesdropping on us," Frank said angrily. "Did you get a look at him?"

"Yes," Joe replied. "Enough to recognize him again. He had on dark glasses—sort of an oldish guy, with long gray hair curling down over his ears."

"Right." Frank had noticed a strange look pass over

71

the Indian's face on hearing the man's description. "Do you know him, Hank?"

The Mohawk shrugged. "We get a lot of people stopping by to watch us. I may have seen him before. Hard to say."

Later, after thanking their newfound friend for his interesting guided tour of the work site, the Hardys drove back to Hawk River. "Did you notice the way Hank reacted when you described that eavesdropper?" Frank asked Joe.

"I sure did—as if he was covering up something." Joe added wryly, "Something tells me he was attempting to be a poker-faced Indian, only he didn't get his poker face on fast enough."

"You think he was lying?"

"I think he was trying *not* to lie."

"Same here," Frank said thoughtfully. "But I still like him."

The Hardys arrived at the cottage around noon and found Chet working on his birchbark canoe. It lay overturned on the ground in front of the cabin.

"How're you coming along, Chet?" Joe asked.

"Great! It's almost done. Just have to finish sewing these strips of bark together, which isn't easy on the fingers, I might add."

Just then they heard the phone ringing. Frank dashed into the cabin to answer it. The caller was Alena Tabor.

"How would you boys like to come on a picnic?" she asked.

"Sounds great!" Frank replied. "When and where?"

"Soon as you're ready. I took a chance and told Pokey to pack a lunch for us." Alena suggested a quiet curving branch of the Hawk River, not far from the cottage, as a place to hold the picnic, and described a particularly pleasant spot on the riverbank where she would meet the boys.

"I'd better confess right now that I have an ulterior motive for suggesting this picnic," she added, lowering her voice. "Something has come up that you should know about. We can talk privately at this spot I've picked, without running the risk of someone snooping on our conversation."

"Smart idea. We'll be there," Frank promised.

Chet was in a dilemma when he heard about the invitation. Although eager for another chance to see his new dream girl, he was also desperately anxious to finish his canoe.

The stout youth stood scratching his head for a moment, with a look of frustration on his freckled moonface and perspiration glistening on his tubby torso. "Listen," he said finally, "you go ahead, and I'll join you as soon as I can."

"Okay," the Hardys agreed.

"Just one thing," Chet added as they turned away.

"What's that?" Joe asked.

"Don't start lunch till I get there!"

The boys hiked to the picnic spot and found Alena waiting for them on the bank of the sparkling stream with her red miniwagon parked nearby. She wore jeans and a pretty embroidered cotton blouse and was holding a copy of the local paper, the *Hawk River Herald*.

"Big news?" Joe inquired.

"Bad news, I'm afraid. At least it's not very pleasant from my family's standpoint." She handed him the paper.

Frank and Joe saw its banner headline: "ANOTHER WEREWOLF ATTACK!" But Alena pointed to a different story, splashed all over the front page. It was a lengthy report of the Tabor family's werewolf tradition, and pointed out that young Tabor was a seventh-generation descendant of the last alleged werewolf, Jan Tabor. This, the story implied, automatically made him a prime suspect in the local outbreak of lycanthropy.

"That's a shame," Frank said with a sympathetic frown when he finished reading. "But I'm not really surprised."

Alena's eyebrows went up. "What do you mean?"

"That nasty little werewolf masquerade at your barbecue yesterday evening. Whoever was wearing that outfit was limping as if he'd been shot in the leg—like your ancestor, Jan Tabor."

"So you noticed, too!"

Frank nodded. "The author of a book on werewolves told us about those oldtime cases. And if someone here at Hawk River has found out about your ancestor, and was malicious enough to play that prank last night, it seemed pretty likely the story would soon get around."

"Can you imagine how all the neighbors will be talking now?" Alena said unhappily. "If people start picking on John or he imagines they suspect him, I hate to think how he'll react. I'm afraid he'll end up in a worse state than ever!"

The Hardys tried to comfort the girl as best they could. Luckily, there was soon a distraction to take her mind off the subject. Frank and Joe saw her eyes widen, and she pointed toward the stream.

"Look!" she exclaimed.

A majestic figure clad in a buckskin hunting shirt was paddling toward them in a birchbark canoe.

"It's Chet!" Joe cried out.

Their beefy chum made a striking sight in his wilderness costume as he swung his dripping paddle from one side of the canoe to the other.

"He's even wearing an Indian headband!" Frank muttered.

Chet was sitting rigidly upright like a stalwart mountain man or impassive redskin brave. Presently he paused from paddling and struck a gazing pose, as if scanning a distant shore for a sign of friend or foe. The Hardys stifled wild chuckles, realizing their pal was doing all this to impress Alena.

Suddenly Frank frowned. "Am I seeing things, or is that canoe getting lower and lower in the water?"

"You're not seeing things," Joe confirmed. "Chet's sinking!"

Both boys realized that their pal must be feeling very

uncomfortable with the water rising higher and higher around his hips. Nevertheless, his chubby face retained its dignified expression, with no sign of panic. The only hint of anxiety was that he began paddling faster and faster.

Could he reach shore before his craft capsized? The Hardys wondered. The answer was soon apparent, however. In a few moments the canoe had sunk practically out of sight! Chet cast his dignity to the wind and tried to leap overboard. Unfortunately his foot caught on the gunwale and he plopped headfirst into the river in a resounding belly flop that sent water splashing high in the air!

The canoe corkscrewed over on one side, upending for a moment, then once again sinking from view. Chet, meanwhile, was flailing the water with his arms and legs, trying to get his bearings and strike out for shore.

Alena had run to the river's edge with Frank and Joe. "Is he all right?" she asked anxiously.

"Sure, no problem," Frank replied. "Chet's the best water polo player at Bayport High."

"But it looks as if he may lose that canoe he sweated so hard over," Joe added.

Without another word, the plump, apple-cheeked girl kicked off her rope-soled espadrilles and dove gracefully into the water.

"For crying out loud," Joe groaned. "She's making us look like backward chumps!"

Frank chuckled. "Never mind. They don't need our help."

Apparently the river was about five or six feet deep at this point. Between them, Alena and Chet managed to retrieve the canoe and haul it ashore. The Hardys helped them drag it up on the bank.

Chet was dewy-eyed with gratitude and astonishment that Alena had jumped in to help him. "That's the bravest thing I ever saw!" he blurted.

Alena smiled. "Well, I couldn't let you lose that beautiful canoe your friends say you worked so hard to make," she told him and gave him a consoling kiss on the cheek.

To Chet, all the labor he had put into his canoe had paid off beyond his wildest dreams! He never stopped smiling while he and Frank examined the damage to the craft. Joe and Alena, meanwhile, went off to lay out the picnic lunch.

"Here's your problem," Frank pointed out. "You sewed this row of stitches right in line with the way the bark splits. As a result, the bark is already starting to tear. Same down here. That's probably what caused the leaks. You should have staggered the stitch holes, or else run your stitches across the grain, so to speak."

"Guess you're right," Chet said. "But who cares?" Lowering his voice and glancing over his shoulder, he added, "Boy, hasn't Alena got spunk, though! I think she likes me a little!"

"Could be," Frank said with a straight face.

Pocahontas had packed chicken sandwiches and chocolate cake, and the picnic lunch proved to be a great success, despite the discomfort of Chet's and Alena's wet clothes. Afterwards, Frank steered the conversation back to the werewolf mystery and the feature in the *Hawk River Herald*.

"Any idea how the editor might have gotten hold of all that information?" he inquired.

Alena hesitated, her brow puckering. "As I told you, my father once mentioned it jokingly in a magazine interview—"

"What magazine?"

"*Worldweek*. I suppose the editor of the *Herald* ran across that story. I can't imagine where else he could have learned all those details," Alena said.

"We'll find out," Joe promised.

Frank nodded. "Another thing. Now that this old-time werewolf yarn has come out in the open, I think it's time Joe and I talked directly to your brother. He may know something important."

A worried look flickered over Alena's face. "Is that really necessary? Both Dad and I are afraid it may only make John's delusions worse."

"I don't see why. The very fact that Joe and I are trying to *solve* this mystery should prove to him that we don't take any stock in such superstitions, and we certainly don't believe he himself turns into a werewolf when the moon is full!"

Alena smiled. "Very well, then. How soon would you like to see John?"

"This afternoon, if possible. We can visit the *Herald* editor first and then go out to your place, that is, if your brother is in shape to talk to us. How did he act this morning, by the way?"

"He slept like a log and didn't wake up till noon. He seemed fairly normal, but apparently doesn't remember a thing about what happened last night."

Alena drove the boys back to the cabin with Chet's waterlogged canoe on top of her miniwagon. Then she went home. Meanwhile, the Hardys transferred to their own car and drove into Hawk River, leaving Chet to change into dry clothes.

They found the *Herald*'s office on the town's main street. The editor, a red-haired man named Lyle Dunn, recognized them immediately when they introduced themselves as the sons of Fenton Hardy.

"So you're up here to solve our great werewolf mystery!"

"Let's say we'd like to do whatever we can," Frank said evenly.."As you can imagine, that story you printed about the Tabor family is pretty embarrassing to them."

The editor shrugged. "We only print the news."

"What makes you so sure you got your facts right? Apparently you didn't even bother to check them out."

"Didn't need to," said Dunn. "They came from an interview with Karel Tabor himself."

Frank frowned. "You mean the one that appeared in *Worldweek* magazine?"

"Right, and confirmed by additional research data."

"Where'd you run across that?" Joe asked.

"I didn't. It was mailed to me." The editor rose from his chair, pulled a manila envelope out of a file drawer, and showed its contents to the boys. One item was a photocopy of the magazine article, and there were several pages of typewritten notes, stapled together. Each bore the printed initials, D.Q., at the top.

Joe whistled in surprise as he saw the latter. "You said these came in the mail. Who was the sender?"

"No idea. As you can see, there was no name on the envelope, or inside it, either. Just an anonymous tip."

"Well, for your information," Frank said, "that typewritten material was stolen from the author Desmond Quorn."

A faint look of alarm passed over the editor's face.

"Furthermore," Frank went on, "if readers get the impression from your story that John Tabor's responsible for these local werewolf attacks, you might be sued for libel."

"I didn't say Tabor was the werewolf!" Dunn defended himself hastily, looking more alarmed than ever.

"Maybe not directly, but people would certainly get that idea."

"Why should they? This isn't the Middle Ages. There's no more reason why they should think John Tabor is some kind of wolfman than there is to blame the attacks on one of Alec Virgil's wolves."

"Who's Alec Virgil?" Joe asked.

"A naturalist who runs what he calls a 'wolf farm' near here. He breeds wolves, and some of them run pretty big, too!" The redheaded newsman got up from his desk again and fished some more material from another file drawer. "There's a story I wrote about him a week or two ago."

The Hardys read the clipping with keen interest. It reported how Alec Virgil carried on his project as a labor of love to help preserve the buffalo wolf, a species threatened with extinction. It also showed a photograph of Virgil standing beside the stuffed effigy of one of his earliest pet wolves.

Frank rose from his chair. "Okay, thanks for your time, Mr. Dunn. We appreciate your help."

"My pleasure, boys. Stop in any time."

After leaving the *Herald's* office, the Hardys drove back to the cabin, picked up Chet, and went on to the Tabor home.

Parking their car in the drive, Frank and Joe started up to the front door, with Chet tagging at their heels. Directly above, they could see the burly figure of Pocahontas, the half-breed housekeeper. She was perched on a second-floor sill, washing windows.

Frank hesitated a moment, not sure whether he ought to call up to her or draw her attention with a gentle knock. On the other hand, he reflected, Alena was expecting them and was probably downstairs ready to answer the door. He reached out to ring the bell.

His finger had just pressed the button when both he and Joe heard a splashing sound and a muffled gasp and felt something wet splatter them from behind.

Turning around, the Hardys gaped in astonishment. The housekeeper had just dumped her pail of water on Chet!

9

Ghostly Voices

Chet spluttered and gasped, drenched to the skin!

Frank glanced up at Pocahontas, who was leaning outward from the windowsill. From the scowl on her coppery-skinned face, Frank was glad she did not have another pail of water handy. He had a hunch that, otherwise, he and his brother might have gotten the same treatment as Chet!

"Good grief!" muttered Joe, appalled at their stout chum's face. "The poor guy practically drowns before lunch and now gets doused all over again!"

"Serves him right!" growled Pocahontas just as the front door opened. "That'll teach him not to dump my little girl in the river!"

"Pokey!" exclaimed Alena, taking in the scene at one horror-stricken glance. "Chet didn't dump me in the river! His canoe sank and I dived in to help save it!"

"Huh!" The housekeeper tossed her braids defiantly. "Amounts to the same thing! It was on account of him that pretty embroidered blouse of yours got ruined, after all the time I spent this morning, ironing it just so!"

"My blouse isn't ruined!" Alena scolded. "It just got soaked! And another thing, Poca—"

Before she could finish speaking, the housekeeper withdrew from her perch, and the Hardys heard the upstairs window being slammed.

"Oh, brother!" Alena shook her head in vexation and embarrassment. "That bossy old Mohawk! She'll drive me up the wall one of these days." The girl added, "I'm so sorry about this. Come on in, boys, and I'll find some dry clothes for Chet."

The stout youth blushed and mumbled awkwardly, "You d-don't have to go to any trouble, Alena!" He was shivering due to his wetness, but obviously pleased at her concern.

Unfortunately, John Tabor's clothes were too small for Chet's barrel-shaped figure, so Alena dug up an old shirt and a pair of slacks which belonged to her father. After Chet retired to a bathroom to change, it became apparent that they were not a perfect fit, either. But they would have to do until he could get dry clothes of his own back at the cottage.

"Never mind, Chet," said Joe with a sympathetic chuckle. "At least you won't get busted for sneaking around in your underwear!"

The Hardys turned as they heard footsteps on the stairs. John was coming down to join them. The young architect looked more alert than he had when he had returned home in the wee hours of the morning, but he was obviously in poor spirits.

He shook hands with the visitors, smiled wanly on hearing about Chet's comical mistreatment at the hands of Pocahontas, then settled himself in a chair.

Frank hesitated, not sure how to begin. Finally he said, "Perhaps you've heard of my father. His name is Fenton Hardy."

John nodded. "The famous detective. Yes, I rather thought you two might be the Hardy boys I've read so much about. I suppose Alena got you up here to get to the bottom of this werewolf mystery."

"I'm glad you call it a mystery," Frank said. "That means you don't believe in those old superstitions about werewolves any more than we do."

John Tabor shrugged unhappily and ran his fingers through his curly brown hair. "Right now I don't know *what* to believe. I can't remember a thing about last night—either where I went or what happened while I was gone."

"But at least you don't think you turned into a wolf and attacked people or animals?" put in Joe. "Your common sense tells you that's impossible?"

"Maybe so," John conceded. "But that doesn't explain what I *did* do. You see, I'm not afraid of turning into a wolf. What worries me is that I may become insane, and, if that happens, I might wind up *acting* like a werewolf!"

"Where did you first get the notion that you might be going out of your mind?" Frank inquired.

"While I was studying for my architect's license. I'd be deep in my books, or bent over the drawing board, and then I'd get these calls—"

"What sort of calls, and from whom?"

"Don't ask me. From people I never heard of before. Maybe people I just made up in some sick part of my mind. I used to imagine they were—they were accusing me of being a werewolf!"

Joe frowned. "How do you know you just imagined it? Maybe you really did get such calls."

"Sure," said Chet, trying to be helpful. "It could've been someone playing a dirty trick on you!"

Tabor gave another helpless shrug. "Maybe. But I find that pretty hard to accept. Why would anyone want to play such a trick on me?"

"You can't think of anyone?" Frank prodded.

"Nobody at all. I don't have any real enemies. I'm just not that important. Besides, the delusions got even worse after I checked into the sanatorium. I suppose Alena or my father told you about that."

"The sanatorium? Yes, your Dad did mention that you'd gone for treatment, to the Pine Manor Rest Home, I believe. What happened? More calls?"

"No. Just voices."

"From where?" Joe asked.

John Tabor rubbed his head in bewilderment at the disturbing recollection. "I don't know. From the walls, I guess, or just out of thin air. I'd hear them in my room, first at night, when I was just drifting off to sleep. Later on, when it got worse, I'd even hear them during the day when I was wide awake."

"What did the voices say?"

"Terrible things, about rending fangs and bloodlust and so on. They said they were the voices of my old werewolf ancestors, like the Jan Tabor who was convicted in Bohemia in 1759."

Seeing that both John and Alena were becoming upset, Frank decided to end the questioning for the time being.

"Look," he said, "would you mind if Joe and I went to that sanatorium and interviewed the doctor who treated you?"

"Of course not," the young architect replied. "If you think it'll help in any way."

"It can't do any harm. But we'll need a letter from you, giving permission to ask questions about your case. And would you write down the name and address of the sanatorium, too, please?"

John nodded and Frank asked for directions to Alec Virgil's wolf farm. After saying good-by to Alena and her brother, the Hardy's drove back to the cabin so Chet could change into dry clothes of his own. Then they took the river road eastward out of town.

The preserve lay spread out on a slope forested with

cedar and hemlock, and was enclosed by a high wire fence. A sign over the gate said:

WOLFVILLE   Alec Virgil, Prop.
Guided Tours $1.00   Please Ring Bell

Joe did, and after a short wait a man drove up in a battered-looking jeep to greet them. He was tall and deeply tanned, with a mane of sandy hair.

"Howdy, boys!" he said, unlocking and opening the gate. "Come to see my lobos?"

"That's right, Mr. Virgil," Frank grinned. "We heard about your place this afternoon. I never knew anyone who actually raised wolves."

"Someone's got to protect the species! In most places everyone's against them. There's a wonderful preserve on the Olympic Peninsula of Washington State, where they breed five times as many wolves as I've got here. Still, I'm doing my bit."

Because of the rough terrain, Virgil suggested the boys ride with him in his jeep. They paid their admission and climbed in.

"Where'd you get your wolves?" Joe asked.

"The original stock came from the Great Plains. They used to run in packs when huge herds of buffalo dotted the plains, but they're all gone now. I bought half a dozen from the descendants of the last few caught by the government trappers in the late 1920s. Now I have thirty-seven."

"Good for you. Must take a lot of work, though."

Virgil laughed. "True. I have to be the general handy-man, the vet, the animal feeder, the yard cleaner-upper, the purchasing agent, and a few other things. But my wife helps me, and we find it a lot more satisfying than the kind of life we used to lead back in the city."

As they drove along, more and more wolves came bounding out from among the trees. Virgil slowed the jeep, and several lobos jogged alongside, their tongues lolling. They were magnificent beasts, ranging in color from silver gray and blond to cinnamon brown. Some were seven feet long from nose to hind legs.

At one point, Alec Virgil stopped the jeep and got out to play with his charges. They surged around him, wild with delight at the chance for a romp. He wrestled with them and even rolled on the ground while they nipped playfully at his arms or legs, yet never doing him any harm with their huge jaws and fearsome-looking teeth.

"Are they—er, dangerous?" Chet asked.

"Yes and no," Mr. Virgil replied. "Most of the stories about wolves attacking men are nonsense. They're actually shy creatures. But they're not lapdogs, either. They should be *respected*."

The boys decided to stay in the jeep. They found the wolves' yellow-eyed stares a bit disconcerting. Finally Virgil drove to his house and invited the guests in for coffee. When he found out that Frank and Joe were the sons of the famous Fenton Hardy, he wanted to refund their admission. But the boys refused, knowing from

Alena that the naturalist was often hard-pressed to keep his farm going.

Mrs. Virgil, a smiling, motherly woman, served coffee and doughnuts, then went outside. While the boys sat around the fireplace, her husband told them more about the sad story of the plains wolves.

"When hunters killed off the buffalo herds and thinned out the elk and antelope and deer populations," he related, "many wolves starved. Others took to preying on livestock. So the ranchers and settlers went after them with poison and traps. It was a long, desperate duel. The wolves learned to refuse the poisoned bait and became incredibly cunning at avoiding traps. But finally the humans won, and the lobos disappeared from the plains."

As he finished speaking, the distant howl of a wolf was heard from outside, then others joined in. The boys were thrilled by the eerie chorus. But gradually it changed to wilder yelping and barking.

Alec Virgil rose from his chair in alarm. Just then his wife hurried in, her face pale with excitement.

"Someone's cut the fence wire!" she cried. "Our wolves are getting out!"

10

Skyscraper Caper

"What part of the fence?" Virgil asked his wife.

When she told him, he moved into action swiftly, like a man used to handling such crises. He slipped a small whistle into his pocket, got some meat from a freezer in the shed, then climbed behind the wheel of his jeep. With the boys accompanying him, he careened off through the trees toward the section of cut fence.

Some of the wolves, more cautious than dogs might have been, were merely nosing around and sniffing at the freedom that lay beyond the opening. Others had already plunged through and were exploring the brush along the road.

Virgil leaped out of the jeep and blew his whistle. Even though it did not make a sound audible to the human ear, the escaped wolves instantly turned and loped toward the enclosure—slowly at first, then faster and faster as he waved handfuls of meat in the air. Soon he was the center of a frenzied mass of leaping, snapping lobos. Virgil flung the meat in several directions, but all of it away from the fence. The pack raced off, each animal eager to fight for his share.

Satisfied that all his wolves were accounted for, Virgil hastily moved the jeep so as to block any further escape through the hole in the fence. Then, using tools and wire from a repair kit mounted on the back of the vehicle, he and the boys wired the ripped fencing back in place. There was no doubt that it had been cut deliberately.

"Who'd do such a thing?" Frank asked.

"You'd be surprised," Virgil said wryly. "I've had all sorts of trouble ever since I started my wolf farm. Most people hate wolves and think they should all be wiped out."

"Maybe they would be, if it weren't for people like you and your wife," said Joe.

Alec Virgil smiled and nodded. "Yep, Mary and I love the critters. When the mother wolves bring out their pups to show us every spring, the little ones are rather like our own grandchildren."

He explained that the she-wolves burrowed underground dens in which to raise their litters. At night, the wolf "families" were kept in separate pens or runs, instead of ranging freely over the whole preserve.

"Which gives you double protection against a break-out?" Joe remarked.

"That's right. Good thing, too, with this werewolf foolishness going on. I don't intend to give people around here any excuse to blame those so-called werewolf attacks on my critters!"

"How come we didn't hear that whistle you blew?" Chet asked as they drove back to the house. "Was it ultrasonic?"

"Yep, it's inaudible to human ears, but my lobos hear it! Usually it's the signal for feeding time, but they're trained to respond any time I whistle."

"Hey!" Frank suddenly snapped his fingers. "That may explain it!"

"Explain what?" Joe inquired.

"What happened Saturday night at the Bayport Diner! Look, Mr. Virgil blew that ultrasonic whistle for his wolves to come, and he used the meat as an extra scent lure."

"So?" Joe looked puzzled.

"Maybe that phony werewolf we saw was trained like an attack dog, and its owner swiped my jacket as a scent guide to clue it in to our group!"

"I'll bet you're right!" said Joe, catching on. "He let the animal sniff your jacket so it would know to attack you when we came out of the diner. Then Chet and the others rushed to help us, and he blew an ultrasonic whistle to call his critter back."

"What are you talking about?" Alec Virgil asked.

After they went into the house again to finish their

94

doughnuts and coffee, they explained what had happened, and Virgil agreed that Frank's theory was a very likely one. Joe inquired about the stuffed wolf that had been shown in the newspaper photo. "I don't see it anywhere," the boy remarked.

"I sold it—or *thought* I did," Alec Virgil replied. "Turned out to be just another dirty trick."

He explained that he had received a phone call after the picture appeared in the *Hawk River Herald*. The caller, pretending to be a wealthy donor, said he wanted to buy the wolf and present it as a gift to the Mountain View Natural History Museum.

"That lobo had been a special pet of Mary's and mine," Virgil went on, "and we hated to part with it. But the caller offered us a thousand dollars."

Since the wolf farm existed on occasional grants and donations from animal lovers and the admission fees paid by sightseers, meeting the monthly bills was often a struggle. So the couple finally agreed to sell their beloved specimen.

"A truck came and picked it up," Virgil told the boys, "and the driver left a check which turned out to be worthless. When I called the museum, the curator knew nothing about it and said he had never received the wolf."

Later, back at the cabin, the boys were about to sit down to an early supper when the telephone rang. Joe answered and recognized Hank Eagle's voice.

"Hi, Hank," he said cordially. "Where are you calling from?"

"New York City. I flew back at lunchtime in Mr. Tabor's helicopter. He told me where you're staying."

The Mohawk explained that, during the afternoon, he had rejoined his regular high-steel construction crew working on the Manhattan skyscraper which Chelsea Builders were erecting.

"And I spotted something I think you ought to see," Hank went on. "It may be important to that case your father's investigating. Could you come to New York right away?"

"You mean tonight?"

"Yes. Something may happen here that you'll want to keep an eye on."

Joe checked with Frank, and they decided to follow Hank's suggestion. He gave them precise instructions on where to meet him. Then the boys called Bayport to inform their father, only to learn that he was gone for the evening. However, their mother told them that they had received an anonymous phone message about three o'clock."

"It was a man," she reported. "He said he was the person with dark glasses whom you saw at Eagle's Nest this morning."

"What did he want?" Frank asked excitedly.

"He wants to meet you. Call 555-3621 and ask for Mr. Nest. The area code is 212."

"Thanks for the info, Mom," Frank said and hung up.

"It's a New York number," Joe pointed out. "That fits in nicely with our trip tonight."

"Right," Frank agreed, and dialed the number. An answering service responded, but the operator was unable to arrange a meeting. "Mr. Nest," she said, "calls in every so often to see if there's any word from the Hardy boys. In fact, I heard from him just about twenty minutes ago, so I don't know how soon he'll call again."

"Okay," Frank said. "If he checks in, tell him we'll be in New York tonight. I'll contact you again around ten o'clock."

After a hasty meal, the Hardys started the long drive to New York, leaving a somewhat nervous Chet to keep watch on the Tabors' house after dark. Dusk had fallen as they sped southward on the New York State Thruway, and it was well past nine when they arrived in Manhattan. They parked in a midtown lot, as Hank Eagle had suggested, and walked a block or so to the meeting place.

The Mohawk was waiting for them in a doorway across the street from the skyscraper which was under construction by Chelsea Builders. He quickly told the boys the reason for his call.

"Just before I quit working," Hank said, "I noticed a lunch box stashed against a girder."

"You mean somewhere high up on the building skeleton?" Joe asked.

"Right. The twenty-first floor to be exact. Often, when the men are working, they don't bother coming down to the street for lunch. Anyhow, I figured one of the construction crew must've forgotten it when he left.

So I opened it thinking there might be something in it to clue me in to whom it belonged." Hank shook his head as if still slightly incredulous. "Boy, you'll never guess what I found inside!"

"Something suspicious?" Frank suggested.

"You better believe it! There was a drawing like a building floor plan, with an X mark and some numbers. At first I thought it might have something to do with the skyscraper we're working on, but then, as I looked at it closely, I realized that it was a layout of our company offices on Seventh Avenue!"

"What about the X mark?" Joe questioned.

"That's what made me call you. It indicated the location of the company safe! Those numbers were probably the combination. What's more, there was also a·key in the lunch box, perhaps to the outside door of the office suite!"

Joe whistled. "Wow! That sounds like a preparation for a robbery—an inside job! But who could have left the lunch box? Any idea?"

Hank related that a group of company officials had visited the structure that very afternoon. "Some had on loose cotton dust coats, so one of them might have smuggled up the lunch box and left it, or at least stashed the paper and key if the box was already planted there. Then, tonight when it's dark, maybe the crook who'll pull the robbery is supposed to pick it up!"

"Smart thinking, Hank," Frank agreed. "That could be their plan, all right."

"And the guys who set it up," Joe added, "may also be involved in those three Chelsea building cases Dad's investigating!"

"Right, which is why I tipped you two off," said the Indian high-steel worker. "But what do we do about it?"

The Hardys exchanged thoughtful glances.

"Think we should warn Mr. Tabor?" Joe asked his brother. "After all, he's the head of the company."

"I know," Frank said, deciding to trust the Mohawk and speak openly in front of him. "But we still can't be sure he himself isn't mixed up in all this. Was he one of the company officials who came here today to inspect the structure?"

Hank nodded ruefully. "I'm afraid he was."

"Looks as if we'll have to play it by ear, then, and use our own judgment," Frank decided.

"How do we know the lunch box is still there?" Joe asked.

The Mohawk shrugged. "We don't. I've been hanging around here ever since it got dark, trying to keep my eyes peeled for anything suspicious, but that doesn't prove much. Maybe we'd better check."

"Isn't there a watchman on duty?" Frank inquired.

"Sure, but he's a lazy bum. Spends most of the time with his feet up, reading the paper. Anyone could sneak by him."

"Okay then, if it won't stir up any trouble, let's have a look!"

The skyscraper was going up between two other buildings. The base of its structural skeleton was enclosed by a high board fence. After cautious glances to see whether the coast was clear, the three darted across the street. Hank Eagle gave each of the Hardys a boost up the fence, then leaped for a handhold and swung over easily by himself.

In a lighted booth just inside the access doorway through the fence, they could see the watchman snoring with a newspaper on his lap and a thermos of coffee on the table next to him.

"See what I mean?" Hank grinned.

"How do we get to the twenty-first floor?" Joe inquired.

"There's a freight hoist, but it makes a lot of noise when you switch on the motor. It'd probably wake even *him* up. Better walk."

Temporary wooden stairways had been erected for the workmen, leading up through the building skeleton. The Hardys and their Mohawk friend felt leaden-legged as they neared their destination in spite of their trim physical condition.

Suddenly they heard a metallic clink in the darkness. "Hold it!" Hank Eagle hissed, putting a hand on each boy's arm.

They were ascending a connecting stairway on the right side of the structure. Peering outward and upward, they discovered that someone had heaved a line from a window of the adjoining building to hook onto the floor of the skyscraper skeleton somewhere above them. As they watched, they could see the dark figure of a man silhouetted in the moonlight, shinnying his way up from the window along the rope.

"I'll bet he's going after the lunch box!" Joe whispered.

"Right! Let's get him!" Frank urged.

All three dashed up the stairs on tiptoe. As they reached the twenty-first floor, they saw the intruder scramble over the edge and onto the temporary flooring of the skyscraper. Then he darted silently across the wooden planks.

"That's what he's after, all right!" Hank muttered to the boys. "The lunch box is over that way!"

They moved to cut off the stranger's retreat to the hook and line. But evidently he heard them. With a fleeting glance over his shoulder, he ran nimbly over an open girder toward another part of the structure. The very thought of his reckless flight, hundreds of feet above the ground, made the Hardys dizzy.

Hank Eagle set off after him without hesitation. "Wait—don't try it, you two!" he told the Hardys as he dashed over the girder in pursuit. "Leave this to me!"

Watching the two figures intently in the moonlit gloom, the brothers saw the fugitive reach another stairway. Instead of heading downward to street level, he started up, bounding two or three steps at a stride.

"Keep an eye on him while I try to cut him off!" Joe blurted and darted back to the stairway they them-

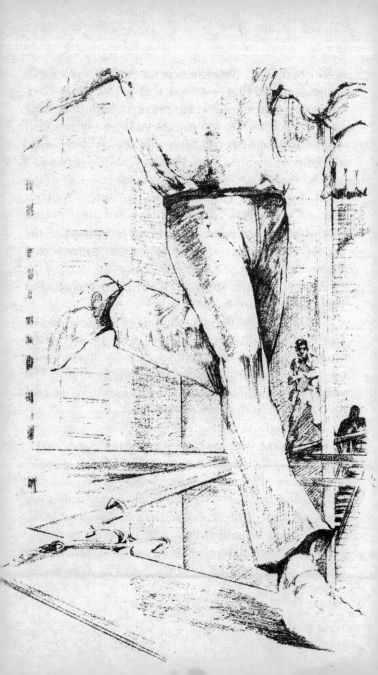

selves had used. Construction on the skyscraper had progressed only three stories higher, with the unfinished skeleton ending on the twenty-fourth floor.

As he reached it, Joe caught sight of the intruder, who was running across the wooden planking toward the edge of the structure. Joe sensed his intention at a glance. He was going to leap down onto the roof of the adjoining building from which he had emerged only a few minutes before!

The Hardy boy rushed to stop him. He grabbed the fugitive by the arm. But the man broke loose with a muttered oath. They grappled wildly at the brink of the planking. Too late, Joe saw the man's fist swinging at him in the moonlight.

The blow caught him on the side of the head and he lost his balance. With a startled cry, Joe toppled into the yawning darkness below!

11

Xavier's Story

Plummeting downward, Joe saw a rope flash past his eyes. He grabbed it desperately, and the jerk on his arm confirmed that his fall had been broken.

As he collected his wits, Joe realized he had managed to grab hold of the line which the intruder had hooked onto the skyscraper.

What a lucky break! Joe thought. With a prayer of thanks on his lips, he got a two-handed grip on the line. Then he swung his legs around the rope as a further safety measure and made his way downward cautiously, hand over hand.

The line slanted outward, away from the skyscraper skeleton into the adjoining building. As Joe shinnied down the rope and wriggled through the window, a new thought occurred to him.

Perhaps the contents of the room he was now in would enable him to identify the unknown intruder or maybe indicate whom he worked for, if others were involved.

But when Joe groped along the wall and found a light switch, he was disappointed. The room was empty, evidently an unrented office. The line had been tied to a radiator underneath the window. Hastily he switched off the light again so as not to make a target of himself.

"Better not stick my head out the window, either," Joe reflected. The safest way would be to go down to the street and wait for Frank and Hank Eagle.

Luckily the building corridors were still lighted and the elevators were working. A night attendant glanced at Joe curiously as he stepped into the lobby, but said nothing.

Joe went out into the street and was greeted with excited relief by his brother and their Mohawk friend a moment or two later.

"Thank goodness you're okay!" Frank exclaimed, putting an arm around his brother's shoulder. "Boy, I thought you were a goner when I saw you go over the side!"

"I never even got a good look at the guy before he punched me," Joe grumbled. "What happened to him?"

"He jumped on the roof of the building you went into," Frank reported, "and then took off via the fire escape."

"Well, at least he didn't get what he came for," Hank Eagle added, displaying the lunch box. The paper and key were still inside it.

"That's a break!" Joe said with satisfaction. "Whatever he and his pals were up to, we seem to have spoiled their plans."

"Right," Frank agreed. "So I guess we don't have to worry about warning anyone till we get a chance to talk to Dad." He looked at his watch. "But maybe we should give Mr. Nest another ring."

When he dialed the number from a nearby phone booth, the answering-service operator said there had been no further word from their mysterious caller. Frank promised to check again the following day and hung up. Hank Eagle invited the boys to stay overnight at his apartment in the Manhattan neighborhood known as the East Village, and they gladly accepted.

Next morning, Frank phoned Bayport. Fenton Hardy answered. When he learned his son was calling from New York City, the detective exclaimed, "Great! You couldn't have timed it better!"

"How come, Dad?"

"I've just had word from the insurance underwriters that the offices of Chelsea Builders were broken into last night. The safe was cracked and looted. I'd like you and Joe to go there and get a full report."

Frank was startled by the news. When he related their adventure on the skyscraper skeleton, Mr. Hardy agreed with Hank Eagle's suspicions. "I'd say last

106

night's burglary proves your Mohawk friend was right. The crooks probably had to break in and crack the safe because you fellows stopped them from getting the key and combination."

The detective said he expected to leave the house shortly to pursue his investigation. So rather than phone back, Frank promised that he and Joe would stop off in Bayport before returning to the Adirondacks and report what they had learned about the burglary.

Chelsea Builders were located in an office building on Seventh Avenue near 38th Street. The Hardys found the premises swarming with police and newsmen. After identifying themselves as the sons of the famed private detective who had been retained by the firm's insurance underwriters, they were admitted at once to the office of the president, Karel Tabor.

With him was a younger man, whom Mr. Tabor introduced as his executive assistant, Neal Xavier. Tabor's manner seemed rather curt and worried.

"Can you tell us what was taken from the safe, sir?" Frank asked.

"Luckily less than a thousand dollars. Just the usual petty cash that we keep on hand."

"Anything else of special value?" Joe inquired.

Mr. Tabor looked slightly uncomfortable. "We—er—don't have an exact list of the safe's contents just yet. The treasurer's secretary is compiling one," he replied, then stole a hasty glance at his wristwatch. "Look, if you'll excuse me, I have a rather urgent appointment to attend to. Perhaps Mr. Xavier here can answer any other questions you may have."

The Hardys refrained from showing their surprise. "Whatever you say, sir," Frank said politely.

Neal Xavier, a sharp-eyed, hawk-nosed man with dark hair, conducted the boys into his own office next door and invited them to be seated.

"You're probably wondering why Mr. Tabor had so little to say," he began, sitting down behind his desk. "Well, he had his reasons."

The Hardys waited for Xavier to explain.

"The fact is, he suspects another firm of architects may have had a hand in the robbery," the executive aide went on, "namely, Upton Associates. But Mr. Tabor feels it's unethical to make any accusations without proof."

Xavier thumped his fist angrily on the desk and added, "Well, I can tell you right now that won't stop *me* from speaking out. I think a crook is a crook and deserves whatever happens to him!"

"Assuming you're both right," said Joe, "that Upton Associates *are* crooks, why would they want to rob your safe?"

"Very simple," Xavier replied. "For some time now, my boss has suspected Upton of taking illegal kickbacks and bribes."

"From whom?" said Frank with a frown.

"From a crooked contractor with mob connections. Whenever Upton Associates designs buildings, they use their influence to see that that particular contractor gets hired to do the work, even though they know his firm is partly run by gangsters."

"And in return," Joe said, "you mean the crooked contractor hands some of the money he is paid for the job back to Upton Associates?"

"Right. Under the table, as they say. Since the contractor overcharges the customer, he can afford to return a share of the take to Upton. It so happens Mr. Tabor's been collecting secret testimony about such payoffs on tape. But now those tapes are missing from the safe!"

Before leaving, the Hardys asked if they could look at the company safe. Its door was hanging loosely by the hinges.

"Expert job," Joe remarked to his brother. "Evidently the safecracker used just enough nitro to blow it open without damaging anything else."

Frank nodded and knelt down to scrape some shreds of pinkish substance off the metal with his fingernail. He sniffed it and pulled it apart.

Joe puckered his forehead. "What is it?"

"Believe it or not, it's chewing gum!"

As the Hardy boys left the Chelsea Builders suite of offices and started down the corridor toward the elevators, they suddenly heard footsteps darting up behind them.

The next moment, each felt something jabbed in his back and a voice snarled, "Hold it, you two!"

12

Restaurant Meeting

Frank and Joe whirled around. From the speaker's snarling tone, they expected to find a hard-eyed gunman behind them.

Instead, they saw a smiling, freckle-faced young man in his early twenties. He held up a pen in one hand and a keychain flashlight in the other.

"Excuse the funny stuff, fellows," he apologized. "Just wanted to make sure you didn't get away. You two are the famous Hardy boys, aren't you?"

"That's right," Frank said.

"I'm Matt Dawson of the *Daily Star*. Just new on the job, to tell you the truth. But I'd sure like to impress the city editor, and getting an interview with you guys would be a step in the right direction. How about it?"

The Hardys exchanged dubious glances. Then Frank shook his head. "Thanks, but we'd rather not."

"Are you or your father working on this case?"

"If we were, we couldn't talk about it."

"Look, that doesn't matter. You wouldn't have to discuss the Chelsea Builders burglary," the young reporter assured them. "Just an interview for a general feature story will do. Things like how you first got interested in solving mysteries; whether or not you expect to become professional detectives like your father; how your sleuthing fits in with your schoolwork, and so on."

Frank hesitated. After consulting briefly with his brother, he said, "Okay, it's a deal, if you'll do us a favor in return."

"Sure thing, if I can. What do you have in mind?"

"The *Star* is one of the city's biggest newspapers, I believe," Frank said. "You cover all the arts, don't you, including architecture?"

"You bet! We've got as big an editorial staff as any paper in town, and one of the best in the country. A man named Earl Bruce writes a regular column on architecture in the *Sunday Star*."

"Fine. We'll give you an interview if you can persuade him to give us some information in exchange."

Dawson grinned. "You've got it, fellows!"

The Hardys accompanied the reporter several blocks through midtown Manhattan to the *Star* building. Once there, Matt Dawson called the paper's architectural critic on an office phone to confirm the bargain. Frank and Joe were then interviewed and photographed for half an hour. Afterward, Dawson took them to Earl Bruce's office on another floor of the building and left the two to talk to the editor in private.

"Well, boys, what is it you want to know?" the genial, white-haired newsman inquired.

"First of all, sir," Frank requested, "we'd like you to keep this conversation in strict confidence, if you don't mind."

"Agreed."

"Thanks. To get right to the point, then, what can you tell us about an architectual firm called Upton Associates?"

"Hm." Bruce leaned back in his chair and began filling his pipe thoughtfully. "Well, they've been in practice for about fifteen years, as I recall. Do quite a sizable volume of business. Commercial stuff, mostly. Office buildings, factories, that sort of thing. Plus several bridges and occasional government projects."

"Who runs the firm?" Joe put in.

"A man named Zachary Upton."

"What's he like?"

A quirky grin shaped itself on Bruce's lips. "Let's say he's a man of strong individuality."

"Has there ever been any trouble between Upton and Chelsea Builders?" Frank asked.

"Not trouble, exactly, but I believe there has been considerable rivalry between them. I know they've often put in competing bids on the same job; no doubt that may have led to a certain amount of hard feelings. After all, they can't both win out on the same project."

"Have Upton Associates ever been accused of anything crooked or illegal?"

Bruce, who was just lighting his pipe, looked up sharply at Frank's question. "Not that I know of, although I believe Upton has a son who was convicted of some crime and sent to prison."

"On what charge?"

The white-haired newsman thought hard for a few moments, then shook his head. "I'm afraid I don't recall. It didn't happen here in New York City. I just heard it mentioned in a conversation."

After a few more questions, the Hardys thanked Earl Bruce for his help and left the office. In the lobby, Frank paused near a pay telephone.

"Maybe we should try to get in touch with Mr. Nest again," he suggested.

"Good idea," Joe agreed.

Frank slipped a coin into the instrument and dialed the number. When the answering service replied, he asked if Mr. Nest had checked in yet.

"Let me see," the operator replied and consulted her notes. "Yes, he called this morning and suggested meeting you at the Soup Bowl restaurant on East 49th Street. He said he'd contact me again at eleven-thirty to see if you'd gotten the message."

113

"Good enough," said Frank. "Tell him we'll be there."

Hanging up, the boy glanced at his watch. It was now ten minutes after eleven, so the Hardys decided to go directly to the restaurant and have an early lunch. After looking up the address in the phone book, they hailed a taxi, which deposited them in front of the Soup Bowl a few minutes later.

The restaurant was already quite busy, but the brothers found a vacant booth and ordered hamburgers and French fries. While they were waiting to be served, Frank mused. "I wonder if that gum on the safe got there strictly by accident, or if it may not tell us something more."

"Good question," said Joe. "You think it might have turned up on other jobs the guy's pulled?"

Frank nodded thoughtfully. One of the first principles of detection that the Hardys had learned from their father was that a crook's *modus operandi*, or operating procedure, was often the best way to identify the person responsible for a given crime.

"You may have something there," Joe said. "Why don't you call Sam Radley? There's a phone booth over by the counter. You might catch him in if he's not working with Dad today."

"Good idea." Frank got up and placed a long-distance call to Bayport.

Sam Radley was one of Fenton Hardy's top operatives. As it turned out, he was writing a report at his

114

desk and answered immediately. "What can I do for you, Frank?"

"I'm calling from New York, Sam. I wonder if you could check the files and see if you have anything on a safecracker whose known habits include leaving traces of chewing gum on the safe."

Sam chuckled. "I don't have to look. It so happens your Dad wanted a rundown on the same crook recently, in connection with his investigation of those three building disasters."

"No kidding!" Frank felt a surge of excitement.

"The guy in question is a young fellow, a regular technical and electronic whiz," Radley went on. "Got out of prison not long ago. He has a habit of chewing bubble gum while he's working on a job."

"And sometimes the bubbles burst and gum splatters the safe?"

"Right. That's how he got his nickname 'Bubbles'. His real name is Lew Upton."

"Thanks a lot, Sam!" Frank hung up and hurried back to pass on the information to his brother.

The waitress had brought their orders, and Joe was already munching a hamburger. "*Upton?*" he echoed with his mouth still half full. "He could be Zachary Upton's son!"

"Check! The one who was convicted and sent to prison!" Frank said.

The two discussed the latest development eagerly as they ate lunch. Then Frank happened to glance toward the door. He signaled to Joe and said in a low tone, "Here comes our man!"

The mysterious eavesdropper who called himself Mr. Nest had just entered the restaurant and was approaching their table. Gray-haired, with a rather shrunken, wrinkled face, he was wearing sunglasses as before and an expensive-looking bronze silk suit.

"So you kept our appointment. That's good!" he remarked hoarsely, sliding into the booth beside Joe. "Maybe we can do business."

"What kind of business?" Frank asked cooly.

"Don't stall around, Sonny!" the elderly man rasped. "I've got just one thing to discuss with you, and that's the tomahawk! Can we work out a deal or can't we?"

The Hardys stared at him, puzzled. They had no idea what Mr. Nest was talking about.

"First you'd better tell us what tomahawk," Joe demanded, fishing for information.

Instead of answering, however, Mr. Nest leaped up from the booth and hurried out of the restaurant!

13

Toy Boat Trick

"Hey, wait!" Joe called, but the gray-haired mystery man had disappeared before the boys recovered from their surprise.

"Come on, let's go after him!" Frank exclaimed, springing to his feet.

He dashed toward the door, but as he passed the counter, the cashier reached out and grabbed his arm. "Just a minute!" she protested indignantly. "You can't sneak out of here without paying!"

Frank started to explain, but saw that it would be useless, so he fished money out of his pocket and hastily settled their bill.

Meanwhile, Joe brushed past him to pursue Mr. Nest. As he ran out the door, a cane was suddenly thrust in front of him. Joe tripped and sprawled full-length on the pavement!

Angrily he got up and turned to let off steam at the person responsible for the mishap. Then he saw that the cane was held by a poorly dressed man clutching a tin cup with pencils, evidently a blind beggar.

"Sorry if I got in your way," the man mumbled.

Joe stifled the angry remark that had risen to his lips. "Never mind," he said, and hastily collected himself to renew the pursuit. His eyes swept the throng of passing pedestrians and picked out a gray-haired man in a bronze-colored suit near the next corner, about to cross the street.

Joe dashed after him, shouldering his way deftly through the crowd, muttering apologies whenever he bumped into someone. He reached the curb and started across just as the light was changing. With a blare of horns, a pack of cars surged into motion and roared straight at him in the typical impatient fashion of New York traffic.

Joe leaped and hopped across the street, dodging a taxi, a station wagon, and a delivery van. His pulse was racing as he reached the opposite corner but there was no time to stop and cool his jangled nerves. He could see the man in the brownish suit not far ahead.

Joe darted and swivel-hipped his way through the stream of pedestrians. He reached his quarry and grabbed him by the arm. "Okay, Mr. Nest, if that's your real name. Hold it!"

The man turned. He had a large, red nose, veiny jowls, and bushy-browed blue eyes, which at the moment were sparking dangerously. "Let go of my arm, young fellow!" he growled. "Just who do you think you are?"

Joe's eyes widened in chagrin as he saw his mistake. "I—I'm terribly sorry," he stuttered. "I thought you were someone else."

"Hmmph!" The man grunted. "Next time don't grab people before you see who they are!"

Apparently mollified by Joe's apology, he strode off. The younger Hardy plodded back dejectedly toward the restaurant. Crossing the street, he encountered his brother.

"Any luck?" Frank inquired.

"Yes, all of it bad!" Joe said wryly and related his two brief adventures. As if to rub in his humiliation, he saw that the man with the cane had disappeared. "I'll bet that blind beggar was just a phony!" Joe blurted. "Nest probably planted him there to slow us down, in case we came after him."

"Very likely," Frank agreed. "Nest's name is phony, too, for that matter."

"Sure, from the name of that old wooden mansion where you spotted him, Eagle's Nest!"

"Well, never mind, Joe. We can't win 'em all. Let's go back and finish our hamburgers."

But another letdown was in store. When they returned to the restaurant, they saw that their table had already been cleared. The rest of their meal was probably in the garbage by now.

Even Frank was disgusted. "Want to order something else?" he asked his brother.

"Forget it. I just lost my appetite."

Frank decided to use the phone booth again. He called Chelsea Builders and asked Karel Tabor's secretary for the name and address of the client for whom the firm was restoring Eagle's Nest.

Frank jotted down the information she gave him, then hung up and turned to Joe. "Let's look him up when we get a chance. He might be able to give us a lead on Mr. Nest."

"Good hunch. But what'll we do right now?"

"Call Zachary Upton and ask for an interview. Not here, though. Let's go to a place where I can carry on a phone conversation without all this babble and clatter of dishes."

In the lobby of an office building down the street, they found a pay telephone in a quiet, secluded corner. Joe leafed through the Manhattan directory for Upton Associates, and Frank dialed the number. Luckily the head of the firm had not yet gone to lunch, and by quiet persistence, Frank finally got through to him.

"My name's Frank Hardy, Mr. Upton," he began. "My father is Fenton Hardy, the detective. You may have heard of him."

"Well, what is it you want?" the rumbling bass voice challenged.

"My brother Joe and I would like a chance to talk to you, as soon as possible."

"What about?"

"A case which our father's investigating. It involves Chelsea Builders."

"Nothing doing," the architect replied grumpily. "We have no contact with that firm."

"You may still be able to help us, sir."

"I said nothing doing!"

"Very well," Frank said, and on a sudden impulse added, "Then may I speak to your son Lew?"

There was a slight pause, and Frank sensed that Zachary Upton had been taken aback by the sudden mention of his son's name. "He's not here," Upton finally responded.

"Can you tell us how to get in touch with him?"

"This isn't a secretarial bureau—I'm running a firm of architects!"

Frank decided to apply a little pressure. His voice hardened. "It's very important that we speak to Bubbles," he said, emphasizing the nickname slightly. "We want to question him about a burglary that occurred at Chelsea Builders last night. The safe was cracked."

Frank could hear a faint gasp at the other end of the line. "A s-safecracking, you say?"

"That's right, Mr. Upton. My brother and I went there this morning and examined the scene of the burglary. We discovered a clue that *may* link your son to the crime. Now, we'd like to give him a chance to explain. However, if you prefer, we can simply call the police and let *them* follow up."

"No, er, don't do that just yet!" Zachary Upton said hastily. "If you'll call back in half an hour, I'll do my best to arrange an interview with my son."

"Fine. Thank you, sir," Frank said politely. Hanging up he turned to his brother with a dry grin. "That changed his tune in a hurry!"

While waiting to phone back, the Hardys returned to the skyscraper from which Joe had taken his terrifying tumble the night before. The construction crew were still on their lunch break, as the two young sleuths had hoped, so they were able to have a brief chat with their friend, Hank Eagle.

Joe described their frustrating meeting with the so-called Mr. Nest. As he mentioned the man's strange remark about the tomahawk, Frank saw Hank's eyes flicker, as if he were startled but trying not to show any sign of recognition.

"Any idea what the man was talking about?" the older Hardy boy inquired casually.

Hank Eagle shrugged. "None."

For the rest of the conversation he seemed rather taciturn and withdrawn, masking whatever was going on in his head behind a deadpan face.

"Did you notice how Hank clammed up all of a sudden when you asked him about that tomahawk?" Joe remarked to his brother later as they walked away from the construction site.

122

"I'll say I did," Frank replied. "He knows more than he's telling us, that's for sure."

"But why? You don't suppose he's in cahoots with Mr. Nest?"

Frank shook his head. "That doesn't stack up with what we know about Hank, not with our previous opinion of him, anyhow. I've got a hunch about why Mr. Nest set up a meeting with us and tossed out that crack about the tomahawk."

"Why?"

"He wanted to find out from our expressions if we *knew* anything about it. When he saw our blank faces, he realized we didn't, and that's all he was interested in. So he took off and left us sitting there like dummies."

"That figures, all right," Joe agreed.

At a nearby drugstore, Frank made another call to Upton Associates. This time Zachary Upton was much less hostile. He was still vague and uncertain about arranging a meeting between the Hardys and his son. However, he agreed readily to see the boys himself and discuss the matter further.

"I'd like to keep this confidential," he added. "Could we meet somewhere away from my office?"

"You name the time and place, Mr. Upton," Frank said.

"Very well, then. How about two-thirty this afternoon, at the boat pond in Central Park?" The architect added directions, in case the Hardys were not familiar with the layout of the park, and a description of himself.

"We'll be there," Frank promised and hung up.

The boys had left their car overnight in a parking garage, so after some window-shopping on Fifth Avenue, they took a bus north and went into Central Park at the East 72nd Street entrance.

The pond at which they were to meet Upton lay just a short stroll away. The architect was easily identifiable from the description of himself that he had given Frank, a big, shaggy bear of a man with a closely trimmed dark beard streaked with gray.

Several toy boats were being sailed on the pond. As the boys approached, they realized that Upton was playing with one of them, steering it by means of an electronic remote-control device which he held in one hand.

"Mr. Upton?" said Frank.

The bearded man turned to look at the two youths. "Hm, eh, yes. You must be Frank and Joe Hardy."

"Yes, sir. Let's get right to the point, if you don't mind."

"Whatever you say, son."

"First of all, we'd like to learn more about your relationship with Chelsea Builders. And then we want to know how soon we can talk to your son."

"Well, now, that's a fairly big order. Just what did you mean by that first question? Are you implying that Upton Associates or I may have something to do with that burglary you mentioned?"

Frank attempted to reply diplomatically. But Upton paid little attention. He seemed more interested in steering his toy boat across the water, and the Hardys had the odd impression that he was stalling for time.

Suddenly, as his boat reached the opposite side of the pond, they saw a young man stoop and snatch it up. Frank and Joe thought he slipped something into the little craft, but he acted so quickly and unexpectedly that neither could be sure.

As suddenly as he had picked up the boat, the youth put it back in the water. Then he turned and darted off among some trees.

Upton was already steering the boat back to their own side of the pond. As soon as it came within reach, he stooped down and plucked out a rolled-up slip of paper, which he handed to the Hardys.

"That young man you saw just now was my son Lew," he informed them.

Frank hastily unrolled the note. It bore a message scrawled in ink:

Mob job! Tell your father to watch out or we're both dead men!

14

The Mustached Stranger

The Hardy boys gasped as they read the strange warning that Lew Upton had sent them in the toy boat.
Frank shot a puzzled glance at the bearded architect,
who stood by watching them somberly.

"What's this all about, Mr. Upton?" he asked.

The man shrugged. "Don't ask me. I assumed you'd
know. The message is meant for you."

He explained that, ever since getting out of prison a
few weeks ago, his son had been living by himself,
apparently somewhere in the city, but avoiding contact
with his family.

"Lew said it was better that way for all of us, that he
didn't want any of his underworld troubles brushing
off on his mother and me," Zachary Upton went on.

"However, he would call us every so often, and he gave me a number where I could reach him in case of emergency. That's how I got in touch with him after you called today."

Upton related that his son had sounded very disturbed when he heard that the Hardys wanted to talk to him about the Chelsea Builders' burglary. "He told me that it was important to get a message to you fast, but he didn't want to be seen with any of us. That's why we arranged this toy boat gimmick."

Despite his gruff front, Upton was obviously very much worried about Lew's safety, especially in light of the first two words in the message. Mob job implied that some gangster setup was behind the safecracking.

Frank and Joe were also concerned about their father, although they knew he was usually well able to protect himself from criminals. But for the moment, neither the Hardy boys nor Zachary Upton could guess what had prompted the message.

The two young sleuths said good-by to the architect and retrieved their car from the parking garage. Soon they were heading homeward.

Arriving in Bayport, they learned that Fenton Hardy had not yet returned, so they decided to stay overnight before starting for the Adirondacks again.

"Maybe we'd better let Chet know our plans," Joe suggested.

"Good idea," said Frank and called the cottage. Before leaving Hawk River, the Hardys had cautioned their stout chum to speak cagily over the phone for fear of their conversation being overheard by the gossipy local operator. Keeping this in mind, Chet managed to let Frank know by his remarks that he had kept a midnight vigil outside the Tabor house, but that nothing unusual had happened.

"Okay, Chet," Frank replied. "Same deal tonight. We'll see you tomorrow. We want to talk to Dad, so we're going to stick around in case he shows up this evening. Meanwhile, take care of yourself."

"You think I won't?"

Frank chuckled and hung up.

Before dinner, the boys drove to Wild World, an animal park outside Bayport. They asked their elderly friend, Pop Carter, who operated the establishment, if they could borrow a tranquilizer dart gun.

"We may need it to capture a werewolf, Pop," Frank explained.

"If anyone else had told me that," Pop replied, "I'd suspect that he was crazy. But with you Hardys I'm ready to believe anything!" He gave them the gun, and the brothers returned home.

By the following morning, there was still no word from their father. Hiding their own worried feelings, the boys did their best to reassure their mother and Aunt Gertrude. Soon they were on their way once more to the Adirondacks.

En route, the Hardys detoured to the Catskill Mountain area to visit the Pine Manor Rest Home. They asked at the reception desk if they could speak to the doctor who had treated John Tabor.

The receptionist smiled in surprise. "That's a coincidence!" she remarked. "Another visitor came in fifteen minutes ago asking the same thing. He's with Dr. Benton right now."

Frank and Joe sat down to await their turn, wondering who the visitor could be. When the receptionist finally escorted them down a hallway, they saw a man with a thick black mustache coming out of the doctor's office. The Hardys were curious if he was the person who had inquired about the young architect and his nervous breakdown.

Dr. Benton was a thin, fussy-looking individual. His manner seemed rather curt and impatient, as if he were tired of answering questions about the Tabor case. However, when the boys showed him the letter signed by his former patient, he agreed to spare them a few minutes.

"Do you mind telling us who that man was who just left here?" Frank asked.

"He came here for the same reason you did. It wouldn't be proper for me to discuss his business with you."

The physician told them briefly about the treatment which young Tabor had received at the sanatorium. He scoffed at any notion that his apparent breakdown might have been purely imaginary and brought on by outside enemies.

"That's ridiculous!" the doctor snapped. "John was definitely suffering from delusions. Even while he was here, he reported hearing the voices of his werewolf ancestors."

"They wouldn't be hard to fake," Joe pointed out. "With a few electronic gimmicks, we could make any patient here imagine the same thing."

Frank nodded. "That's true, sir. By hiding one or more miniaturized radio receivers in his room, we could be miles from the sanatorium and still broadcast such voices to a patient. By planting both a bug and a receiver, we could even make him think he was carrying on a two-way conversation with a ghost."

The doctor frowned. "To do that, you'd first have to get to his room. And I can assure you that none of John's so-called enemies had a chance to do that."

"A staff employee might have been bribed to plant the radio gimmicks," Joe reasoned.

"I resent any such suggestion, young man!"

"If you'll let us check the room John Tabor occupied while he was a patient here," Frank said, "we can soon tell you if it contains any bugs or other devices."

Dr. Benton seemed somewhat upset, but reluctantly agreed. The Hardys got a kit of detection gear which they had brought along in their car and proceeded to make an electronic sweep of the room in question. They not only checked the walls for hidden devices, but also the bedside lamp, furniture, and other items.

"No luck!" Joe grumbled.

"That doesn't prove the trickery didn't happen," Frank pointed out. "Whoever planted the gimmicks may have removed them as soon as John Tabor checked out of the sanatori—"

The older Hardy boy suddenly broke off speaking, shoved the chair he had been examining out of the way and darted toward the door.

"What's wrong?" Joe exclaimed.

"I saw a guy peeking at us!"

The two young sleuths rushed out in pursuit. As they emerged into the corridor, a door slammed shut down the hall. It appeared to lead to another wing of the sanatorium, but when the boys tried it, it would not open.

"He must've pushed the lock button as he went through!" Frank fumed.

"What did this eavesdropper look like?" Joe asked.

"I only got a brief glance at him. He was rather heavyset with light blond hair, dressed in white. Probably a male nurse or attendant."

"He could have been the guy who planted the radio gimmick!"

When Dr. Benton heard their story, he seemed more upset than ever. Instead of offering to help find the culprit, he insisted that the Hardys leave the sanatorium, pointing out that they had utterly failed to prove their suspicions.

The boys stopped at a roadside diner for sandwiches. Frank pulled out the name and address of the

owner of Eagle's Nest. "He lives near New Paltz, which isn't far from here," the boy stated. "Should we stop in and see him?"

"What have we got to lose?"

The client, whose name was Crawford, proved to be a wealthy retired businessman. A balding, courtly mannered old gentleman, he seemed delighted by the Hardys' visit.

"Come into my study, boys," he invited them. When they were comfortably seated, he said, "Now then, what can I do for you?"

Frank explained how they had happened to visit Eagle's Nest. Then he told about the gray-haired man in dark glasses who had eavesdropped on their conversation with Hank and later arranged to meet them at a restaurant in New York.

Mr. Crawford snapped his fingers. "I know exactly whom you're talking about!"

"Really, sir? We'd like to learn more about him. He called himself Mr. Nest, but Joe and I are certain that name is an alias."

"You bet it is! His real name is Marburg. He's an antique dealer who specializes in old manuscripts and autographs, or so he says."

"How did you meet him?" Joe asked.

"Well, shortly after I bought Eagle's Nest, there was a story in one of the New York papers. It reported that I was having the old mansion restored, how I planned to make it into a historic showplace. Next day I got a call from Marburg. He offered to buy any old documents that turned up during the restoration. I tried to be polite, *and* honest. Told him I didn't expect to find anything of value. After all, the house has been sitting up there in the woods for years, an empty shell just rotting away.

"But Marburg refused to take no for an answer. He kept pestering me with calls," Mr. Crawford went on. "Even drove all the way from New York City just to see me. Finally I became fed up. Didn't trust him, anyhow. He sounded like a crook to me. I told him I wanted nothing to do with him, and if he bothered me any more, I wouldn't even give him the chance to *bid* on anything that turned up."

"I wonder why he lied to us about his name," Frank mused.

"In my opinion," said the elderly businessman, "it merely confirms what I suspected all along. The man's dishonest. He's ready to go to any lengths to lay his hands on whatever valuable items come to light. But he recognized you as the Hardy boys. So he's trying to cover himself, hoping you won't be able to trace him if he has to resort to theft or trickery."

"What about the tomahawk he mentioned?" Joe asked. Mr. Crawford shrugged. "No telling. Wouldn't surprise me if it were part of some elaborate confidence game he's playing."

The Hardys thanked their elderly informant and resumed their drive to the Adirondacks. When they arrived at Hawk River in midafternoon, Chet burst out of the cabin to greet them.

"You really missed some action here last night!" he blurted.

Joe hopped out of the car and stretched his arms and legs. "What happened?"

"Plenty! For openers, there were more wolf howls and werewolf attacks."

"Were you keeping an eye on the Tabors' house?" Frank put in anxiously.

The chubby boy nodded and threw out his chest. "You bet I was. In fact I came near solving the mystery all by myself!"

"Well, don't keep us in suspense!" Joe urged. "Give us a blow-by-blow!"

"Okay, okay. If you'll listen and give me a chance, I will. I was up in the tree, same as before, see? Something seemed to be moving in the shadows, and all of a sudden I caught on. There was *another guy* keeping watch on the house!"

"Did you get a look at him, Chet?"

"Not right away. It was too dark where he was standing. As I told you, he was in the shadows. Let's just call him Mr. X."

"Suits us. But what happened?"

Chet related that shortly before midnight he had seen John Tabor sneak out of the house.

"Was this before or after the howls started?"

"Right after." The chubby youth shuddered. "Boy, it

was weird! Almost as if he heard the wild wolves calling him and was going out in the woods to join them! Anyway, Mr. X started tailing him. So naturally I followed both of them. And when they got out in the open more, out in the moonlight, I finally got a chance to see what Mr. X looked like. He was a thickset guy with a dark cap and a big droopy dark mustache."

The Hardys exclaimed almost in unison, "Same guy we saw at the sanatorium!"

Frank added more cautiously, "At least the description fits. Go on with your story, Chet."

Their stout chum reported that he had followed the two men up a wooded hillside. "We were going along quietly," he continued, "when suddenly I heard a twig crack, as if someone stepped on it. Not in front of me, *behind* me!"

Joe said, "Oh, oh, you mean someone was following *you?*"

"That's what it sounded like." Chet gulped as he recalled his feelings at that scary moment. "Man, I was really shook up!"

"What did you do?" Joe asked tensely.

"I froze for a moment, then crouched down in a clump of brush. I figured if somebody *was* shadowing me, I'd waylay him and grab him as he came by."

Frank waited for the climax of the story. "Any luck?"

"Oh, I caught him all right," Chet said ruefully. "But I'm not sure how lucky I was. The guy fought like a wildcat. We were rolling all around in the dark, then he grabbed a stone and conked me on the head. When I came to everything was silent. So I came back here to the cabin. And I never even got a good look at the fellow I was scrapping with!"

"Never mind. You did fine, Chet, and showed plenty of nerve in a tight spot." Frank clapped the boy on the back, then frowned thoughtfully. "But this gives the case a new twist. Two other guys keeping John Tabor under surveillance!"

"Any hunches about who they are?" Joe asked, eyeing his brother hopefully.

"No. But I'd sure like to know where John was going. Could you show us the route he took, Chet?"

Chet Morton shrugged. "I could try."

The three boys drove to a spot near the Tabor house, then parked and got out, with Chet leading the way. He guided them away from the road, through a ragged patch of woods and over a rough, uneven stretch of terrain. Finally, they clambered up a hillside.

"Hey, look!" Joe exclaimed, pointing ahead.

Beyond the trees, they glimpsed a small hut.

"Wow! I didn't see that last night!" said Chet. "That must be where John Tabor was heading!"

The Bayport trio pressed forward and entered the hut. It was littered with books and papers. Besides a table, chair, cot, and wood stove, there was a drawing board with an architectural sketch pinned to it, and various drafting instruments. Electricity was supplied by a small generator.

"This must be where John comes to study and sketch out ideas for his designs," said Frank, glancing around with interest.

"Hey! Look at this!" Joe said, holding up what appeared to be a fur rug.

"It's a wolf skin!" gasped Chet.

"Right! Complete from nose to tail. The head even has glass eyes!"

Frank, who hurried to his brother's side, turned it over. "And leather straps with buckles are on the underside, so a person can strap it on!"

In their excitement over the find, the boys failed to hear footsteps approaching outside the hut. Suddenly the door burst open and a voice bellowed:

"You're all under arrest!"

15

Paleface Archer

The boys whirled to face the speaker. He was a tall, rawboned man wearing a stetson felt hat and a sheriff's badge pinned to the olive-gray jacket of his uniform.

"Under arrest for what?" Frank asked.

"Breaking and entering'll do for a start."

"We didn't break in, Sheriff. The door was open." Frank identified himself and his brother, as well as Chet, and explained that they were investigating the werewolf mystery.

On hearing that two of the youths were the sons of the famous detective, Fenton Hardy, the lawman relaxed his angry expression somewhat and even shook hands. "I'm Sheriff Kennig," he told them. "You can forget what I said about being under arrest. But that still doesn't excuse you for poking around without permission. I'm the local law officer. If you're up here to work on a case, you should've checked in with me first."

The Hardys thought it best not to argue.

"We're still fairly new at detective work, Sheriff. We don't have your experience at crime-fighting," Frank said diplomatically. "I guess we have a few things to learn."

The rawboned police officer seemed mollified by Frank's attitude and shrugged a bit pompously. "We all have to start somewhere," he said. "What's that you're holding, young fellow?"

"A wolf skin," Joe said, handing it over.

"Hm." Kennig examined the hide, obviously mystified but doing his best to look professional. "I'll take charge of this. It may be important evidence."

"How did you know we were here, Sheriff?" Joe inquired.

"I didn't. Just got a phone tip that it might be worth while to take a look in John Tabor's cabin." He added, "As your Dad may have told you, that's one of the most important techniques in police work—gathering leads from informers."

"Any idea who the caller was?" Frank asked.

Sheriff Kennig cleared his throat. "Actually, no. He didn't leave any name. But he spoke with a foreign accent."

The lawman fished a gleaming metal pellet from his

jacket pocket and held it out to show the boys. "Here's something else that may interest you fellows, strictly off the record, you understand."

"A silver bullet!" Joe exclaimed. "Where'd it come from, Sheriff?"

"When that werewolf was prowling around last night, someone took a shot at it. I dug this out of the bark of the tree where it hit. Didn't get too mashed up."

Chet started to say something. Frank sensed that he might be about to mention the bullet fired into the Hardys' front door in Bayport, which might have led to lengthy questioning by the sheriff. So he silenced his chum with a quick frown. Instead, Chet said, "Er, silver bullets are what people used to say it took to kill a werewolf, right?"

The sheriff nodded. "Uh-huh. And this isn't the only one that turned up."

Frank flashed him a startled glance. "Where else?"

"Somebody fired one at Karel Tabor this morning. Happened just as he was climbing into his helicopter to take off for New York."

"Did anyone spot the gunman?"

"Nope. The shot came from the woods near the Tabor's house. Whoever it was, looks as if someone around Hawk River may figure the best way to get rid of werewolves is to wipe out the Tabor family!"

"After telling the sheriff where they could be reached, the Hardys headed back to their car with Chet. Both Frank and Joe were worried that the furry

141

clue they had discovered in the hut might cause fresh trouble for the Tabors.

"You think the sheriff would go as far as tossing John in the clink?" Chet asked owlishly.

"He just might," Frank replied, "if people around here get worked up enough about the werewolf attacks."

"I still don't see how anyone could be deceived by that wolf skin , though," Joe argued. "Even if someone strapped it to his arms and body, I wouldn't be fooled into thinking it was a real werewolf!"

"Neither would I," Chet chimed in.

"And it sure wouldn't explain that glowing wolf creature we saw at the Bayport Diner," Frank pointed out.

Suddenly Joe snapped his fingers. "Hey! I'll bet I know where that pelt came from!"

"Where?"

"Off that stuffed wolf that got stolen from Alec Virgil! That would explain the glass eyes!"

"Right," his brother agreed. "Someone just emptied out the stuffing. I think you've hit it, Joe."

Frank was thoughtful when they arrived at the cottage. "Do you suppose the Mohawks knew anything about werewolves?" he mused.

"Sure," Joe replied. "That book by Desmond Quorn says that American Indian tribes had lots of folktales about people turning into animals. Why?"

"Hank Eagle said his uncle's a medicine man, remember? Just for the fun of it, I'd like to hear what

142

he has to say about this werewolf scare. Who knows, he might come up with some kind of Indian lore or wolf-hunting gimmick that we could use to distract people around here and take some of the heat off the Tabors." Frank looked at his two companions. "Are you game to drive to Hank's village?"

Joe nodded, and Chet was positively enthusiastic about the idea. A visit with the Indians, he felt, would give him a chance to soak up some real wilderness know-how. When the trio set off in the car again a short time later, the stout youth was clad in his fringed buckskin hunting shirt and headband, and even brought along his bow and arrows.

The Mohawk village, as they found out by asking directions, lay only a few miles from Hawk River. To Chet's disappointment, it consisted only of a few weatherbeaten houses and cabins, and the people, aside from their coppery complexions and, in some cases, braided hair, seemed no different from other local Americans.

"Chet looks more Indian than they do," Joe remarked with a chuckle to Frank.

The Mohawks seemed to think so, too. When the boys climbed out of the car, a group of children who had been playing in front of the general store immediately surrounded the chubby visitor, admiring his bow and arrows and asking questions about his costume.

Meantime, Frank and Joe asked where Hank Eagle's

uncle lived. His name was Adam Eagle, and he proved to be a thin, gnarled-looking old man with a beaky nose and high-cheekboned face. When he heard that his callers were friends of his nephew he greeted them with a firm handshake.

"*Say-go! Skaw-non-gowa*, my friends. How are you?"

The boys chatted with him and found out that Adam Eagle, too, had been a high-steeler in his youth. He had helped build the George Washington Bridge across the Hudson River and the Empire State Building, but now worked as a carpenter and odd-job man.

"Hank told us you were a medicine man," Joe remarked.

The elderly Mohawk shrugged. "Sometimes I make herbal remedies for my neighbors when they are ill, and perform tribal ceremonies."

It turned out that he had already heard about the werewolf attacks at Hawk River. When Frank asked his opinion about them and how the trouble could be stopped, at first Mr. Eagle would say little.

But finally, as a favor to the boys, he donned an Indian costume and built a small fire of twigs in the fireplace of his cabin. He played eerily on a red cedar flute. Then, shaking a pair of gourd rattles and speaking in the Mohawk tongue, he began calling on *Ga-oh*, the Spirit of the Winds. Frank and Joe got goose pimples listening to the weird chant.

Afterward, the old man said to them, "The woods are

144

full of mystery, my friends. Most people have lost touch with nature. Who can say whether or not men may become like animals? Still, I think the trouble you speak of comes not from any wolf. I see you in the fire, hunting down evil persons!"

Somewhat mystified but impressed, the Hardys thanked the medicine man and went out to look for Chet. They found him showing off his skill at archery, taking turns with some of the village teenagers, shooting arrows at a makeshift target. The Indian youths clapped when he managed to hit the bull's-eye every time.

But none of the Bayporters could match the Mohawks when it came to hurling a hickory lance at a rolling ring. Later they played the deer-button game. The buttons, made of polished horn, were each charred on one side. The players shook the buttons in one hand like dice, then threw them on a blanket, trying to make six or more buttons land with the same side turned up.

Much to his delight, Chet won more games than anyone else. He and the Hardys were invited by the villagers to stay for supper. It was a feast of corn soup, fried trout, venison, succotash, squash, cornbread and blueberry pie.

Before the visitors left, some of the village girls presented Chet with a beaded headband they had sewed, as a prize for his marksmanship with bow and arrow.

"*Ohna-ghee-wahee!*" the Mohawks called, waving good-by.

Chet was so proud of the trophy he wanted to show it off to Alena. He asked the Hardys to stop by the Tabors' house when they returned to Hawk River. However, when it came to ringing the bell, he seemed a bit nervous.

"What's the matter?" Frank asked. "Feeling shy?"

"That goofy housekeeper doesn't like me," Chet confessed sheepishly as he got out of the car. "What if *she* answers the door?"

Dusk had fallen and the boys saw Alena pass in front of a lighted window. Then the light went out.

Chet had a sudden inspiration. He wrote a note to Alena, tied it to an arrow, and strode halfway up the drive while Frank and Joe waited in the car. He aimed at Alena's still open window and let the arrow fly.

Unfortunately, his nervousness must have spoiled his aim. There was a loud tinkle of glass, and Chet froze in horror. His arrow had crashed into the wrong window!

Next moment the front door burst open and Pocahontas charged out, bellowing and brandishing a broom!

16

Tomahawk Reward

"Clear outa here, you no-good!" the huge housekeeper roared, shaking her broomstick weapon. "I'll teach you to come breaking windows in this house!"

Chet pounded down the drive in panic as fast as his chubby legs could carry him. "Gun the engine!" he shouted while still ten yards from the car.

"How come?" teased Joe, who was at the wheel. "Don't you want to stick around till Alena reads your note?"

"Never mind the wisecracks, just get going!" Chet leaped aboard, bug-eyed and puffing. "Think I want that giantess to brain me with her war club?"

Once back in the safety of their cottage, the stout youth began stoking up on cocoa and doughnuts.

"Having someone like Pocahontas chase after him is hard on a guy's nerves," he said plaintively. "I have to recharge my batteries!"

"Good idea," said Frank. "We may need your full power tonight."

"What for?" Chet blurted, eyeing the Hardy boy suspiciously.

"All three of us are going to stake out the Tabors' house. If any of those guys who were out there last night show up again, we'll nab them!"

Around nine-thirty, just as the boys were about to leave the cabin, the phone rang. Joe answered. The caller was Hank Eagle.

"I just got home from New York," the Mohawk high-steeler said. "My uncle told me you were here at the village this afternoon. Sorry I missed you."

"Same here," Joe said. "But we sure enjoyed the visit. Your uncle's a fine man, Hank."

"He thinks you Hardys are pretty special, too. When he 'made medicine' over the fire, he says *Ga-oh* told him you could be trusted, so he advised me to tell you the truth."

"About what?"

"About that sneaky dude you met in the restaurant, the one who called himself Mr. Nest. His real name is Marburg."

"We already found that out," Joe said. "But if you've got something more to tell us, wait till I get Frank on the line, so he can hear it, too!"

The Hardys were fascinated as they listened to the story Hank Eagle related. After the Revolutionary War, his ancestor, Dark Eagle, had sailed on a British troopship, carrying redcoats home to England. In London, King George had presented his fierce Indian ally with a silver tomahawk in reward for his services to the Crown. Made by a famous English silversmith, the tomahawk was decorated with a gold design and embossed with several diamonds.

"Wow! What happened to it?" Joe exclaimed.

"Nobody knows," Hank replied. "Remember, that was two hundred years ago. Somehow, the tomahawk got lost or disappeared from sight during those two centuries. But when you told me what Marburg said in the restaurant, I knew right away that's what he was after."

Frank said, "How would he know about the tomahawk?"

"From history books. It's no secret. Anyone who's interested in antiques could have heard about it."

Hank went on to tell that his family possessed an old journal or diary kept by Dark Eagle. "Many pages are too faded and moldy to read, but from various legible remarks, I'm sure the tomahawk is hidden somewhere at Eagle's Nest."

"Would Marburg know about that diary, too?" Joe asked.

"Probably. We've tried our best to keep it secret; in fact, it's stored in a safe deposit box. But several historians know Dark Eagle kept such a diary, so the news may easily have leaked out to Marburg."

Hank said he became more and more convinced of this when Marburg came to see him and tried to work his way into the Mohawk's confidence. "Then when he saw you guys talking to me and recognized you from news pictures as the sons of Fenton Hardy, he probably figured you were after the same prize he was."

Frank told the high-steeler about the chat he and Joe had had with Mr. Crawford, and added, "Probably Marburg figured if you didn't have the diary, it might just turn up when the old mansion is restored."

"Quite likely," Hank agreed, "and he's hoping if he can lay hands on it that the diary will clue him in to what happened to the tomahawk."

The Hardys thanked the construction worker for telling them his family's secret. They also promised to let him know if they gleaned any clues to the whereabouts of the tomahawk. Then they set off with Chet for the Tabor estate.

Parking their car out of sight, the boys chose a different tree from the one Chet had used for his lookout post. All three found places to perch themselves in its sturdy branches. In the moonlight, they could see the house clearly.

Less than half an hour later, Joe hissed a soft warning and pointed to the left. A stealthy figure had just emerged from among the trees and was moving closer to the house.

"You stay here, Chet," Frank whispered, "and keep your eyes peeled for any other intruders. Joe and I'll go get this guy, okay?"

"Check!" their stout chum agreed.

Letting themselves down from the tree, the Hardys closed in fast and silently on their quarry. He had taken up a position in a clump of shrubbery, which gave him a view of both the patio and the front of the house.

But he was unprepared for an assault from behind. Before he realized what was happening, Frank hooked an arm around his windpipe and clamped a hand over his mouth. Joe grabbed the man's wrist and twisted it painfully behind him.

Between them, they marched him well out of earshot of the house. He was the mustached man whom they had seen leaving Dr. Benton's office at the Pine Manor Rest Home!

"Suppose you tell us what you're doing here, spying on the Tabors," Frank said.

"Why should I tell you anything?" the prisoner retorted.

"Because if you don't we'll call Sheriff Kennig and you can try explaining to him!" Joe warned.

The mustached man scowled and hesitated, then shrugged. "Okay, you win. My name's Elmo Yancey. I'm a private eye."

"Prove it," snapped Frank.

The man pulled a billfold from his inside coat pocket. He opened it and presented them with his private investigator's license for the State of New York. The Hardys inspected it, and Frank nodded. "Good enough."

Yancey said he had been hired by a client to investigate and report on the Tabor family, especially the son. After coming to Hawk River, he heard about the werewolf who was said to be haunting the area. Then he read the news story hinting that John Tabor might be the culprit due to a family taint. Next day an unsigned note came to his motel in the mail, informing him that the young architect had been a mental patient at the Pine Manor Rest Home. So he went there to try to interview John's doctor.

"What about last night? And don't hand us any baloney," Frank added. "You were under surveillance."

"Then why ask?"

"We want to hear your version. It's one way to find out if you're leveling with us."

Yancey said he had decided to keep watch on the Tabor house to see if John slipped out after dark and had anything to do with the werewolf attacks. "He showed, all right, and he was acting pretty odd."

"How do you mean?" Joe said.

"He was moving like a sleepwalker, almost as if he were in a trance. I followed him for a while. He headed up a hillside, a little way north of here. I lost sight of him for a moment or two, but then I saw a gleam of light appear up near the top of the hill."

Frank frowned on hearing this. Chet had made no mention of any light. However, Frank reflected that it might not have been visible from their chum's position farther down the hillside.

"Right after that," Yancey went on, "I heard a scuffle break out somewhere below me. John Tabor must've heard it too, because the light went out, and then I caught sight of him again."

Yancey said that the young architect had headed homeward by a different route. The investigator himself had followed in order to make sure of where John was going. Afterward, Yancey had returned to the hillside to check on the scene of the scuffle, but found no one there. He had then discovered the hut near the top of the hill, from where the light had come.

"You looked inside?" Frank inquired.

"Naturally. It wasn't locked."

"Did you see a wolf skin in there?"

The private eye seemed startled by the question, but shook his head. "Nope, just books and architectural drawing gear. It looked as if John had used the place as a private studio where he could go off to study or work on plans."

"You're sure there was no fur pelt lying around?" Joe persisted.

"Positive. If there'd been anything like that, you can bet I'd have spotted it."

The Hardys exchanged glances. If Yancey's testimony was true, then the wolf skin must have been planted in the hut later, maybe by the same person who had tipped off the sheriff!

"How come you're back tonight?" Frank inquired.

Yancey shrugged. "I didn't really learn anything last evening. I figured tonight I might be luckier. But it sure didn't turn out that way," he added ruefully.

"Who is your client?" the older Hardy asked abruptly, hoping he might catch the detective off guard.

"You don't expect me to answer that, do you? No ethical private investigator reveals his client's identity without permission."

"We understand." Frank grinned and introduced himself and Joe.

Elmo Yancey's attitude changed immediately on learning that they were the sons of Fenton Hardy. He promised to tell them his client's name if and when he was allowed to do so. Meanwhile, he stayed with the Hardys and Chet, keeping watch on the Tabor's house. But when nothing happened by midnight, he abandoned his vigil.

The Bayport trio maintained their stakeout an hour longer. Then they, too, gave up for the night.

Next morning, Frank and Joe were relieved to get a radio call from their father. They filled him in on all that had happened, both in New York and in Hawk River.

Fenton Hardy, in turn, revealed that Bubbles Upton,

the son of the burly architect, was now working on the side of the law, trying to make up for the crime that had led to his jail sentence and thus redeem himself in the eyes of the authorities.

"Is he helping you on this case, Dad?" Joe inquired.

"Yes, he's checking out the possibility that a crooked contractor may be mixed up in those building disasters."

"Same angle Neal Xavier mentioned to us?"

"Right. But now I want you fellows to check out a brand-new lead for me in New York City. It may be urgent, so I'm sending Jack Wayne to fly you there."

The detective gave his sons careful instructions and on Chet's request, agreed that their stout chum could go with them.

"One other thing, Dad," put in Frank. "Could you give us the name of a psychiatrist in New York that we could talk to while we're there? I'd like to get another opinion on John Tabor's behavior."

"Good idea," said Fenton Hardy. He named a reliable expert whom he himself had consulted in connection with various criminal cases.

"Thanks, Dad, and watch yourself. Remember the warning note Bubbles sent to us in Central Park."

"Right, son, and you do the same. This assignment could be dangerous."

Jack Wayne often flew Mr. Hardy's private plane, *Skyhappy Sal*. An hour after the detective's call, the small craft landed at an airfield near Hawk River. The boys greeted the friendly pilot, then all set off for LaGuardia Airport in New York.

From there they taxied to the address Fenton Hardy had given them in a slummy area of the Bronx. It was a narrow-fronted, two-story brownstone house, squeezed between half-ruined tenement buildings. The boys scouted the scene first, then rang the bell. No one answered.

"Door's open," Joe noted. "Let's go in."

Frank led the way cautiously, through a dirty, tiled vestibule into the first-floor living room. All three gasped at the sight of a motionless figure lying bound and gagged on the floor.

"It's Bubbles Upton!" Joe exclaimed.

Chet blurted in dismay, "He's dead!"

17

The Flying Chicken

Frank rushed across the room, with his two companions close behind, and they examined the man on the floor. It was apparent from his bruised face and torn, red-stained clothes that young Upton had been badly beaten. But he was still breathing, and Frank was able to detect a fairly strong pulse.

"He'll be okay, if we get him to a doctor," the older Hardy boy declared. "Help me untie him."

He took off Bubbles' gag while Joe and Chet removed the rope from the young man's wrists and ankles. Then they lifted him onto a sofa.

Joe hurried into the kitchen to fetch a glass of water. A few swallows were forced between the victim's lips as Frank chafed his wrists. Soon young Upton opened his eyes.

"H—how did you guys get here?" he asked weakly.

"My father sent us," Frank informed him.

"Thank goodness. Then he—he must have clued in to my code signal." Bubbles explained that he had paid a ham radio operator to broadcast a call when he could not reach Fenton Hardy by phone.

Joe said, "Feel strong enough to tell us what happened?"

"I'll t—try," Bubbles responded. He said he had been hired by mobsters to crack the Chelsea Builders safe. "And I'm sure those same crooks who hired me are in cahoots with the contractor your father's investigating!"

"What did they want out of the safe?" Frank asked.

"Some sound tapes."

A look flashed between the Hardys. Once again Neal Xavier's charges seemed to be confirmed by outside testimony!

"Do you know what was on them?" Frank pursued.

Bubbles shook his head painfully. "No. I tried to play them to find out, but the mobsters caught me and beat me up. They planned to dump me in the river after dark."

Both Hardys wondered if young Upton realized the tapes might incriminate his own father. But they decided not to risk upsetting him while he was in such condition.

"We'll call an ambulance and get you to a hospital pronto!" Frank promised, looking around for a telephone.

But Bubbles insisted that it would be safer all around if the Hardys stayed out of the picture completely, so that no one could connect him with them or their father. "Besides, I'm not in bad enough shape to need an ambulance," he gasped hoarsely. "A taxi will do."

He protested so anxiously that the Hardys gave in. Joe hurried to the nearby corner and flagged a cruising cab. Bubbles Upton was helped into it, and the driver instructed to take him to the closest hospital.

The three Bayporters then proceeded by subway to the office of the psychiatrist that Fenton Hardy had recommended. The receptionist told them that the detective had already phoned for an emergency appointment, and after a short wait, they were waved into the doctor's consulting room.

Dr. Fizzoli, a bespectacled man with thick, dark hair fringing his bald head, asked the boys how he could help them.

Frank described John Tabor's weird behavior. "Is there any way a person could be influenced to do such things?" he went on, "and then not even remember what happened?"

"Of course," the doctor nodded. "Almost anyone could be made to behave that way, by post-hypnotic suggestion."

To accomplish this, he explained the person would first be hypnotized, then given an order to carry out after he woke up from his trance, perhaps quite a while afterward.

159

"The more often a person is hypnotized," Dr. Fizzoli went on, "the easier it comes to control him. Yet, when he's snapped out of his trance, he may not even remember being given any orders."

"Would he recall carrying them out?" Frank asked.

"Not if he'd been programmed to forget them."

Joe said, "But how would he know *when* to carry out the order?"

"Usually, the programming involves some sort of signal," replied the doctor. "For instance, the hypnotist may say, 'When you see me scratch my ear, you will do so and so.' And later on, after the patient's been brought out of his trance, the hypnotist scratches his ear and the patient does exactly what he was told to do."

With a smile, Dr. Fizzoli added, "If you ask him *why* he did such a thing, he'll make up all sorts of reasons. It never seems to occur to him that he may be carrying out a post-hypnotic suggestion."

Suddenly Frank remembered how John had been called to the phone during the barbecue party. A little later, when he came out of the house again, he had acted like a zombie.

"How about a signal over the phone?" he inquired. "Would that work?"

"Perfectly," said Dr. Fizzoli. "In fact, the phone voice, if it *is* a voice, could be used to reinforce or strengthen the original command. But the signal could just as easily be a buzzer or a handclap or a certain bit of music, whatever."

"What if the person didn't *want* to carry out the command?"

"Once he's been hypnotized, he has no choice."

Chet had been listening with a skeptical expression. "Hm, maybe some people are like that," he scoffed, "but I'd like to see somebody make *me* do something I didn't want to do!"

Dr. Fizzoli smiled. "Shall we try?"

"Go ahead," Chet challenged him.

The doctor held up a shiny coin on the end of a chain. He asked the chubby youth to gaze at it as it swung to and fro. Then, in a monotonous voice, he began to suggest that Chet was feeling relaxed and drowsy, that his limbs were growing heavier and losing all feeling, and finally that Chet would do whatever he was told.

Chet carried out several simple commands, such as shivering as if he were cold, barking like a dog, and dancing around the room. But later, after the doctor snapped his fingers to bring him out of his trance, Chet insisted he had never even been *in* a trance.

"I was wide awake all along. I knew what was going on. When you asked me to do something, I cooperated, but I didn't have to do it."

The doctor shrugged and smiled. "Perhaps so. Many subjects feel that way. The fact remains that you did what I told you to."

The Hardys grinned and thanked Dr. Fizzoli for his information and demonstration. Before leaving the

161

office, Frank asked the receptionist if he might use her phone.

"Of course," she said. "Let me get you an outside line first, then just dial the number."

Frank had Jack Wayne paged at LaGuardia Airport. When the pilot answered, the young detective told him to start warming up *Skyhappy Sal*. The boys would be ready for takeoff as soon as they taxied to the airfield.

"Maybe not as soon as you think " Jack replied. He said that an urgent message had been relayed from Bayport.

"From whom?" Frank asked.

"Some guy employed by Chelsea Builders, named Neal Xavier. He phoned your home, your aunt broadcast his message, and I picked it up on the radio."

"What does he want?"

"To see you and Joe as soon as possible. He says it's very important, but the meeting must be kept secret. You're to come to his apartment on Central Park West instead of the company office."

The boys were soon on their way by taxi to Xavier's address.

"Who is this guy?" Chet asked en route.

"Karel Tabor's executive assistant," Joe told him.

When they arrived at his apartment, the trio were surprised to find themselves facing a big, powerful, snarling Doberman guard dog held on a tight leash by Neal Xavier, who seemed tense and frightened.

"I rented him from a trainer last night for pro-

162

tection," Xavier told the boys. "Sit down, please, and I'll explain."

Pacing nervously back and forth while his dog sat watchfully eyeing the three visitors, Xavier began, "I've made a very unpleasant discovery. Much as I hate to say so, I now believe that the real criminal behind the firm's troubles is none other than my boss—Karel Tabor!"

The Bayporters were shocked by the news.

"What makes you think so?" Joe asked keenly.

Xavier explained that Tabor, despite his brilliant reputation, had long been at odds with Chelsea Builders' board of directors. He had, therefore, deliberately arranged the three building disasters which Mr. Hardy was investigating, in order to force down the price of Chelsea Builders' stock.

Frank frowned. "Why would he want to do that?"

"So he can buy it up cheaply and gain control of the company."

"How did he arrange the disasters?" Joe asked.

"Through that crooked contractor I mentioned. All three were due to sabotage carried out by mobsters. He told me those tapes contained evidence linking the contractor with Upton Associates. But now I'm sure they implicated Tabor himself. He was keeping them as insurance, to make sure the contractor didn't double-cross him."

"How did you find all this out?" Frank inquired.

"Just a lucky break, if you can call it lucky." Xavier

explained that, by chance, he had overheard a phone conversation between Tabor and the contractor. "They were setting up a meeting at ten o'clock tonight, at a house near Hawk River. If they get wise that I was listening in, my life won't be worth a plugged nickel!"

After learning the cabin's location, the boys taxied to LaGuardia and flew back to the Adirondacks. Frank and Joe had left their car parked at the airfield near Hawk River. On landing, they drove to the cabin.

Frank braked to a stop and said, "Well, here we are!"

Chet immediately leaped out of the car, flapping his arms. "Look! I'm a chicken!" he cried, cackling loudly. "I can fly!"

"Good for you!" said a girl's voice. "May I watch you take off?"

Chet whirled and saw Alena Tabor walking toward them!

18

Nine O'Clock Shadow

Chet's face blushed fiery red with embarrassment when he suddenly realized what he was doing. The Hardys burst out laughing.

"Good grief!" Chet moaned. "Whatever made me do such a goofy thing?"

"A post-hypnotic suggestion, that's what!" said Joe.

"Huh?"

"You were just doing what you were told to do," Frank added.

Chet stared at the Hardys, his cheeks still flaming. "What're you guys talking about?"

Frank explained that, while under hypnosis in the psychiatrist's office, Dr. Fizzoli had ordered their chum to act like a flying chicken when they arrived at their cabin.

"Cheer up, Chet." Joe chuckled. "He only did it to convince you such things are possible. Frank signaled you when he said, 'Well here we are!'"

To save Chet further embarrassment, Frank turned to their visitor. "What's up, Alena?"

Her face fell after her momentary amusement. "Oh, I'm so worried about John!" she replied. "Sheriff Kennig's been grilling him all afternoon. He's even warned him not to leave Hawk River. Dad and I are afraid he may soon be arrested!"

"Well, you can stop worrying," Frank told her. "I think we've just found out what makes your brother take those midnight strolls."

"What do you mean?" Alena exclaimed, her eyes widening in surprise.

Frank reported what they had learned from the psychiatrist about post-hypnotic suggestion, and went on, "I'm convinced something like that must have happened to John. Someone has hypnotized him deeply and ordered him to leave the house in the middle of the night. Do you remember whether he got a late phone call just before bedtime on Wednesday night?"

"Yes, as a matter of fact, he did. Why?"

"Same thing happened the night of the barbecue. Those calls may be from the person who hypnotized him, to give him reinforcing suggestions. Later, a wolf howl outside, even if it's a fake howl, is the signal that prompts him to leave the house."

"It would also explain why he acts like he's in a trance," said Joe. "Chet's just demonstrated to you how the whole thing works."

The plump girl's face broke into a happy smile. "Oh, that's wonderful!" she gushed. "You've no idea how relieved Dad will be when I tell him! Thank you all so very much!"

Before Chet realized what was happening, Alena flung her arms around his neck and kissed him a resounding smack on the cheek.

The chubby Bayporter's cheeks turned flaming pink again, but this time with bashful pleasure rather than embarrassment.

Meanwhile, Frank and Joe exchanged hasty glances of amusement mixed with concern. Both were thinking the same thing, that they had better not tell Alena about Neal Xavier's accusation against her father, and thus spoil her happiness of the moment. She drove off in her red miniwagon soon afterward, eager to tell her father the good news.

Later, as the boys were finishing supper, they heard a knock. Frank got up to answer the door. Their visitor proved to be Elmo Yancey.

"Come on in!" Frank said. "You're just in time for a cup of coffee."

"Thanks. Don't mind if I do." The private eye joined them at the table and proceeded to tell the news that had brought him to their cabin. "I just got a cablegram over the phone from my client. It's in reply to one I sent him this morning, and it gives me permission to use my judgment about telling you his name. But the information must be kept in strict confidence, of course."

"We understand," Frank assured him. "You can count on us to keep our lips zipped."

"Who is he?" Joe asked eagerly.

"A wealthy European businessman who lives in Paris. His name is Gustav Tabor."

"Tabor?" Joe echoed, and shot a glance at Frank. "That must be the distant cousin Mr. Tabor mentioned to us, the one who escaped to the West just before Czechoslovakia went Communist."

"Right," Frank agreed, and turned to Elmo Yancey. "How come he hired you to report on the American branch of the family?"

"Because he's old and rich and looking for an heir. He has no children of his own, so he's decided to leave his fortune to the youngest male Tabor over here. But first he wants a character check on both John and his father, Karel Tabor, to see if John is worthy of inheriting."

Chet whistled and murmured, "Well, what do you know!"

The Hardys thanked Yancey for the information. Later, after he had gone, Joe said to his brother, "You realize this may explain the whole werewolf business?"

Frank nodded thoughtfully. "I'll say I do! It could mean someone's deliberately trying to smear John and ruin his chances of inheriting Gustav Tabor's fortune."

"Right! But who?" Joe mused.

"You want a suggestion?"

"Let's hear it."

"How about the Frenchman who called on Desmond Quorn for information about the Tabor family werewolves?"

"Hey! You're right!" Joe exclaimed, socking his fist into his palm. "Then he steals the file and mails it, along with a copy of the magazine article, to the editor of the local newspaper, just to make sure everyone gets the message that John's slightly nutty and gets wolfman delusions every full moon!"

"Which wouldn't help John's chances of becoming Gustav Tabor's heir," Frank agreed.

"And to put him even deeper into the soup," Joe went on, "the Frenchman gets hold of a wolf skin and plants it in John's studio hut."

"Just two things wrong with your theory," Frank mused.

"What?" spoke up Chet, who was munching doughnuts and listening to the Hardys' conversation with great interest.

"One, it doesn't explain the glowing wolf-creature." Joe cocked a quizzical eyebrow. "And two?"

"Even if we're right," said Frank, "why is the culprit doing it, and how do we find him? We don't know a thing about him."

"Wrong," said Chet, between mouthfuls of pastry. "You know at least *one* thing about him."

"Name it," Frank said.

"He said his name was Julien Sorel."

"So what?"Joe shrugged. "It's not likely he'd use his real name."

Frank puckered his forehead. "Probably not. But Chet may have a point there. That name might just mean something to a member of the Tabor family."

"Hm, could be. Let's give it a whirl." Picking up the telephone, Joe called the Tabors' number. Alena answered. After telling her who he was, Joe said, "Does the name 'Julien Sorel' mean anything to you, Alena?"

"Of course!"

"Who is he?"

"The hero of a famous French novel by Stendhal, called *The Red and the Black*."

Joe groaned. "Thanks anyhow, Alena, but forget I asked."

Shortly before nine o'clock, the Hardys set out by car for the house where Karel Tabor was to meet the crooked contractor. Xavier had told the boys its exact location, which he had overheard while eavesdropping on the plotters' telephone conversation. The Hardys hoped to arrive in time to stake out the place before the meeting took place. Meanwhile, they left Chet to hold the fort and keep watch on the Tabors' house.

Frank was at the wheel as they tooled along the forest-fringed highway in the moonlight. "Don't look now, Joe," he murmured, "but I think we're being tailed."

"Lights in the rearview mirror?"

"No. Its headlights are out. That's what worries me, but I can see the car fairly well as long as the moon doesn't go behind a cloud. Whoever it is, he's been keeping the same distance behind us for almost ten miles."

Joe proposed a plan which Frank thought might work although it had possible dangers. The older Hardy slowed his speed somewhat, keeping an eye peeled for any turnoffs.

Presently he wheeled right onto a rutted lane which wound among a stand of oaks and evergreens, interspersed with clumps of underbrush. The growth was dense enough to screen the glow of their headlights from the highway.

Soon Frank veered again, swinging the car off the lane and into the first narrow space among the trees that presented itself. Then he switched off their lights and the boys waited.

In a few minutes the tail car came along the lane in cautious pursuit. Its driver had been forced to turn on his parking lights to see his way ahead.

No sooner had the car gone by than Frank vroomed his engine and backed out of their parking space, blocking the lane. As he switched on his lights, they saw the tail car slow to a halt, almost, it seemed, with an audible groan of despair. Its driver obviously realized that he was trapped. To keep going would have meant the risk of getting lost or disabled in the back country wilderness at night, well off the main artery.

It seemed simpler to give up the game as Joe and Frank gambled it would. There was a minute or two of silence. Then they saw the door of the tail car open. The driver got out in the glare of their headlights, with his hands up in a gesture of surrender. He was a young man in his twenties with wavy brown hair. His clothes seemed of foreign cut.

The Hardys stayed in their seats, letting the stranger approach the front of their car. Then Frank switched on his high beams, dazzling the stranger still more. If he thought they had him covered with a gun, so much the better.

"Don't come any closer," Frank growled. "Just toss us your identification and you won't get hurt."

The stranger threw what looked like a thin, leather-bound booklet. Frank caught it. It was a French passport in the name of Paul Clermont. Then came a letter of introduction in English from a bank in Paris.

"Oh, oh," Joe muttered as the Hardys glanced over the letter. It mentioned that the bearer, Paul Clermont, was a brother-in-law of the well-known financier, Gustav Tabor.

Frank turned down his high beams, and the boys got out to confront the Frenchman. Realizing the two young sleuths had him cornered, Clermont glumly admitted what they had already guessed. Namely, that he was attempting to spoil John's chances of inheriting Gustav Tabor's fortune by making the young architect seem like a dangerous lunatic.

"But surely that is no great crime," Clermont insisted. "The worst you can call it is a cruel prank."

"A prank to cheat John out of his rightful inheritance!" Frank retorted.

"You also stole a folder from Desmond Quorn's files," Joe added, "and swindled Alec Virgil out of his stuffed wolf."

Clermont became frightened when he saw how much they knew. "I promise you I will make amends," he pleaded, "if you don't turn me in to the police."

It was clear that he was afraid of getting into trouble which might be reported to Gustav Tabor. He explained that he was the young brother of Tabor's late wife, but Gustav had never liked him. Under the old man's present will, he would inherit only a small part of the estate. He had plotted to ruin John's chances as heir in hopes of getting a larger share of the fortune himself. Instead, he might be cut out of the will altogether if Gustav learned what he was up to.

Knowing Gustav was hiring Elmo Yancey to investigate John, Clermont had flown to this country before Yancey took the case. He already was familiar with the Tabor family's werewolf tradition, and when he learned of the werewolf scare at Hawk River, he decided this would be a good way to discredit John. He had found out from local gossip about John's hospital stay and had sent an anonymous note about this to Yancey.

Frank said coldly, "Are you sure you didn't start the werewolf scare yourself?"

"No! I swear it!" the Frenchman exclaimed. On Wednesday night, he said, he had sewn straps on the wolf skin and had come to plant it on the patio of the Tabor home. Then he saw John leave the house, with Yancey trailing him and Chet trailing both of them. So he, too, had followed. After getting into a scuffle with Chet and knocking him out, he had discovered John's studio hut.

He decided the hut would be the best place to plant the wolf skin, and did so the next day. Following that he tipped off the sheriff.

"What made you trail us tonight?" Joe asked.

Clermont shrugged ruefully. "I was shadowing Yancey and saw him come to your cabin. So I wanted to find out what you two were up to and how you fitted into the picture."

"Now you know," Joe said with a dry grin.

The Hardys decided to let the Frenchman go. As an alien, he would not be hard to trace, especially since they knew his car license.

Continuing their journey, they found the rendezvous house empty. With their car parked out of sight from the road, they sat waiting for Tabor and the crooked contractor to arrive.

Suddenly a red light flashed on the radio. Chet was calling.

"What's up?" Frank asked.

"Karel Tabor and his son drove away from their house about ten or fifteen minutes ago," the boy reported. "I just got back to our place."

"Any idea where they were going?"

"Looked to me like they were heading north to get on Route 30," Chet replied.

"Okay, Chet. Thanks a lot," Frank said and turned off the radio.

"Route 30?" Joe muttered. "That would be in the opposite direction from here!"

A cold suspicion began forming in Frank's mind. He looked thunderstruck. "Joe! Something tells me we have been decoyed from the real action!"

"You mean Neal Xavier conned us?"

"Sure do! But he may have spun us that yarn for his boss's sake!"

"Where could the Tabors be heading, Frank?"

"If they're taking Route 30, I can only think of one place."

"Eagle's Nest!" Joe exclaimed.

"Right! Let's not waste any more time hanging around here!" Frank revved the engine and they headed back the way they had come, then swung off on a shortcut which skirted Hawk River. Soon they were rolling north on Route 30 as fast as the law would allow.

Nearing Indian Lake, they detoured to a side road and parked about a half a mile from Eagle's Nest. By approaching the site on foot through the woods, they hoped to avoid being spotted.

Joe carried a long-range walkie-talkie hooked to his belt for emergency contact with Chet. Suddenly he gripped his brother's arm. "Look!"

In a deep, wooded ravine just ahead, they glimpsed the flickering light of a concealed campfire!

"That may be the Tabors and whoever they came to meet!" Frank declared. "Come on, let's try and get close enough to see their faces!"

The boys pressed forward cautiously. As they started down into the ravine, Joe lost his footing and crashed loudly into the dry brush.

Their quarry heard the noise. Almost instantly the campfire was doused, as if smothered by dirt or a blanket. Figures burst from the little clearing and dashed off in the moon-dappled darkness.

The boys were about to give chase but stopped short with a gasp. A weird, glowing wolf-creature had just leaped into view at the bottom of the ravine! Its fangs were bared in a ferocious snarl as it charged in the Hardys' direction!

"Leaping lizards!" Joe blurted. "It's a werewolf!"

19

The Werewolf

The beast came at them like a demon of the night, its ears laid back, eyes ablaze with savagery! One glimpse of its deadly fangs told the boys they were facing a killer!

"The dart gun!" Frank cried, shaking off an instant of paralyzing fear.

They raced back to their car and around behind it. Frank unlocked the trunk, yanked out the gun, broke it open at the breech and rammed home the tranquilizing dart cartridge that Joe handed him. By now the four-legged fury was close enough to spring for his throat.

Frank whipped up the gun and fired pointblank. *Bla-a-am!* The shot thundered through the night air. He saw the creature shudder and jerk in mid-leap. Then it was upon him. He went down beneath the glowing beast, holding the gun crosswise as a barrier while he struggled to keep its jaws from his throat!

Joe grabbed the animal from behind, clutching it by the nape of the neck. The wolf-creature growled furiously as he sought to wrestle it away from his brother. But in a few moments it began to weaken from the effects of the dart anesthetic and finally it collapsed limply at their feet.

Both boys were trembling violently. It seemed a miracle that neither had been slashed by the beast's rending fangs.

"Boy, you nailed it just in time!" Joe panted.

"Look here," Frank said, pointing with the toe of his shoe toward the animal's belly. Its glowing fur appeared to be *laced up* on the underside of its body, from its throat clear back toward its tail!

For a moment Joe could only stare in amazement. "Well, for crying out loud!" he muttered.

The boys undid the lacing and, after considerable effort, managed to remove the creature's false coat. Its glowing pelt had obviously been made from synthetic fur colored with fluorescent dye and crafted with great care so as to encase the animal snugly, even including a head mask and four "leggings."

The beast itself was a huge, deep-chested Doberman pinscher!

"It's Neal Xavier's guard dog!" Frank exclaimed.

There was no time to assess their amazing discovery.

Both boys felt it was more important to find out what the campfire plotters were up to and, if necessary, thwart their latest move.

"They may be planning to ruin Eagle's Nest or wreck the restoration work somehow!" Joe conjectured.

"Could be," Frank said. "That would make *four* Chelsea building disasters. If that's their game, we've got to stop them, Joe!"

Flashlights in hand, the Hardys hurriedly retraced their steps to the ravine. Probing downward, they reached the site of the campfire and continued on past it, playing their beams cautiously right and left in hopes of picking up the fugitives' trail.

"Hold it, Joe!" Frank called out suddenly.

"What's the matter?"

"Hear that crackling noise?"

Joe listened a moment, then gasped, "Oh, oh! I sure do!"

Both boys had the same thought. A brief reconnaissance soon confirmed their fears! In their haste to douse the campfire, the fugitives had failed to extinguish it completely, and now some of the surrounding leaf litter and undergrowth had evidently caught fire from the embers! Parched from the hot, dry August weather, the brush would go up like tinder and the trees themselves would soon be ablaze!

"Good grief! We'd better get out of here, Frank!"

"You're telling me!"

The boys tried to run back towards their car, but found the way blocked by a wall of flames. Veering in a different direction, they sought to clamber out of the gully by one of its steeper walls. But the night breeze was spreading the blaze fast, and wherever they turned, a scorching, crackling barrier of orange-yellow flames seemed to bar their progress. Soon the whole ravine was ringed with fire!

"We're trapped!" Joe started to exclaim in despair, but he choked back the words in his throat and snatched up the walkie-talkie from his belt. He began beaming out a call to Chet, describing their horrible plight.

"Come on! Over this way, Joe!" Frank called.

Joe hurried to join him. "Where're you going?"

"There's a creek that runs through this ravine. I caught a glimpse of it in the moonlight when we were creeping up on the campfire. That'll give us a fighting chance to survive, if we can find it!"

Blundering about in the firelit darkness, the Hardys eventually reached the shallow, boggy stream. Frank had hoped that, by wading its full length, they might make their way out of the trap. But blazing trees came crashing down across the creek to block their escape. Finally they realized that their only hope was to stay hip-deep in the water and wait for rescue, or else for the fire to burn itself out.

Meanwhile, Joe continued to radio for help. But no response came over the walkie-talkie's loudspeaker.

"What's wrong? Why doesn't Chet answer?" Joe said in frustration.

"This ravine we're in or the heat waves from the fire may be interfering with our reception," Frank guessed.

"Let's hope it hasn't spoiled our transmission!"

The heat from the fire on both sides of the creek was intense. The boys splashed themselves with water to make it more bearable. Suddenly they were startled to attention by a noise from somewhere overhead.

"That's a plane, Frank!"

"I know! There it is!" The older Hardy boy pointed, "Let's try signalling with our flashlights!"

They aimed their beams skyward and waved their flashlights back and forth. Whether such feeble signals could be seen among the flames seemed doubtful, but their hopes were buoyed by the appearance of possible help.

"Look! The plane's circling, Frank!"

"The pilot must have seen us, or at least he's noticed there's a forest fire down here. Maybe *he'll* radio for help!"

What followed seemed like a miracle to the boys. A whitish stream began to spew downward from the circling aircraft. Hissing smoke billowed through the ravine as it hit the trees.

"It's chemical foam!" Frank cried joyfully.

Presently the pilot's voice came through over Joe's walkie-talkie. "Do you read me, Hardys? . . . Come in, please! . . . This is Jack Wayne in *Skyhappy Sal!*"

"We read you, Jack! And do you ever sound good!" Joe responded. "Just keep dumping that foam!"

After a few more passes by the plane, the blaze gradually sputtered out. As soon as the fire-blackened woods cooled enough underfoot to permit their passage, Frank and Joe clambered out of the ravine.

A few hundred yards beyond, they reached the road bordering Indian Lake. Ahead and to the right, they could glimpse Eagle's Nest looming on the hillside in the moonlit darkness. The boys ran toward it. Parked near the roadside was a light-colored four-door sedan. Frank and Joe recognized it as the Tabors' car, which they had seen standing in the driveway of the family's house. Something else lay on the roadway nearby.

"Frank, it's another wolf skin!" Joe exclaimed, pausing long enough to snatch it up. "Wow! Look at those fangs, and the claws feel razor-sharp!"

"This one's got straps, too, for buckling it on!" Frank noticed, playing his flashlight over the furry disguise.

"But never mind all that now, we can examine it later. Let's find out what's going on at Eagle's Nest!"

Flinging the wolf skin over the hood of the car, the Hardys hurried up the hillside. Frantic voices reached their ears.

"Help! Help!"

By this time, they were nearing the old timber mansion. Frank shone his flashlight in the direction of the cries. Two figures could be seen on the upper-story porch.

183

"It's Mr. Tabor and John! They're tied up!" Frank gasped.

The Hardys reached the building, ran inside and up a stairway. Making their way through the ancient structure, they came out on the porch and began untying the Tabors.

"The scoundrels who tied us used guns to *make* us call for help!" Karel Tabor exclaimed.

"Where are they?" Joe asked, working busily.

"You didn't see them?" put in John. "They must have gone out a different way than you came in."

At that moment they heard a resounding thud, and the whole porch quivered. More blows followed.

"Great Scott!" cried the elder Tabor. "This porch is braced with temporary supports, and they're knocking out the props with sledgehammers!"

As he spoke, there was a loud rending, creaking noise and the porch started to give way! The Hardys' hearts were in their mouths as they realized they would be dumped down the steep hillside to their deaths on the rocks far below!

20

Battle Royal

The porch swayed and teetered perilously beneath their feet. "Quick!" Frank cried. "Back inside!"

Mouldy timbers were cracking and splitting, ancient wooden pegs coming loose! Without bothering to finish untying the two prisoners, the Hardys dragged them frantically into the building through the open doorway.

Not a moment too soon! Scarcely an instant after they were inside the old mansion, a deafening *crack* resounded through the night air. The porch broke loose and crashed down the hillside!

With deft fingers, Frank and Joe finished undoing the ropes. "We'd better get out of here pronto!" Frank urged, straightening up from his task. "No telling what those crooks'll do next!"

The answer was soon apparent as the Hardys and the Tabors hurried to the stairway leading to the ground floor. Half a dozen figures were about to swarm up from below. Evidently the gang had realized that their intended victims had escaped destruction, and they were coming up to finish them off in person!

Frank and Joe recognized Neal Xavier's sharp-eyed visage among the upturned faces of their enemies, visible in the glare of the Hardys' flashlights.

"Come on! Grab some of these loose timbers!" Joe yelled to his companions.

The floor of the musty old mansion was strewn with boards, beams and other debris. Together the Hardys seized one good-sized plank and hurled it into the midst of their onrushing foes. Karel and John Tabor followed suit.

All four rained more wooden missiles on the crooks below. Then, before Xavier and his accomplices could recover their weapons and collect their wits, the group rushed down the stairway and leaped on them, kicking out and punching in all directions.

Despite the odds, the four held their own in the wild melee that followed. Even so, the outcome might have gone against them had two more fighters not joined the fray. The newcomers waded in, fists flying. One of the enemy quickly went down for keeps, then another, as punches connected with jaws. In the shadowy gloom, illuminated by moonlight streaming through the gaping windows and open sections of walls that were being replaced or repaired, Frank finally recognized their welcome allies.

"It's Dad and Jack Wayne!" he shouted to Joe.

The fight soon ended as the crooks lost heart. Neal Xavier tried to get away, but Frank brought him down with a flying tackle.

Fenton Hardy explained to his sons that he and Jack had been flying to Hawk River when they picked up Joe's radioed calls for help. Jack had landed at the airfield near Hawk River just long enough to load a tank of fire-fighting foam onto the aircraft. Then, within minutes, they had flown to the scene.

"It took a while to find a place to set down after the fire was out," Jack added, "but I guess we got here in time."

"You couldn't have timed it better!" Frank said gratefully. "Boy, that was some scrap!"

Joe was nursing a set of badly skinned knuckles. "If this joint was Dark Eagle's castle," he said with a wry chuckle, "I guess you could call what happened a battle royal!"

From among the workmen's supplies inside the mansion, Karel Tabor produced several lanterns, and Fenton Hardy proceeded to interrogate the prisoners. Besides Neal Xavier, they included the crooked contractor with whom he was involved and three of the latter's gangster stooges, as well as another man, who proved to be a male nurse from the Pine Manor Rest Home.

Mr. Tabor looked pale and exhausted from the night's hectic events. However, his color gradually returned after taking some of his heart medicine, and he seemed jubilant over the fact that the mysteries troubling his firm and his family were at last being resolved.

The Hardys learned that he had discovered several serious engineering errors in Xavier's architectural work. He also found out that Xavier had taken bribes to let the contractor use cheaper, substandard materials than the specifications called for on construction jobs which he carried out for Chelsea Builders.

"Why didn't you report him?" Fenton Hardy asked.

"I was afraid if the news leaked out it would harm our firm's good name," Karel Tabor replied. "So I agreed to say nothing if he would promise to reform and return the bribes. To ensure this, I recorded his full confession on tape."

"And that's why you said nothing when Joe and I came to your office?" put in Frank.

"Exactly. I left it to Neal's own conscience as to how much he would tell you about the stolen contents of the safe."

Xavier had cleverly twisted this situation to throw suspicion first on Upton Associates and then on his trusting boss, Karel Tabor himself, who was unaware that Xavier had, in fact, arranged the safe robbery with the help of the contractor's gangster associates in order to get rid of the incriminating tapes.

Xavier had joined Chelsea Builders with high ambitions, hoping some day to become the firm's president. Under Fenton Hardy's shrewd questioning, he confessed that he had connived with the same accomplices to cause the various building disasters and thus force Karel Tabor into early retirement.

However, John Tabor posed a new threat to his ambitions. The young architect was so brilliant, it seemed likely he would be chosen to succeed his father as head of the company. So Xavier devised the werewolf plot in order to drive the young man out of his mind, or at least make him appear unfit to run the firm.

From friendly chats with his boss, Xavier already knew about the family werewolf legend, and he gleaned other information by calling Desmond Quorn. At first he had pestered John with disturbing phone calls, disguising his voice. Later, after recommending the Pine Manor Sanatorium to the young man's father, he had harried John further with ghost voices by means of electronic gimmicks planted with the help of a friend who worked there as a male nurse. The latter was an expert hypnotist. While pretending to help John relax, the nurse had implanted post-hypnotic suggestions to make him behave suspiciously when he returned home to Hawk River.

On learning that the Tabors planned to call in the Hardy boys, Xavier had carried out the various incidents in Bayport to try and scare them off the case. He had also been the limping masquerader at the barbecue party—another step in his war of nerves against the Tabors.

Fearing that the Hardys might soon crack the case, Xavier had decided to eliminate both Karel Tabor and his son, John. To do this, he had first decoyed the Hardys off on a false scent, then lured the Tabors to Eagle's Nest with an emergency phone call.

Xavier's plan was to have his savage Doberman attack and kill the elder architect, which he assumed would not be difficult, given Tabor's weak heart. John would be found unconscious nearby with a wolf skin disguise, which Xavier had fashioned from a pelt the gangsters had stolen in a fur warehouse robbery. John would then be blamed for killing his father in a fit of werewolf mania.

"But you two punks had to spoil everything when you spotted our campfire in the ravine!" Xavier snarled at the Hardy boys.

The porch "accident" was his substitute murder plot for getting rid of all four victims, when it turned out Frank and Joe had survived the fire.

"His plan nearly worked, too," Frank remarked to his father as the Hardys strolled outside while waiting for the State Police to arrive and take charge of the prisoners.

"Another second or so, and we'd have taken a plunge with the porch," Joe added, then gasped.

"What's wrong?" Fenton Hardy inquired.

Joe hastily clambered up one of the broken porch

supports toward something that glinted in the moonlight. When he climbed down again, he was clutching a lightly gleaming hatchet.

"It's Dark Eagle's silver tomahawk!" cried Frank.

Next day, Chet and Alena accompanied the Hardy boys to the Mohawk village near Hawk River, where Frank and Joe presented the trophy to Hank Eagle. The Indians gazed at it and examined it with awed reverence.

"Dark Eagle died on the porch when he was very old, looking over the lake," Hank told the Hardys. "The mansion was probably getting pretty dilapidated even then. The tomahawk must have fallen from his hand and embedded itself in one of the supports. You don't know how much finding this means to my people!"

"It will always remind us of our proud past," said his uncle, the medicine man, "and be an inspiration to our young ones!"

"It might even inspire Chet to build a better canoe," Joe whispered to Alena with a grin.

"Listen! She's already promised to come paddling with me, wise guy!" Chet retorted. "But first we're going to stop on the way back to Hawk River for a few hamburgers and a banana split!"

The Hardy Boys Mystery Stories
by Franklin W. Dixon

Look out for these thrilling new mysteries in Armada.

The Mystery of Smugglers Cove (62)

When a valuable painting is stolen, the Hardy Boys are determined to catch the thieves. But the trail of clues soon leads them to the steamy swamps of Florida – and to a deadly encounter with some man-eating alligators!

Coming soon

The Stone Idol (63)

The strange disappearance of an ancient stone statue begins a hair-raising new adventure for the Hardys. But their investigations lead them into a sinister trap – in the freezing wilderness of the Antarctic.

The Vanishing Thieves (64)

Frank and Joe's search for a valuable missing coin takes them to California. But they soon realise that they are on the trail of a particularly nasty bunch of crooks . . .

2
The Mystery of the
Samurai Sword

The Hardy Boys® in
The Mystery of the Samurai Sword

The Mystery of the Samurai Sword
was first published in the U.K. in a single volume
in hardback in 1980 by Angus & Robertson Ltd.,
and in Armada in 1981
by Fontana Paperbacks,
8 Grafton Street, London W1X 3LA.

© 1979 Stratemeyer Syndicate.

Contents

1

Mysterious Flashes

Gusty sheets of rain swept the Bayport airfield. The moon had disappeared behind a heavy overcast sky, but the glare of floodlights lit the airport with almost daytime brilliance.

A little knot of people, huddling beneath umbrellas, watched eagerly as a small jet plane swooped out of the darkness and braked to a screaming halt between the twin rows of landing lights.

"Just a few seconds till ten o'clock," announced dark-haired, eighteen-year-old Frank Hardy with a glance at his wristwatch. "Mr. Satoya's right on the button!"

"Hey, what's going on over there?" muttered his blond brother, Joe, who was a year younger.

Through the rain-washed glass front of the airport

terminal wing, a bearded man could be seen gesticulating wildly. He was waving a long, sheathed sword over his head.

"Looks like a Japanese samurai sword," said Frank.

"Sure does! But what's wrong with the guy?" Joe wondered aloud. "Is he doing a war dance or just trying to attract our attention?"

Before Frank could reply, a policeman appeared and hustled the man away despite his protests.

Meanwhile, an unloading ramp had been wheeled up to the executive jet, which bore the famous red-and-white emblem of the Satoya Corporation—a samurai sword curving beneath the rising sun.

"Have you ever seen Mr. Satoya before, Dad?" Frank asked his father, who stood next to the boys.

Fenton Hardy shook his head. "No. Very few people have in recent years. He runs a worldwide business, but has become almost a hermit. In fact he has seldom been photographed."

"Sounds like quite a mystery man!"

"You could call him that, I suppose. Actually that's what a good many reporters and magazine writers *do* call him—just because he's so hard to see or interview."

"Who do you suppose leaked news of his trip to the press?" put in Joe.

"Good question," his father replied grimly. "I intend to find out the answer. His company wanted this visit to America kept top secret, and we've done everything possible to maintain tight security at this end."

The tall, distinguished-looking detective, formerly an ace investigator with the New York Police Department, had been hired to protect the Japanese tycoon from assassins or terrorists during his stay in the United States. But despite Mr. Hardy's efforts to ensure secrecy, a number of reporters had shown up at the airport to witness Satoya's arrival. Luckily the police were keeping them at a distance.

Two men were allowed through the barrier and joined Mr. Hardy and his sons. One was the detective's longtime operative, Sam Radley, the other a burly six-foot Japanese named Kawanishi. He was a Satoya executive, who had flown to the United States with a colleague a few days earlier to arrange details of the trip.

Just then an erect, gray-haired man with a wispy mustache emerged from the plane.

"Ah! That is my revered employer, Mr. Takashi Satoya," Kawanishi said. After greeting the tycoon in Japanese, he introduced him to the Hardys and Sam Radley.

A younger man had followed Satoya down the ramp. He turned out to be another executive of the firm, but of lower rank than Kawanishi. His name was Ikeda. He was slim and strongly built, and his black hair was cut very short.

"I suggest we get underway as soon as your car is unloaded, sir," Mr. Hardy said to Satoya.

The tycoon nodded courteously. "Whatever you say,

Mr. Hardy. Our security is in your hands from this point on."

A cargo hatch had already been opened in the executive jet, and a sleek black limousine was driven out of the plane's interior and down a ramp onto the airfield. It was bigger and longer than most Japanese cars. Joe whistled admiringly as a granite-faced chauffeur drove it smoothly toward the group. "Some job!"

"You can say that again," Frank agreed. "Must have been specially built."

Mr. Satoya and his junior aide, Ikeda, took their places in the back seat of the limousine. Sam Radley was allowed, rather grudgingly it seemed, to sit in front beside the chauffeur.

The burly senior aide, Kawanishi, was to ride in Mr. Hardy's car behind the limousine, while a state policeman of the highway patrol would clear the way on a motorcycle at the head of the procession.

Frank and Joe, also mounted on motorcycles, had been assigned to act as outriders.

"Keep a sharp eye open for trouble anywhere along the route into town," the detective told his sons before taking the wheel of his car.

"Will do, Dad!" Joe replied.

"I'm glad we wore our raingear," Frank murmured as the two boys started toward their road bikes.

"We'll probably get soaked anyhow," said Joe. "One good thing, though—this rain should cut down the traffic quite a bit."

At a radio signal from Fenton Hardy, the little motorcade got underway, tooling along the exit road that led out of the airport. Once on the open highway, the vehicles picked up speed. The motorcade rolled along smoothly for several miles. But as the expressway wound through a hilly stretch, the state policeman waved his hand in a sudden warning signal.

Frank and Joe heard his voice come over their CB radios: "Looks like a little tie-up!"

Two or three cars had slowed to a halt just ahead. The policeman steered his motorcycle past them to find the reason for the delay. Frank and Joe followed suit. They braked as they saw a tree lying across the road.

"The storm must have blown it down off the hillside," Frank opined.

"What's the trouble, fellows?" Fenton Hardy's voice crackled on the radio.

"Tree down. Nothing serious, Dad," Joe replied. "We'll be moving again soon."

Dismounting, the Hardys lent the policeman a hand in clearing the obstruction. The windfallen tree was little more than a sapling, but somewhat awkward for one man to handle.

As soon as it was out of the way, the cars began to roll again. Frank and Joe were about to climb back on their motorcycles when a brilliant light flashed from the hillside on the right.

"What was that?" Joe exclaimed.

Two more dazzling flashes exploded in quick succession.

"Must be a photographer!" Frank guessed.

"You're right!" Joe blurted. "Snapping pictures of Mr. Satoya, I'll bet!"

As their vision recovered from the flashes, they saw a figure burst from cover and sprint up the muddy hillside in the darkness. The Hardys wanted to leave their bikes and take off in angry pursuit but horns began to honk impatiently as more and more cars lined up behind them.

"No law against taking pictures," said the state policeman philosophically.

"Guess you're right," Frank agreed with a disgusted look. "Too bad we can't prove he planted that roadblock."

The Hardys and the policeman gunned their cycles into action again, and the motorcade resumed its swift journey into Bayport.

They passed through the outskirts and soon reached the downtown area. The rain had subsided, and the wet pavement glistened under the street lights.

As they neared the Bayport Chilton Hotel, Joe saw a short, thickset, broad-shouldered Japanese come out and stand beside the doorman to watch the approaching motorcade. He was Mr. Oyama, who had flown to the USA with Mr. Kawanishi to prepare for their employer's visit.

Oyama was wearing a radio headset and had a small

transceiver tucked in his breast pocket. Joe guessed that Satoya's chauffeur must have transmitted word of their arrival.

The sleek black limousine drew up directly in front of the hotel entrance canopy. Mr. Hardy's car stopped behind it, while his two sons and the highway patrolman found parking places for their motorcycles along the curb.

The chauffeur was the first to leap out. Sam Radley, Fenton Hardy and Mr. Kawanishi followed suit, while a little knot of onlookers gathered to goggle at the VIP in the limousine. Waving the doorman away, the chauffeur moved swiftly to open the back door of the car. He stood stiffly at attention, waiting for his master to get out. But Satoya did not emerge from the limousine!

Fenton Hardy and Mr. Kawanishi reacted simultaneously, guessing that something was wrong. They almost bumped heads as they bent forward to peer into the car's rear passenger compartment.

"What's the matter, Dad?" Frank exclaimed, noticing his father's startled expression.

A moment later, as the Hardy boys pressed closer, they could see for themselves the reason for the men's dismay.

The young executive named Ikeda lay slumped unconscious in the back seat of the limousine, and Mr. Satoya had disappeared!

2

Telltale Splashes

The news spread like wildfire among the bystanders. They pressed closer, exclaiming excitedly.

"What about Mr. Ikeda, Dad?" Joe asked.

"Looks like he's been drugged," said Mr. Hardy after thumbing back the victim's eyelids to examine his pupils. "Go get the hotel doctor, Joe—this man may need attention."

The medic quickly arrived on the scene. He confirmed Mr. Hardy's opinion, but stated that Ikeda would probably sleep off the anesthetic without any ill effects.

Seeing the unconscious Japanese being carried into the hotel stirred fresh excitement among the sidewalk crowd. Luckily the highway patrolman was able to hold them back.

"You've no idea what happened, Sam?" Fenton Hardy asked his operative.

"Not a clue," Radley confessed, looking chagrined and mystified. "The dark partition between the front and back seats is a one-way glass pane. When you're sitting in front, you can't see into the rear passenger compartment at all."

The driver, he explained, relied on a wide-angle roof periscope for his view of the road behind instead of a rearview mirror.

"Could Mr. Satoya have jumped out when we stopped on the highway to remove that tree?" Frank inquired.

Mr. Hardy frowned. "Seems to be the only possible answer, but my car was right behind the limousine. I can't believe he got out without either Mr. Kawanishi or myself spotting him."

The burly Japanese agreed and added, "Unfortunately the chauffeur, Shigemi, doesn't speak much English. But I questioned him while the doctor was examining Ikeda, and he can shed no light on the mystery."

Frank glanced at the stony-faced driver and wondered if he knew more than he was telling. But his impassive expression gave no hint of whatever thoughts might be passing through his head.

"Think you would have noticed if the back door had been opened on either side?" Joe asked Sam Radley.

The private eye hesitated before nodding unhappily. "Yes, I do. But it's hard to be sure."

Mr. Oyama, the other senior aide, exchanged a few words in Japanese with the chauffeur and then turned back to the Americans.

"A red light on the dashboard flashes if either back door is opened, or even if one becomes unlatched," he pointed out. "Shigemi is quite certain no such thing happened."

"That's assuming the flasher works," Mr. Hardy countered shrewdly. "Better have him check it to make sure."

Oyama transmitted the order in Japanese. The chauffeur touched his cap in a silent salute, then closed the car doors and climbed back behind the wheel. He drove the limousine past the hotel, then turned down a ramp which led to an underground parking garage.

By now reporters and television news crews, who had been unable to interview Mr. Satoya at the airport, were arriving at the hotel. They crowded around the detectives and the two Japanese aides, bombarding them with questions and adding to the noisy confusion.

"What do you make of it, Frank?" Joe asked.

"I have no idea," Frank said, "but this sure puts Dad on the spot!"

"I'll say it does," Joe agreed as they made their way into the hotel lobby. "The Satoya Corporation hires him to protect the head of their company—and now Satoya disappears less than an hour after he lands!

211

Boy, that'll really look bad in the news stories wh—"

Frank flashed his brother a quizzical glance as the younger Hardy boy suddenly broke off. "What's the matter, Joe?"

"Over there by the reception desk, " Joe pointed. "It's that nut we saw at the airport, waving a sword!"

"Hey, you're right! Now's our chance to find out what he wanted!"

The bearded man had just peeled off his tan raincoat. He was folding it and laying it on top of his suitcases while he waited to check in behind two other newly arrived guests. As he straightened up, he saw the Hardys striding toward him, and his face took on an embarrassed, furtive expression.

"We're Frank and Joe Hardy, two of Mr. Satoya's escorts," the older boy said. "Would you mind telling us why you were waving that sword at the airport?"

The man's face reddened and his prominent nose seemed to twitch nervously like a rabbit's. He had a wild mop of curly hair, the same sandy color as his whiskers, which somehow added to his look of comic confusion.

"Well, uh, actually it was just a spur of the moment advertising tactic, you might say." The man chuckled, then gulped. "I was hoping I might make a lucky sale."

"A lucky *sale?*" Joe regarded him with a puzzled frown. "A sale of what?"

"The samurai sword you saw. It's a *katana*, or long sword, of excellent workmanship, dating from the early eighteenth century. I thought if I could catch Satoya's eye, he might be interested enough to buy it."

The man bent down and opened the larger of his two suitcases so the boys could look inside. To their astonishment, they saw that it contained a number of sheathed swords and daggers. "That's my business—selling Oriental art objects—but as you see, I specialize in fine blades."

Snapping his suitcase shut again, the man plucked a card from his wallet and handed it to the Hardys. It bore the name *Axel Gorky* with a phone number and cable address in Boston.

Joe said, "How did you know Mr. Satoya was coming to Bayport?"

"But I didn't," Gorky replied, looking surprised at the question. "Had I known, I would have written beforehand to ask for a proper appointment! I myself just arrived in Bayport this evening, a short time before he did. When I saw the TV camera crews, I asked what was going on. Someone told me this famous Japanese industrialist was about to land—so I seized my chance."

Gorky's face went pink again. "Perhaps I did make a fool of myself, waving the sword as I did—but then one has to catch the customer's attention in order to make a sale."

"Any objection to telling us your business here in Bayport?" Frank asked stolidly.

"Of course not. I came to call on several customers—including the dancer Warlord. As you probably know,

213

he uses various knives and swords in some of his dance numbers."

Just then the two guests in front of him finished registering at the hotel desk. Gorky excused himself and moved up to sign for a room. He looked relieved at the chance to get away from the Hardys.

"Think he was leveling with us?" Joe muttered as the boys started back across the lobby.

Frank grinned dryly. "His story's so nutty I'm inclined to buy it. Anyhow, he's checking in at the Chilton, so we'll know where to find him if we want to ask him more questions."

Just then they saw their father and Mr. Kawanishi come into the hotel, accompanied by Chief Collig, head of the Bayport police force. Newsmen swarmed in after them, trying to snap pictures and pick up additional morsels of information for the next morning's headline stories on the Japanese tycoon's sensational disappearance.

"No use trying to talk to Dad," Frank said. "Let's see what's doing outside."

"Okay."

A bigger crowd than before was milling about the sidewalk, a couple of plainclothes detectives circulating among them. The Hardy boys saw Sam Radley conferring with the state policeman and trying to fend off other news hawks.

The boys shucked their raincoats, rolled them up and stuffed them into their motorcycle pouches.

"Oh, oh!" Frank suddenly murmured under his breath.

Joe glanced up at his brother. "What's the matter?"

"Take a look at that photographer."

"Where?"

"Over there. The one snapping a picture of the motorcycle cop."

"What about him?"

Frank drew his brother closer to the man in question. The photographer was using an expensive Japanese-made 35-millimeter camera and a "potato-masher" flash unit powerful enough for long-range shots at night.

Joe looked at Frank, puzzled. "I don't get it. What am I supposed to see?"

"Those mud stains on his pants," Frank whispered.

The man's trouser legs were splashed up to the knees. Even his raincoat bore a few muddy traces.

"Wow!" Joe hissed. "He could've been that guy on the hillside who snapped pictures when we were coming in from the airport!"

Joe's muted exclamation carried farther than he expected. The photographer whirled around and stared at the boys suspiciously. The next instant he dashed off across the street!

"After him!" Frank cried.

The Hardys took off in hot pursuit. Their quarry was already disappearing down the block. He was a healthy-looking young man in his early twenties, and now he was whizzing away from them with long-legged trip-hammer strides. Frank and Joe could hardly keep him in sight!

He rounded the next corner into a dark side street. The Hardys made a skidding turn and continued the chase, though for the moment neither could see the fugitive ahead.

Their pursuit might have ended in failure had Joe not glimpsed a movement out of the corner of his eye. Glancing toward the building on his left, he saw a figure huddled in a darkened doorway.

"Hold it, Frank!" Joe shouted, braking hard with shoe leather. "I think I've found him!"

A moment later, as Joe lunged toward the doorway, he caught a fist square in the face!

3

The Face at the Window

The blow was too hasty to have much force, but it landed hard enough to knock Joe off balance. He grabbed the photographer's raincoat to steady himself, and by hanging on like a bulldog, kept the man from getting away.

By this time Frank had reached the scene. For a few moments fists flew in all directions. But their quarry soon realized he was cornered and gave up.

"Okay, okay, cool it, you two!" the photographer panted.

"You're the one who started swinging!" Frank retorted angrily.

"What did you expect me to do when two guys start chasing me down a dark street? Just stand still and get mugged?"

"Nobody's mugging you. We just wanted to ask you some questions."

"How did I know that?"

"If you had nothing to hide," put in Joe, "why did you run away from us?"

"Why should I have anything to hide? I've never even seen you before!"

"Oh no? How about on the highway tonight, when we were escorting Mr. Satoya's limousine in from the airport?"

The young photographer glared sullenly. "I don't know what you're talking about!"

"Can the innocent act!" Frank growled. "The film in your camera will prove whether or not you're the guy who snapped those flash photos on the hillside."

"So what if I did? There's no law against taking pictures."

"There is against blocking traffic—especially when you deliberately plant an obstruction on the open highway, like that tree you dragged across the road!"

"You can't prove that!"

"Look! We're not going to waste any more breath," Frank declared. "If you'd rather have us call the police, we will—and you can explain to them how it all happened. On the other hand, if you'd rather talk to us, we're willing to listen—and if you're not mixed up in anything crooked, we'll promise not to turn you in."

The photographer hesitated uncertainly, his glance

wavering back and forth between the two Hardy boys. Finally he made up his mind. "Okay, I'll talk . . . Not that I have much to tell you."

"We'll decide that," said Joe. "You know who we are?"

"Sure, you're the Hardy boys. From what I gather, your dad was hired to protect Satoya."

Frank's eyes narrowed. "Who told you that?"

The photographer shrugged. "Nobody in particular. It was just common gossip among the newsmen around here. Actually I heard a couple of reporters talking about it at the airport restaurant earlier this evening."

"Any idea where *they* picked it up?"

"I got the impression someone phoned a tip to one of the papers. He revealed the whole story about Satoya's visit to this country—including the fact that Fenton Hardy was supposed to keep him under wraps."

"You work for the *Bayport Herald*?" Joe asked.

"Nope, just a stringer for the wire services. I'm a freelancer."

The photographer, whose name turned out to be Pete Ogden, said he had devised and carried out his roadblock trick with the aid of a couple of members of the local Gung-Ho motorcycle gang. One had waited at the airport and called Ogden at a roadside phone booth to alert him as soon as the motorcade got underway for Bayport.

The other gang member had helped him maneuver

the fallen tree into position so that it could be toppled across the highway at short notice. Then the same youth had cycled back toward the airport and tipped off Ogden by walkie-talkie when he sighted Satoya's limousine and escorts.

"I figured if I could obtain a couple of good candid camera shots of Satoya," the photographer concluded, "they'd not only bring a high price, they might even help me land a job on one of the major newspapers."

"Wait a minute," Frank said with a thoughtful frown. "Did you *get* any good shots?"

"Dunno, I haven't developed them yet. But I sure hope so. I wanted to shoot some more pictures at the hotel, but it turned out that Satoya had disappeared."

"But do you think you *got* him?" Frank persisted.

Ogden scratched his head. "Well, I got somebody. There was a face in the window when the second and third flashes went off."

"But you're not sure whose? I mean, you couldn't describe the face?"

Ogden shook his head. "No way. It all happened too fast, and I was too excited."

Frank exchanged a look with Joe, who by now had caught the reason for his brother's questions.

"Leaping lizards!" the younger Hardy boy exclaimed. "If we could see those pictures, they might tell us whether or not Satoya jumped out during the traffic tie-up!"

Pete Ogden was not enthusiastic about sharing his

possibly valuable photos with the Hardys. But he realized that if he refused, the police were likely to seize his camera and impound the film as evidence. So he agreed to develop the roll immediately and allow Frank and Joe to inspect the results.

The Hardys and Ogden returned to the photographer's car, which was parked near the hotel. Then the two boys trailed him home on their motorcycles. He lived in a small flat above a bookstore on the edge of the downtown area.

Frank and Joe waited while he developed the film. The negatives were too small for them to recognize the face in the car window, even when viewed under a magnifying glass. So Ogden made an eight-by-ten enlargement of the best shot.

It showed that the person looking out of the limousine was definitely Satoya! He was wide-eyed and his mouth was partly open, portraying the typical expression of a subject surprised by a sudden photoflash.

"So he was in the car all right, even after we removed the tree!" Joe declared.

"And he sure doesn't look like he was about to hop out in the next few moments before we got underway again," Frank added.

Pete Ogden shot an excited glance at the Hardys. "Then you mean this photograph *proves* something about the mystery?"

Frank nodded. "I'd say it proves that Satoya did not disappear on the highway."

"Hey, how about that?" Ogden snapped his fingers triumphantly. "Maybe I can sell these shots for even more than I figured! Thanks a lot, you guys."

Outside Ogden's flat, the boys were about to climb back on their motorcycles when Joe suddenly stopped his brother. "Did you see something move just then?"

"Like what?"

"I don't know. A dark figure over there in the park."

"Matter of fact I did, but I thought I was imagining things. Let's take a look!"

The park was a triangular grassy island at the junction of three streets. The boys darted across to the island and spent several minutes searching among the few scattered trees and shrubbery, but could find no trace of anyone lurking there.

"That's funny," Joe said in frustration. "I could have sworn I saw someone dressed in black from head to toe!"

"Guess our imaginations were working overtime," Frank said. "You'll have to admit not many people except frogmen go around looking like that."

"Where to now?" said Joe, as they mounted their street bikes. "Report to Dad?"

"May as well." Frank hesitated. "You've read the Sherlock Holmes stories, haven't you, Joe?"

"Sure, even Dad likes them. He says Sherlock Holmes and Edgar Allan Poe's detective are the greatest masters of deduction that writers have ever dreamed up. Why'd you ask?"

"If you remember, one of Sherlock Holmes's rules was that when you've eliminated all the explanations of a mystery but one, then that one must be the answer—no matter how far out it seems."

Joe frowned. "So? What're you getting at?"

"Just this," Frank replied. "We didn't hit a single red light coming into Bayport tonight. And the only time we stopped was during the traffic tie-up. If Satoya didn't get out of the car then—"

"He must still have been inside when we got to the hotel!" Joe concluded excitedly. "That's straight thinking, Frank. And if no one could see him when the chauffeur opened the door—"

It was Frank's turn to finish the sentence. "Then he must have been *hiding* inside the car!"

"Which means there would have to be a secret compartment in the limousine. Let's go check it out right now!"

They reached the Bayport Chilton in three minutes. The crowd of curious onlookers had thinned considerably, and neither Fenton Hardy nor Sam Radley was anywhere in sight. The Hardys took an elevator to the parking garage in the basement.

The black limousine was easy to spot, but Joe stopped abruptly as they neared it.

"Hey, we'll probably need a key to get inside."

Without a word, Frank held one up.

"Dad slipped this to me before we left the airport. He arranged beforehand with Mr. Kawanishi to get three extra keys—one for himself, one for Sam, and one for you and me—so any of us could take over in a hurry and drive the limousine out of danger in case of emergency."

"Great!" said Joe. "Let's see what we can find."

Frank unlocked the limousine, and the Hardys proceeded to examine both the front and rear seat areas thoroughly. They marveled at the fine craftsmanship and fittings, but could discover no hiding place.

Finally Joe stepped back and scratched his head. "Hold it, Frank! Did you notice the distance between the back of the front seat and the dividing partition? You sure wouldn't need all that room just for upholstery or springs!"

"Right," Frank agreed. "And what's this little metal button for, right where the glass fits into the lower half of the partition? It can't be a rivet head bec—"

The next moment, as Frank's forefinger touched the metal button, both boys gasped.

The leather-covered lower half of the partition was slowly sliding upward over the glass pane!

4

A Trio of Suspects

The leather panel continued moving upward until the glass pane between the top of the front seat and the roof was completely covered.

The Hardy boys could now see a large hollow space between the back of the front seat and the rear passenger compartment, which the sliding panel had previously concealed!

"Leaping lizards! That's big enough for a man to hide in!" Joe exclaimed.

"Or big enough to stash a body in," Frank said grimly.

"You mean someone may have drugged Satoya, the same way Ikeda was drugged?" Joe frowned doubtfully. "But they were the only two people in the back seat."

"So far as we know," Frank countered. "But suppose someone else was hiding in this secret compartment when the limousine was driven off the plane?"

"You've got a point there," Joe conceded. "So the hidden perpetrator crawls out sometime before we get to Bayport, zaps both Ikeda and Satoya with a hypodermic needle or a whiff of gas and then stuffs Satoya's body into the secret compartment."

"Well, it's one possible scenario," said Frank in a dubious voice.

"Just one catch to it."

"Don't bother telling me, I already know."

"Namely, what happened to the dirty trickster who did all this?"

Frank grinned wryly. "Look, I came up with part of an answer—you're supposed to supply the rest."

"Okay," said Joe, rising to the challenge. "So maybe the guilty party was a midget or a dwarf. He not only stuffs Satoya's unconscious body into the secret compartment—he squirms back inside himself and then closes the sliding panel."

"Pretty tight fit, I'd say—unless he was about the size of Tom Thumb."

"Why not? Dwarfs can come pretty small."

"And after the limousine's parked in the garage, he hops out of the secret compartment again and carries off Satoya on his back."

Joe returned his brother's grin. "If you have a better answer, let's hear it."

"I think we're both getting wacko. Before we come up with any more goofy theories, there's one important point we should clear up, Joe."

"What's that?"

"Do Kawanishi and Oyama know about this secret compartment?"

"Hm, good question. Let's ask them."

The Hardys locked the limousine and returned to the elevator. From their earlier briefings by their father, they knew the location of the suite reserved for the visiting Japanese. They got out at the fifteenth floor and spoke to the security guard who had been stationed there at Mr. Hardy's orders.

"Is Dad around?" Frank inquired.

"Nope. Just Mr. Kawanishi and Mr. Oyama."

"We'd like to speak to them."

"Just a second." The guard announced them over a special phone that had been installed for this purpose, then nodded and gestured for the boys to proceed.

Mr. Kawanishi, the burly senior aide who had met the Hardys at the airport, opened the door to admit the two youths. His colleague, Mr. Oyama, was standing by a window overlooking the street. He turned to greet the boys when they entered.

"We have a question to ask you gentlemen, if you don't mind," Frank began.

"By all means," said Kawanishi. "If you lads or your father can do anything to clear up this appalling mystery, we shall be most grateful!"

"Did you know there's a secret compartment in Mr. Satoya's limousine?"

There was a silence, during which the two aides glanced at each other uncomfortably.

"Yes, we know about that," said Mr. Oyama. The squat, broad-shouldered Japanese gestured toward a sofa. "If you will please be seated, we shall try to explain."

The boys obeyed and waited to hear what their hosts had to say.

"Our revered employer designed that compartment himself," Mr. Kawanishi told them.

"What for?" asked Joe.

"As a way of eluding newsmen and inquisitive crowds."

"Wouldn't it be simpler to curtain the windows," said Frank, "or just have them made out of one-way glass, like the partition pane between the front and rear seat compartments?"

"So it might seem at first thought," Mr. Oyama replied. "But actually that would only whet people's curiosity. You have no idea how much interest and gossip Mr. Satoya has aroused by his secretive ways."

"In Tokyo," Mr. Kawanishi put in, "reporters will sometimes hover for hours around our central office building merely in the hope of glimpsing our employer or snapping his photo."

"If the interior of his limousine were hidden from view," Oyama went on, "they would assume he was inside it, behind the curtains or the one-way glass. So they would try harder than ever to corner him."

"But if they see his car leave or arrive empty—or rather, *apparently* empty," the other aide added, "then his whereabouts remains a mystery. His pursuers are baffled and tend to become discouraged."

"I see." Frank frowned and digested this information thoughtfully.

Joe spoke up. "Why didn't you tell our father all this when the limousine first arrived at the hotel, and he discovered Mr. Satoya's disappearance?"

There was another awkward silence and exchange of glances between the two Japanese.

"You are right to take us to task," said Mr. Kawanishi, bowing his head contritely. "However, it occurred to both of us that Satoya-san might have become—how do you say?—camera shy, because of what happened on the way in from the airport. Therefore he might have chosen to conceal himself in the secret compartment for his own reasons."

"Naturally, in such a case," Mr. Oyama explained, "it would not have been right for us to go against our revered employer's wishes and reveal his hiding place."

This time it was the Hardy boys' turn to exchange glances. The reasoning of the two Orientals sounded logical enough, but it certainly clashed with their own impatient, practical Western outlook.

"What about Mr. Ikeda?" Frank questioned. "How did you think he got drugged or anesthetized? Or weren't you concerned about what happened to *him?*"

"He is very much junior to Satoya-san," Mr. Kawanishi pointed out patiently, as if he were correcting a child or a barbarian whose ignorance could be excused. "We were certainly disturbed to find him in such a condition. But that in itself would not excuse us from respecting our employer's wishes."

"In any case," Mr. Oyama said, "we had no intention of standing by and doing nothing. Perhaps you may recall that I left the scene soon after the chauffeur drove off."

"What did you do?" Joe asked.

"I hurried down to the garage by elevator in order to be on hand when the limousine pulled in. I wished to see for myself whether Satoya-san had concealed himself in the secret compartment."

Frank said, "And what did you find?"

Oyama spread his hands in a helpless shrug. "Nothing. The compartment was empty."

The Hardys thanked the two senior aides for their time and went down to the lobby, where they failed to find their father. As they left the hotel, they encountered a couple of their high school buddies, Tony Prito and pudgy Chet Morton.

Joe hailed them. "Hey, what're you guys doing downtown so late?"

"Checking out the new disco," Tony replied. "Then we heard a midnight news broadcast on the car radio about that Japanese big shot disappearing, so we hustled over to get the scoop. He was a client of your dad's, wasn't he?"

"*Is* a client," Frank corrected. "Tony, don't jinx him by putting him in the past tense!"

"Never mind all that! What happened to the guy?" Chet blurted. "Did some dragon society snatch him for violating its sacred customs?"

Joe grinned. "You're a little mixed up, Chester. The way we heard it, dragon societies and tongs are Chinese. Satoya comes from Japan. There's a slight difference."

"So what? They're both Oriental, aren't they? Quit stalling and give us the lowdown on this case!"

"I wish we could, Chet," Frank confessed wryly. "But if you want the latest bulletin, Mr. Satoya's still missing, and his disappearance remains as much of a mystery as ever. You can quote us."

"You mean you Hardys are baffled?"

"Put it this way," said Joe. "We're working on it."

"How about stopping off at the diner for a couple of burgers and a milkshake?" Chet proposed. "Then you can fill us in on the details."

"Got a better idea," Joe countered. "Aunt Gertrude's probably still up, waiting for a blow-by-blow account of the mystery. How about stopping off at our place, and maybe we can talk her out of some apple pie in return for a firsthand report."

"It's a deal!"

Gertrude Hardy, who lived with Frank and Joe and

231

their parents, was Fenton Hardy's unmarried sister. The tall, bony spinster worried constantly about the safety of the famed detective and her two nephews. Yet, despite her constant prophecies of looming danger, she kept herself avidly up to date on all their latest sleuthing activities.

More important from Chet's point of view, she was also one of the best cooks and bakers in Bayport. The Hardy boys found her fretfully awaiting their return, wrapped in her red bathrobe, with her hair in curlers.

"Chet and Tony are with us, Aunt Gertrude," Joe said. "Mind if they come in?"

"Of course not!" she said sharply. "They're probably as hungry as you two. I'd much rather you all did your late snacking here than out in some rowdy drive-in!"

"Well, if you insist, Miss Hardy!" said plump Chet Morton, eagerly pressing forward into the kitchen behind Frank and Joe.

Soon all four boys were hungrily attacking thick Dagwood sandwiches and slices of fresh apple pie, washing them down with glasses of milk.

"Where's Mom?" Frank asked between bites.

"In bed, where all you young ones should be at this hour!" Aunt Gertrude retorted. "She has to get up early tomorrow to help prepare the Garden Club display at the Bayport Festival. For that matter, where's your father?"

"Dunno, Aunty," Frank replied. "Last we saw of him, he was pretty busy coping with what happened tonight."

"Well, for mercy sakes, what did happen? I couldn't make head or tail out of the news broadcasts!"

The Hardy boys described the strange disappearance of Takashi Satoya, and their own subsequent adventures. The bathrobed spinster listened with keen interest.

"Hmph, sounds to me as though Satoya's been snatched by business enemies!" she declared. "Not surprising either, when you stop to think how big a corporation he's running. That's probably why he's been hiding from public view. He knew someone was out to get him."

"I'll buy that about someone being out to get him," Chet piped up. "If you ask me, it's probably a mysterious gang of Oriental killers!"

"Such as?" Joe said.

"How do I know? Maybe that creep you spotted who was all in black could be one of them!"

"*If* we spotted him," Frank amended. "But none of that explains how Satoya vanished."

"Those flashes in the darkness could have blinded everyone for a second or two while you were stopped on the highway," Aunt Gertrude pointed out. "Perhaps that was long enough for a kidnapper to drag him out of the car before you got going again."

"What about his aide Ikeda, who was drugged?"

"Perhaps the kidnapper had a confederate who jabbed him with a hypodermic needle."

"Hm, it's an interesting theory," Frank said politely if a bit skeptically.

Just then a car was heard pulling into the driveway. Soon afterward Fenton Hardy strode into the house. He greeted everyone in his usual friendly fashion, but Frank and Joe could see that their father was both angry and deeply concerned over the night's events. However, his sons' report about the limousine's secret compartment made him feel somewhat better.

"What was Mr. Satoya planning to do in this country, Dad?" Frank inquired.

"Among other things, confer with officials of the Road King Motorcycle Company. There's talk of a merger between Road King and Satoya's own motorcycle division."

"You see? What did I tell you!" Aunt Gertrude cut in triumphantly. "A move like that could easily have stirred up business enemies!"

"Quite true," Mr. Hardy agreed. "What I'd like to lay hands on fast is the enemy in Satoya's own corporation."

"How do you mean, Dad?" Joe queried.

The detective rose from his chair to pace the kitchen floor. "Someone tipped off the press that Satoya was coming to this country. The tip came in the form of anonymous calls to the news services and networks, and naturally, since Satoya's such a mystery man, they were all eager to get a look at him. Yet I'm absolutely sure there was no leak in my security setup!"

"Then where did the leak occur?"

"It has to be in the Satoya Corporation," Mr. Hardy

replied. "Aside from the jet plane crew and his chauffeur, the only other people who knew in advance about his visit were Kawanishi, Oyama and Ikeda—though I'll admit it's hard to believe Ikeda would deliberately have landed himself in such an unpleasant predicament."

"So right off the bat," Frank reflected grimly, "we have at least three important suspects!"

Next day, the Hardy boys decided to check up on Axel Gorky's story. The best way to do this seemed to be to interview Warlord. The famous dancer and his troupe were to perform at the Bayport Summer Festival and were staying at Bayshore College, which was sponsoring their appearance.

The boys arrived on campus about 10:30 in the morning and were directed to the gymnasium, where the troupe was working out. As they entered the building vestibule, a loud, angry voice reached them from the gym floor.

"Maybe we came at the wrong time," Joe said. "Think we should go on in?"

"May as well," Frank said wryly. "I don't see any receptionist to announce us."

The boys had just started to walk through the doorway leading to the gym when a man came charging out, almost knocking them down in the process!

5

A Breakneck Race

Joe was the first to recover. "Watch it, mister!" he exclaimed. "Where's the fire?"

The man, who was strongly built, with freckled skin and thinning red hair, merely snorted and brushed past the two boys without the slightest apology.

"How do you like that?" Frank muttered in a taut voice. "The big ape doesn't even have manners enough to say 'Excuse me'!"

"I should've belted him one!" Joe fumed. "In fact maybe we ought to go after him and *demand* an apology."

"Forget it," Frank said, choking back his own temper. "That's not why we came."

The Hardys went on into the gymnasium, where half

a dozen dancers were going through various exercises—mostly practicing ballet movements or doing warm-up calisthenics. Two others were engaged in acrobatic flips and leaps under the critical gaze of a man with a lionlike mane of long black hair.

The boys recognized him from the festival posters as Warlord, whose real name was Yvor Killian. They caught his eye and he came over to see what they wanted.

Frank introduced himself and his brother and got an immediate smile of greeting.

"Of course! You're those famous young sleuths, the Hardy boys!" Warlord offered them each a handshake. "It's a pleasure to meet such noted manhunters! Don't tell me you're here on the trail of a new mystery?"

"Matter of fact we are," said Frank. "It involves the disappearance of a Japanese businessman named Satoya. Maybe you heard about it on the news broadcasts this morning."

"Indeed I did! But how can I help you?"

"For one thing," said Joe, voicing a sudden impulse, "you can tell us who that turkey was who came barreling out the door just a minute ago."

Warlord broke into a chuckle. "What happened—did he run you down?"

"He sure tried to. Call it a nasty collision. If he'd hung around for a few seconds, there might've been another collision—between one of our fists and his jaw!"

Warlord's chuckle became a hearty laugh. "Excuse

me for seeing the funny side, but that sounds just like Humber. He's one of the most pompous, arrogant louts I've ever run into."

"Who is he?" Frank inquired curiously.

"A wealthy collector."

"Of what?"

"Exotic weapons. And not only wealthy, but spoiled rotten. He thinks whenever he wants something, everyone should rush to oblige him. In my case, what he wants is a *yataghan*."

"What's that?" said Joe.

"A rather short Turkish saber with a double-curved blade," Warlord explained. "As you probably know, I use various knives and swords in my dance routine, and that *yataghan* happens to be one of them—quite a fine example of its kind, I might add. Humber wants to add it to his collection, and naturally he thinks I should sell it to him immediately at any price he cares to name."

"But you refused," Joe deduced, "so he went storming out with a bee in his ear."

"You've got the picture." Warlord grinned.

Both Hardy boys were thinking that Yvor Killian was much different from what most people might have expected a dancer to look like, especially one who had anything to do with ballet. Instead of seeming dainty or girlish, he had a square-jawed, rugged-featured face and appeared to be lithe and well muscled enough to be a fast-punching lightweight boxer. His ready grin and magnetic manner also impressed the Hardys.

238

"Actually, the person we meant to ask you about," said Frank, returning to the purpose of their visit, "is a man named Axel Gorky."

"Ah, yes," Warlord nodded. "The dealer in Oriental objets d'art."

"You've met him?"

"Once or twice."

"He told us last night that he came here to Bayport to call on several customers, including yourself."

Again Warlord nodded. "He wanted to show me an eighteenth-century Japanese *katana*, or long sword. In fact he called me about it this morning, but I told him I wasn't interested."

"How come," said Frank, "if I'm not too inquisitive?"

"Not at all. It just happens that I've got my heart set on another samurai sword, a really beautiful blade that I recently saw in New York. It's to be sold at auction next week at the Palmer-Glade Galleries in Manhattan, and I intend to get in the top bid!"

Frank rubbed his chin thoughtfully. "Just one thing more, sir. When we spotted this fellow Gorky at the airport, he was acting like an oddball."

The Hardys described the incident, and Frank went on, "Gorky claims he was trying to attract Mr. Satoya's attention, because he hoped Satoya might offer him a good price for the sword."

Glancing at Warlord with a frown, the older Hardy boy added, "Does that sound plausible to you? I mean, why should Gorky assume that a businessman like

Mr. Satoya would be interested in buying old samurai swords?"

"Oh yes, that strikes me as perfectly plausible," the dancer replied. "You can take my word for it, Gorky's a smart salesman. In fact I believe Satoya was planning to bid on that very sword I just mentioned—the one at the Palmer-Glade Auction Galleries."

"Well, I guess that clears Gorky, then," Frank said. "Thanks for your time and help, Mr. Killian."

"My pleasure, boys. I hope you'll come and see my troupe dance."

"We intend to," the Hardys replied.

"Good! Just phone in and tell the box office which performance you prefer. I'll see to it that tickets are reserved for you and your dates."

The boys drove off in high spirits, but their bubbling enthusiasm was somewhat deflated on arriving home. Fenton Hardy was pacing the living room floor, while their slim, pretty mother sat on the edge of a sofa trying to comfort him. From their parents' faces, Frank and Joe could tell at once that unhappy news must have struck the Hardy household.

"Something wrong, Dad?" Frank ventured cautiously.

"I've been ordered off the Satoya case!"

"What!" both boys exclaimed incredulously.

"Who did the ordering?" Joe asked.

"The U.S. government," Mr. Hardy replied. "Supposedly the FBI wants me to handle another investigation. But reading between the lines, the message is perfectly clear, namely, *get off the Satoya case!*"

"For crying out loud! They can't do that!" Frank exploded.

"They not only can, they've already done it. And I have no choice except to obey, or else risk getting my license lifted." The famed detective resumed his pacing, grim and tight-lipped.

"But won't they give you a reason?" said Joe.

"Just a lot of nonsense about government policy and more urgent priorities."

"Meaning what?"

"You figure it out. It beats me." Mr. Hardy paused and punched his fist into his other palm. His face was a study in angry frustration. "Hang it all, Satoya's disappearance reflects directly on my worth as a security expert and a private investigator. Unless I can clear up the case, my reputation may be permanently damaged. It amounts to a matter of honor! But what can I do when my hands are tied?"

"Fenton dear, you must keep calm about this," Mrs. Hardy urged soothingly. "I'm sure your reputation is well enough established to survive whatever may happen in this case. In any event, losing your cool won't help."

"You're right, Laura, as usual. All the same, it's not easy to walk away and do nothing when it's clear that all our security measures were sabotaged by someone on the inside!"

"Don't worry, Dad," Frank said. "Joe and I will do our best to solve this case."

"You bet we will!" Joe chimed in. "That's a promise!"

"I'm sure of it, sons," Mr. Hardy said proudly, putting an arm around each of the boys. "And no one could ask for a better backup team!"

Frank and Joe had little chance to discuss the case further with their father. A motorcycle meet was to be held that day as part of the Bayport Summer Festival, and Frank was scheduled to ride in an event called a Hare Scrambles. The Hardy boys had souped up a dirt bike for the race.

The brothers had a hasty lunch, then hitched up the bike trailer to their car and sped off to the scene of the meet, on the outskirts of town. Shouts of greeting went up from a group of their high school friends, who were on hand to watch the race. Among them were Chet Morton, Tony Prito, Phil Cohen, Biff Hooper and several others. The Hardys' eyes lit up when they noticed Chet's pretty sister Iola, who was Joe's favorite girl, and Callie Shaw, a brown-eyed blond whom Frank considered special.

"Looks like we've got our own cheering section," Joe chuckled.

The five-mile course had been laid out through open country in the form of a three-leafed clover and was marked with lime. The starting and finishing points were at the stem of the clover, where the judges' stand was located and most of the spectators had gathered.

Observers were stationed at checkpoints around the course.

The three cloverleaves were on rising ground, and the middle leaf extended on a fairly steep hillside. This way much of the race could be watched by viewers at the starting point.

More than a dozen participants would compete head to head. The one favored to win was riding an experimental model bike newly developed by the Road King Motorcycle Company with a revolutionary frame and suspension. But Frank and Joe had worked hard on their own bike, equipping it with a special magneto and tuned exhaust system, and they felt sure it would at least make a good showing.

One rider wore the special helmet and insignia of the Gung-Ho motorcycle gang. "Watch that guy," Biff warned Frank. "He's Lenny Boggs, the head of the gang, and I'll bet he'll pull every dirty trick in the book!"

"Thanks for telling me," Frank murmured. "I'll keep an eye open for him."

Joe, as the one-man "pit crew," gave the bike a final check. Then Frank took his place at the starting line.

A "rubberband" starting gate had been stretched across the track. At the drop of a green flag, a pin was pulled releasing the gate, and the riders took off with a roar!

Frank found himself bunched among four or five racers, which hampered his performance. As they rounded the first cloverleaf, he gradually moved up among the leaders. In doing so, he smoothly outmaneuvered and passed Lenny Boggs.

The gang leader scowled furiously and gunned his machine to top power. Bit by bit he gained ground, then tried to crowd Frank off the course.

The Hardy boy, however, refused to be scared aside, even though they were riding neck and neck. Boggs kept kicking his bike and made threatening passes trying to nudge him over. Instead, Frank concentrated on all-out speed. Once again he began to outdistance the gang leader.

"Okay, wise guy! You're asking for it!" Boggs shouted.

At this point they were passing among scattered trees, and Frank saw a broken branch hanging down from one of them. A moment later he heard a sharp crack as the gang leader reached up and yanked off the branch.

Boggs gunned his engine to full throttle. From the corner of his eye Frank saw the young hoodlum drawing abreast on his right, trying to crowd him off course, but the Hardy boy refused to let himself be unnerved.

This time, however, Boggs had a new weapon, the broken tree branch. He reached out, trying to poke it in among the spokes of Frank's front wheel!

"Knock it off!" Frank cried, turning his head. "Are you crazy?"

Not only was Boggs's trick a flagrant violation of rules and good sportsmanship—it could cause a dangerous accident!

The only way to keep the stick out of contact with his wheel was to give ground and swerve off course to the left. As Frank glanced forward again and veered his handlebars, a gasp of alarm escaped his lips. He was heading straight for a huge oak tree!

6

Flat-Out Finish

There was no time to weigh the odds. Frank had a choice of either crashing into the tree or turning back on course, which would expose him to the original danger of a shattered wheel and a possible high-speed accident!

Frank made a split-second decision. He avoided the tree, but instead of merely turning back on course, he swung hard right. He knew this meant risking a collision with Len Boggs. But by skidding his rear wheel to the left, it would also help keep the spokes out of reach of Boggs's threatening tree branch.

His move caught the gang leader utterly unprepared. Boggs yelled in fear, dropped the branch, and grabbed both handlebars in blind panic.

The next instant the two bikes collided with a loud crash! Both youths were jolted from their saddles and went sprawling on the ground!

The collision had taken place near the hairpin curve between the first and second cloverleaves, at a point where the course dipped back close to the starting point.

"That dirty rat!" gritted Joe, who had watched the incident. He started off at a run across the open field to help his brother, in case Frank had been injured. Several of the Hardys' friends followed close behind to offer whatever assistance they could.

Half a dozen members of the Gung-Ho gang also sprinted out from among the spectators and headed for the scene.

Meanwhile, other racers were veering around the two tumbled riders in order to avoid running them over. But Frank and Len Boggs were already scrambling to their feet bruised, scratched, and shaken up but otherwise uninjured.

Boggs glared with rage at the Hardy boy. "You smart punk! You're gonna pay for this!" he threatened and charged at Frank with his fists cocked.

Frank's lip curled in scorn. He did not bother to waste breath pointing out that Boggs had brought the accident on himself. Instead, his left fist swung in a whistling uppercut that connected hard with the gang leader's jaw!

Len Boggs reeled backward from the blow and landed flat on his back, too dazed to collect his wits for the next few seconds.

Without giving his foe another thought, Frank picked up his bike and hastily checked it over. The Gung-Ho's, who had seen him knock down their leader, yelled threats and abuse, and ran as fast as they could to stop him.

Frank ignored them. Swinging aboard his bike, which seemed to be in working condition, he toed the shift lever back to neutral. Then he kicked the starter, gunned his engine and roared off in pursuit of the pack!

In baffled fury, the motorcycle gang members turned to pick a fight with Joe and the Hardys' friends, who were only too willing to oblige. Phil Cohen, in fact, was already swapping punches with one of the leather-belted hoodlums.

Luckily, just then a checkpoint observer, two other race officials and a policeman reached the scene. They forced their way between the two belligerent groups, and managed to stop what might otherwise have turned into a nasty brawl.

Frank saw little of this. He was bending all his efforts toward making up for lost time. The accident with Len Boggs had been a costly interruption. Except for one lagging rider, he was now at the tail of the pack. But the second cloverleaf wound upward along the face of a steep hillside, and his souped-up dirt bike was a good climber.

Yard by yard, Frank closed the gap and regained lost ground. When he was halfway down the side of the cloverleaf, he had already nosed his way forward to the middle of the pack.

The third cloverleaf was the roughest part of the course. The terrain was not only wooded, but dotted with thick patches of brush that forced the marked-out course to zigzag crazily. The ground was bumpy and rutted and was traversed by a meandering, muddy creek which had to be crossed at two points.

Three riders had taken spills on the hillside, and two more went spinning or careening out of action on this third leg of the course.

As the first bikes in the pack came whizzing out from among the trees and into view of the spectators and judges, Joe saw that the leader was the Road King entry. But Frank was only a dozen yards behind and slowly gaining!

"He's got a chance!" Joe blurted out.

"He'll make it yet!" said Chet Morton, whose face glistened with sweat and excitement.

"Come on, Frank! *Come on!*" cheered Iola and Callie, while Tony Prito was literally gnawing his knuckles in breathless suspense.

The other riders were well back, and the race was now clearly between the Road King entry and Frank Hardy as they roared home along the final stretch of the course.

But the miracle was not to happen. As the winner's front wheel crossed the finish line, and the black-and-white checkered flag came sweeping down, Frank had not yet drawn abreast of his lone opponent!

"What a great ride!" said Joe, rushing forward to hug and congratulate his brother. "I'll bet you'd have won, if that meathead Boggs hadn't fouled you!"

"Never mind, I can't complain," said Frank, grinning happily as he pulled off his helmet.

"Not after the way you decked him with one punch." Biff chuckled. "That alone was worth a silver loving cup!"

As further consolation, Frank's girlfriend, Callie Shaw, awarded him a public kiss.

Later, after a lengthy consultation on the judges' stand, the meet referee stepped to the microphone and announced:

"Although Dave Stewart, riding the Road King entry, is the official winner, we feel that special recognition should be given to Frank Hardy. Despite a deliberate foul that slowed his time considerably, he refused to give up. As most of you saw, he plunged back into the race and, by a great display of heart and skill, he still managed to achieve a close second place!"

The announcement was greeted with cheers and thunderous applause. Frank was called to the judges' stand to be photographed with the winner and received a fresh ovation from the crowd.

Later, when the Hardys were strapping the dirt bike into the trailer, Biff joined them.

"Better keep an eye on that creep," he muttered, nudging Frank.

The older Hardy boy followed Biff's glance and saw the Gung-Ho leader talking to a tall, hawk-faced, squint-eyed man. From the dirty looks they gave the two boys, it was not hard to guess the subject of their conversation.

Frank nodded thoughtfully. "You're right, Biff. Maybe I haven't heard the last of Len Boggs."

As soon as they had showered and changed at home, Frank called the director of the Palmer-Glade Auction Galleries long distance in New York City.

"I was told by the dancer Warlord that you have an especially fine samurai sword that will soon be placed on auction," Frank began.

There was a pause. Then the director cleared his throat and replied, "Yes, that *was* correct."

Frank was puzzled. "You mean it's been removed from sale—or already sold?"

"No," came the reply. "Apparently you haven't heard the news."

"What news?"

"Our building was broken into last night and the sword you just mentioned was stolen!"

7

Cat Burglars

Frank's eyes widened on hearing this unexpected development. He flashed his brother a startled look. "Was anything else taken?" he asked.

"Luckily, no," replied the voice at the other end of the line. "It appears that whoever did it was interrupted before he or they could snatch anything more."

"I see." Frank paused a moment to consider, then said, "This may tie in with a case my brother and I are investigating. If we come to New York, could we check out the details of the break-in?"

"Of course! If you Hardys can do anything to help catch the thieves, we'll be more than happy to cooperate!"

As Frank put down the phone, Joe exclaimed, "Don't tell me the sword's been stolen?"

The older Hardy boy nodded. "You guessed it. Happened just last night."

"Boy, that sounds like more than just a coincidence, Frank! Satoya disappears—we get a lead that he may have wanted to buy a certain rare sword—and now the sword's gone too!"

"I agree, Joe. I think the burglary's worth looking into."

"Check. Let's head for New York first thing in the morning."

Frank and Joe made good time on the highway, and by ten o'clock they were parking their car in a garage just two blocks from the Palmer-Glade Auction Galleries on the Upper East Side of Manhattan.

Mr. Sanders, the gallery director, proved to be a balding, bespectacled man. He received the boys in his office and called in his security chief to help answer their questions.

"First of all, sir," Frank began, "just how valuable was this sword?"

"We expected it to bring at least twenty-five thousand dollars at auction," Sanders replied.

"Wow! That's a lot of money!" Joe murmured.

"True, but you must remember—Japanese swords have the finest blades ever produced, and many are exquisitely decorated. Today they're increasingly sought after by Western collectors."

"How was the robbery discovered?" Frank asked.

"Quite by chance," the security chief said. "A police

254

scout car happened along about 3:00 A.M., and the officers spotted a hole in the pane of a third-floor window. We keep a guard on the premises at night, but by the time he answered their knocks and then rushed up to the third floor to investigate, the thieves had escaped."

"You have an alarm system?" put in Joe.

"We sure do. Had the window been forced open, the alarm would have gone off. But this job was pulled by a pro—or pros. Part of the pane was cut out, using tape to keep the loose glass from falling and making any noise. Then whoever did it reached inside and disconnected the window alarm."

Frank turned back to the gallery director. "We're investigating the disappearance of that Japanese businessman you may have heard about—Takashi Satoya, the head of the Satoya Corporation. We were told he was probably planning to buy the sword that was stolen from you last night. Can you tell us if that's true?"

Sanders frowned and toyed with a bronze paperweight on his desk. "You must understand, our business requires us to be very discreet. Many customers will only deal with us because Palmer-Glade guarantees that no information will be given out about them and their bids or their purchases."

"We understand, sir. All we're trying to find out is whether there may be any connection between your burglary and what happened to Mr. Satoya."

"Let me put it this way," the gallery director said

after a brief silence. "We did receive a cabled bid from Japan."

"Any name?" Frank pursued.

"No. Just a cable address to which we were asked to send our reply. But for various reasons, I believe the offer may have come from Satoya."

"Mind telling us how much was bid?" Joe asked.

"Forty thousand dollars."

Joe whistled in awe. "But you didn't accept?"

The director shrugged. "It wouldn't have been ethical. We had already advertised the sword for auction, so we could not back out."

"Do you by any chance have a picture of the sword that we could see?" Frank queried.

"Matter of fact, I do. We had one made for our sale catalog." Mr. Sanders plucked an eight-by-ten color print from a drawer and handed it across the desk.

The Hardys studied it closely.

"Hm, the scabbard doesn't look like much," Joe remarked.

"Quite right," Mr. Sanders agreed. "The sword itself is a *tachi*, the kind that's designed to be slung from a belt, instead of merely thrust through the wearer's sash, like the kind called a *katana*. Its blade is absolutely superb. Our expert dates it as probably of sixteenth-century workmanship by a swordsmith of Mino Province. But the scabbard is what's called *shin-gunto*, or army style, just leather-covered metal, of the kind issued to military officers beginning in 1937."

"That's interesting," said Frank. "How do you explain the difference between the two?"

"It's really not all that unusual. Many officers who came from good families and owned fine old samurai swords carried them on active service—but in army scabbards, instead of the original decorated mountings." With a slight puzzled frown, the director added, "But there is one thing rather odd."

"What's that, sir?"

"When a samurai sword was converted for military wear, the owner would usually switch to a plain military hilt as well."

"How could he do that?" asked Joe.

"It's quite simple. The metal blade is held in the hilt by a peg which fits clear through the hilt and the tang, or handle end, of the blade. Remove the peg, and the hilt comes right off. But in this case, our expert couldn't figure out *how* to get it off."

"Why would he want to do that, anyhow?" said Frank.

"To examine the tang—that's where the swordsmith's signature is usually inscribed. But with this one he couldn't. However, even without knowing the maker, the fine quality of the sword was readily apparent, not only from the workmanship of the blade, but also from the hilt and the *tsuba*, or hand guard. The hilt, as you can see from the picture, is inlaid with mother-of-pearl, and the *tsuba* is embellished with intricate carving and cloisonné enamel."

"They're really beautiful," Frank agreed, then rose from his chair. "Thank you very much, Mr. Sanders, for all the information."

As Joe got up also, Frank turned to the security man. "I wonder if we could see the scene of the crime?"

"Sure thing."

The Palmer-Glade Galleries occupied a four-story building which had once been a wealthy New Yorker's town house. The merchandise was divided into departments, with Oriental *objets d'art* being grouped at the front of the third floor.

The cut windowpane had already been replaced.

"The facade of the building is quite smooth," Joe mused thoughtfully. "How do you suppose the burglar or burglars got up to the window?"

"Good question," the security man said wryly. "We still haven't figured out the answer."

"I guess they wouldn't have dared to use a ladder, even that late at night," Frank said. "How about a grappling hook and a line, to scale up the front of the building?"

"It's possible, but by heaving up the hook they would have risked making enough noise to attract the attention of the guard inside. Also, the windowsill shows no markings from a hook."

"Could a line have been dropped from the roof?" Joe asked.

The security man shook his head. "No way. The alarm system would have detected any intruder on the roof."

"And nothing else was taken but the sword?" Frank asked.

"As far as we can tell. I'm convinced they got scared off. At that time of night with the streets fairly quiet, they probably heard the scout car pull up, and they certainly would have heard the police pounding on the door. Also, an alarm *did* go off just a little later, when the guard and the cops were rushing up to the third floor to investigate."

"How come?" said Frank.

"What triggered it was the trapdoor to the roof being opened," the security man explained. "Apparently that's how the thieves got away—over the roofs of some adjoining buildings to the nearest fire escape."

The Hardy boys left the gallery soon afterward, promising to pass along any leads they might uncover.

"We still don't know for sure if the gallery heist ties in with our own case," Joe complained. "We can't even be certain Satoya did want the stolen samurai sword."

Frank nodded. "Maybe it's high time we went right to the horse's mouth."

Stopping at a public phone booth, he made a long-distance call back to Bayport, and managed to catch Mr. Oyama at the Bayport Chilton Hotel.

"Can you tell us if Mr. Satoya was planning to buy a certain samurai sword at the Palmer-Glade Galleries in New York?" Frank asked.

From the momentary silence that followed, and from Oyama's tone of voice when he finally replied,

Frank got the impression that the Japanese was surprised by his question, and especially by the fact that the Hardys had found out about the sword.

"Yes, that is correct," Oyama confirmed. "It may even have been the most important reason for his trip to America."

"How so?"

"Something must certainly have caused him to make such an unusual decision—and I am not sure that business reasons alone can explain it. Perhaps you do not realize what a drastic move this was for Mr. Satoya. Even at home in Japan, among his own people, he shuns all crowds and public appearances. Yet by flying to America, he was willing to expose himself more to the public eye than ever before."

"I understood he was coming over to discuss a business merger," Frank said.

"Yes. That is so. There is a chance the Road King Company may combine with our own motorcycle division. But if Mr. Satoya had wished, I am sure their officials would have agreed to visit Japan and talk with us, instead of Mr. Satoya coming here. For that matter," the aide added, "I believe Mr. Kawanishi and I could well have carried on the negotiations under Mr. Satoya's supervision."

"If that's so," Frank pointed out, "couldn't he have sent someone over here to buy the sword for him?"

Over the line, Frank could hear Oyama's worried

sigh. "Yes, that too seems sensible. I am afraid I do not know the answer."

Frank thanked the Japanese, then hung up and reported the conversation to his brother.

"Sure doesn't help us much," Joe grumbled.

Frank agreed and added, "We'll just have to keep scratching for leads, that's all."

New York's skyscraper office buildings were letting out their employees for lunch, and both streets and sidewalks were crowded. Everyone seemed in a hurry. Frank and Joe enjoyed watching the sea of faces all around them as they made their way back to the parking garage.

To avoid having their car jockeyed by careless attendants, the boys had purposely picked a garage which allowed them to park and lock up. But as Frank was about to insert the key in the lock, he let out a startled gasp.

"What's the matter?" Joe asked.

"Take a look! The window's been pried open, and the door's unlocked!"

The Hardys hastily checked for signs of theft and discovered that the glove compartment had been jimmied and its contents ransacked. But so far as they could determine, nothing had been taken. The trunk showed no signs of forcible entry.

Frank and Joe looked around angrily for the parking attendant on duty. The cashier's window was near the exit, well out of view of their car, but they saw a cigar-chewing man in coveralls coming down the next aisle.

"Hey!" Frank called out. "Did you see anyone monkeying with our car?"

"Nope. Why?"

"It's been broken into."

The attendant hurried over. When he saw what had happened, he scowled and snapped his fingers. "So that's it! I spotted a guy snooping around here about twenty minutes ago and chased him out. He's probably the one who did this."

"What did he look like?" Frank asked.

"Some kind of Oriental wearing shades. A tough-lookin' mug, Japanese, I think."

8

Invisible Men

Frank and Joe exchanged slightly startled looks. Both felt sure that the parking attendant had correctly spotted the guilty party.

"No doubt he was our man," Frank told the attendant.

"You want to report this to the police, or make an insurance claim? The garage is covered for any damage to a customer's car."

The older Hardy boy shook his head. "It's not worth bothering with. The only thing damaged is the glove compartment lock, which doesn't amount to much— but you ought to be more careful about keeping out intruders."

The attendant scowled again, somewhat sheepishly

this time, and removed his cigar long enough to clear his throat. "I know, I know. We try to, but there's always creeps around, waitin' to rip off anything they can get their hands on."

Joe was about to climb into the car when Frank said, "Wait a minute. We passed a drugstore on the corner, didn't we?"

"Yes. Why?"

"Let's go there before we take the car out. I've got an idea."

Leaving the garage, they walked back down the block. When they got to the drugstore, Frank led the way inside and gestured toward the soda counter. "Order me a chocolate milkshake, will you, Joe? Be right with you. There's something I want to check out first."

"Okay," said Joe, thoroughly mystified.

He saw his brother head toward a telephone booth at the rear of the store and leaf through the yellow pages of the directory.

Presently Frank returned to the counter and slid onto a stool beside Joe. "Know what kendo is?" he asked.

"Sure, it's one of the Japanese martial arts like judo or karate. Only kendo is the art of swordsmanship—right?"

"Correct. I figured there might just be a place in New York that teaches kendo, and it turns out there is. Want to go check it out? We might learn something about samurai swords that would help us on this case."

"Sure, great idea!" Joe was enthusiastic. "Even if we don't learn anything, it sounds like fun!"

After downing their milkshakes, the boys started out for the kendo studio on foot. It was on the West Side and could soon be reached by cutting across Central Park. On the way, they discussed the incident of the Japanese thug breaking into their car at the garage.

"What do you suppose he was after, Frank?" asked the younger Hardy boy.

"Maybe nothing special," Frank guessed. "Could be he was just looking for anything that might clue him in to how much we know about this whole mystery."

"Which is practically zilch at this point," Joe gloomed. "Another thing, it's not likely he just happened to spot us going into that garage or coming out. Which means he must have tailed us here all the way from Bayport."

"Right." Frank nodded. "And that tends to confirm Dad's theory about the leak in Satoya's own company."

"How do you mean?"

"If that garage creep's not American, and he's involved in the Satoya case, then he must have come here from Japan because he knew in advance about Satoya's trip. So he sure couldn't have found out through any of Dad's security arrangements over here. Someone in the Satoya Corporation must have hired him or tipped him off."

"That figures," Joe agreed.

The kendo studio was located on the ground floor of

a converted storefront building. Inside, there was a sound of whacks and feet thumping the floor as students in masks and padded garb practiced with bamboo swords. A calm-faced, middle-aged Japanese gentleman in cotton jacket and loose trousers came over to find out what the boys wanted. On learning that they were the sons of the famous Fenton Hardy, he smiled and bowed.

"Ah, so! My humble *dojo* is honored by your visit." He introduced himself as Ryu Shimada. The boys learned that he was attached to the Japanese Mission to the United Nations, and conducted his school in kendo as a way of introducing this ancient art to Americans.

Both Frank and Joe sensed at once that he was a man of honor who could be trusted implicitly. They told him about their work on the Satoya case. Then Frank asked his opinion about Mr. Satoya coming to the United States just to bid on a sword, despite his intense dislike of appearing in public.

"Indeed, that does not surprise me," Mr. Shimada replied. "His family belonged to the samurai, or warrior class, and in Japan it is said that the sword is the soul of the samurai. To such men, the sword is an object of veneration beyond price. Therefore he might go far to obtain a particular blade, especially if it held any family tradition."

"What about the fact that the sword had just a plain army scabbard?" Joe asked.

"Your informant was correct," said Mr. Shimada.

"Many fine antique blades were carried into battle during the war. Some were lost in combat when their owners were killed or taken prisoner. Others were sold as souvenirs during the American occupation of Japan. I am sure that many samurai swords have turned up in secondhand shops or among art dealers in this country."

But Mr. Shimada was surprised to learn that the sword still retained its original beautiful hilt that could not be removed.

"This I cannot explain," he said with a shake of his head.

To give the Hardy boys the "feel" of kendo, Mr. Shimada had them try on the equipment worn by his students. It consisted of heavily padded gauntlets, a leather apron, slatted breastplate armor and a steel-grilled helmet. The latter looked like a catcher's mask and was worn over a towel to keep perspiration from running down in the fencer's eyes.

The boys were required to kneel while the armor was being tied on. This was an important part of *reigi*, the discipline or etiquette of kendo.

"The purpose of kendo, you see, is not merely to train a fierce fighting man," Mr. Shimada said, then tapped his head and chest. "More important is its effect on mind and heart."

By teaching the student to overcome the "Four Poisons of Kendo"—fear, doubt, surprise and confusion—it also helped to develop character and self-control.

"The training that your distinguished father is giving you in the art of detection," he added, "has probably much the same effect."

Frank and Joe tried some of the basic attacks and parries of kendo, using *shinai*, or bamboo practice swords. They were shown how to leap forward and swing the sword in a fierce downward chop, then skip backward out of range, and also how to crouch and slash.

The explosive *kiai*, or shouting, that accompanied these blows was meant to put spirit into the swordsman and shock his opponent off balance.

"Like the rebel yell the Confederates used during the Civil War," Joe chuckled.

Both boys felt they had been through a real workout when they finally shucked their armor. Afterward, they listened with keen interest as Mr. Shimada and his pupils discussed other Japanese martial arts, such as kyudo or archery, judo, karate and aikido—as well as special weapons such as the *naginata* or curved-bladed spear, the *bo* stave and the iron fan.

Frank and Joe pricked up their ears at the mention of a special class of warriors called *ninja*, who were experts at *ninjutsu*—the art of remaining invisible. They dressed all in black, and in olden times were often used as spies.

"Do *ninja* still exist?" Frank asked.

"Oh, yes," the kendo master replied. "But their art was always so secret that no one can be sure how much of it was real and how much just hearsay. Some actually think *ninjutsu* involved magic. Others say it depended on trickery or hypnosis."

As the Hardys started back to the parking garage, Frank said, "Remember that sneak in black we thought we saw outside Pete Ogden's house?"

"I'll say I do!" Joe exclaimed. "And you're probably wondering the same thing I am—namely, if he could have been a *ninja*."

"Right now I'm ready to believe almost anything," Frank said, "including the fact that someone's tailing us."

Joe shot his brother a startled look. "Are you serious?"

"You bet I am! Don't look now, but keep your eyes and ears open, Joe."

The boys entered Central Park just south of the American Museum of Natural History. As they crossed a wooden bridge, they paused to look down at the water of the lake. Joe used the opportunity to steal a cautious glance behind them.

"Yes. I see the guy," he muttered. "Looks Oriental, all right—and he's wearing dark glasses, like the crook who broke into our car!"

Beyond the bridge, the Hardys turned onto a paved walk which wound through the park. They discussed a plan of action as they strolled along. A dirt path led off among some craggy rocks. Frank and Joe took this path, and as it turned sharply through a sort of rocky gorge, they scrambled hastily up the slope and flung themselves flat.

Moments later they heard footsteps approaching, and their Oriental shadow came into view. He had crew-cut dark hair and wore a loud checked sports coat.

"*Now!*" hissed Frank, and the two boys leaped down at him! Each grabbed one of his arms.

"Now, mister," Frank gritted, "you're going to tell us why you're following us!"

Instead of answering, their opponent fought furiously. He seemed as strong as a bull and was clearly adept at unarmed combat. Twisting and turning, he wrested his arms free, using them like flails.

Joe thought he saw an opening and swung at the man with a hard right hook. But the man was no longer there. Joe's fist merely sailed past his jaw and hit Frank on the side of the head, sending him sprawling backward!

An instant later Joe himself caught a sword-hand jab in the pit of the stomach. As he crumpled, gasping for breath, he saw the Oriental flee from the gorge!

9

Lurking Shadows

Frank was the first to recover. Scrambling to his feet, he dashed after their unknown enemy. But the Oriental had a long head start. By the time Joe rejoined his brother, the man was already out of sight. He was either lost from view among the trees and rocks, or else had managed to blend in among other park strollers and loungers without attracting attention.

"Oh, rats!" Frank fumed. "We had the guy in our clutches and let him go! He might've given us a clue to whatever happened to Mr. Satoya!"

"Sorry I decked you," Joe apologized. "That punch was meant for our attacker."

"It wasn't your fault. He was one tough cookie. At least we'll be able to identify him if we ever see him again. Did you notice his tattoos?"

"I'll say I did! Oriental dragons and evil spirits sticking out of both sleeves; they probably run clear up his arms. And did you notice his little fingers?"

Frank nodded grimly. "You mean what's left of them. They were both missing the top joints!"

Back home in Bayport that evening, the boys described the attacker to their father. From Fenton Hardy's expression, it was clear that he recognized the description at once.

"The fellow must have been a *Yakuza!*" he declared.

"What's that?" Joe queried.

"A Japanese gangster. They're almost a separate caste over there. The crew cut and dark glasses and loud clothes sound typical. So do the tattoos and especially the amputated finger joints."

"How come, Dad?"

"It's a ritual," Mr. Hardy explained. "Whenever a gang member does something wrong in the eyes of his leader, he is required to cut off a finger joint. This proves that he is still loyal and shows that he regrets his mistake."

The younger Hardy boy shuddered. "Sounds sick to me!"

"I warned you two! You were asking for trouble when you went poking around New York looking for bloodthirsty Oriental criminals!" Gertrude Hardy scolded. She was hovering within hearing distance as she finished setting the dinner table.

"If you mean the art gallery thieves, Aunt Gertrude,

272

there's no way of telling whether or not they were Orientals," Frank pointed out.

The tall, thin woman sniffed scornfully. "Who else would want to steal a Japanese sword?"

"Quite a few crooks, I imagine, if they knew it was worth twenty-five thousand dollars."

"Don't argue with me, young man! Just come to dinner!" Miss Hardy disappeared into the kitchen to bring out the roast, muttering darkly, "Tattooed gangsters! Chopped-off finger joints! Next thing we'll be getting poisoned fortune cookies in the mail!"

After dinner, Frank and Joe found time to glance through the evening paper. Joe had the front section, which carried stories about Takashi Satoya's baffling disappearance, and also the break-in theft of the samurai sword from the Palmer-Glade Auction Galleries.

"Hey, get a load of this!" Joe muttered to his brother.

"What?" said Frank, scarcely looking up from the comics page.

"Remember that klutz who bumped into us when we went to see Warlord?"

"Humber? Sure, what about him?"

"There's an interview with him in the paper."

Frank put down the comics page with an expression of interest. "What's he got to say?"

"He thinks there may be a connection between Satoya disappearing and the gallery theft—*because the stolen sword belonged to the Satoya family!*"

"Hey! Let's see that!" Frank exclaimed, springing up

from the sofa. Taking the newspaper from his brother, he ran his eyes hastily over the story that Joe was pointing to.

Apparently Humber had been interviewed as an expert on swords because of his own collection of exotic weapons.

"I would not care to speculate on why the sword was stolen, or who may have engineered the theft," he was quoted as saying, "but the timing and coincidence are certainly interesting!"

"Boy, Humber's taking a chance, making a crack like that!" Frank remarked thoughtfully.

"You said it," Joe agreed. "Almost sounds as if he's accusing Satoya. The Satoya Corporation might decide to sue Big Mouth!"

"He's probably banking on Satoya being too publicity shy to take him to court. Or maybe he just likes to hear himself talk, and let his mouth run away with him."

From the pompous tone of the interview, Humber did indeed sound as if he enjoyed basking in the limelight, however briefly or unimportantly.

"We still ought to check this out," Frank said soberly as he handed back the paper to his brother.

"Right." Joe nodded. "If he knows something we don't know, the sooner we find out the better!"

Mr. Hardy had gone out again after dinner to resume his own investigative work, so the boys were unable to ask his advice. Frank, therefore, took the most direct approach. He called the wealthy collector for an appointment.

"Hm, haven't I heard your name before?" Dobert Humber said.

"Our father's a private investigator," Frank replied. "He's quite well known."

"Oh yes. And you and your brother run some kind of boyish detective service, I believe."

"That's right. We're trying to find out what happened to Mr. Satoya. That's why we'd like to talk to you about that stolen sword."

"I see. Well, if I can be of any help, I shall be glad to spare you a few minutes. It's quite possible my knowledge and expertise may shed some light on the mystery."

Joe flashed his brother a questioning glance as Frank hung up the phone a few seconds later.

"Well?"

"He'll see us tonight," Frank said with a grimace. "Sounds like a real fathead!"

The boys drove out to see Humber, who lived in a beautiful wooded area outside of town. His home, built of gray stone, looked like a huge old English manor house. As they started up to the front door after parking their car, Frank suddenly put a hand on his brother's right arm.

Joe guessed at once that Frank had noticed something unusual. "What is it?" he murmured.

"Left side of the house. Thought I saw a movement in the shadows."

Without any hasty action that might telegraph their intentions, Joe casually returned to the car and got a flashlight. Then he and Frank darted in opposite directions, trying to cut off the intruder's escape. But the flashlight beam failed to reveal any lurking figures.

"Maybe I was seeing things again," Frank fretted.

"Maybe and maybe not. Never hurts to check."

A butler admitted the boys to the drawing room where Humber was waiting. If their host recognized the Hardys as the two youths he had bumped into at Bayshore College, he gave no sign. Instead, he offered them refreshments and insisted on showing them his collection of rare weapons.

Most of them were displayed in glass cases or hung on the walls of his study. Frank and Joe were fascinated as Humber pointed out his treasures. Among them were an ancient Saxon war axe dating back before the Norman Conquest of England, a knobkerry or African throwing club, a two-bladed scissors dagger from the Middle East, and a *katar* or punch dagger from India. The latter had a handle with twin crossbars, which the user could hold in order to jab an enemy, the same way a boxer punches with his fist.

"And this curious weapon also comes from India," said Humber, holding up a small but vicious-looking device. "These curved steel blades are called 'tiger claws.'"

The claws were attached to a steel bar with a little ring at each end. Humber showed the boys how the wearer could slip his first and little fingers through these rings in order to slash an opponent.

"Wow!" Joe muttered. "I'd hate to tangle with anyone wearing *those!*"

"A very nasty weapon," Humber agreed. "I'm told these were often used sneakily, to attack an enemy off guard."

He seemed pleased by the boys' interest in his collection and answered all their questions. Frank maneuvered the conversation around to the reason for their visit.

"We're wondering how you knew that stolen samurai sword belonged to Mr. Satoya's family," he probed.

Their host said he had been told so. "The fact wasn't mentioned in the sale catalog for the auction, but I'm a valued customer of the Palmer-Glade Galleries," Humber said smugly. "I daresay that's why their Oriental expert confided the information to me."

Frank threw a glance at Joe. Both boys had the same idea. No doubt this explained why the gallery director believed the anonymous Japanese offer to buy the sword might have come from Satoya. But he had not revealed his reasons to the boys in order to protect his gallery's reputation for being discreet about its customers' affairs.

"Matter of fact, that dancer Warlord told us Mr. Satoya was probably interested in purchasing the sword," Joe said. "I wonder how *he* found out?"

"Hm! Good question," Humber sniffed disdainfully. "In my opinion that Warlord fellow's not to be trusted—especially about anything connected with the Satoya Corporation."

Frank frowned alertly. "Why not, sir?"

"Because I've reason to believe he's involved in a nasty feud with the company."

"What sort of feud, Mr. Humber?" Joe asked.

Their host shrugged as if he found the subject too unpleasant to talk about. "It started when Warlord was over in Japan. There was trouble of some kind—actual physical violence, or so I've heard. But I wouldn't know the details."

Again the Hardys exchanged thoughtful looks.

As they were leaving, Humber said, "By the way, I may need some detective work done myself one of these days."

Frank politely inquired the reason.

"Because I suspect thieves may have their eye on my collection of weapons," Humber replied. "Possibly professional burglars."

"Do you have any definite grounds for your suspicions?" Frank persisted.

"Indeed I do, though you may think I'm worrying about shadows. This evening at twilight, just before it got dark, I'm sure I saw someone spying on the house. It was a man dressed all in black!"

10

Trouble in Tokyo

Joe was about to blurt out that Frank, too, had glimpsed a dark figure, as a result of which they had made a hasty search for any lurking spy just before ringing the doorbell. But he stifled his remark at a slight frown from his brother.

"If it happens again, Mr. Humber, please give us a call," Frank said. "We'll come right over and try to trap whoever's watching your house."

"Thanks! I'll certainly do that." Humber sounded genuinely grateful for the offer of help.

As the boys drove away, Frank explained, "No sense worrying the guy—that's why I signaled you not to mention what we saw. Or what *I* saw, anyhow."

"Guess you're right," Joe agreed. "At least we know it

wasn't your imagination." He added after a pause, "You think it was a *ninja?*"

Frank nodded thoughtfully. "It's sure beginning to look that way. What do you make of that trouble Humber mentioned, between Warlord and the Satoya Corporation?"

"Sounded to me like he's peeved at Warlord, so he's raking up some old business to make him look bad."

"I got the same impression. On the other hand, if Warlord really does have a grudge against the company, I'd like to know more about it."

"Same here. Maybe we ought to have another talk with Warlord."

It was not yet 9:30, so the Hardys felt there might still be a chance of seeing the dancer before he retired. Frank pulled into a gas station. Leaving Joe to deal with the attendant, he dialed the number of Bayshore College on the pay telephone inside and asked for Warlord's extension in the dance troupe's quarters on campus.

Another member of the troupe answered. "Yvor's not here right now," he said, using Warlord's given name. "May I help you?"

Frank told the dancer who was calling and said, "My brother and I would like to ask him about something that happened when he was in Japan."

"That must've been before he formed our troupe, so I wouldn't know about it, myself," the dancer replied. "But look, you're the fellows who were here before, aren't you, investigating the disappearance of that Japanese businessman?"

"That's right."

"Well, the campus is still lit up, and things seem pretty lively around here. Yvor should be back soon— so if you want to take a chance and come on over, I imagine he'll see you."

"Great! Thanks," Frank said. "We'll be there in about fifteen or twenty minutes."

The Hardys drove to Bayshore. With many students on vacation during the summer term, two of the dormitories were empty, and the dance troupe had been assigned rooms in one of them. But the boys were in for an unpleasant surprise.

When they knocked on Warlord's door, it was opened by another member of the troupe. From his look of instant recognition, Frank guessed that this must be the person he had talked to on the phone.

"We're Frank and Joe Hardy," he said. "We've come to—"

"I know—I know who you are," the dancer interrupted hastily, with an embarrassed expression on his face. "But I'm not too sure th—"

He was pushed aside before he could finish speaking, and Warlord himself appeared in the doorway, looking furious.

"I have nothing to say to you two!" he exclaimed. "So kindly leave!"

The Hardys stared in astonishment. Unlike his

friendly manner that morning, the dance star was red-faced with anger.

"What're you upset about?" Frank asked in a reasonable tone, hoping to calm him down. "All we want to do is ask you a few qu—"

But Warlord cut him short and growled, "Get out!" and slammed the door in their faces!

The Hardys returned somewhat glumly to their car.

"Boy, I sure wasn't expecting anything like that," Joe remarked.

"Neither was I," Frank concurred. "Whatever happened in Japan must still be a mighty sore point with him. Maybe Humber was right."

When the boys arrived back at the Hardys' house on Elm Street, they found their father home again. They learned that he had gone to the airport to confer with an FBI official, who had flown from Washington expressly to brief him on his new assignment.

"What do they want you to do, Dad?" Joe asked. "I mean if it's not too secret to tell us."

"Actually it may well be connected with the Satoya case," Fenton Hardy replied. "The Road King Motorcycle Company has received certain threats."

"There's a chance they may merge with the motorcycle division of the Satoya Corporation," Frank put in. "That's what Mr. Satoya came over to discuss."

Mr. Hardy nodded. "Right—and that's what the threats are all about. Road King's been warned to forget the merger, or they'll regret it."

"Any leads to go on, Dad?"

"Not really—just suspicions. I have a hunch the threats may have come from another Japanese firm, Gorobei Motors. They'd like to take over the Road King company themselves. In fact they've already made an offer. If my suspicions are correct, I may have to fly to Japan to prove them, but so far I'm not sure."

After hearing about the unpleasant incident with Warlord, Mr. Hardy offered to cable the Japanese police for information. "I know several of the top police officials in Tokyo," he said. "I've even handled a few investigations for them. If Warlord was ever in trouble over there, I'm sure they could check out the facts."

"Great! Thanks, Dad," his sons responded.

Next morning, Frank and Joe went to the Bayport Chilton Hotel to see Takashi Satoya's two senior aides. They noticed his rugged-looking, poker-faced chauffeur sitting in the lobby. He returned their nods politely.

"Looks like he's keeping an eye out for trouble himself," Joe remarked in a low voice as they headed for an elevator.

"Yes, backing up the regular security guards," Frank agreed. "And if any trouble does come up, he sure looks as if he could handle it."

Mr. Kawanishi and Mr. Oyama received them in the sitting room of the company's hotel suite.

"We're wondering if you could tell us anything about

284

an American dancer called Warlord," Frank began. "It happens he's in Bayport to perform, and we were told he once had trouble with the Satoya Corporation when he was in Japan."

Satoya's aides regarded the Hardy boys with fresh respect.

"You two young men do, indeed, carry out thorough investigations," Mr. Kawanishi said. "And what you say is correct. I recall our company having trouble of some kind with the dancer called Warlord, although it happened several years ago."

Mr. Oyama explained, "He had a fight with one of our employees—a grudge fight, I believe, in which our employee was seriously injured and had to go to the hospital. As you may know, in Japan, companies take a keen interest in the private lives of their workers, as well as in how they perform their jobs. Therefore, the Satoya Corporation took legal action against Warlord, on behalf of our injured worker."

As a result, he went on, the dancer had been forced to leave Japan. However, all this had been handled by company lawyers, and neither Mr. Oyama nor Mr. Kawanishi knew any of the details. Nor, up until now, at least, had they considered it very important.

"Are you suggesting that Warlord may know something about our revered employer's disappearance?" Kawanishi inquired.

"It's one possibility we wanted to look into," said Frank. "We'd also like to know a little more about this samurai sword that was stolen in New York. Mr. Oyama told me on the phone that the sword may have been Mr. Satoya's main reason for coming to America."

Both aides nodded seriously as though they had discussed the matter between them, following Frank's phone call.

"Our employer wore the sword as a young officer during World War II," Oyama related, "but he lost it when he was taken prisoner by your soldiers, sometime before Japan surrendered. Apparently the sword was 'liberated,' as the saying goes, by a GI. At any rate, it disappeared. Perhaps you know how much a Japanese samurai values his blade?"

"We've been told," said Frank.

"This one was especially treasured because it had belonged to the Satoya family for many generations," Mr. Kawanishi added. "For that reason, our employer has had agents looking for it all over the world, feeling that one day whoever took it might decide to sell it for money."

"And events proved him right," said Mr. Oyama. "He was delighted when the sword turned up for sale at the Palmer-Glade Galleries. He was able to identify it from their sale catalog. But, alas, I fear the news of its theft may come as a very unpleasant blow to him—that is, assuming Mr. Satoya himself is still alive and safe."

"You think he disappeared of his own accord?" Joe asked shrewdly.

Once again, the Hardys saw a troubled glance pass between the two aides.

"I must confess we do think so," Mr. Kawanishi admitted, "even though we are at a loss to explain how or why it happened."

"If you're right, his chauffeur must have been in on it," Frank pointed out.

Both aides agreed. "But there is no hope of learning anything from him," said Oyama.

"Why not, sir?"

"Because he is fanatically loyal to his master. You see, he has a small daughter, who was born with a heart defect. Mr. Satoya had her flown to a hospital in Texas and paid for an expensive operation that saved her life. Now that fellow would die before he would betray anything which his master wished to keep secret."

On a sudden impulse, Frank decided to phone Warlord from the hotel lobby. As he had hoped, the dancer accepted his call.

"We've found out about the fight you had with a Satoya worker, and how you were forced to leave Japan," Frank said. "We'd like to hear your side of it, just out of fairness."

There was a brief silence. Then Warlord said, "Okay, you win. Come on over to the college and I'll tell you the whole story."

11

A Crooked Offer

"We'll be right over," Frank promised and hung up.

Joe was excited when he heard the news. "Maybe something'll break now!"

"Maybe. But we'd better not get our hopes too high. This may turn into another blind alley."

The boys sped to Bayshore College. After parking their car in the student lot, they found Yvor Killian and his troupe practicing their numbers in the gymnasium again.

The dancer's manner was somewhat embarrassed as he greeted the Hardys.

"Come over and sit down, please, where we can talk in private," he said, gesturing toward some folding chairs in one corner of the gym.

When they were all seated, Killian began, "About three years ago, before I formed my present troupe, I studied the martial arts in Japan."

"How come?" Joe asked.

"Because I thought they might add an important touch to the kind of dance spectacle I was interested in creating. I enjoyed learning the Japanese fighting skills and the way they were taught, partly because it was all so different from our American self-defense sports like boxing, for example. But there was one student, named Noguchi, with whom I never got along. He hated me— maybe because his father had been killed fighting the Americans during the war."

Killian said the bad feelings between them erupted one day during a practice match. Noguchi had refused to "pull" his blows. This enraged Killian. They were soon fighting in deadly earnest, and before their instructor could stop them, Killian hit his opponent with a karate chop, seriously injuring him.

The dancer's head drooped for a moment and his face took on a bleak expression as he recalled the unpleasant situation.

"I instantly regretted it," he went on, "and I tried to make amends by visiting Noguchi at the hospital and apologizing. But by then the damage was done. Noguchi worked for the Satoya Corporation, and their company lawyers pressed charges against me with the police. As a result, I was asked to leave the country."

"Tough break," Frank sympathized.

Warlord shrugged. "Just one of those things, I guess. Noguchi recovered, but I still feel guilty about what happened, so I've tried to forget the whole business. If the news ever came out, it probably wouldn't do my career any good, either."

"Don't worry, it's not going to leak out through us," said Joe.

"No, I'm sure of that—now. But at the time I got your call and heard what you wanted to see me about, I guess I lost my head. I thought you were going to drag up that old scandal and try to pin something on me. Sorry about that."

"Forget it," Frank said. "But we do have another question . . ."

"Shoot."

"You told us you thought Satoya intended to bid on that sword at the Palmer-Glade Auction Galleries, and it turns out you were right. How did you know?"

"That sword's been stolen, by the way," Joe added.

Warlord nodded. "So I've heard. Well, I felt Satoya would be interested in it, because when I looked at the blade while it was on display, I noticed the name *Satoya* inscribed on it. You see, while I was in Japan, I learned to read Japanese characters. And when you mentioned that dealer, Gorky, trying to sell him a samurai sword, it just seemed likely he'd be more interested in buying one that belonged to his own family." The dancer rose from his chair and began to pace the floor. His manner seemed vaguely uncomfortable.

"There's something else I'd better tell you," he said after a few moments.

"We're listening," Frank said.

"Last night I had an anonymous phone call."

"What about?" Joe asked.

"That samurai sword. Apparently the person who called was the thief who stole it from the auction gallery—or maybe a fence. He offered to sell me the sword—for ten thousand dollars."

Warlord's startling news caught the Hardys by surprise. They stared at him, wide-eyed.

"How did you handle it?" Frank asked.

Warlord ran his fingers nervously through his mane of long black hair. "To tell the truth I didn't know *what* to say. He only gave me a few moments to make up my mind, and I was afraid if I said no, that would be the last I'd hear from him. So I said I'd accept, and he named a time and place to complete the deal."

"You bring the money, and he'd hand over the sword?"

"Right."

"When and where is this supposed to take place?"

"Midnight tonight at Seaview Park."

"Did you intend to go through with it?" Joe put in.

The dancer shrugged helplessly. "I don't know *what* I intended. The whole thing's been on my mind ever since I got the call. Guess that's why I was glad to hear from you fellows again—so you could advise me."

"If you buy stolen goods, that makes you as guilty as the thief," Frank pointed out.

"I realize that. But I wasn't planning on just keeping the sword and saying nothing. It wouldn't be any use to me, anyhow, if I had to keep it hidden. I thought if I returned it to the auction gallery, they might be willing to sell it to me for a bargain price—I mean, to make up for the ransom money I'd already paid out."

"You might find a lot of people would suspect you were the guy who swiped it in the first place," Joe remarked dryly.

From the dismayed look on Warlord's face, the boys could see that this possibility hadn't even occurred to him. "So what choice do I have at this point?" Killian asked the Hardys.

"Use the payoff meeting as a chance to catch the thieves," Frank shot back.

"They warned me I'd regret it if I tipped off the police—and not just myself, my whole dance troupe!"

"You agreed not to tell the police?"

"The caller made me swear it before he named the time and place for the exchange."

"Leave it to us," said Joe after a questioning glance at his brother, who responded with a nod. "That way you'll be keeping your word, and Frank and I will try to set up a trap on our own."

Warlord's expression showed relief at getting out of his dilemma, and he readily agreed to the Hardys' proposal.

"One more thing," said Frank. "How would the thief or thieves have known *you* might be interested in buying that stolen sword?"

"The gallery's public relations man had a publicity photo taken of me examining the sword," Killian replied. "It turned up in a couple of newspapers, and the caption under the picture said I planned to bid on the sword when it was auctioned."

"That would explain it, all right," Frank agreed.

"Besides," Warlord added, "everyone who's seen my show knows that I use swords and knives in my dance act—and each one's an authentic example of its kind."

As the Hardys returned to their car in the parking lot, Frank murmured, "Oh, oh! Something must be up!"

A red light was flashing on their instrument panel. Frank switched on the specially licensed transceiver mounted under their dashboard.

"H-1 here," he said into the hand mike.

"G calling!"

Something in the tone of the woman's voice as it came over the speaker struck a note of alarm in the hearts of both Hardy boys.

"What's wrong, Aunt Gertrude?" Frank asked.

"Sam Radley's been hurt!" she reported. "I just had a call from Shoreham. He was found unconscious in the street there—with a head wound!"

12

A Meeting at Midnight

"Oh, that's terrible news!" Frank exclaimed with an anxious glance at Joe. "Where is Sam now?"

"They've taken him to Shoreham Hospital," Miss Hardy replied. "The police recognized him as your father's top aide, so they called here. But so far I haven't been able to reach Fenton and give him the bad news. That's why I called you boys."

"Good! I'm glad you let us know, Aunty. Joe and I'll drive to the hospital right now and see how Sam is. Over and out!"

Frank switched off the set and hung up the mike. Then he gunned the engine and maneuvered smoothly and swiftly out of the parking lot. Soon they were pressing the speed limit over the Shore Road, en route to the nearby town of Shoreham.

"Do you suppose this is connected to the Satoya case?" Joe asked his brother.

"I don't know. I'm not sure what kind of assignment Dad had him working on."

At the hospital they were directed to the emergency room. Sam Radley had already regained consciousness. The boys found him sitting up on the examining table while a doctor bandaged his head.

"Wow! What a relief!" Frank exclaimed. "We weren't sure what had happened, or how seriously you were hurt!"

Joe added, "What did happen, Sam?"

"Got conked." The detective grinned wryly. "Fortunately I seem to have a hard head."

Frank gave the medic a questioning glance. "How is he, Doctor?"

"Nothing too serious, apparently. Just a bruise and a slight scalp laceration. Bit swollen now, but that'll be down by tomorrow morning. However, I want him to stay here at the hospital overnight, to make sure he's suffered no concussion."

The doctor allowed the Hardys to talk to Sam Radley for a few minutes before he was taken to one of the hospital wards.

"Any idea who hit you, Sam?" Frank inquired.

"No name, if that's what you mean—but I've got a general idea."

Although Radley was the only investigator who worked regularly for Fenton Hardy, there were other operatives whom the sleuth employed from time to time as the need arose. Sam told the boys that their father had asked all his associates to keep their eyes open for any possible *Yakuza*, or Japanese gangsters, in the area.

"I spotted a guy here in Shoreham with all the earmarks," the private detective went on. "Tattooed arms, flashy clothes, amputated finger joints, the works. So I started tailing him."

"Where'd he go?" Joe asked eagerly.

"To a cafe down on the waterfront. And he met a man there, an American, from the looks of him, anyhow." Sam paused for a moment, his brow creasing in a thoughtful frown.

"Did you recognize him?" Frank prompted.

"I don't know. And that bothers me a bit." Sam hesitated, still frowning. "He looked familiar, but I can't place him. Anyhow, the two of them gabbed for a while, then the *Yakuza* got up and left. And I followed him—which turned out to be a mistake."

"How do you mean?"

"I figure he may have suspected he was being shadowed, so he told the American to keep watch. Or maybe the American saw me follow him out of the cafe, and took action on his own hook, or tipped off one of the *Yakuza*'s pals. Whichever it was, the Japanese led me down a narrow street near the wharves. Next thing I knew someone jumped me from behind!"

"Did you get a look at the person who attacked you?" put in Joe.

"Nope." Sam Radley shook his head in disgust. "Not even out of the corner of my eye. He just grabbed my coat long enough to slow me down, then let me have it with a blackjack, or whatever it was he hit me with. All I remember after that is waking up here in the hospital emergency room."

Sam speculated that his assailant might have been hiding in a doorway as he passed.

Frank and Joe started back to Bayport in a somewhat grim mood. Both were disturbed over the attack on Sam Radley. Partly to get their minds off the subject, Joe switched on the radio and tuned in the police frequency.

The first calls were routine and not very interesting. Then the boys heard the dispatcher say, "Car Seven, proceed to 119 Ardmore Avenue, corner of Dean Street. Investigate report of an escaped monkey."

"Escaped monkey?" The man responding from the scout car sounded startled.

"That's right. It got loose from a pet shop."

There was a burst of static and a blurred mutter of voices. Then the man exclaimed, "That must have been what we saw!"

"What do you mean 'what you saw'?" the dispatcher queried irritably.

"A man running down the street with a monkey on his head!"

"What?"

"We saw this guy running down the street with a monkey on his head," the officer repeated. "He did look kind of excited, and we wondered what was going on, but. . . ."

"For crying out loud!" the dispatcher sounded angry. "What did you *think* was going on—that the monkey was prospecting for coconuts?"

"No. We figured the animal was the fellow's pet, and they were just having fun, or else he was taking it out for exercise, something like that."

"Listen! Next time you see someone with a monkey on his head, *find out* what's going on, understand? Now get moving and round up the critter before it attacks someone else!"

"Roger."

Frank and Joe were shaking with laughter as they neared the outskirts of Bayport. Before driving to their house on Elm Street, they stopped off at the Morton farm, where they found their chubby friend, Chet, squaring off against lanky Biff Hooper in the barnyard.

"What's this? A grudge match?" Frank asked, noting Chet's intense scowl of concentration. Although he spoke half jokingly, he was ready to step between the two youths instantly if the fight turned out to be real.

"No, haven't you heard?" Biff asked, not taking his eyes off his pudgy opponent.

"Heard what?" Joe asked.

"Chet's taking up the martial arts," Biff explained. "He's showing me the fine points of karate or kung fu or wing ding or something."

"Think I'm kidding, huh?" Chet retorted. "Well,

watch this, wise guy! It's a combination. First a feint, then a move backward to draw you off balance, then a series of blows to finish you off, using a mixture of two different Oriental fighting styles. *On guard!*"

Chet took a couple of quick, shuffling dance steps and flailed out with both arms before leaping backward out of range. The next instant Biff's long left snaked out in a fast jab, and their plump chum landed flat on his back!

"No fair!" Chet grumbled loudly as he scrabbled back up on his feet. "You weren't supposed to get that close!"

"How do I know what I'm supposed to do?" Biff retorted. "I'm just defending myself."

"Then do it right, meatball!"

"Meatball, eh? Look who's talking!"

The Hardys, who had a hard time to keep from howling with laughter, hastily intervened before the exhibition could, indeed, turn into a grudge match.

"Listen, you guys!" Frank said. "How'd you like a chance to show off your fighting styles tonight?"

"What's up?" Biff asked.

"A ransom stakeout. Joe and I are going to try and catch a thief. If he makes a run for it, we may need help in stopping and subduing him."

The Hardys explained about the anonymous call Warlord had received, offering to sell him the stolen samurai sword, and the meeting that had been set up at Seaview Park.

"Count me in!" Chet exclaimed. "Boy, this'll really

give me a chance to show you how they do it in the Orient. If this guy makes one false move, I'll have him hollering uncle so fast that his head'll swim."

"Great! But don't take any chances," Frank cautioned. "If the man's armed, or comes with pals who may be armed, none of us makes any move. Just watch for a signal from me."

Biff was as eager as Chet to lend a hand in the nocturnal trap baiting.

That night, after a final phone check with Warlord to coordinate their movements, the Hardys picked up Chet and Biff in their car. Then, shortly after 10:30, the boys headed down Ardmore Avenue. It connected with a cinder road that wound through the full length of Seaview Park.

The park itself was a pleasant wooded stretch, bordered on one side by the coastal highway and on the other by the water. Officially it closed at eleven every night, but there was no gate or roadblock. Youngsters and dating couples often sneaked in later by moonlight or stayed after the official closing time.

Frank, Joe and their two friends parked the Hardys' yellow car out of sight among some trees. Then they found a comfortable spot where they could sprawl and listen to music on Biff's transistor radio or tell yarns to pass the time.

At about a quarter to twelve, they took up hiding places around the point where the meeting had been set up. It was a short dirt turnoff which ended in a parking site near two or three picnic tables.

Shortly before midnight, they heard the low hum of a car engine and saw a glow of headlights. They were doused as a sleek white car pulled to a stop on the parking site.

"Warlord," Joe hissed to his brother, who was crouched in a crevice between two rocks.

Soon afterward, the *putput* of a motorboat drifted over the water. It died away abruptly, as the engine was shut off, but moments later the boat could be heard pulling alongside the shore embankment. Apparently its operator had allowed the craft to coast toward the park.

At that moment there was a loud commotion from a tree a dozen yards away, where the Hardys' chubby friend was perched among the branches.

"Something's wrong with Chet!" Frank exclaimed.

13

Masked Riders

In the shadowy moonlight, the Hardys could clearly see the tree in which Chet was hiding. Its branches were swaying violently.

"What is going on?" Joe gasped.

"Help!" their fat chum yelled in fright.

Before either of the Hardys could respond, there was an explosive *crack* as one of the tree limbs snapped under its heavy load. The next instant, Chet tumbled down into view!

Frank and Joe hesitated no longer. They knew their stakeout would be ruined, but they ran to help their friend. Warlord was jumping out of his car at the same time.

"Chet!" Frank cried. "Are you all right?"

Their roly-poly pal struggled painfully to his feet and dusted off the seat of his pants. "D-D-Don't ask me!" he stuttered. "I was attacked by some wild animal up in the tree!"

"Wild animal?" Joe gaped at Chet, not quite sure he was serious.

"You heard me!" Chet retorted. "Boy, it was really savage! Is my face all clawed up?"

"Not a scratch as far as I can see!" Joe declared.

"Well, stop staring at me as if I were nuts! I'm telling you th—"

Whatever Chet was about to tell his baffled audience was drowned out by the sudden roar of a motorboat engine being revved into action.

At the same instant something plopped out of the tree onto Chet's head. *It was a live monkey!*

Chet screeched in fright and hopped about, clutching wildly at his excited furry rider!

Frank and Joe did not wait to watch the uproarious spectacle. Half amused, half furious at the wreckage of their carefully laid plans, they turned and darted down the park's wooded slope toward the water's edge.

Too late! The motorboat they had heard was already speeding off into the darkness. Its pilot cautiously hugged the shadow of the hillside in order to avoid being silhouetted in the moonlight. The Hardys could not even tell whether the boat held more than one occupant.

"Great!" Frank fumed. "So much for our stakeout!"

"Not only didn't we catch the thief," Joe added in disgust, "we didn't even get the sword back!"

"Never mind. Maybe the whole thing was a con job anyhow, just to help someone get his hands on ten thousand dollars."

"Guess you're right." Joe did his best to emulate his brother's example and swallow his disappointment. "Blowing our stacks won't do us any good."

The Hardys headed back up the slope toward the meeting place. Biff had joined forces with Warlord to try and pry the chattering monkey loose from its perch on Chet's head.

A passing policeman, who had heard the noise, hurried into the park to investigate.

"What's going on here?" he demanded suspiciously. Then he did a double take as he recognized Frank and Joe. "Hey! You two are the Hardy boys, aren't you?"

"That's right, officer," Frank replied. "We're working on a case for our dad. We had a trap set for a suspected thief, but then another fugitive showed up and spoiled everything."

Grinning, he pointed at the monkey, who was now nestling contentedly in Biff's arms, scratching itself and staring at the circle of faces watching it.

"Well, I'll be a monkey's uncle!" said the policeman. "You mean that's the one that escaped from the pet shop?"

"Must be," said Joe. "The last time it was seen, I believe it was heading down Ardmore Avenue, which leads right into the park."

"People's heads must be its favorite mode of transportation," Frank added with a chuckle. "That's how it was proceeding on Ardmore Avenue when last observed."

"Next time it tries hopping up and down on my noggin," Chet steamed, "I'm going to tie a knot in the little creep's tail!"

"Relax, and knock on wood, pal," said Joe, patting Chet on the head. "That's probably what confused the poor critter. It thought that round thing on top of your shoulders was part of the tree!"

Joe's wisecrack brought a general round of laughter. Even Chet joined in, with his usual good nature.

The policeman used his walkie-talkie to report the monkey's capture to the station house. The sergeant on duty promised to dispatch a squad car to pick up the escaped animal, so the officer took the monkey and headed back to the park entrance to await its arrival.

Yvor Killian had remained silent in the policeman's presence, which might have been one of the reasons the officer had not recognized him.

"Sorry our trap didn't work," Frank apologized as the boys accompanied the dancer to his car.

Warlord grinned wryly. "Doesn't matter. To tell the truth, I'm a bit relieved. If we had caught the crooks, it might've made the headlines, but I'm not sure how I'd have ended up looking in the eyes of the public. A lot of people might figure I was crooked myself. Plus, I'd be worrying about the thief's pals trying to get even with me for setting him up."

"We'll nail him eventually," Joe promised.

"I don't doubt it." Warlord offered the Hardys and their friends a handshake and added, "Are you coming to see my show?"

"Joe and I'd like to catch the matinee tomorrow," Frank said. "If we can get in."

"No problem. There'll be tickets waiting at the gate for you and your dates."

Frank and Joe looked forward to the performance enthusiastically. Joe invited Iola Morton, and Frank brought Callie Shaw. Arrangements had been made to stage the show in the auditorium in case of rain, but sunshine prevailed so the outdoor performance was to go on as planned.

Since Bayshore College had no football stadium, chairs and a stage had been set up in the grassy quadrangle at the center of the campus.

The show began with two numbers by the college symphony. Then Warlord and his troupe bounded on stage, amid excited shouts and handclapping.

"Ooh, what gorgeous costumes!" gasped Iola.

Warlord was garbed somewhat in the style of a Japanese samurai knight, though in much more brilliant colors. His face was whitened with powder and streaked with war paint, and he was literally armed to the teeth with a variety of knives and a long-bladed sword. The other dancers looked equally stunning and barbaric.

From the first note of their opening number, they held the audience spellbound. The whole troupe formed a pulsing spectacle in color, but Warlord especially riveted all eyes with his breathtaking leaps and twirls as he brandished his blades in gleaming arcs.

"It looks so dangerous!" Callie murmured.

"You're right," said Frank. "But what a showman he is!"

Suddenly Joe became aware of a noisy hum that seemed to clash with the music. As it grew louder, he glanced questioningly at his brother. "Hey, what's that?"

"Sounds like motorcycles!"

The words were hardly out of Frank's mouth when, with an earsplitting din of exhaust, a column of motorcyclists appeared between two buildings and started to charge across the lawn. The riders were masked and leather-jacketed, and bestrode powerful black-and-chrome choppers!

"Are those guys crazy?" Joe blurted, hardly able to believe his eyes.

There were shouts and screams of panic as the audience leaped up and jostled each other in a mad rush to get out of the way. The motorcyclists roared in among them, knocking over chairs and frightening people out of their wits!

Soon the audience and orchestra were scattering in all directions as the masked riders circled around and around the quadrangle. Several of them even roared up the side ramps and across the stage, forcing Warlord and his troupe to take cover.

"Those nuts should be locked up!" Frank shouted. "Come on, Joe. Give me a hand!"

"What can we do?"

Instead of straining his voice to be heard above the engine roar, Frank merely pointed to a coiled firehose on a nearby building. Joe's face lit up.

The Hardys swiftly broke out the wide canvas hose from its wall brackets. Then, while Frank gripped the nozzle and braced himself, Joe spun the valve wheel. A powerful gusher of water shot across the quadrangle as the valve was opened.

"Hang on!" Joe shouted and grabbed the hose before it got away from Frank.

The rogue motorcyclists were enraged by the Hardys' tactic. Some tried to run down the two boys, but the blasting force of the water at pointblank range almost knocked them out of the saddle and forced them to veer away!

Frank and Joe played the hose back and forth, dousing the riders thoroughly. One by one, they scooted out of the quadrangle, rather than get soaked further. The approaching whine of police sirens sped them on their way.

Several police cars soon converged on the campus. The Hardys learned later that an alarm had been telephoned in by a college official who had witnessed the scene from a window overlooking the quadrangle. Unfortunately, the masked riders had fled at top speed before roadblocks could be set up, and there seemed little hope of collaring and identifying any of them.

"Good work, you two!" Sergeant Burton congratulated the Hardy boys. "Did you get a look at any of their faces?"

"No chance, with those masks they were wearing," Frank replied. "But they could have been the Gung-Ho gang."

"I'd bet on it!" said Joe.

"So would I," the burly police sergeant agreed. "Those punks are the worst bunch of motorcycle hoods around here. But there's not much hope of proving it unless the highway patrol manages to nail one of them."

Warlord and his troupe were willing to resume the show. But half the audience had dispersed, and the orchestra was in disarray due to scattered sheet music and several damaged instruments, so it was announced that the performance would be rescheduled at a later date.

"Sorry the show was ruined," Frank said when they took Callie home.

"It certainly wasn't your fault," the pretty blond girl told him with a cheerful smile. "I think it was wonderful the way you and Joe drove off that vicious gang!" Iola agreed.

After a stop at the Mortons' farm, the Hardys drove back to Elm Street. On the way, Joe remarked thoughtfully to his brother, "Think there was any special reason for that motorcycle attack?"

"Good question," Frank responded. "I've been wondering the same thing myself. Breaking up the show that way was really asking for trouble with the police. Seems to me even the Gung-Ho gang wouldn't go that far just for kicks. They must've had a definite motive."

"That's how it looks to me, too. And here's another question," Joe went on. "Did you get the impression any of those punks were gunning for us in particular?"

"Matter of fact I did," Frank said. "When they first showed up, I thought for a while the leader was deliberately steering our way. But there was so much confusion and milling around, he got sidetracked."

Joe flashed his brother a quizzical glance. "So what does it all add up to?"

"If you're asking for a hunch, I'd say it could be more than a coincidence that this should happen right after last night's stakeout. . . . Check?"

"Check! In other words, Warlord helps set up a trap for whoever stole the samurai sword, so the next day his show gets wrecked for revenge!"

"And if you and I were seen last night," Frank added, "that would be enough reason for including *us* in the revenge."

"Right. Assuming our hunch about the identity of the masked riders is correct, it would also mean the Gung-Ho gang must be in cahoots with the gallery thief, who—"

As the Hardys turned up Elm Street and could see their home, Joe broke off with a slight exclamation. A familiar blue sedan was parked in front of their house. "Hey! That's Sam Radley's car. I wonder what's up?"

The boys hurried inside and found the operative chatting with their mother. Aside from a much smaller bandage than they had seen him wearing at the hospital, he seemed none the worse for wear.

"No concussion?" Frank queried as they shook hands warmly.

"Nope." Radley grinned. "I woke up this morning raring to go, so they had to turn me loose."

Mrs. Hardy excused herself to attend to some chores, and Sam Radley hastily briefed the two boys on the reason for his visit. He told them that ever since his release from the hospital that morning, he had been keeping watch on the waterfront cafe where he had seen the Japanese gangster meet the American.

"Did you spot the *Yakuza* again?" Joe asked eagerly.

"No, but I did spot the guy he met yesterday." Sam related that his attempt to shadow the man had failed when his quarry leaped aboard a passing bus. "But this time I got a really good look at his face—and I was surer than ever that I'd seen him somewhere before! I drove straight home and checked my files, and sure enough I got a make!"

"Then his photo would probably be in Dad's files, too," Frank put in.

"Of course. I'll show it to you."

Fenton Hardy's study was lined with file cabinets bulging with dossiers on every known criminal who had come under his scrutiny. Besides data from his own cases, information had been gleaned from police and FBI sources as well as newspaper accounts.

Sam Radley quickly pulled out a picture from the K drawer and handed it to the Hardy boys. "There's the bird I'm talking about. He's an expert burglar and second-story man named Krunkel."

The photo showed a squint-eyed, hatchet-faced man about forty years old with a receding hairline. As they studied the picture, both boys gasped.

"Hey! That's the guy we saw right after the motorcycle race!" Joe blurted.

"Right," Frank concurred. "He's the man Len Boggs was talking to!"

14

A Siren Shrieks!

Radley was keenly interested to learn that the Hardys had already come across Krunkel in their investigation of the Satoya case. He was also startled when he heard about the anonymous phone call offering to sell Warlord the stolen samurai sword, and the outcome of last night's stakeout.

"Tough break," the private detective commented. "But at least we've got a definite lead now. I'd say this makes it pretty certain that Krunkel must figure in the case."

Frank and Joe also felt that it confirmed their hunch that the Gung-Ho gang might be in cahoots with the criminals behind the theft of the samurai sword.

"Incidentally, I've got an idea how that gallery heist might have been pulled," Frank added.

"Let's hear it," said Radley.

"The thief couldn't have dropped a line from the roof of the Palmer-Glade Galleries because there are some kind of detectors or sensors up there that would've triggered the alarm. But suppose there are *two* thieves—and they went up separately on the roofs of the buildings on each side of Palmer-Glade."

"Then what?"

"They heave or shoot a line from one to the other, so that it passes over the gallery building without actually touching the roof. They make it fast at both ends and let the middle of the line droop down in front of the Palmer-Glade building's facade."

"I get it!" Joe exclaimed, snapping his fingers. "And then they simply go down the line, hand over hand, to the third-story window where they want to break in."

"Right, or they could use a pulley with a handgrip and slide down. That would give the first man something to hang onto while he cut the pane."

"Pretty smart," said Radley. "I think you've hit on the answer, Frank. What's more, it ties in with Krunkel's usual M.O."

The boys knew that among detectives M.O. stood for *modus operandi*, or a crook's known working methods.

"He generally works with a partner," Radley explained, "and he always comes up with some cute trick to avoid setting off the alarm."

"Does Krunkel operate in the Bayport area?" Joe inquired.

"Not that I know of. Most of his robberies have been around New York or Boston, although he pulled one job in Miami. But now that I've seen him in Shoreham two days in a row, it looks as if he's staying here. I'll check the hotels and motels in this area."

"Good idea," said Frank.

Soon after Radley left, the telephone rang. Joe answered. His face tensed and he beckoned his brother to listen in as a whispering voice came over the line.

"You interested in that Jap sword that got heisted in New York?"

"You could say that," Joe replied. "Who's calling, please?"

"Never mind who I am. And don't bother trying to trace this call. I won't be on the line long enough." The whisperer paused for effect before adding, "I just thought you might like a tip."

"Go ahead. I'm listening."

"Ever hear of Dobert Humber?"

"Sure. He collects rare weapons."

"That's the guy. And he may soon be adding that stolen sword to his collection."

"How come?" Joe asked, exchanging a startled glance with Frank.

"Because he just made a secret deal to buy it from the thief who swiped it!"

There was a click at the other end of the line as the

unknown caller hung up. Joe whistled softly and put down the phone. "What do you make of that, Frank?"

"Looks like the thief couldn't make a sale to Warlord last night, so he's trying another customer."

"Right. But how do we find out if the tip's on the level?"

"There's one simple way," said Frank. "Let's get hold of Humber and ask him while we watch his face."

Frank called the collector and requested an appointment. Humber was willing to see the Hardys immediately, so they drove to his house. He invited them into his sitting room.

"Mr. Humber," Frank began, "would you have been interested in bidding on that samurai sword that was stolen from the Palmer-Glade Galleries?"

"Oh, definitely. In fact, I intended to do so. It would make a splendid addition to my collection. Why do you ask?"

"Because we got a tip that you've arranged to buy it from the thief."

Humber's reaction to Frank's bombshell was plain to see. Surprise was written all over his face, but neither boy could see any sign of guilt.

"Why, that's the most ridiculous thing I ever heard!" Humber exclaimed. "How on earth would I be able to get in touch with the thief, when I don't even know who stole the sword? Or is he supposed to have contacted me? Just who told you this fantastic tale, anyhow?"

"An anonymous phone caller."

"No wonder! He wouldn't dare make such an idiotic charge in public, where I could have the law on him! I'd like to get my hands on that lying sneak! I'd soon teach him not to go smearing my good name!" Their freckled host was becoming red-faced with anger as he responded to the charge.

Frank held up his hand with an apologetic smile. "Okay, you don't have to convince us, Mr. Humber. We received the call, so we got in touch with you right away to give you a chance to refute his story. Apparently whoever contacted us either has a screw loose, or has it in for you."

"Any idea who it might be?" Joe asked.

Before Humber could answer, the phone rang. He scooped up the handset impatiently, but a few seconds later the Hardys saw his expression change dramatically.

He beckoned frantically to the boys. Frank and Joe sprang up from their chairs and bent close to listen as he held the receiver slightly away from his ear.

"You can have the sword for ten thousand in cash!" a man on the other end said.

Humber flashed a glance at Frank, who nodded.

"And to whom would I—er, pay this money?" he said into the phone.

"To me."

"How?"

"Ever heard of Lookout Rock?"

"Hm, yes. On the outskirts of Bayport, I believe. In any case, I'm sure I can find it."

"Do that. And be there tonight, at twelve sharp, with the money in a flight bag. Got that?"

"I think so. Midnight at Lookout Rock, and bring the ten thousand dollars in a flight bag," Humber repeated.

"In unmarked bills!" the voice added sharply. "Now listen carefully. Wear a watch, and make sure it's adjusted to the telephone time signal. Lookout Rock's on top of a hill, but when you first arrive, just go halfway up the hillside and wait there. Then, at twelve, start walking toward the rock."

"I understand."

"Good. That's where the exchange will take place. The money for the sword, assuming you're not dumb enough to try doublecrossing me. Any tricks and you'll regret it!"

The receiver was slammed down as the caller rang off. Dobert Humber hung up with a somewhat stunned expression.

"It appears your anonymous tipster wasn't so far wrong after all!" he murmured to the Hardys.

Frank nodded thoughtfully. "He evidently assumed you'd already received the call and accepted."

"If he knew the call was going to be made, he must be one of the thieves himself, or at least in with them somehow," said Joe. "Which sounds like *he's* pulling some kind of doublecross—squealing on his own pals."

"B-B-But should I have agreed?" Humber asked a trifle nervously.

"Sure! It'll give us a chance to trap the thieves and recover the sword!" said Joe.

Frank frowned and tugged his lower lip. "They may be having your house watched, Mr. Humber, to make sure you don't go to the police. They may even have your phone bugged or your line tapped. Would you mind if Joe and I stay here till you leave?"

"Of course not, do by all means! But if the thieves are watching my house and see you Hardys drive away right after me, isn't that likely to put them on guard?"

"It would if they saw us, but I intend to make sure they don't. Your car's in the garage, isn't it?"

"Yes, of course, but—"

"And the garage is attached to the house, so Joe and I could go there without being seen."

Humber's eyes lit up with enthusiasm as he caught on. "You mean you and your brother can be hidden in my car when I drive away!"

"Right, sir."

"Splendid idea, my boy! By jove, how clever. I wish I'd thought of that!"

At quarter after eleven that night, Humber's expensive limousine was driven out of the garage and away from the estate. Humber was at the wheel, the only visible person in the car. A flight bag filled with newspaper sat on the passenger seat next to him. Frank and Joe were huddled on the floor of the back seat compartment.

Meanwhile, two boyish figures could be seen in silhouette through one lighted window of the wealthy collector's mansion. They appeared to be watching the late TV news. Actually they were dummies which Humber had helped the boys rig with great glee. They consisted of stuffed suits of clothes with marble statuary busts fitted in place to serve as heads.

The hill on which Lookout Rock was situated had been the site of the middle cloverleaf in the motorcycle race. A narrow dirt lane ran along the foot of the slope.

Humber parked in a secluded spot and got out without saying a word. Frank and Joe crawled out the other side, which was concealed from view by the surrounding shrubbery. Earlier they had disconnected the courtesy light switch, so that no glow would be visible to give them away when the back door was opened.

Humber started up the hillside first and settled himself to wait at a convenient spot about halfway up the slope. The Hardy boys followed cautiously, keeping low and squirming through the underbrush. Rather than risk going too high and giving themselves away, they picked a hiding place which would afford them an equally clear view of Humber and the massive rocky outcrop on the brow of the hill.

"Got the time?" Joe whispered after a lengthy wait.

"About one minute to twelve," Frank responded softly. "It won't be long now!"

Seconds crept by.

"Now!" Frank hissed as the illuminated dial of his watch showed twelve o'clock.

The Hardys saw Humber rise to his feet, clutching

the flight bag, and start slowly up the slope. Both boys braced themselves to make a sprint toward the rock and try to seize the thief once the exchange was underway.

Suddenly a siren shrieked somewhere below them! Frank and Joe glimpsed Humber's startled reaction, but their eyes were mainly fixed on Lookout Rock.

In the moonlit darkness they saw a figure bolt from cover and dart toward a motorcycle. Its engine roared to life and the rider sped off!

The Hardys raced up the hillside. It was too late to catch the thief, but Frank whipped out a flashlight, playing its beam on the ground. Then he stopped short. "Joe! Take a look at this!" he cried.

15

Police Tip

Joe gasped as he saw the object revealed by the flashlight beam—a sheathed, long-bladed sword lying near the base of Lookout Rock! Its scabbard was of plain, leather-covered metal, but its hilt was beautifully inlaid with mother-of-pearl!

"Just like the photo they showed us at the gallery!" Joe exclaimed, kneeling down for a closer look. "This must be it, all right!"

"Watch out for prints!" Frank warned.

"Don't worry, I'm not going to handle it," Joe replied. "Got some twine here that should do for a carrying handle."

He fished in his pocket and brought out some stout string salvaged from a package, then tied one end to the hilt and the other to the sheath. By gripping the string, the sword could now be picked up without danger of smudging any possible fingerprints.

"Hey! What happened to Humber?" Frank blurted.

His brother glanced down the slope but could see no one. "The car's gone, too!" Joe noted. "He must have taken off the same time as the guy on the motorcycle— that's why we didn't hear him go!"

Frank chuckled dryly. "That siren must've scared him out of his wits. He was probably afraid the police might nab him for buying stolen goods!"

"Speaking of the police—where are they?" Joe wondered aloud.

The boys hurried down the hillside to obtain a better view, unobstructed by trees. After surveying the moonlit lane in both directions, they could see no car of any kind, either police or civilian.

Joe frowned and scratched his head. "Boy, that's funny. Maybe the siren noise we heard was just a police car going by on the main highway."

"Sounded closer than that," Frank said doubtfully.

"Next question. What do we do for transportation? Looks like we're stuck out here with no car."

After a hasty conference, the Hardys decided that one of them would go back to Humber's house to retrieve their car, while the other kept watch on the ransom site, in case the thief or thieves returned to look for their abandoned loot. The boys flipped a coin, and Joe got the job of staying.

"Don't take any chance of being seen," Frank warned his brother. "Pick a spot where you'll be out of sight, and stay there till I get back!"

"Will do," Joe promised.

His wait was shorter than expected. In less than an hour, their yellow car appeared on the dirt lane that bordered the foot of the hillside. Joe scrambled down from his hiding place to join his brother, bringing the samurai sword with him.

"You made good time," he commented, climbing into the car.

"Yes, I had a lucky break," Frank said as he maneuvered to turn the car around. "Phil Cohen tooled along shortly after I made it out to the highway. He was on his way home from a date and gave me a lift to Humber's house."

"Was Humber there?" Joe queried.

"Probably. But the garage was closed and the place was dark, as if everyone had turned in." Frank grinned. "Guess he was trying to give himself an alibi in case the law did come around."

"That guy's a real nitwit," Joe declared. "I wonder what he thought *we'd* say if that police car had picked us up?"

"No telling. He didn't stick around to find out! I guess Warlord had him sized up right," Frank reflected. "Humber's only interest is looking out for Number One. The rest of the human race isn't all that important."

Joe was silent for a minute or two as they drove through the residential suburbs on their way to the downtown area of Bayport. Finally he said, "Now that we've got the sword, do you think it had anything to do with Satoya's disappearance?"

"My hunch is yes," the older Hardy boy mused thoughtfully. "But I can't prove it. Before we'll know the answer to that, we've got to find out whether he disappeared on his own accord or was kidnapped."

"Right! I was thinking about that while I was waiting for you," Joe said. "I've got an idea how Satoya could have pulled his vanishing act."

"Let's hear it."

"It's so simple," Joe explained. "Say the chauffeur is as loyal to his boss as Oyama claims. When he turned into the underground parking garage, he could have stopped the limousine halfway down the ramp, just long enough to let Satoya pop out of the secret compartment. Then he could have continued on and pretended he knew nothing when Oyama searched the car. Meanwhile, all Satoya had to do was turn up his coat collar and slip away through the crowd. At that time, there was a mob of people around the hotel. None of them knew what was going on."

Frank was impressed by his brother's theory. "When you put it that way, it sure sounds obvious, Joe! That's so simple, it's *got* to be the right answer!"

"But where's Satoya hiding?"

"If your deductions are right, he must have arranged

for a place before he ever flew over here. Perhaps a house in an out-of-the-way spot!"

"That figures, with no nosy neighbors to wonder who he is. He could have had somebody rent it for him under a phony name before he arrived."

Frank nodded, keeping a watchful eye out for late-hour traffic as they slowed and crossed an intersection with a blinking yellow light. He looked as though he were already turning over another idea in his mind.

"Joe, suppose Satoya knew beforehand that something was going to happen to the sword—"

"You mean, that someone might try to steal it?"

"Could be. Anyhow, say he went into hiding so he could try to get hold of it himself without anyone knowing what he was up to."

"I'd buy that," said Joe, "especially if the sword had belonged to the Satoya family. Remember what Mr. Shimada told us about how much the samurai class prizes their swords."

"Right! But now that we're turning the sword over to the police, the whole thing's out of his hands. I mean, now there's no possible way Satoya can latch onto it secretly, and nobody else can, either."

The younger Hardy boy shot his brother a keen glance. "What are you getting at, Frank?"

"Just this. If our reasoning is correct, Satoya will no longer have any motive for staying undercover."

"You're right!" Joe snapped his fingers. "Once he

hears the news on television, or reads it in the papers, maybe Satoya will turn up again!"

"Suppose the police decide not to release the news for a while, in order to keep the thieves in the dark."

"Hm. Then how would he find out?"

"We could tip him off."

Joe looked startled. "Are you kidding? How could we do that?"

"Look," Frank replied. "If Satoya disappeared on his own accord, the chauffeur must have helped him. Right?"

"Sure, but how does th—" Joe broke off suddenly as he caught on. "Oh, oh! I get it. If our theory is correct, the chauffeur probably knows where his boss is hiding, so if we tip *him* off, he'll pass the word on to Satoya!"

"Check. But we'd have to do it very casually and naturally. Otherwise the chauffeur might get the notion that we're just trying to trap his master."

"Any ideas?"

"We'll use the sword itself," said Frank. "I just hope we can find him this late at night."

Joe pointed out that every time they had gone to the Bayport Chilton, the chauffeur had been seated in the hotel lobby. "Come to think of it," the younger Hardy boy mused, "maybe Satoya posted him there to report what goes on."

"You could be right," Frank agreed. "If you are, we've got a good chance of finding him there now."

When the boys entered the lobby after parking outside the hotel, the granite-faced chauffeur was sitting in his usual spot. The Hardys hurried toward him. Frank noticed his eyes widen in surprise when he saw the samurai sword that Joe was carrying by the twine handle.

"Do you speak English?" Frank asked.

The chauffeur nodded. "A little."

"Do you know if Mr. Kawanishi or Mr. Oyama is still awake?"

The reply was a shrug. "I do not know. Maybe so."

"Well, look," Frank went on smoothly, "we just recovered this sword that belonged to Mr. Satoya, the one that was stolen in New York. We're taking it to police headquarters, but we thought his company officials might want to know. Only it's late and we're in a hurry, so could you please give them the news?"

The chauffeur looked eager for more information, but seemed at a loss for words. Perhaps, the boys thought, it was because he did not speak English very well.

Instead, the man merely rose from his chair and bowed to the young detectives. "Thank you. I will tell them."

The Hardys strode toward the door.

"Pretty neat, the way you handled that, Frank!" Joe murmured out of the corner of his mouth. "I'll bet he gets on the phone to Satoya as soon as we're out of the lobby!"

As the boys emerged from the hotel, they turned and

headed toward their parked car. The downtown area of Bayport looked almost deserted at this late hour. A policeman who was coming along the street eyed them with interest.

Suddenly the young officer's face took on an expression of excitement. He quickened his pace so as to intercept the Hardys before they reached their car.

"Hold it, you two!"

Frank and Joe halted in surprise.

"What's wrong?" Frank inquired.

"Hand over that sword!" the policeman snapped.

Joe started to explain. "We're just taking it to police headquarters."

But the officer cut him short. "Don't give me that! Just hand it over! You're both under arrest for possessing stolen goods!"

Frank guessed that the policeman was probably new to the force and had never heard of the Hardy boys or their famous father. Calmly he advised his brother, "Do as he says, Joe. We'll straighten things out at the station."

The policeman summoned a patrol car by radio, and within a few minutes the Hardys found themselves at police headquarters. Here, after exchanging friendly remarks with the surprised desk sergeant, they were ushered into the office of Police Chief Ezra Collig. The sword was already lying on his desk.

"Sorry about this, fellows!" Looking slightly red-faced, Chief Collig rose to shake hands with the boys. "The whole thing's a mix-up!"

The chief explained that the police had received an anonymous phone call shortly after midnight. The unknown caller reported spotting two teenage youths in the Bayport area in possession of the valuable Japanese sword that had been stolen from the Palmer-Glade Galleries in New York.

"We put out a radio bulletin telling all officers to be on the lookout," Collig continued, "and I came to the office on purpose to supervise the search, because the tipster knew what he was talking about. But I certainly never expected that you Hardys would be caught in the dragnet!"

"Neither did we," Frank said wryly. "Matter of fact we were on our way here when we got nabbed." He filled the chief in on the night's events and added, "We were hoping the lab might turn up some prints, either on the sword hilt or the sheath."

"Good idea. I'll have them both dusted," the chief promised. "But first, there's someone I want you to meet. He just walked into the station tonight, literally out of the blue sky!"

Collig picked up the phone and gave a brief order. A few moments later, a young Japanese man was escorted into his office. The newcomer, who had glasses and long, dark hair, was well dressed in a gray silk business suit and looked studious but athletic. The police chief introduced him as Toshiro Muramoto.

"Mr. Muramoto has flown over here from Japan, at his own expense, I might add," Collig continued. "I think you fellows ought to hear what he has to say."

Muramoto bowed politely to the Hardys, who

331

returned his gesture. "I understand you two are attempting to solve the disappearance of the man who calls himself Takashi Satoya."

"That's right." Frank frowned. "But why do you say the man who *calls* himself Takashi Satoya?"

"Because that person who landed here in America three nights ago was an impostor!"

16

A Startling Challenger

The Hardys stared in amazement at the Japanese.

"That's a pretty drastic statement," Frank said, "especially if you're asking us to believe that he could fool Satoya's two top senior aides!"

"You raise a good point," Muramoto acknowledged. "One would have to draw one's own conclusions as to whether the two gentlemen were truly deceived."

The young detectives exchanged quick glances.

"Can you prove what you're saying," Joe asked, "about the missing man being an impostor?"

Muramoto nodded firmly. "I can, indeed. What is more, I shall do so, using that sword on the police chief's desk as the main evidence."

He declared he would give the man who called himself Satoya until ten o'clock the next morning to come to police headquarters and answer his accusation. "If he fails to appear," Muramoto added, "I shall then be forced to expose him to the press as a fraud!"

After leaving police headquarters, the Hardys sped back to the Bayport Chilton Hotel to report this startling development to Mr. Kawanishi and Mr. Oyama.

On the way, Joe muttered suspiciously, "Does the timing of all this strike you as a bit fishy, Frank?"

"I'll say it does! If Muramoto needed that samurai sword to prove his accusation, how did he know we'd get it back tonight?"

"Right! That's exactly what I'm wondering. What would he have used as proof without it? Did he just fly over here on the chance that the sword would turn up by the time he landed in Bayport?"

Frank puckered his forehead thoughtfully. "When you come right down to it, it almost sounds like a put-up job, doesn't it?"

"You think Muramoto could have been mixed up in the theft of the sword, and that ransom deal tonight?"

"You've got me, Joe. But I'd like to know the answer. To quote that word you used a minute ago, there must be something fishy somewhere!"

However, when the Hardys reached the hotel and expressed their suspicions to the two senior aides, neither Japanese agreed.

"It is most unlikely that Muramoto would take part in

any criminal plot to have our employer branded as an impostor," Kawanishi pointed out. "To do so would harm his own financial interest."

"How come?" Frank inquired.

The aide explained that the value of a company's stock partly depended on how well the company was managed. If news came out that the Satoya Corporation was run by some fraudulent mystery man posing as the real Takashi Satoya, many investors would lose confidence in the company and would try to sell off whatever shares they owned. This would cause the value of the stock to fall sharply.

"It so happens that young Muramoto owns a large block of stock in the Satoya Corporation," Mr. Kawanishi continued. "So he would suffer a heavy loss. His stock would be worth many millions of yen less than it is worth now, perhaps several hundred thousand dollars in your own money."

"Wow!" Joe whistled softly. "That's a lot of money to lose, just for spilling some bad news!"

Mr. Oyama nodded, confirming what his associate had just told the boys. "You see, young Muramoto's uncle, Akira Muramoto, was an army general in the Second World War. He was also a good friend of our employer. After the war, he became head of a Tokyo bank and lent Mr. Satoya enough money to start his company. In return, he was given a large block of stock in the Satoya Corporation."

The aide added that General Muramoto was now dead, but that his stock had been inherited by his nephew whom the Hardys had just met.

"Naturally," Mr. Oyama concluded, "we find it hard to believe that young Muramoto would cause any scandal that might harm our company. In fact, he would be far more apt to try and cover up any bad news, if he could properly do so."

"It is difficult to guess what has given him this wild idea that our employer is an impostor," said the other aide. "But I think he must sincerely believe it is so."

The Hardys drove home from the hotel thoroughly mystified by this latest surprising twist in the Satoya case. Both were eager to find out what would happen the following day.

Shortly before ten o'clock the next morning, they returned to police headquarters. Toshiro Muramoto was already waiting in Chief Collig's office, and Satoya's two senior aides, Mr. Kawanishi and Mr. Oyama, arrived soon afterward.

Presently Muramoto glanced at his wristwatch. "It is now almost one minute past ten o'clock," he announced. "The deadline has expired."

Chief Collig looked at the two company aides, who merely shrugged. Then his gaze turned back to Muramoto. "We're all waiting to hear what you have to say, sir."

"Very well. I had hoped to give the man who calls himself Takashi Satoya a chance to defend himself.

336

Since he is not here, I can only assume that he is afraid to face me. This confirms my suspicion that he is an impostor."

"You still haven't told us why you suspect him in the first place," Frank Hardy put in.

"Is the reason not obvious?" Muramoto shot back. "Here is a man who heads one of the world's greatest corporations—yet he is afraid to be seen in public. For years now he has avoided reporters and cameras and hidden himself away from the outside world. Why else would he be so secretive, except that he fears being exposed as a fake!"

Joe spoke up. "Then what do you think happened to the *real* Mr. Satoya?"

Muramoto's eyes flashed at the two company aides, and he pointed his finger at them accusingly. "I think those two can answer your question better than I can."

"Why, sir?"

"Because I believe they have done away with the real Takashi Satoya! They were his closest associates, so they are the only ones who could have pulled such a crime and still escaped detection. In his place, they have substituted an impostor who is completely under their control. Through him, they have been able to run the company for their own profit!"

There was a moment of startled silence as Muramoto finished speaking.

Then Frank said, "If you're right, why has this so-called impostor disappeared?"

"Probably because they knew he would soon be exposed as a fake. So long as they keep him out of sight and pretend he has 'disappeared,' no one can prove they've committed any crime."

All eyes swung toward the two aides. Both looked perfectly calm.

The tall, burly Mr. Kawanishi spoke first. "You ask why our revered employer became a hermit who prefers to keep out of the public eye. The reason is no mystery. Ten years ago, his wife and children were killed in an air crash."

"Their deaths were a terrible blow," said Mr. Oyama. "For a time he felt he had nothing more to live for. Ever since then he has shunned the outside world and lives mostly at his villa, where he devotes himself to gardening and studying the way of life called Zen."

"It is true that he runs the company by issuing orders through us," Kawanishi went on. "But that is his own wish, because it enables him to keep his privacy. However, he telephoned us last night, and we are happy to announce that he will reappear in Bayport this morning, to answer your charges in person."

Mr. Kawanishi, who was seated near the office windows, had been glancing out at the street below, and now he spoke with a slight smile. "In fact, I believe our revered employer has just arrived."

There was a stir of excitement. Moments later the telephone rang on Chief Collig's desk. Soon after he answered, an erect, gray-haired man with a wispy mustache was ushered into the office—the same man Frank and Joe had seen alight from the Satoya jet plane in the Bayport airfield!

Toshiro Muramoto stared keenly at the elderly newcomer, who responded with a polite bow.

"I understand you accuse me of being an impostor," he said to Muramoto.

"I do, indeed! And I shall now *prove* my accusation!"

"Pray do so, by all means."

It was Muramoto's turn to bow. "Very well. I shall do so by means of a test—using that beautiful samurai sword, which has belonged to the Satoya family for over four hundred years."

As Muramoto moved to pick up the sword from the police chief's desk, Frank asked if the sword had been dusted for prints. Chief Collig reported that this had been done, but that no fingerprints had been found, indicating that sheath, hilt and blade had all been carefully wiped clean.

Muramoto then proceeded with his demonstration. "It is well known to many close friends and business associates of the *real* Takashi Satoya," he went on, "that this sword has a secret compartment concealed in its hilt. It was designed centuries ago by the expert swordsmith who forged the blade."

The gray-haired tycoon nodded. "That is so. The secret knowledge of how to open it was passed down only to male members of the family."

His two aides murmured their agreement.

"Good!" said the bespectacled Muramoto. "If there is no argument on that score, it will give you a way to prove that you are, indeed, the real Takashi Satoya. I suggest you show us that you can open the secret compartment."

He held out the sword.

"Of course! I am happy to accept your challenge," said the tycoon, taking the weapon.

His face was calm as he began to finger certain points on the hilt. But his expression slowly changed—at first to a frown of surprise, then to bewilderment, and finally to outright dismay.

"Something is wrong!" he exclaimed.

"So it appears," said Muramoto sarcastically.

Satoya's two aides appeared dumbfounded.

Their employer made one or two final desperate attempts to open the secret compartment before giving up. "This cannot be the real sword!" he declared. "Someone has substituted a forgery!"

"Indeed?" Muramoto sneered. "How strange that you did not notice the switch until it turned out that you were unable to discover the mechanism of the secret compartment!"

Glancing at the Hardy boys and Police Chief Collig, he added, "I believe these impartial witnesses will now agree that I have proved my accusation beyond any doubt."

All three stared at the man who called himself Satoya. His only response was a helpless, tight-lipped shrug.

"In that case," Muramoto continued, "I shall now issue an announcement to the press, telling how I have proved this man to be an impostor. I shall then cable the Japanese government in Tokyo, officially requesting that they take over control of the Satoya Corporation, until the police can find out what happened to the real Satoya."

Kawanishi and Oyama both sprang to their feet, with looks of consternation on their faces.

"Wait! If you do that, it will play havoc with the operation of the company!" one cried.

"Not only that—the value of our company stock will plunge disastrously on the stock exchange! People who have invested heavily in shares of the Satoya Corporation will lose millions of yen!"

"You are quite right, gentlemen," Muramoto said regretfully. "As a major stockholder, I myself shall be one of the biggest losers. But my honor demands no less. My late uncle, General Akira Muramoto, was a longtime friend of Takashi Satoya's. If you two or anyone else have harmed him or done away with him, my uncle would certainly wish justice to be done and the guilty parties punished, no matter how many millions of yen it might cost."

Suddenly Frank cut in. "Mr. Muramoto, may I make a request?"

The bespectacled young Japanese said, "I promise nothing, but I am certainly willing to listen."

"From what my brother and I have just heard, it may

341

wreck the company if you go ahead and make your accusation public. But I think even you will admit that this whole situation is a mystery."

"The only mystery, I'm afraid, is what has happened to the real Takashi Satoya."

"Put it that way if you like," Frank said. "But at least give Joe and me a chance to solve the mystery. All we ask is twenty-four hours before you take such a drastic step."

Chief Collig added, "What they're asking certainly sounds reasonable to me, sir. I can assure you these young fellows are no mean sleuths. They've been trained by their father—who's probably the greatest criminal investigator in America—and they've solved a number of important cases."

Muramoto hesitated before replying, his forehead creased in a frown. But at last he nodded reluctantly. "Very well. I shall wait until this same time tomorrow morning before calling in the press or cabling my government—but no longer!" Bowing to everyone, he turned on his heel and strode out of the office.

Satoya, or the man who was impersonating him, flashed Frank and Joe a grateful look.

"Young men, I am much indebted to both of you— perhaps even more than you realize," he declared. "If you care to accompany me back to my hotel, I shall explain the reason for my disappearance."

342

17

Jungle Nightmare

Frank and Joe were eager to hear Satoya's story and readily accepted his invitation. His black limousine was waiting at the curb, with the stony-faced chauffeur at the wheel. The Hardy boys rode in the back seat with the tycoon, while his two senior aides—Kawanishi and Oyama—followed in a separate car.

"My story begins many years ago, in the closing months of World War II," Satoya told them. "Your General MacArthur had begun to recapture the Philippines, and it was only a question of time before the Americans would invade Japan herself."

A certain group of Japanese officers, he related, felt that an honorable surrender was the best course to take, rather than wait for their country to be devastated by bombing and invasion.

One of the group was Takashi Satoya. Although he was only a young lieutenant, he volunteered to carry the group's written, signed surrender offer to the Americans, concealed in the secret compartment of his sword hilt. But on the way he was badly wounded during a strafing attack by American fighter planes, and then taken prisoner.

"For weeks I lay unconscious or delirious in a jungle hospital," the tycoon went on. "By the time I recovered, my sword was gone. Either it was still lying back at the spot where I was wounded, or perhaps it had been picked up by some American GI or Filipino resistance fighter."

"And the surrender offer was lost with it?" Frank inquired.

"Precisely."

"Didn't you tell the Americans who captured you about the surrender document you'd been carrying?" asked Joe.

"I tried to, but no one would believe me. I imagine they thought I was still out of my head with fever, or else that my story was a trick to help me gain special treatment."

Because the surrender offer never reached the proper U.S. authorities, the war wound down to its grim conclusion, including the atom-bombing of Hiroshima and Nagasaki.

"Later, after the war was over," Satoya said, "the

officers who had taken part in the surrender plan met in Tokyo and agreed to keep the whole story secret."

"But why?" said Frank. "By that time I should think most people would have felt you were absolutely right."

"So it may seem to you now, in the United States, but there were still many in Japan who felt otherwise, especially among the samurai class. Some of the older, stiff-necked military men thought we should all have died for the Emperor. They would have called us cowards and traitors had the truth leaked out."

Even today, the Japanese tycoon told the Hardys, some of his countrymen might react the same way.

"For myself, I do not care," Satoya added. "I am an old man. What other people think of me is no longer important. For that matter, most of the senior officers who were involved in the surrender attempt, such as General Muramoto—are now dead. But even so, the truth might cause shame to their families if it became known."

"Then in a way," said Joe, "you're actually protecting the general's nephew, Toshiro Muramoto, who's over here calling you a faker."

Satoya smiled dryly at Joe's remark. "That is so. Life plays strange tricks at times. In any case, the only way I could make sure that the story never came out was to find my lost sword and destroy the surrender document hidden inside the hilt."

"So that's why you were so eager to buy the sword!" Frank commented.

"Exactly. It was also my main reason for coming to the United States, rather than risk entrusting the job to someone else. I intended to make sure that no one outbid me at the auction, and then to destroy the surrender document as soon as the sword was in my hands."

The limousine had now arrived at the Bayport Chilton Hotel. Frank and Joe accompanied Mr. Satoya inside and went up in the elevator to his private suite. He telephoned room service to order tea and resumed his story without inviting Mr. Kawanishi or Mr. Oyama to join them.

"You still haven't told us how or why you disappeared," Frank reminded the gray-haired industrialist.

"I was just coming to that," Satoya replied. "The fact is, I had begun to suspect that there was a traitor in the company—probably a top-rank executive."

The Hardys were startled. The tycoon's words seemed to confirm their father's theory!

"What gave you that idea?" Joe asked.

"Two things. First, someone has recently been leaking information on our business to a competitor, a company called Gorobei Motors. The information included data that was only known to me and my two top aides."

"You mean Mr. Kawanishi and Mr. Oyama?"

Takashi Satoya nodded grimly. "Correct. Also there have been several attempts on my life."

"Wow!" Joe blurted. "You actually think one of them might have tried to kill you?"

"To tell the truth, I do not know what to think. But one thing seemed clear. This trip to the USA would give the guilty party a good chance to have me murdered—and then to blame the crime on American terrorists or assassins. That is why I decided to disappear. It seemed the best way to ensure my own safety. Also, by secretly watching Kawanishi and Oyama, I hoped to discover which one was the traitor."

To accomplish this, Mr. Satoya had arranged to have the hotel rooms of his two senior aides electronically bugged.

"When your limousine arrived at the hotel from the airport," Frank put in, "your other aide, Mr. Ikeda, was unconscious. Did you anesthetize him somehow?"

The gray-haired Japanese nodded. "Yes, I must confess that I did. While he was busy looking out the window on the other side of the car, I suddenly jabbed him with a hypodermic needle, using a quick-acting anesthetic. It started to take effect almost immediately, before he could collect his wits enough to make any outcry. I am ashamed to tell you this, but it seemed the best way to carry out my scheme."

Once Ikeda was unconscious, the tycoon had vanished exactly as the Hardy boys had deduced. He had hidden in the limousine's secret compartment and then had his chauffeur let him out of the car when it was halfway down the ramp, out of sight from both the street and the basement parking garage. The chauffeur, in fact, had been his only confidant, and was the

347

one who had bugged Kawanishi's and Oyama's hotel rooms.

"One more question, sir," said Frank. "Have you any idea at all as to how or why a duplicate sword could have been substituted for your family sword?"

Mr. Satoya shook his head helplessly. "I am relying on you two young men to solve that mystery. I can only assume that it is part of a plot to wrest the company away from my control."

The Hardys promised to do their best to solve the case as soon as possible. Satoya's chauffeur drove them back to police headquarters to pick up their car.

As they headed homeward, Joe switched on the car radio to check the time. An announcer was reading the news. Suddenly he said:

"A flash has just been handed to me. That missing Japanese businessman, Mr. Takashi Satoya, has now turned up again—or at any rate, a person who calls himself Satoya has turned up. He's reported to have walked into Bayport police headquarters just a short time ago. But now he's accused of being an impostor! A major stockholder in the Satoya Corporation has flown here from Japan to make the charge."

The announcer added, "This is the second report to come over the news wires this morning on this strange case. For those of you who missed our earlier story—it was learned this morning that the valuable Japanese samurai sword stolen from the Palmer-Glade Auction Galleries in New York was found last night somewhere near Bayport. According to one unconfirmed report, this sword belonged to the real Takashi Satoya. We will keep you posted on any further developments in the story as they come in."

"Sufferin' catfish!" Joe exclaimed. "I wonder if Muramoto broke his promise about giving us twenty-four hours to crack the case?"

"Sure sounds that way," Frank gritted. "This means we've really got to work fast!"

When they arrived home on Elm Street, Aunt Gertrude was waiting eagerly to quiz them about what had happened at police headquarters. Before the boys could satisfy her curiosity, the telephone rang. Frank answered. The caller was Sam Radley.

"What's up, Sam?" Frank inquired.

"I've finally run down Krunkel and his partner!"

"You mean you've got them under arrest?"

"Not yet. I figured it might be better to keep them under observation for a while and see what we can learn from them."

"Smart idea!" Frank agreed.

Radley explained that he had shown Krunkel's photo to the desk clerks of various hotels and motels in the Shoreham area, and had finally located the place where the squint-eyed burglar was staying. He and another man named Darbold, who was a known accomplice of Krunkel's, had registered at the Seneca Motel on Main Street.

"I've got the place staked out," Sam added, "but

there'll be two suspects to watch—so I may need help. Could you and Joe lend me a hand?"

"You bet!" said Frank. "Tell us where to meet you, and we'll be there in a jiffy!"

A short time later the two youths walked into a coffee shop across the street from the Seneca Motel. Radley was seated in a booth by the front window, nursing a cup of coffee.

"Great work, Sam!" Frank congratulated the operative as the Hardys joined him.

"Have either of them shown yet?" asked Joe.

"Not yet, but it's past noon, so they ought to be coming out soon to get something to eat. When I showed the desk clerk Krunkel's mug shot, he told me they were still in their room."

"Any chance they could have slipped out when you phoned us?"

"No way. I called you from that booth in the corner, which has a clear view of the motel."

The boys ordered hamburgers and wolfed them down with hearty appetites. They tensed with excitement as Radley suddenly exclaimed, "There's our man!"

A tall figure had just emerged from the motel. Sure enough, it was the hawk-faced man whom the Hardys had seen talking to Len Boggs after the motorcycle race! He made his way toward one of the cars in the motel parking lot.

Radley flipped a coin to see who would follow him. The Hardy boys won.

"Maybe it's just as well," Sam commented. "I think Krunkel might recognize me quicker than he would you two. But be mighty careful, fellows! This guy has no record of violence, but you never can tell."

"We'll watch it, Sam," they promised.

Frank and Joe hurried outside and reached their own car just as Krunkel was pulling away in a sleek, silver-colored, foreign-made coupe.

He headed for the road leading southwest out of Shoreham. It was not a main highway, so the Hardys had to keep a considerable distance behind their suspect to avoid arousing wariness, especially when he turned off on a wooded, dirt road.

As a further precaution, Frank drove past the turnoff, then U-turned a little way farther on. Coming back to the dirt road, he nosed their yellow sporty-looking car slowly along the same route Krunkel had taken. Soon they sighted the silver coupe some distance ahead.

"There it is!" Joe exclaimed.

Apparently Krunkel had pulled off the road and gotten out. Frank maneuvered their own car in among some trees where it would be well concealed from view. Then the boys hastily closed in on Krunkel on foot.

Krunkel's destination turned out to be an old abandoned farmhouse. The house itself was a weather-beaten, ramshackle structure with a sagging roof and boarded-up windows, and the surrounding fields were overgrown with weeds.

Creeping up through the tall grass and underbrush, the Hardys saw Krunkel shining a flashlight down a well.

"What's he looking for?" Joe hissed.

"Search me," Frank whispered back.

Presently the tall, hawk-faced crook straightened up and returned to his car. As soon as they heard him drive away, the two boys rushed toward the well. Frank pulled out a pocket flashlight and aimed it downward.

"Jumpin' Jupiter!" Joe gasped as they saw what the beam revealed.

At the bottom of the well lay a long, sheathed Japanese sword!

18

Gang Wheels

The glimmering light revealed the sword's beautifully decorated hilt.

"It's the *real* sword that Satoya lost during the war!" Frank declared. "It must be!"

"Check," Joe agreed. "There can't be more than two that look that much alike. Wait a minute—!" He broke off suddenly and snapped his fingers. "Frank, I'll bet Krunkel heard the news about that other sword turning up in Bayport—so he came to make sure this one was still here!"

"That makes sense, all right," Frank nodded. "All we have to do now is fish it out of the well."

"Wonder how Krunkel stashed it there and expects to get it up again?"

"Dunno. He's an expert cat burglar. Maybe he's got

some kind of folding ladder in his car. But my guess is one of us will have to go down on a rope."

"You're right," said Joe. "We've got some in the car. Let's go get it."

However, after hiking back to the spot where they had parked, they discovered the red radio signal light was flashing on their dashboard. Joe quickly switched on the transceiver and spoke into the microphone.

"H-2 here. Come in, please."

"This is L calling," said his mother's voice. "You two just had an urgent call from your foreign client at the hotel. He wants to see you as soon as possible."

"Thanks, Mom! Will you phone him back, please, and tell him we're on our way."

"Roger. Ten-four."

Joe hung up the mike and shot a questioning glance at his brother. "She must mean Satoya! Think we should take time to recover the sword first?"

"Better not," Frank voted. "It may be a tricky job and that call sounds urgent. I'm sure the sword will be safe if we leave it here for a while."

"Right! Let's get going!"

The Hardys crowded the speed limit on their way back to Bayport. At the Bayport Chilton Hotel, they phoned Satoya's room from the lobby and were told to come right up.

"I received a startling phone message about half an hour ago," the tycoon informed the boys when they arrived in his suite.

"From whom, sir?" Frank asked.

"From my junior aide, Haruki Ikeda. He told me he has established contact with the gallery thief, and that he can get my real sword back for one hundred thousand dollars in ransom money!"

The Hardys gaped in astonishment at this unexpected news.

"Did he give you any details?" Joe queried.

Satoya shook his head. "No. From the noises in the background, there seemed to be other people around, and he told me he could not speak freely."

"What did you say?"

"I stalled him off by saying that I needed time to decide whether or not it was wise to deal with a criminal. So he said he would call back in a little while to get my answer."

Frank and Joe exchanged shrewd glances. As often happened because of their close relationship, the two brothers could almost tell what the other was thinking. Frank cocked a quizzical eyebrow, and Joe responded with a slight nod.

"Look, sir!" the older Hardy boy said, turning back to Mr. Satoya. "When Ikeda calls, our advice is to tell him you accept the deal."

It was the tycoon's turn to look astonished. "Are you asking me to trust a thief? What if his offer turns out to be a fraud?"

"As a matter of fact, it probably is," said Frank. "But

if our hunch is right, we may be able to trap the thief, and get back both your sword *and* the money!"

The telephone rang even before Frank finished speaking. Mr. Satoya frowned and plucked nervously at his wispy mustache, then scooped up the handset and answered.

The short conversation that followed was in Japanese. When it was over, the tycoon hung up and turned to face the Hardys again.

"As you have no doubt guessed, that was Ikeda. I have authorized him to draw out the ransom money in cash from the account which our company has opened at the local bank."

Although Satoya did not say so, both boys knew what he was leaving unsaid—namely that he was risking one hundred thousand dollars to back their hunch.

It was not a very comfortable thought.

But Frank replied confidently, "If you'll come with us, sir, Joe and I have something important to show you. When you see it, I think you'll agree the risk is worthwhile."

Satoya's dark eyes were keen and cold, but he inclined his head politely. "Very well, young man. I shall do as you say."

Joe got into the back seat of their yellow car, leaving the Japanese tycoon to sit in front beside Frank. Soon they were on their way out of town.

As they retraced the route they had traveled not long

before, the Hardys explained to Mr. Satoya where they were taking him.

"Joe and I know where the Satoya sword is hidden," Frank began. "So if the offer Ikeda phoned you about is on the level, that means the thief will have to go there to get the sword."

"And that's when we'll nail him!" Joe added zestfully.

Mr. Satoya digested this news with a thoughtful frown. "Do I gather you already know who the thief is?"

Frank nodded as he steered the car along the country road. "Yes, sir, I think we do."

"Yet at the hotel you implied the ransom offer was a fraud."

"I was simply referring to the story Ikeda told you."

"Perhaps you'd better explain that remark, young man."

"Well, sir, the only thing that seems fairly certain," the elder Hardy boy reasoned, "is that whoever planned this whole caper must have known beforehand that you were coming to America, and that you wanted that sword at the Palmer-Glade Galleries."

"I agree," Satoya nodded.

"We can probably count out your jet crew," Frank went on, "and I guess your chauffeur is too faithful to be suspected."

"Yes, that is so."

"Which leaves only your aides as suspects."

"Of course," the tycoon responded impatiently. "I have already told you that the traitor in my company must be either Kawanishi or Oyama."

"You're leaving out somebody," Joe reminded him.

"You mean . . .?"

"Ikeda, sir."

Satoya frowned again. "But as I informed you this morning, only my two *senior* aides would have known the data that was leaked to Gorobei Motors."

"But isn't it possible," Frank pointed out, "that someone else in your company may have gotten hold of the same information, either by tapping their phones or rifling their desks and files?"

"Hmm. . . . Now that you put it that way, I suppose such a thing is possible."

"Anyway, there's no use guessing," Frank concluded. "If we're lucky, we may soon know the ans—"

He broke off suddenly, and Joe saw his brother staring keenly into the rear-view mirror.

"What's the matter, Frank?"

"We've got company!"

Almost at that same moment, Joe's ears caught a rising engine sound. Turning his head, he saw a group of motorcyclists behind them.

"Gallopin' guppies! That looks like the Gung-Ho gang!"

"You guessed it," Frank gritted. "And something tells me they've recognized our car!"

The Hardys were skilled auto mechanics and kept their car engine tuned for top performance. Frank made sure everyone's seat belt was fastened, then stepped on the gas. He was too good a driver to take foolish chances, but Fenton Hardy had trained his sons carefully in evasive driving tactics, and the boys knew every street in the Bayport area.

By dodging and circling back and forth through a network of back roads, Frank gradually managed to shake off their pursuers. Joe flashed his brother an approving grin in the rear-view mirror, and even Mr. Satoya murmured, "Well done, young man!"

At last they reached the dirt lane to which they had trailed Krunkel. Frank parked in the same concealed spot they had used before. Then Satoya and the Hardys walked toward the deserted farmhouse. The sword was still in the well.

The group hid but had not long to wait before an approaching car was heard. A compact green station wagon pulled to a halt on the now rutted, weed-choked path that had once been the entrance lane to the farm. A man got out of the car.

It was Haruki Ikeda!

19

The Fearless Three

At the sight of his crew-cut junior aide, Mr. Satoya gave an angry gasp and started to burst out of their hiding place in a clump of shrubbery and underbrush. But Frank restrained him.

"Let's see what he does first," the elder Hardy boy whispered softly.

Opening the station wagon's tailgate, Ikeda took out what seemed to be a ladder of lightweight, flexible metal cable. He carried this up the lane and lowered it into the dried well shaft after hooking it securely to the lip of the well.

As the hidden trio watched, they saw the slim Japanese maneuver cautiously for a footing, and then disappear from view as he climbed down the ladder.

When he reappeared several minutes later, he was clutching the samurai sword! Ikeda wore a smug grin of satisfaction.

This time there was no holding Satoya back. The gray-haired tycoon sprang to his feet, shouting angrily in Japanese. Frank and Joe jumped up and ran after him, seeing that there was no point in continuing to hide.

Ikeda stood motionless for a moment, then his face took on an expression of dumbfounded dismay. But suddenly he seemed to pull himself together and dashed toward his station wagon!

He was still clutching the sword as he reached his car and yanked open the door. Flinging the weapon inside, he slid behind the wheel and tried to gun the engine to life.

In his eagerness to get away, he apparently flooded the engine, and twice it failed to start. Frank and Joe felt afterward that they might have reached the car in time to stop him.

But just then the whine and roar of motorcycle engines caught their attention. The noise was rapidly swelling in volume, and a second later a horde of riders blasted into view between the scattered trees fringing the abandoned farm.

"It's the Gung-Ho gang!" Joe cried, recognizing the mounted hoodlums for the second time that afternoon.

The same thought was going through both boys' minds. *Somehow the gang must have picked up their*

362

trail after Frank thought he had given them the slip, and now the Hardys and their companion were in for trouble!

Obviously the first tactic of Len Boggs and his street punks, Frank realized, would be to try and run them down.

"Come on! Head for the farmhouse!" he cried to Joe and Mr. Satoya.

The trio reached the farmhouse porch only yards ahead of their pursuers. Frank kicked open the door that was hanging by a single hinge, and they plunged inside!

Len Boggs, leading the motorcyclists, tried to chase them right up the porch steps and into the house. But the rotten structure collapsed under the weight of his heavy bike!

There were moments of confusion. Boggs was scarlet with fury as he extricated himself and his motorcycle from the debris.

Realizing that their machines were no longer of any use for purposes of attack, the Gung-Ho's dismounted and began smashing their way into the farmhouse through every possible opening. Most of the gang swarmed in through the windows, after ripping away the boards. Several others gained entry through the long-since stairless back door.

As a seasoned warrior, Mr. Satoya calmly took charge—somewhat to the Hardys' surprise—and suggested that the boys stand back-to-back with him to repel their attackers, though not too close together. Instead of the famous British square, favored by the oldtime redcoats when surrounded and outnumbered, the three formed a human triangle, each several feet away from the others.

Frank and Joe were astonished at the elderly Japanese gentleman's fighting ability. It was clear that he was expertly trained in the martial arts. The boys were too busy swinging their fists or throwing occasional karate kicks to do more than throw him a hasty glance from time to time, in case he required help.

From the looks of things, no such help was likely to be needed. Mr. Satoya coolly whirled and weaved and ducked with the smooth precision of a ballet dancer—and at every move, another attacker seemed to go flying!

Frank and Joe grinned, recognizing his slick evasive technique as that of aikido, by which the attacker's own momentum is turned back against himself.

The Hardys relied more on old-fashioned American punches to discourage their opponents, and these seemed to work equally well.

One by one, the panting Gung-Ho's seemed to lose heart and fall back to let others do the fighting. At last they were actually watching, more like spectators than participants.

Moments later, as Frank uncorked a hard right that sent an attacker spinning back against the wall, one gang member exclaimed admiringly, "Hey, man! These dudes are *good!*"

When Joe also decked an opponent with his fist, and Mr. Satoya sent another man flying over his shoulder, the gang suddenly burst out laughing and applauding.

The Hardys could scarcely believe their eyes and ears. They and their elderly companion had fought the Gung-Ho's to a standstill, and now they were getting cheers instead of blows. Like Horatius defending the bridge of Rome with his two friends, by their spunky fight they had actually won over their enemies!

"If you can't lick 'em, join 'em!" one motorcyclist chuckled and stuck out his hand toward Frank. "Put 'er there, pal!"

Frank hesitated a moment, suspecting a trick, but then grinned and responded to the offered handshake. "Suits me."

Other gang members crowded around to join in the handshaking and smoke the figurative peace pipe.

"Hey, Pop!" one said to Satoya. "Where'd you learn all those trick judo throws?"

"Aikido, actually," the Japanese tycoon corrected. "I learned it in a martial arts *dojo* in my native land, many years before you were born, young man. If you too wish to learn the art, perhaps that can be arranged. My company may soon open a plant here in the Bayport area. When this happens, I shall give orders for an instructor to be sent over as part of the staff. He will teach you young men to be true samurai—not dangerous jackals or bullies."

The Gung-Ho's took his reproof with good-natured

respect and heartily applauded the announcement. Mr. Satoya was clearly pleased. He seemed more at ease with these high-spirited, roughneck gang members than he had in the polite surroundings of the Bayport Chilton Hotel.

"What did you guys jump us for, anyhow?" Joe asked.

The motorcyclists grinned sheepishly and shrugged.

"No special reason," one said. "We were just tooling along when we spotted your car. Len Boggs talked us into chasing you. I think he's still sore 'cause your brother beat him in the Hare Scrambles race."

The gang leader reddened at this, but finally and reluctantly came forward to shake hands with the Hardys.

"What're you guys doin' out here?" another motor-cyclist asked. "Solvin' another mystery?"

"Trying to," Frank replied. "We almost had a crook collared before you Gung-Ho's showed up. Now he's taken off."

Suddenly an idea occurred to Frank, "Hey, how would you like to give us a hand?" he said.

"Why not?" a gang member replied. "What's the deal?"

"Did you notice that green station wagon that was parked near the road when you first got here?"

"Sure, what about it?"

"Have you guys got CB radios on your bikes?"

"Most of us have. Why?"

"How would you like to fan out from here," Frank proposed, "and see if you can spot where that wagon went?"

"I will pay a one-hundred-dollar reward to the first man who sights it," Mr. Satoya promised.

The Gung-Ho's exploded with enthusiasm. They all hurried out to their motorcycles. Soon the gang was roaring off in all directions in pursuit of the fugitive.

Frank and Joe returned to their car with Mr. Satoya. Frank tuned in their radio to the proper frequency, and the three waited tensely for news.

At last a voice crackled over their speaker. "Len Boggs calling the Hardys!"

"Hardys here. We read you," Frank replied. "Come in, please! Any luck, Len?"

"You bet! I've spotted your green station wagon!"

20

Black Commandos

The Hardys felt a thrill of excitement at Len Boggs's report. Both sensed that the case was nearing a climax, and that luck was giving them another chance to trap the traitor inside the Satoya Corporation, the culprit behind the mystery of the samurai sword!

"Where're you calling from, Len?" Frank spoke into the microphone.

"The Pine Glen area near Shoreham. Know where that is?"

"Sure, west of town. It's not much built up."

"Right. Just a few scattered houses and farms. The station wagon's parked outside a house on Locust Road."

"You think it's the same one you saw here?" Frank inquired, trying to avoid a false alarm.

Len Boggs sounded confident. "Sure looks like it. The license number starts with an X7."

"That's it!" Joe exclaimed excitedly as the combination clicked in his memory.

"Okay. Give us directions," Frank said.

Len Boggs complied, describing enough landmarks to make sure they found the spot.

Soon the Hardys sped off in their car with Takashi Satoya. The gray-haired Japanese recluse seemed to be enjoying the adventure thoroughly, coming more and more out of his shell as he traded remarks with Frank and Joe.

In less than fifteen minutes they sighted Len Boggs signaling to them from the road ahead.

"Any signs of life or new developments?" Frank said out the window as he braked to a gentle halt.

"Nope. The station wagon's the only car parked outside, and no one else has shown up," Len reported.

"Great! That sounds as though we ought to be able to handle the situation," Joe opined.

"Let's not take anything for granted," Frank cautioned. "Ikeda may have pals inside."

Satoya nodded. "It is always wise not to rush into danger."

After a hasty conference, they parked off the road and approached the house on foot. Well screened from view by trees, it was a modest white bungalow, bordered by tall shrubbery.

Len Boggs had agreed to ring the bell, since his face

presumably would not be recognized by Haruki Ikeda. The others waited out of sight nearby, huddled behind shrubbery.

Presently the door opened. Ikeda looked out with a suspicious frown. "Yes?"

The next moment he gaped in surprise as the others burst into view. Satoya called out what sounded like a command in Japanese and dashed toward the front door with the Hardy boys. Len Boggs stepped aside.

Ikeda tried to slam the door in their faces, but Satoya flung himself forward to push it open with his shoulder. The Hardys were close behind.

Suddenly Ikeda seemed to stop resisting their push. The door flew open under their combined weight, and all three went plunging inside. Their momentum carried them well into the front room, and they wound up sprawling headlong on the floor.

As Frank and Joe scrambled to their feet, they heard Len Boggs chuckle gleefully as he yanked the door shut behind them. The room seemed to fill with menacing figures, and the Hardys realized they had been lured into a trap!

Takashi Satoya rose calmly to his feet beside them. From his impassive expression, the gray-haired industrialist seemed utterly unperturbed by what had happened. But Frank and Joe felt no such confidence as they eyed the enemies who confronted them.

Besides Ikeda, there were five men, ranged in strategic fighting positions. Two were Americans—

Krunkel and another man, no doubt his partner in crime, Darbold. The other three were tough-looking Orientals with tattooed arms—obviously *Yakuza*, or Japanese gangsters. Among them the Hardys recognized the crook who had tried to shadow them in New York.

Satoya spoke coldly in Japanese, but his words drew a jeering response.

"Let's not waste time!" Krunkel growled in English. "Just grab 'em and tie 'em up—then we can figure out what to do with them!"

One of the *Yakuza* reached inside his suitcoat, as if to draw a weapon from a shoulder holster and cover the three prisoners.

But Satoya moved like lightning. He swept up a small table that stood within reach and hurled it through the air! It caught the threatening Japanese gangster on the side of the head and knocked him off his feet!

With angry oaths, the other crooks swarmed into action. But the Hardys and their gray-haired companion did not wait helplessly to be seized. They met the attack with flying fists and swirling aikido counter-moves.

In a minute the room was a bedlam of noise and violent activity. Ikeda, the gangsters and the two American burglars were far more dangerous opponents than the awkward, roughneck Gung-Ho gang had been. Also, the Orientals were expert enough in the martial arts to offset Satoya's fighting skill.

372

Whether the outnumbered trio could survive the battle looked doubtful. Frank and Joe realized the odds were heavily against them.

But suddenly the front door flew open and three black-clad figures burst in! A man in a business suit was with them.

"It's Sam Radley—and the *ninja!*" Joe cried.

The newcomers waded in, swinging punches and karate chops in all directions. In a few minutes the fight was over, and all six crooks, including Haruki Ikeda, were being lined up against the wall and frisked.

"What a break!" Frank panted. "You sure showed up at the right time, Sam! How'd you find this place?"

"Easy." Sam grinned. "Krunkel returned to the motel, then he and his partner came out again about an hour after you and Joe left. I think they may have gotten a phone order to come to this house. Anyhow, I trailed them here and then went off to find your dad."

"Where is he?" Joe asked.

"Three guesses," said a familiar voice.

One of the black-clad figures peeled off his hood, and the boys saw that the speaker was none other than their father, Fenton Hardy!

"Good night!" Frank exclaimed in astonishment. "When did you become a *ninja*, Dad?"

Mr. Hardy chuckled and gestured toward his black-clad associates. "I'm not sharp enough to call myself a *ninja* yet, son. But these two gentlemen have been giving me some mighty useful training. They're old army buddies of Mr. Satoya's. He uses them as his private security team."

"So that's where they came from!" said Joe.

Mr. Satoya explained that because at first he had suspected either Kawanishi or Oyama of being the traitor in his company, he had also been suspicious of the American detective whom they had hired to protect him.

The two *ninja* had been sent to the USA before his own arrival in order to prepare for his "disappearance." Later they had been instructed to keep an eye on the Hardys, and after Humber's newspaper interview, the wealthy collector had also been placed under observation, in case he might have been involved in the gallery theft.

It was through Satoya's secret request to the Japanese ambassador in Washington that the FBI had pulled Fenton Hardy off the case. Eventually, however, the famed private eye had convinced the two *ninja* agents of his trustworthiness—and since then he had been cooperating with them.

"But there's still a good deal we don't know about this case," Mr. Hardy concluded. "I'm hoping you boys can clear things up."

"I think we can explain part of the puzzle," Frank volunteered. "Ikeda hired the three gangsters to come over to this country beforehand, just like Mr. Satoya sent his two *ninja*. My guess is that the gangsters then hired Krunkel and Darbold to steal the sword from the Palmer-Glade Galleries."

"Right," said Joe. "But they also had a duplicate made, so they could switch it for the real sword and make Mr. Satoya look like a phony when he couldn't open the secret compartment, because the hilt of the fake sword *had no secret compartment!*"

The ransom ploy, so the Hardy boys reasoned, had been a clever way of getting the fake sword accepted by the police without anyone questioning its authenticity.

Had Warlord bought the fake sword, the police would no doubt have been tipped off by a secret phone call that they would find the stolen weapon in his possession.

When this move failed to work, the Hardy boys and Dobert Humber had been lured to Lookout Rock for a second ransom ploy. This time the crooks had taken no chances on anything going wrong, or themselves being trapped by the police. The siren trick had been used to make it look as though the thief had fled in panic, with the fake sword being left at Lookout Rock, where the Hardys would be sure to discover it.

"Smart thinking, boys," Mr. Hardy congratulated his two sons.

"A brilliant explanation, indeed!" Mr. Satoya agreed. "And now I think it is time to hear what my dishonest, worthless aide has to say for himself."

Haruki Ikeda seemed to shrivel under his employer's scorn as Satoya berated him bitterly in Japanese.

He confessed that for some time he had been engaged in crooked double-dealing, selling company secrets to its business competitors—especially Gorobei

Motors. The latter had used every means possible, including attempted murder, to keep the Satoya Corporation from merging its motorcycle division with the Road King Company.

In a last-ditch effort to prevent this from happening, Gorobei Motors had been pressing Ikeda to do something drastic. This had led to his clever scheme to have Takashi Satoya branded an impostor and removed from control of his own company.

The scheme had occurred to Ikeda partly because Toshiro Muramoto was worried that the company might already be in the hands of some crook who was merely impersonating the real Satoya. In fact, Muramoto had already been paying Ikeda for inside information on the company. He had done this in a sincere attempt to uncover any plot to take over the Satoya Corporation, without knowing that Ikeda was crookedly conniving with business competitors against his own firm.

But Ikeda admitted that the main motive for his scheme had been to make as much money as possible. He had planned to buy a lot of company stock after leaking the news story that Satoya was an impostor. This announcement would drive down the value of the company stock, so that he would be able to buy it cheaply.

He would then deliver the real sword to Satoya for a hundred thousand dollars in "ransom money." Once Satoya was able to clear himself and prove that he was the rightful head of the firm, the value of the stock would rise again. Ikeda would then be able to sell at a huge profit.

"How do these two birds fit into the picture?" Sam Radley asked the boys with a jerk of his thumb toward Krunkel and Darbold. "I mean, why were they hanging around this area after they'd pulled the museum heist and delivered the loot to Ikeda or his hired gangsters?"

"He probably promised them a share of the ransom money, besides whatever he paid them to steal the sword in the first place," Frank replied.

"Of course he'd have kicked in part of the ransom," Krunkel growled. "You think we're stupid enough to let him keep it all for himself?"

"Being criminals at all is stupid enough," Frank retorted coolly.

As Krunkel and his accomplice began talking, the Hardys learned that it was Sam Radley who had scared them into hiding the sword down the well. Once Krunkel started worrying that Sam might have identified him, the two thieves became alarmed that the sword might be found in their possession while they were waiting for Ikeda to take it to his employer under the pretense of having paid out the hundred thousand dollars in ransom money.

And as Joe had guessed, it was the news story about the recovery of the sword that had prompted Krunkel to check the well, because he and his partner had been told nothing about Ikeda's scheme involving the fake sword.

"Well, that seems to clear up the whole mystery," said Fenton Hardy.

"Except for a certain document hidden in the hilt of Mr. Satoya's sword," Frank put in with a glance at the Japanese tycoon.

"Which I am quite impatient to check on," Satoya admitted.

After fleeing from the deserted farm in his rented station wagon, Ikeda had brought the sword into the house on Locust Road. It was lying in plain sight on the mantel.

The tycoon's expression was tense as he took down the sword. Frank and Joe watched in fascination as he gave the pommel cap a slight twist, then pressed two small metal decorations on the hilt, called *menuki*. Instantly the mother-of-pearl inlay on one side of the hilt swung open like a flap!

With a smile of relief, Satoya reached two fingers into the opening and plucked out a folded piece of paper. Without opening the paper, he borrowed a pipe lighter from Mr. Hardy and held a flame to the document. In seconds it caught fire and shriveled to ashes!

Frank watched him, suddenly feeling depressed. This was the end of their case. Would there ever be another one? He did not know that soon the boys would be called upon to work on *The Pentagon Spy*.

Suddenly a thought occurred to him, and he turned

to his father. "Dad, you didn't happen to see a motor-cyclist riding away from here, did you, or notice where he was going?"

"Matter of fact I did," said Fenton Hardy, "and the answer is nowhere—at least not for a while, till he spends some time under a pump, cleaning up."

"How come?" Frank queried.

"Because he ran into a farm truck and got trampled by a load of very annoyed pigs."

Once again the detective was mystified as he saw his sons burst out laughing!

The Hardy Boys Mystery Stories
by Franklin W. Dixon

Look out for these thrilling new mysteries in Armada.

The Mummy Case (61)

The Hardys are en route for Egypt – as chaperones to a mummy! But some cut-throat thieves are out to seize the priceless relic. In a deadly war of nerves, the Hardy Boys fight their enemies under the burning desert sun.

The Mystery of Smugglers Cove (62)

When a valuable painting is stolen, the Hardy Boys are determined to catch the thieves. But the trail of clues soon leads them to the steamy swamps of Florida – and to a deadly encounter with some man-eating alligators!

Coming soon

The Stone Idol (63)

The strange disappearance of an ancient stone statue begins a hair-raising new adventure for the Hardys. But their investigations lead them into a sinister trap – in the freezing wilderness of the Antarctic.

Armada

3
The Pentagon Spy

The Hardy Boys® in
The Pentagon Spy

The Pentagon Spy
was first published in the U.K. in a single volume
in hardback in 1981 by Angus & Robertson Ltd.,
and in Armada in 1981
by Fontana Paperbacks,
8 Grafton Street, London W1X 3LA.

© 1980 Stratemeyer Syndicate

Contents

1

Spies, Submarines, and Sailboats

"This case is a tough one, boys," said Fenton Hardy, the famous private detective, after he had settled himself comfortably behind the desk in his study. "It concerns our government and possibly a foreign power. Espionage in Washington, that's what it looks like at this point."

His sons, Frank and Joe, who were seated in two leather chairs facing their father, perked up.

"Can you tell us more about it, Dad, or is it classified?" asked dark-haired Frank, who was a senior in high school.

"If so, we won't ask any questions," added Joe, who was blond and a year younger. But he sounded disappointed.

Mr. Hardy smiled. "I've cleared you with the Defense Department," he said, "because you may be in on this before it's over. I may need your help."

"Great!" Joe said excitedly. "What's your case about?"

"A spy in the Pentagon," Mr. Hardy replied.

The boys looked at one another in amazement.

"How could a spy get through all that clearance?" Frank asked. "They check everybody in the Pentagon, from the brass on down."

Mr. Hardy nodded. "That's what the Defense Department wants me to investigate. How did a spy manage to operate under their noses?"

"Any suspects?" Joe inquired. Like Frank, he was always eager for a mystery.

Mr. Hardy nodded. "A civilian employee of the navy named Clifford Hunter has disappeared. So has a top-secret navy document. It appears that Hunter sneaked the document out of the files and smuggled it out of the Pentagon."

Frank whistled. "He must be a cool customer! Any clues, Dad?"

"Yes. The FBI traced Hunter to Chesapeake Bay. We know he shoved off into the bay aboard his sailboat. Since then—nothing. The navy's asked me to enter the case because I've done investigations for them in the past."

"Tell us about this guy Hunter," Frank urged.

Fenton Hardy explained that the suspect was a physicist assigned to computer programming for underwater guidance systems. "This is a real breakthrough by navy scientists. It gives our commanders of nuclear submarines pinpoint navigational accuracy on around-the-globe voyages half a mile below the surface of the ocean."

"Wow!" Joe exclaimed. "A sub could leave Bayport and hit Easter Island right on the nose without taking a single breath! I'll bet it would make those stone heads talk to one another!" He was referring to the South Pacific island whose ancient population was known for carving remarkable stone monuments.

Fenton Hardy smiled at his son's enthusiasm. "The scientific details are even more dramatic than that, Joe. But you boys know enough now to realize what the navy's up against. The document Hunter took must be recovered before it reaches a foreign government."

"Maybe a gang of foreign agents is mixed up in the case!" Joe said. He was more impetuous than Frank, who did not jump to conclusions so quickly. They had solved many cases together and had helped their father with some of his investigations.

Fenton Hardy was a former member of the New York Police Department, who now worked out of Bayport as a private investigator. He had achieved national fame and put many notorious public enemies behind bars.

Joe's exclamation made his father frown. "It's possible that foreign agents are involved," he said. "That's why I may need you and Frank to help me. If Hunter's planning to turn the sub document over to them, we must stop him before he succeeds. Here's an identification card for each of you. Carry it with you wherever you go." He handed the boys two plastic-encased cards with their pictures on them.

Just then Mrs. Hardy entered the room. She was an attractive, pleasant woman who often worried about the cases her husband and sons investigated.

"Fenton," she announced, "your suitcase is ready. I've packed everything you'll need for a week."

"Thank you, my dear," the detective replied. Rising to his feet, he handed Joe a piece of paper. "Here's the telephone number at the Pentagon where you can reach me. Check with me tomorrow and I'll let you know how the Hunter case is progressing."

He started to leave, then remembered something and turned back to his sons. "By the way," he said, "I have an appointment here this morning with a man named John Hammerley. Make my apologies, will you?"

Then he went out of the room. Shortly afterward, the sound of his car rolling down the driveway into Elm Street indicated that he was on his way to the airport to catch a plane to Washington.

Frank and Joe discussed the mystery of the spy in the Pentagon, who had disappeared with the classified navy document.

"I wonder where he went," Frank said thoughtfully. "He couldn't really go too far in a sailboat."

"People have sailed all the way to Europe," Joe reminded him.

"While carrying a classified stolen document?" Frank shook his head. "Hardly. But he could have met a foreign agent out on the bay."

"We won't know until we get an SOS from Dad," Joe said. "And then we'll have to be ready to move in."

"I hope that won't be necessary," Mrs. Hardy said in a worried tone.

"It's all right, Mom," Frank reassured her. "Dad's got the navy behind him. And I'd sure hate to buck the U.S. Navy."

Mr. Hardy's sister, who lived with the family, stuck her head through the open door. "Spies, submarines, sailboats!" she exclaimed. "What's next?"

The boys grinned. They knew their aunt was very fond of them even though she had a tart tongue and often criticized her nephews.

"How about a piece of chocolate pie, Aunt Gertrude?" Joe suggested.

"Humph! It's certainly better for you than getting involved with spies!" Miss Hardy declared. Then she smiled and led the way to the kitchen, where she served her nephews a sample of her excellent culinary skills.

"You two mind the store now," Aunt Gertrude commanded. "Your mother and I have some shopping to do."

"Don't worry, we will," Joe said as he took a soda out of the refrigerator.

Fifteen minutes later the doorbell rang. Frank went to answer it. A dignified man in a brown suit stood outside. He was wearing a deerstalker hat with a high crown and a peak in front.

"He must have borrowed that hat from Sherlock Holmes," Frank thought while he greeted the stranger with a smile.

The man removed his hat. "Is this the Hardy residence?" he inquired.

"It is, sir," Frank replied.

The visitor handed him a card bearing the name John Hammerley, Lancaster, Pennsylvania.

"Young man, may I come in?" he asked in a troubled tone of voice.

"Of course, Mr. Hammerley. We've been expecting you." Frank stepped aside and ushered their

394

visitor into the living room. There he introduced himself and Joe, and the three sat down.

"I'm a Pennsylvania farmer with an office in the city of Lancaster where I deal in grain," Hammerley announced. "I've come to see Fenton Hardy, the private investigator."

Frank explained that their father had suddenly been called away on another case. "He asked us to say he's sorry he couldn't wait for you. But he's on a top-secret assignment for the government."

Hammerley looked crestfallen. "That's too bad. I wanted him to handle a case for me. I came all the way from Pennsylvania just to see him."

"Mr. Hammerley, what's your case about?" Joe asked.

"Weather vanes!" Hammerley exclaimed.

The Hardy boys were mystified.

"What have weather vanes got to do with a criminal investigation?" Frank inquired.

"They've been stolen!" Hammerley informed him.

Joe scratched his head. "Who would want to steal weather vanes? And what for?"

Their visitor threw up his hands in astonishment. "Young man, I see you don't understand. These are not ordinary weather vanes. They come from the Pennsylvania Dutch country, where we have them on our houses, barns, churches, and public buildings."

"We have some around Bayport," Joe pointed out.

"I'm sure you do," Hammerley agreed. "But the Pennsylvania Dutch weather vanes are special. Many are large, ornate heirlooms up to two hundred years old. They are immensely valuable as antiques. My neighbor's missing weather vane, the figure of a man on horseback called the *Galloping Rider*, would bring twenty thousand dollars, and more than that if it could be smuggled out of the country. American antiques sell for a king's ransom abroad."

Joe whistled. "Twenty thousand bucks just to tell which way the wind's blowing!"

"That would bring the crooks running," Frank declared.

"Right," Hammerley said. "I represent a group in my county who have lost their valuable weather vanes and want them back!"

"Did you have one stolen yourself?" Frank asked.

The visitor shook his head. "No. My own is still on the barn, and I want it to stay there. It's called the *Flashing Arrow*, an arrow with a two-foot eagle perched on top. The whole thing is of beaten copper. A beautiful work of art! Thieves could sell it for a fortune!"

"But why don't you take it down?" Joe asked. "That way the crooks won't get it."

Hammerley gave him a sly look. "I'm setting a trap for the thieves. My foreman sleeps in the barn loft, and he'll sound the alarm if anyone tries to seize the *Flashing Arrow*. So far, nothing has happened. But other people have lost their valuable antiques. I was hoping your father would find them before they disappear into private collections or leave the country."

"How and when were they taken?" Frank asked.

"The thieves who raided my county worked quickly and precisely," the farmer replied. "They struck on four consecutive nights, grabbing the weather vanes before anyone realized what was happening. They knew what they were doing. They took only the most valuable ones."

"How did they get the weather vanes down?" Joe wondered aloud.

"They took the stairs to the roof whenever they could, as in the case of the county courthouse. Then they broke a window and got in while the building was empty. Otherwise, they used ladders to climb up on the outside of buildings. That's how they got the *Galloping Rider*. The police found the marks of the ladder in the mud near the foundation of the barn."

Hammerley sighed, then went on, "Some owners were away at the time, others did not notice at first that their weather vanes were gone from the roofs.

A few angry people who were robbed called the police, and then the story broke on the radio. About twenty were taken. The sheriff and his men inspected every site without finding a clue to the thieves. We're up a tree, so to speak, and there aren't enough officers to stay on the case until it's solved. That's why we need a private investigator."

"Sorry Dad isn't here," Frank said.

"I'm sorry, too," Hammerley confessed. "I was depending on him."

"Maybe he can take your case when he finishes the one he's on," Joe suggested.

Hammerley shook his head vigorously. "Young man, we cannot wait. The trail will grow cold and the thieves will get away. We need a detective right away." He balanced his deerstalker hat on his knee with one hand, tugged on his earlobe, and looked hard at Frank and Joe. "I've heard you boys are detectives, too," he remarked.

"We've worked on several assignments," Joe said modestly, not adding that he and Frank had been involved in more than fifty investigations.

"And you solved them all, I am told," Hammerley commented shrewdly.

"We've got a pretty good batting average," Frank admitted.

Hammerley looked hopeful. "Perhaps you'd be willing to take my case? Judging by your success in the past, I'm sure you could handle it."

Frank pointed out that they would have to check with Mr. Hardy first. "If Dad doesn't need us, it's okay with me."

"Me too!" Joe exclaimed. "I'd like to lasso in the *Galloping Rider* and get it back for you."

"That suits me," Hammerley declared. "How soon can you begin?"

"If we take the case," said Frank, emphasizing the first word, "the timing will depend on our father. He told us to call him tomorrow."

Hammerley brightened up. "Then you could start the day after tomorrow?"

"Maybe," Joe agreed. "How do we get in touch with you?"

Hammerley took a road map of Pennsylvania from his pocket and spread it on the coffee table. "Fly to Lancaster," he said. "Then take Route 222 south to Quarryville. About a mile beyond Quarryville, turn east on a dirt road between two tall pine trees. Keep going for about ten miles, and you will see a sign reading 'Hammerley Homestead.' Drive right on up to the house. I'll be waiting for you."

"You live in the middle of Pennsylvania Dutch country," Frank said with a smile. "That's where people still ride around in buggies drawn by horses, right?"

"That's right," Hammerley said. "Good people, the Amish. We're proud to have them."

The Hardys and their guest chatted for a while

about the Germans who arrived in William Penn's colony back in the eighteenth century. Although Germans, they were called "Dutch" because they referred to themselves with the German word "Deutsch."

"The Pennsylvania Dutch are still there," Hammerley told the boys. "The Amish are the most restrictive group among them. They teach separation from the rest of the world and that you shouldn't go to war, swear oaths, or hold public office. They strive for a simple way of life without modern conveniences and technology."

"I understand they don't even use telephones or electricity on their farms," Joe put in.

Hammerley nodded. "And if someone's property gets damaged, the whole community pitches in and rebuilds it. The barn that belongs to me now was erected in this manner over a century ago."

Hammerley stood up. "I'd better go now. If you want to call me, the number is on my card." Before he walked out the door, he hesitated. "I suppose I should tell you one more thing," he said.

"What's that?" Joe asked eagerly.

The farmer's voice sank to a hoarse whisper. "Beware of the hex!"

2

The Hex

Joe raised his eyebrows in surprise. "The hex?" he repeated. "That's a magical spell, isn't it?"

Hammerley nodded. "That's right. The hex can kill or cure!"

Frank looked puzzled. "Do people still believe in that stuff?"

Hammerley answered him in a stern voice. "The hex may be stronger than you think. Strange things have happened in the Pennsylvania Dutch country, and the local people attribute them to the hex."

"But what has that to do with the stolen weather vanes?" Joe wanted to know.

"There are hex signs on many buildings in our county, including my barn," Hammerley went on.

"But the people who lost their weather vanes also lost their hex signs. They believe that the thieves employ a more powerful hex, since they have been so successful. There are also witches who cast spells—white witches who cure illnesses and black witches who harm their victims. Many people feel that the thieves have at least one black witch among them!"

He adjusted his deerstalker hat in a mirror on the wall. "Are you willing to face the hex?" he asked.

Frank and Joe grinned. "I think so," Frank replied.

"Good. I'll be hearing from you then," Hammerley concluded and walked out the door.

Frank and Joe returned to the living room. "Well, brother, what do you think about this hex business?" Joe asked, flopping into an overstuffed chair.

"Let's read up on it," Frank suggested and went into his father's study. He returned with a large, leather-bound tome on mystical lore and found a chapter on the hex. He flattened the book on the coffee table and began to turn the pages, while Joe peered over his shoulder.

They learned that the hex originated in Germany. People believed that hex signs could ward off danger from those who used them. Or, the signs could be applied to focus uncanny forces on victims. German immigrants brought these ideas to America in colonial days, and they have survived to this day in the Pennsylvania Dutch country.

"The owl is the bird of the hex," Frank read, "and talking owls are frequently the pets of witches."

"Talking owls!" Joe marveled. "I wonder what they say."

"To-whitt, to-whoo, the old woodoo," Frank joked. He turned more pages of the book until he reached a plate showing hex signs. Many were geometrical forms in various colors, squares surrounded by a series of triangles, sunbursts inside concentric circles, and so on. The chief hex sign, they learned, was the pentagram, a star pattern of five points that can be drawn without lifting a pencil from a piece of paper.

"We learned how to do that at school and called it a star," Joe said. "But they never told us it was a hex sign."

"Well, it isn't always a hex sign," Frank pointed out. "But when it is, it's a good luck charm, like a rabbit's foot."

"Unless it's being used against you," Joe stated. "That's what the book says. When two people are using the hex, I suppose the winner is the one who's got the toughest witch for a friend."

"Like those weather vane thieves," Frank grumbled and closed the book.

"Hey, what if they steal ours?" Joe said.

"You mean the tin arrow atop our lab over the garage?" Frank grinned. "The one Aunt Gertrude picked up at a tag sale? I'll let you have it for three bucks."

"I'll pass."

Just then the phone rang. "Maybe that's Dad!" Frank exclaimed, jumping to his feet and lifting the instrument from its cradle.

"Is this one of the great Hardys?" a familiar voice inquired.

Frank smiled. "The greatest. What's up, Chet?"

"Arrows!" their friend announced. "I'm getting so good at it I shot ten straight bull's-eyes in a row earlier this morning!"

"You should. After all, you've practiced archery long enough!"

"You really know how to put a guy down," Chet complained. "Even an expert archer doesn't get ten bull's-eyes in a row every day!"

"Okay, okay. Congratulations. Want us to bring you a medal?"

"No, but you could bring yourselves. How about it, Frank? We've got a contest going on here."

Frank conferred briefly with his brother, then promised their pal to be over in fifteen minutes.

Chet Morton, their best friend, was a roly-poly youth who preferred eating to danger. But the Hardys knew he would never let them down if they were in a tight corner. Chet had proved that when he helped them on a number of dangerous investigations.

"Maybe Chet will come up with an idea on those weather vane thefts," Joe said as the brothers drove across Bayport to the farm where their friend lived with his family.

Frank laughed. "You've got to be kidding! All he's interested in is food and his hobbies."

They turned into the driveway to the Morton home and saw a large target with a number of arrows in it on the front lawn near the house. Several of their friends were standing near the gate, watching Chet go through excited motions with his arms and hands.

Frank stopped the car and the boys got out.

"The Hardys have arrived!" Chet announced as the brothers walked toward the group. "Now we can proceed!" He was dressed in dungarees and a corduroy shirt, two buttons of which remained open because his expansive waistline would not permit them to be closed. A quiver was slung across his left shoulder from which protruded the feathered ends of a dozen arrows, and a baseball cap perched jauntily on his head.

Chet obviously relished the role of director of the archery contest. "Go ahead, Phil," he said to the boy next to him. "Let's see what you can do."

Phil Cohen, dark-haired and slender, enjoyed reading as much as sports, even though he was famous for his quickness and agility. He released his arrow with a determined motion. It flew through the air and hit the target in the third ring surrounding the bull's-eye. "Aw, that's not good enough," he grumbled disgustedly.

"Don't worry, you're getting better!" Tony Prito said cheerfully. "A few minutes ago you didn't even hit the target!"

"Thanks, pal," Phil replied, looking at Tony darkly. "Do you have to advertise my mistake? I explained to you that it was only a momentary lack of concentration."

Tony grinned. "Some mistake! You almost killed Biff!"

"He was in my way," Phil said.

Biff Hooper, a husky football player for Bayport High, winced. "I think you did it on purpose, because I ate your sandwich."

Chet interrupted the friendly banter and raised his hand for silence. "We're not here to gab but to learn the skills of archery!" he announced. "Joe, how about trying a shot?"

Joe glanced quickly at Chet's pretty sister Iola, who sat in the grass watching the boys. The vivacious, dark-haired girl was often his date, and he did not want to appear anything less than perfect in front of her.

"Come on, Joe," Tony kidded. "Show Iola what a terrific shot you are!"

Joe shrugged and hefted the bow. He fitted the feathered end of an arrow into the bowstring, took aim, and let loose. He struck the bull's-eye, although not in dead center.

The boys cheered. "Good shot, Joe!"

"Best yet," Tony said.

"The best is yet to come," Chet told him. "The best is me!"

He took his place in the circle occupied by each contestant in turn. Casually, he pushed his cap back on his head, flexed his fingers, and peered across the lawn at the target.

"Ready, Robin Hood?" Frank joshed him.

"Let's see you split Joe's arrow," Iola teased him. "That's what Robin Hood did."

"Don't rush me," Chet said. "This sport needs plenty of concentration." Tightening the bowstring, Chet snapped it until it twanged like the string of a guitar. Then he whipped an arrow over his shoulder from the quiver, with the gesture of an expert showing the amateurs how to do it. Raising the bow, he took aim.

His friends waited expectantly, their eyes glued to the target. Seconds ticked away, but nothing happened.

Then Chet lowered the bow. "Something is wrong with this arrow," he declared.

"Oh, no!" Biff groaned.

"Getting nervous?" Tony teased.

"I'll ignore the boos from the gallery," Chet said nonchalantly and picked another arrow from his quiver. Again he took aim as his friends watched in expectant silence.

Chet took his time and shifted his feet to get better balance. Suddenly he hit a slick spot in the ground. He skidded and went over backward, losing his grip on the bow!

Twang-g-g! The string snapped and the arrow lofted high over the Morton house. Chet's yell of dismay was answered by a scream in the backyard.

"The arrow hit somebody!" Joe cried out in alarm. "Come on!" He raced around the house, followed by the others.

3

Trapped in a Tent

There was no one in the backyard but the Mortons'
farmhand, Mr. Osborn, who stood at the edge of a
pumpkin field. He had his hands on his hips and
looked very angry.

When the boys came closer, Mr. Osborn pointed
to a big pumpkin neatly pierced by an arrow.
"Who did this?" he thundered. "And what's the idea
of ruining my vegetables?"

"I—slipped and missed my target," Chet stammered. "But I d-didn't do it on purpose, Mr.
Osborn."

The man shook his head in disbelief. "What
target? I was weeding around my garden when the
arrow flew over here. It could have hit me!"

Chet was crestfallen. "I'm really sorry, Mr. Osborn."

"Tell you what, Chet," Phil suggested diplomatically. "Why don't you finish weeding for Mr. Osborn, and maybe he'll forgive you."

Mr. Osborn seemed more pleased with that idea than Chet. "Well, now, that would be real nice. My back's hurting me anyway. If you do my weeding, I'll take this pumpkin in to Mrs. Osborn and ask her to make a pie. Later you're all invited to have a piece."

Chet's eyes lit up. "It's a deal!" Then he turned to his friends. "You'll help me, won't you?"

To tease Chet, the boys pretended to run away, but then everyone pitched in. While working in Mr. Osborn's garden, the Hardys told the others about Mr. Hammerley and the missing weather vanes. They also mentioned the farmer's antique called the *Flashing Arrow*.

"Sounds like an exciting case!" Chet spoke up. "I'd like to be in on it."

"You should be," Biff said dryly. "You're the expert on arrows!"

"Aw, stop picking on me!" Chet complained.

Frank chuckled. "Don't let it bother you. And if we need help, we'll certainly let you know!"

After breakfast the next morning, the Hardy boys turned on a scrambling device that made it impossible for anyone to listen in on a conversation by tapping their telephone. Joe stood next to his brother so that both could speak to their father, then Frank dialed the number Mr. Hardy had given them. The detective answered at once.

"Oh, I'm glad you called," he said. "I'm on my way out."

"How are things progressing, Dad?" Frank asked.

"So far all right. I'm following a clue that will take me out of town for a while."

"Will you need our help?"

"Not at the moment. Tell me about your meeting with John Hammerley. What did he want?"

Frank described the mystery of the stolen weather vanes, then added, "He wants us to go to his farm tomorrow. If you won't need us in the next few days, is it all right if we take his case?"

"Go ahead," Mr. Hardy said. "But be careful. The gang may be dangerous if so much money's involved. Where can I get in touch with you if I have to?"

Frank gave him Hammerley's number, adding that the farm was close enough to Washington for them to get there in a hurry.

"Fine," Fenton Hardy said. "And good luck on your case."

After their father had hung up, Joe called Mr. Hammerley to say he and Frank would be coming the following day. Hammerley was relieved by the news. "No one has tried to steal the *Flashing Arrow* yet," he reported. "But I'll be glad to have you and your brother on the case."

"Would you mind if we brought a friend along?" Joe asked. "He's helped us on other assignments in the past."

"Of course not. The more the merrier," John Hammerley said with a chuckle.

The following morning, Frank, Joe, and Chet flew from Bayport to Lancaster, where they rented a car. Frank got behind the wheel, with Joe next to him, while Chet climbed in the back. He spread a road map out on his pudgy knees to monitor their way. Soon they were driving along Route 222 through a farming area.

They passed a barn decorated with a green triangle inside a blue square, with straight lines extending out from each of the four corners.

"That's a hex sign," Joe commented.

Chet was suspicious. "What's that mean?"

The Hardys explained the occult geometrical forms used by the Pennsylvania Dutch to ward off evil spirits.

"I don't like it," Chet grumbled. "It's spooky."

"Better get used to it," Frank advised him. "We'll run into more hex signs as we go along."

Recognizing the two tall pine trees mentioned by

413

Hammerley, Frank turned east on a narrow dirt road flanked by heavy vegetation on both sides. About a mile on, they noticed a cloud of dust approaching.

"Great Scott! It looks like a tornado heading right toward us!" Chet cried out.

"Calm down." Joe grinned. "Tornadoes don't stick to the road."

Frank pulled over into the underbrush. "Let's see what this is all about," he suggested.

The cloud came closer. Finally the boys could make out a line of horses and carriages moving rapidly along in single file. Dust puffed up under the hooves of the animals, who were guided by bearded men dressed in plain farmer's clothing. Beside each driver sat a woman in a long gray dress and an old-fashioned bonnet.

"They're Amish," Frank concluded.

When the caravan came abreast of the car, the men and women waved. The boys waved back. Twelve carriages passed in this manner and vanished down the road.

"They're pretty friendly people," Chet commented. He had scarcely spoken when more sounds of galloping hooves could be heard up the road. A creaking wagon careened through the dust and pulled to a crunching halt next to the car.

Its horse was flecked with foam and tossed its

mane back and forth. The boys stared in astonishment at the driver, a wild-eyed woman whose hair was flying in the wind.

"Are ye natives or outlanders?" she challenged them in a harsh voice.

"Outlanders," Frank replied. "We are from Bayport."

"Then go back," she grated, "or the curse of the hex will get ye! Do nor forget Mad Maggie's warning!"

"Who's Mad Maggie?" Chet asked.

"That's what people call me!" She uttered a screeching laugh, whipped up her horse, and dashed off down the road.

"She must be a local character," Frank guessed.

"She's got the right name," Joe remarked. "She sure looks like Mad Maggie."

Chet mopped his brow with a handkerchief. "She's putting the hex on us. Let's go back to Bayport!"

Frank started the car. "Chet, we promised Mr. Hammerley we wouldn't let the hex scare us."

"*You* did," Chet muttered. "I never promised any such thing!"

Driving on, the boys came to an area where broad fields and meadows extended for miles on either side of the road. Smoke rose into the air from farmhouse chimneys, and farmers were plowing their fields or storing grain in silos next to barns marked by large, multicolored hex signs.

A large tent stood in one field by the side of the road. Stout guy ropes attached to pegs along the sides held it in place, and the canvas roof sloped down from a central high pole that supported it on the inside. People were coming and going through the opening in the front.

A sign over the door proclaimed in large letters:

JOSHUA KORBO, AUCTIONEER

Chet spotted a refreshment stand at the side of the tent. "I vote we invest in a hot dog and a bottle of soda!" he spoke up. "What do you say?"

"Okay," Joe agreed, and Frank added, "Sounds like a good idea." He drove to a grassy knoll that served as a temporary parking lot. Leaving the car, the boys strolled over to the stand.

"What's going on?" Joe asked the youth in charge of selling the food.

"Biggest auction of the year in these parts. Folks come from all over the county."

He flipped a hamburger on the grill and began serving another customer.

"Let's stay awhile and watch," Frank suggested. Joe and Chet agreed, and after having their snack, the three walked into the tent. Collapsible chairs were arranged in two groups, about fifty to a group, separated by a narrow aisle. Halfway down the aisle was the tall center pole that kept the tent up. People were milling around, chatting in low voices.

Spotting three unoccupied chairs in the back row, the boys sat down. They had a clear view of the platform where the auctioneer was running his business. He was a medium-sized man, clean shaven, wearing steel-rimmed glasses pushed up on his forehead. A nameplate over his breast pocket identified him as Joshua Korbo.

An assistant carried articles from the back of the tent to the platform, where Korbo offered them to the highest bidder in the audience. There were antiques, china, crystal, paintings, sculptures, and beautiful pieces of jewelry.

"He seems to have enough stuff back there to stock the Bayport Department Store," Chet commented.

"Aunt Gertrude should be here," Joe added. "She loves auctions."

Frank shook his head. "She'd empty her bank account. The price of some of this stuff is far out."

As he spoke, a Colonial silver service went for ten thousand dollars. Next, the assistant placed an antique lamp in front of Korbo, who banged his gavel and started the bidding. People raised their hands to indicate they were interested, and Korbo announced the increasing price as the bids came fast and furious.

"Five hundred, six hundred, seven hundred," the auctioneer called out. "Will anyone bid eight hundred for this valuable lamp? Do I hear eight hundred? Nobody bids eight hundred? Going, going . . ."

Suddenly a fly buzzed past Chet's ear. He swatted at it with his hand.

"Gone!" Korbo boomed. "Sold to the young man in the back row for eight hundred dollars." He pointed his gavel at Chet. "Come forward, sir."

Chet turned pale under his freckles. He seemed mesmerized as Korbo gestured at him sternly with the gavel. Unsteadily Chet rose to his feet and moved up the aisle to the platform. The Hardys followed him.

"Please write out a check for eight hundred dollars," Korbo instructed Chet, "and the lamp is yours."

Chet gulped. "But I didn't bid for it!"

"Of course you did," said Korbo severely. "I saw you raise your hand."

"B-but I was just swatting a fly!" Chet stammered.

"That's right," Frank said. "That's all he did."

An argument started, with Korbo insisting that Chet pay up while the Hardys insisted that the auctioneer had made a mistake. At last the boys convinced Korbo, who disgustedly ordered them to step away from the platform while he got on with the auction.

Relieved that the argument was over, the boys walked toward the back of the tent. Chet mopped his brow. "Thanks for the assist, fellows."

"That's okay," Frank said with a grin. "We only sprung you because we might need you!" As he spoke, he noticed a shadow cast on the wall of the tent by the bright sunlight. Someone was moving along outside, cautiously avoiding the guy ropes attached to the pegs. Frank watched the shadow until it turned the corner and a man appeared in the entrance.

He was a small, wizened figure dressed in the overalls of a farmhand. He sat down near the boys and peered intently at Frank and Joe. Chet had gone ahead and disappeared into the crowd.

Frank nudged Joe. "That guy who just came in seems to be watching us!"

Joe looked at the man out of the corner of his eye. "Why should he? We don't know him from Adam."

Frank shrugged. "I have no idea."

Chet interrupted them by calling out from the back of the tent, where he was standing amid an array of chairs, china, mirrors, rugs, athletic equipment, and other objects. "Boy, we could use this stuff for the Bayport baseball team," he marveled as he pawed through a pile of gloves, masks, and spiked shoes.

The Hardys joined him, forgetting the stranger for a moment. Joe noticed something that caught his attention. Shifting a small table to one side, he lifted the object and examined it. Then he held it up for Frank and Chet to see.

"Look at this!" he exclaimed excitedly.

He was holding a weather vane shaped in the form of a man on horseback. On the base was the descriptive title: *Galloping Rider*.

"It's the stolen weather vane!" Joe surmised.

"Sure looks like it," Frank stated. "What'll we do now?"

"Let's bid for it," Joe proposed.

"Not me!" Chet retorted. "I'm not bidding for anything. Not even a hot dog."

Before they could work out a strategy, they heard footsteps coming in their direction. They turned and saw the stranger in overalls, who had bounded out of his chair and was plunging toward them in a headlong attack!

The man barreled into Joe, wrenching the weather vane from his hands and knocking him over backward. The Hardy boy fell against his brother and both went down in a heap. Chet got a bear hug on their assailant, but the latter twisted around, hit him on the head with the weather vane, and made him see stars.

Breaking loose, the man bolted up the aisle carrying the weather vane. He elbowed his way through the crowd and hastened toward the exit.

"Stop thief!" Joe yelled. "Don't let him get away!"

Realizing that no one could make out what was happening, the Hardys leaped to their feet and dashed after the fugitive, with Chet close behind them. Frantically they tried to push their way through the bidders in the aisle.

Striving to get around one group, Chet stumbled and crashed into the tent pole, knocking it loose. The tent swayed crazily for a moment, then started to collapse!

4

Vanishing Weather Vanes

Cries went up from the crowd as the tent fell down like a cloud, enveloping everyone in its folds.

"Let me out!" a woman screamed.

"We'll be smothered!" someone else yelled over the excited shouts of other people.

Frank pushed up the limp cloth over his head and looked around for Joe and Chet. They were right next to him.

"Come on, let's try to crawl out of here," he urged and began to scramble forward on his hands and knees. The other two followed. Reaching the side of the tent, they wriggled underneath, loosened a guy rope by releasing it from its peg, and lifted the canvas above their heads.

"This way, everybody!" Frank shouted.

Those trapped in the tent struggled clear, aided by the boys from Bayport.

"Good thinking!" one man complimented them.

"I believe no one was hurt thanks to you," said another.

Korbo, who had been on the auctioneer's platform when the tent collapsed, was the last to escape. He railed furiously at Chet's clumsiness in barging into the pole.

"What Chet did wasn't as bad as auctioning stolen property!" Frank interjected.

"Everything that I handle is legitimate!" Korbo snapped.

"What about that weather vane called the *Galloping Rider?*"

"There were no weather vanes at this auction. Look for yourself." Korbo took a list from his pocket and handed it to Frank, who checked the "W" entries.

"Wagon, warming pan, washing machine, wheelbarrow, writing desk," Frank read. "No weather vane. I guess we owe you an apology, Mr. Korbo."

"But the weather vane was in the tent!" Joe protested. He explained how he had found it and how the stranger had snatched it away from him.

"I don't know anything about a weather vane or that man you're talking about," Korbo said, "but I do know who knocked the tent down." He pointed an accusing finger at Chet, who turned red with embarrassment.

"We'll put it up again," Frank offered. Korbo accepted the suggestion with a curt nod, and the boys set to work.

Wriggling back under the canvas, they reached the center of the tent, where they found the pole tilted at an angle but still attached to the roof. They took hold of the support, straining to get enough leverage, then gradually eased it into an upright position and wedged the base against the ground where it had been. Then, with the help of some other young people, they righted the chairs and tightened the guy ropes outside.

The auction resumed while the Bayporters drove on toward the Hammerley farm.

"Maybe that guy stole the weather vane and hid it in the tent for some reason," Joe observed. "He might have come back to pick it up on the sly, but we got there first."

"That would explain why it was stashed behind the table," Frank agreed.

A sign loomed ahead of them in the distance:

HAMMERLEY HOMESTEAD

Frank turned a few feet beyond it and drove toward the big house. A barn with a tall silo attached to it stood behind the place, and moving in the wind atop the barn was the copper-colored figure of an eagle perched on an arrow.

"The *Flashing Arrow!*" Joe pointed.

Frank nodded. "And it's up to us to see it stays where it is." He parked in front of the house and the three went up to the front door. Chet punched the bell. Hammerley appeared and smiled happily when he saw his callers. Frank introduced Chet as the friend who would be on the case with them.

Hammerley was pleased. "An extra member always strengthens the team," he said. He was surprised when Joe told him about the *Galloping Rider.* "You mean the thieves were about to auction it off?" the farmer thundered.

"Mr. Korbo didn't even have it on his list," Frank explained. "He didn't know how it got there or who took it."

Hammerley sighed. "Too bad you couldn't catch the man who ran off with it. Well, let's go over to the barn and I'll show you my prized possession on the roof."

He led the way through the yard. The boys saw hired hands dumping corn from a truck onto a conveyor belt leading into the silo. Some distance away, a line of horses looking out from their stalls indicated the building where the livestock were kept. Chickens clucked in a coop nearby, and a hawk wheeled in the sky overhead.

Hammerley stopped in front of the barn. "This is where I keep the hay, feed, and farm implements," he informed his visitors.

Looking up, the boys saw a hex sign over the front door. It was a bright red pentagram in a white square, which was inside a black circle.

"The original owner put the hex sign there to protect the barn," Hammerley explained.

"Wouldn't it also protect the *Flashing Arrow?*" Frank queried.

Hammerley scowled. "Maybe, but some hexes are stronger than others, and I'm not taking any chances. The thieves might be using the pentagram hex too. Now follow me."

He led them around the barn, explaining that, because of its height, anyone climbing up to the roof would have to use a fireman's ladder. "There's a staircase inside. It leads to that skylight above the gutter, which is the only exit from the loft to the roof."

The boys craned their necks to see where he was pointing. They noticed a man glaring down at them from the skylight with a sinister expression. He pulled back when he saw them looking at him.

"I wouldn't want to meet him in a dark alley," Chet muttered.

"Cheer up," Joe encouraged their rotund friend. "No alleys on the farm."

"Very funny!" Chet growled.

The group circled the barn and arrived back at the front door. "You can see how the other weather vanes vanished," Hammerley noted. "They were left unprotected. Here, as long as somebody is in the loft, the *Flashing Arrow* is safe. My foreman has been sleeping in the barn for the past few nights, as I told you in Bayport."

Just then the man they had seen at the skylight came out of the door. Hammerley introduced him as Crow Morven, the foreman of the farm.

"I was in the loft all night," Morven reported to Hammerley. "Nothing happened. I guess the crooks aren't thinking of stealing your weather vane."

"Could be a setup," Chet said. "Make you forget the *Flashing Arrow's* in danger, and one night— whammo—it'll be gone."

"You got it figured out, haven't you, wise guy?" Morven scoffed. "The *Flashing Arrow* is safe as long as I'm foreman. You can bet on it."

"Nobody's betting against you, Crow," Hammerley soothed his employee. "Now, suppose you take our visitors up to the roof and let them inspect the weather vane."

The farmer went back to the house, while Morven led the way into the barn. They climbed the stairs past two landings into the loft, which was a broad room with a low ceiling. A pile of hay filled one corner. The skylight window admitted the rays of the sun.

Morven pushed open the skylight, allowing the boys to see how the roof dropped away at a steep angle toward the gutter. There was nothing beneath it but a long fall down to the ground.

The foreman gave the boys an evil grin. "Want to follow me out there?" he challenged them.

"Sure," said Frank and Joe.

Chet poked his head out the skylight, blanched at the height, and quickly pulled back. "I think I'll pass," he gasped. "I'll check out the loft instead."

Frank and Joe climbed through the skylight after the unfriendly foreman, pressing their feet against the gutter to get a toehold. Then, doubled over and clutching the wooden shingles with their fingers as they went, they worked their way up the steep incline of the roof.

Although Morven was used to the barn, he fell behind Frank and Joe in the climb to the apex, where the other side of the roof dropped away in the opposite direction. Joe was in the lead. Halfway up, a shingle snapped in his hand, but he managed to steady himself.

When they reached the apex, they stood up. They could see the surrounding area. A stream meandered through a woods, and a row of small hills rose beyond it.

"Time to go back," Morven said after they had taken in the view. "I haven't got all day!"

"We'd like to inspect the weather vane first," Frank replied. "Mr. Hammerley said we should."

"Is there some reason you don't want us near it?" Joe asked suspiciously.

"Of course not," Morven snarled. "Come on."

The Hardys were used to heights. They had done some mountaineering, and many of their cases had forced them into death-defying feats high above the ground. But both felt rather uneasy on the roof of Hammerley's barn.

To reach the weather vane, they had to crouch on their hands and knees, then edge their way along the apex, with disaster on either side should they slip. Finally the trio reached the middle of the roof, and the Hardys had a close-up view of the *Flashing Arrow*.

A Pennsylvania Dutch craftsman had beaten flat copper into the likeness of an eagle with its head back in a defiant gesture, its beak open as if to attack, and its wings spread for flight. The eagle's talons gripped the arrow on which it perched. One end of the arrow was pointed, while the other end expanded into simulated feathers. A bar through the center of the arrow held the weather vane in place on the roof.

Frank and Joe edged their way around Morven and sat on opposite sides of the *Flashing Arrow* so that they could inspect it together. They were struck by the beauty of the workmanship.

"Look, it's loose," Frank said, lifting the weather vane from its bar. "How come?"

Morven shrugged. "Beats me. It had a collar that held it on the bar."

"Where's the collar now?"

"Search me," Morven said. "Maybe the workmen who fixed the roof took it."

Frank replaced the weather vane on the bar, noting that it could still turn in the wind without falling off. Joe swung it around until the arrow pointed in his direction. He wiggled to sit next to Morven, with his legs dangling down one side of the roof, and explored the pointed end with his fingertips.

"Say, this arrowhead isn't welded on," he said. "It's screwed on." Grasping the arrowhead between his thumb and forefinger, he gave it a sharp twist that caused it to move.

"Let's see," Morven said. He rose and leaned toward Joe. Just then his foot seemed to slip and he fell heavily against the young detective. With a cry of surprise, he righted himself with his hand, but Joe was knocked off balance and toppled from the apex of the roof.

While Frank stared in horror, his brother slid down the steep slope and plunged over the side of the barn!

5

Joe's Close Call

Without hesitating, Frank skidded down the roof to a point where he could brace his feet against the gutter. Joe was hanging onto the gutter by his fingertips! The force of his fall had swung one foot against the wall, where the sole of his shoe had come to rest on a fastening that held a drainpipe against the side of the barn.

Quickly Frank grabbed his brother's wrists. Joe swung one knee over the gutter and with Frank's help hauled himself back onto the roof. He lay there for a moment, breathing heavily after his near-fatal accident.

"That was some ride you took," Frank said, his voice still tense.

"I'm glad I didn't finish it," Joe puffed. Catching his breath, he followed Frank back to the apex of the roof where Morven was waiting.

"I'm sorry about your fall," the foreman said apologetically. "My foot slipped. Are you all right?"

"Don't worry, I do this all the time," Joe said coldly. He suspected that it had not been an accident. Carefully wedging himself next to the weather vane, he resumed unscrewing the arrowhead and noticed that the arrow formed a hollow tube.

"That makes it light enough to turn with the wind," he reasoned. After peering in and finding the tube empty, he screwed the arrowhead back on.

Deciding that they had seen enough, Frank and Joe descended the roof with Morven, dropped through the skylight, and rejoined Chet in the loft. Their roly-poly friend, who had watched Joe's close call, was pale, and his hands trembled slightly.

"You sure know how to scare a guy," he said to Joe, trying not to show how upset he was.

"Sorry about that," Joe said. "I didn't know you were watching. What'd you find in the loft?"

"Nothing but a telephone," Chet replied and pointed to the instrument that was mounted on the wall. "I checked it out. Connects with the house. Matter of fact, Mr. Hammerley wants you to call him up."

Frank lifted the phone and heard it ring at the other end. Hammerley answered.

"Did you find anything?" he inquired.

"Yes. The *Flashing Arrow* is loose. I lifted it clear off its rod. Why is that?"

Hammerley was puzzled. "I don't know. It always had a collar holding it in place. I'll talk to Crow about it. Tell him to come to the house with you."

The group entered through the front door and Hammerley ushered them into the living room. He ordered Morven to put a new collar on the weather vane, and the foreman promised to take care of it in the morning.

"What's our next move?" Harmmerley asked the boys.

"Tomorrow we'd like to talk to the people whose weather vanes have been stolen," Frank said. "Meanwhile, perhaps we could sleep in the barn tonight. I'm sure Mr. Morven wouldn't mind having some time off."

Hammerley liked the idea, and Morven gave no indication that he objected in any way. He took a flashlight from a shelf on the wall, stuffed it into his pocket, and said he would see about the cows in the pasture. As he was leaving, he turned to the boys with a smirk and added, "Pleasant dreams!"

Hammerley showed his guests around the house,

then entertained them with tales of the Pennsylvania Dutch and the plain ways of the Amish. He was interested to hear that they had seen Amish couples in their carriages on their way.

"We also met Mad Maggie," Frank said but did not mention the woman's warning.

"Oh, she's a harmless old crone," Hammerley told the boys. "No one takes her seriously."

Frank decided not to press the subject any further, when Chet suddenly sat bolt upright. His eyes became wide, and his nose quivered.

"What's the matter, Chet?" Frank asked.

"Food!" Chet exclaimed. "I smell it! And I just remembered that we haven't eaten in a long time!"

The familiar aroma of roast beef wafted in from the kitchen, and the Hardys grinned.

"Mr. Hammerley, please excuse Chet," Frank said. "He has this thing about food—"

"I can tell." Hammerley chuckled. "And I assure you he'll enjoy tonight's meal."

An hour later their host served onion soup from a large green tureen at the head of the table. The roast beef came next, with vegetables and potatoes, and finally Mrs. Smith, the housekeeper, brought in homemade ice cream. Chet took a double portion of everything.

Hammerley was amazed at the spectacle. "My

goodness, young man, you really know how to do justice to a meal!" he commented.

"Chet's had a lot of practice," Joe stated.

Later, as night was falling, the boys left the house and went to the barn. They climbed up to the loft and discussed their strategy. They agreed to rotate one-hour watches—Joe first, Chet second, Frank third, and then back to Joe to repeat the series.

Then they went to the skylight and peered out. Dark clouds drifted across the face of a full moon, causing the trees in the woods to throw ghostly shadows over the landscape. From down below came the scream of a wildcat hunting for its prey in the underbrush. Bats flitted in the night sky, zooming through the moonlight and disappearing into the darkness. Far off, a bell tolled mournfully in a church steeple.

"Let's keep the light out," Frank suggested and sat down. "It might scare the thieves away."

"But I'm scared without it!" Chet declared. "This place gives me the creeps."

"Want to sleep in the farmhouse?" Frank needled.

Chet looked at him darkly but didn't reply. Finally he said, "What if the thieves outnumber us?"

"We have a phone to send an SOS," Frank told him. "Besides, the hex is on our side."

Being reminded of the hex sign over the barn door made Chet feel more uneasy than ever. Frank and Joe could not help but tease their pal, and they began to discuss how witches used hex signs to cast spells on their victims.

"Strange things happen at the crossroads in the dark of the moon," Joe intoned. It was a sentence he had read in the book on mystical lore.

Chet shivered. "Please, fellows, let's talk about something else. The only thing I want is—"

His companions never found out what he wanted because he was interrupted by a sound on the roof in the vicinity of the weather vane. They jumped to their feet and quickly opened the skylight. They were about to climb out onto the roof, when they realized what had made the noise.

A large horned owl sat on the arrow beside the copper eagle. It glared at them, hooted hoarsely, spread its wings, and sailed off into the moonlight.

Frank and Joe broke out into relieved chuckles. "Some thief!" Joe said.

"It certainly didn't do my nerves any good," Chet grumbled, wiping perspiration from his face.

The three settled down again to wait in the darkness. Chet yawned. He kicked some of the hay in the corner into a makeshift mattress. "I'm going to sleep," he announced and lay down. He closed his eyes and soon only his snoring disturbed the silence of the barn loft.

Joe glanced at the luminous dial of his wristwatch. "Time for me to stand guard, Frank. You can turn in if you want to."

"Good idea," Frank said. "I could use a little shut-eye."

But before he could get comfortable, a creaking noise came from downstairs. "Sh!" Frank warned, putting a hand on Joe's right arm. The Hardys sat motionless, straining their ears.

"It must have been the door," Joe whispered. "Maybe the wind did it." But then they heard a step creak on the lower stairs, then another, and another!

"That's not the wind," Frank hissed. "Someone's coming up the stairs!"

In their detective work, the boys had developed a technique for dealing with situations like this. Noiselessly they tiptoed to the door and positioned themselves on either side of it.

The stealthy footsteps drew closer and stopped on the landing outside. Frank and Joe felt their spines tingle and they breathed in muted gasps, while their eyes remained fixed on the door.

It began to swing inward very slowly, inch by inch. When it was half open, a dark form slipped through into the loft! The Hardys could see the intruder was a man but did not recognize him. They sprang into action. Joe grabbed the stranger by the elbows, pulling his arms behind his back, while Frank got him around the waist.

However, their adversary was quick and strong. He wrenched free of Joe's grip and jumped clear of Frank. Then he bolted out the door! Frank hit him with a flying tackle, and the two rolled over and over down the stairs to the landing below.

The kicking and pounding had awakened Chet. He and Joe rushed down the stairs after the two combatants to join the fray. Seconds later Chet immobilized the intruder with a headlock!

6

Helicopter Caper

"All right, I give up!" the captive sputtered. "Just let go of me!"

The voice sounded familiar to the boys, so they quickly pushed the intruder up the steps and into the loft where they shone the light on him. He was Crow Morven!

"What in the world are you doing here?" Frank exploded.

"I came for my jacket," the man replied. "I must have left it in the loft."

"But why did you sneak up the stairs?" Joe demanded. "Why didn't you just call out and let us know you were here?"

"I figured you were asleep, and I didn't want to

wake you up. Did you have to pounce on me like that?"

"You threw a few punches yourself," Chet accused him. "And if you'd let us know who you were in the beginning, we all could have saved ourselves a lot of bruises!"

"I know," Morven muttered. "But after you jumped me I wasn't sure whether it was you or the gang of thieves. After all, they could have come in and subdued you. Anyway, have you seen my jacket?"

"You were wearing it over at the house," Joe reminded him. "I saw you put the flashlight in your pocket."

"Oh . . . yes. Now I remember. I must have left it out in the pasture," Morven said, slapping his forehead with his hand. "Well, sorry about the bruises. I'll see you in the morning." With that, he turned on his heels and left.

Joe snapped the light off again. "I don't trust that guy," he declared. "He didn't forget his jacket. He was up to no good when he came sneaking in here!"

"And remember how he tried to keep us away from the *Flashing Arrow*?" Frank asked. "Why would he do that if he was on the level? Maybe *he* took the collar off and didn't want us to find out."

Chet nodded. "Joe, when he bumped into you, it

wasn't an accident, either. He was probably trying to knock you off the roof."

"I felt that all along," Joe admitted.

The boys agreed to keep an eye on Morven. After the excitement of the fight, none of them felt like sleeping. It occurred to Frank that it would be a good idea to check out the rest of the barn. "Morven could have dropped something downstairs before coming up," he said. "One of us can stay here while the other two investigate."

They decided that Joe would remain on guard while Frank and Chet scouted through the lower levels. Frank took out his pencil flashlight. Using its narrow beam, he led the way down the stairs.

At the bottom, they found a dozen stone steps, descended them, and ended up in a basement constructed from large cinder blocks. Chet yelled as something jumped onto his shoe. Frank whipped the flashlight around and the beam picked up a rat scurrying out of sight.

Pressing on, the boys discovered farm machinery and a long bench holding tools for working on the machines.

"This must be the repair shop," Frank judged.

Chet slapped a tractor with the palm of his hand. "Boy, I'd like to drive this baby out in the field! I'd show them how to make furrows!"

He got into the driver's seat of the tractor and

began to experiment with the controls in the darkness, while Frank played his light on the ceiling.

Varrooom! Suddenly the tractor engine sprang to life and the machine began to move, plowing forward into a pile of crates before Chet managed to brake to a halt! It all happened so fast that Frank could only stare at his friend, who was now festooned with straw that had fallen over him from one crate. The pile tilted at crazy angles over his head, and Chet looked horror-stricken at a broken crate in front of him.

"I just turned on the ignition, and it took off!" he declared defensively.

"You must have kicked it into gear without noticing it," Frank said, suppressing a chuckle.

"I guess so." Chet backed the tractor to its original position and jumped down to inspect the crates he had hit. "Only one is smashed," he said with relief.

"They can use it for kindling," Frank encouraged him.

Chet pushed his hand through his hair to remove the straw and ran a finger around his collar. Then the two boys continued around the basement in the darkness. The flashlight showed dust and cobwebs everywhere except over one cinder block, where the mortar around the block had been pried loose and removed.

"This looks like a hiding place!" Frank exclaimed excitedly. "Let's see what's in it."

Together they shifted the block back and forth and drew it from its position in the wall. Frank shone his beam into the cavity. They saw a parcel wrapped in brown paper inside.

"Maybe it's a bomb!" Chet said in alarm.

"I won't take any chances," Frank promised. Picking up a long, thin stick from the floor, he stood to one side of the cavity and prodded the brown paper off the parcel. Underneath was a white cube about six inches square on each side.

"That's no bomb," Frank muttered. Reaching in, he lifted the cube out, examined it, and began to chuckle. The whiteness was the reflection of waxed paper. Removing it, he held up a couple of sandwiches.

"One of the farmhands must have put it behind the cinder block to keep the rats away," Frank surmised.

He put the sandwiches back in the paper covering, replaced them in their hiding place, and with Chet's help pushed the cinder block into its old position. Then the boys proceeded toward the rear door of the barn, where the machinery entered and left. It was locked. Slowly, they continued along the wall and finally arrived back at the steps.

"Let's go up to the next level," Frank suggested.

"I don't think there are any clues down here."

Chet nodded, and they climbed the stone staircase to examine the ground floor. This part of the barn was used for storing grain. Frank and Chet shuffled forward cautiously, passing bins of wheat, oats, rye, and corn.

At the end of the row of bins, Frank turned right in the darkness, guided by the narrow beam of his flashlight. Chet, who was behind him, had caught his sleeve on a nail, which held him up for a moment. When he reached the place where Frank had turned, the light was too far away for him to see. He went left, expecting to catch up with his friend. Suddenly something clapped him on the shoulder, making him stop in paralyzed fright.

"Is th-that you, Frank?" Chet whispered tremulously.

There was no answer. He reached up and felt a soft pressure inside burlap sacking. The truth dawned on him. The corner of a large sack of grain had shifted under its own weight, sloped over as he passed, and struck him on the shoulder!

Running the back of his hand across his forehead, Chet hurried on until he saw a dim light in the wall of the barn. He figured it must be the open door to another room and that Frank was in there. Quickly he stepped through and, with a terrified scream, plunged into darkness! He landed on a pile of corn in the silo.

Groggily he struggled to his feet and discovered that the aperture of the silo was too high for him to climb through. "Frank!" he yelled. "Frank, help me!"

The older Hardy boy, having circled the room, was near enough to hear Chet shouting. Hastening to the spot, he shone his light down into the silo. Chet stood there, ankle-deep in corncobs. His mouth was open and his eyes were glazed.

"Chet, are you inspecting the corn for the horses and cows?" Frank asked with a chuckle.

"Just get me out of here!" Chet pleaded.

Frank spotted a rope on a hook and lowered one end to his friend. Then he wound the opposite end around a pulley used in lifting heavy sacks of grain and helped Chet scramble out.

"I've had it!" Chet declared emphatically. "I want to get out of here pronto!"

"We haven't finished investigating," Frank pointed out. "There's the second floor—"

"Oh, all right," Chet grumbled. "But don't lose me again!"

They ascended the stairs to the next level of the barn. Here they made a rapid inspection of lighter farm implements—shovels, hoes, rakes, crowbars, pruning hooks, and so on.

"Nothing here either," Frank said finally. "Let's get back to the loft and see what Joe's doing."

But when the two arrived, Joe was gone!

"Where in the world is he?" Frank said worriedly as he put on the light and looked around the loft. "He wouldn't leave without letting us know!"

"Maybe the thieves got to him while we were gone," Chet said nervously.

"It's possible," Frank replied somberly. "We were in the basement long enough that they could have hustled him down the stairs without our knowing it! If so, I'd better get on their trail. You stay here, Chet, while I run outside and see if I can find out what happened!"

Frank was heading for the door when a dark shape loomed on the roof against the rising moon. The figure raised its arm as if to spring through the skylight!

"Frank!" Chet quavered. "Don't go!"

Frank turned. "What's up?"

Speechlessly Chet pointed to the dark shape on the roof. As they stared, the figure swung down through the skylight into the loft. It was Joe!

"I thought that owl we spotted might have knocked the weather vane off center," he said. "So I went out to see before it tumbled down to the ground. What a windfall for the crooks that would have been! Did you find anything downstairs?"

"Nothing," Frank reported. "Chet even checked out the silo."

Their rotund pal squirmed as Frank described the incident to Joe. "Knock it off, fellows, will you?" Chet pleaded.

"Don't worry, we know we can count on you," Frank mollified him. "And now it's your turn to stand guard."

Chet parked himself on the floor with his back to the wall, while the Hardys lay down to sleep. Squinting through the skylight, he could see dismal clouds scudding across the moon. A rising wind shook the shingles of the roof with a mournful sound. Chet shuddered and felt relieved that he was not alone in the darkness of the barn loft.

The minutes slipped away slowly. Everything was still, and Chet began to nod. Soon a snore arose from his corner. Fast asleep, he did not hear a faint sound in the night sky that grew louder as it approached.

Suddenly a terrific clatter erupted overhead, waking the three boys. The noise continued past the barn, started to die away, then came back with a thunderous roar that shook the building.

Frank and Joe leaped to their feet and rushed over to the skylight. Chet dived under the pile of hay. The noise diminished once more, and the Hardys climbed onto the roof. In the moonlight, they could see a helicopter circling for another approach to the barn. Again the clatter became deafening.

"What's that chopper doing?" Frank shouted in consternation over the noise.

"I don't know!" Joe yelled back. "The pilot must be a complete fool! He'll hit the barn!"

The helicopter came directly toward them. Someone on the inside played out a cable on a winch. It dropped ten feet and swayed back and forth under the chopper, which hovered over the roof. Four curved prongs spread out at the end of the cable.

"He's got a grappling hook at the end!" Frank shouted. "They're after the *Flashing Arrow!*"

The chopper moved slightly and the cable swung toward the weather vane. Then the grappling iron struck the copper eagle with a loud clang. It missed. The whirlybird passed over the barn with only feet to spare, flew off far enough to circle around, then started back toward the weather vane, lower than ever. Joe could see the painted legend on its side: JF333.

The boys were scrambling up the roof in a frantic effort to reach the weather vane first. At the apex, they edged their way along the route they had taken with Morven during the day. It was even more dangerous in the darkness, but the boys gritted their teeth and pressed on as fast as they could, with Frank in the lead.

As he approached the *Flashing Arrow*, the chopper came directly toward him. It was so near that

449

he could see the face of the pilot at the window, but the darkness prevented him from distinguishing his features.

Frank had almost reached the weather vane when the grappling iron swung toward it from the opposite side. The metal claws closed beneath the arrow of the weather vane and grabbed it as the man at the winch jerked the cable upward!

Desperately Frank lunged forward, his arm outstretched and his fingers grasping for the weather vane. But he missed by inches as the grappling hook plucked the *Flashing Arrow* from its bar. The winch rolled in the cable, drawing its prey into the interior of the chopper.

Then the helicopter moved up and disappeared into the darkness!

7

The Charging Bull

Frank slumped over the apex, breathing heavily. Joe almost lost his balance from the wind caused by the chopper's blades, and for a few moments the brothers rested in silence. Then they made their way back to the loft.

"I hate to tell Mr. Hammerley what happened," Frank muttered.

"I know," Joe said. "But we have no choice." He lifted the phone and listened. Then he jiggled the instrument. "It's dead!" he declared.

Frank walked to the skylight and hauled in the wire. "It's been cut. Judging by the length, it was severed down below. I'll go over to Mr. Hammerley and tell him. You and Chet might just as well stay here."

He left the barn and walked to the house, where he pressed the doorbell. Getting no response, he pushed the bell several more times. Then he banged the knocker and hammered on the door with his fist, at the same time shouting, "Mr. Hammerley! Mr. Hammerley!" Still, no answer came from inside the house.

Frank walked around the building knocking on the windows and at the back door, all to no avail. He was wondering what to do next when out of the corner of his eye he noticed a movement in the underbrush flanking the woods. A man was sneaking away!

Frank called out for him to stop, but the stranger started to run. Guiding himself by the sound of crashing through the underbrush, Frank ran after him. He caught up with the fugitive about twenty yards into the woods. Panting for breath, the man swung around, and his face became visible in the beam of Frank's flashlight.

He was Crow Morven!

"What were you doing hiding in the bushes?" Frank demanded.

"I was on my way home. When I saw you sneaking around the house, I thought you were a burglar, so I watched you."

"Didn't you hear me call Mr. Hammerley and recognize my voice?" Frank asked.

Morven shook his head, pulling loose of Frank's grip. The young detective realized he had no right to stop the foreman, so he let him go and watched him disappear into the woods. Then he returned to the loft. Dawn was just breaking.

"Morven's our prime suspect," Joe said after hearing Frank's tale.

His brother agreed. "Unfortunately, we still don't have any proof."

The boys decided there was no point in remaining in the loft, now that the weather vane was gone. They moved to the front porch of the house and sat on wicker chairs around a small table until the housekeeper arrived at 8:00 A.M. She let them in with her key, saying she was surprised that Mr. Hammerley was still in bed. "He's always up when I get here," she added, shaking her head. She went upstairs, calling the farmer.

At last he appeared, breathing slowly and with his face flushed. Yawning drowsily he invited the boys to have breakfast with him. "Anything exciting happen during the night?" he asked.

"I'm afraid so," Frank said hesitantly. "The *Flashing Arrow* was stolen!"

"What!" Hammerley exploded.

Frank explained how the thieves had managed to remove the weather vane, and he watched Hammerley's angry face with apprehension.

"You knew the thieves might try to steal my antique. Why did you let them take it from under your noses?" the farmer thundered.

"We didn't expect a chopper," Chet pointed out. "Neither did you."

Hammerley simmered down. "You have a point there, young man. This is the first time I ever heard of robbery by helicopter." He frowned thoughtfully, then sat down at the table. "So the crooks changed their method of operation. Is my hex sign still there?"

"It's there," Joe confirmed. "They had no chance to take it."

"We tried to phone you after it happened," Frank said, "but the line was cut." He explained how he had attempted to deliver the message in person, only to find complete silence at the house.

"I can't understand why I didn't hear you," the farmer said. "I'm usually a light sleeper. But I didn't hear the helicopter you described, either. And I overslept this morning. Couldn't seem to wake up when Mrs. Smith called me. It's mystifying."

"Not if you were slipped a drug," Frank declared. He looked closely at the farmer. "You were breathing rather slowly when you came down, and your face was red," he added. "Those are symptoms of chloral mixed with alcohol. Did you take anything before you went to sleep last night?"

"Only my nighttime cocoa."

"Where's the cup?"

"It was on my bedside table. Mrs. Smith may have taken it to the kitchen by now."

"We'd like to see it before she washes it."

Hammerley led the way into the kitchen. The housekeeper was just about to put the cup into the sink.

"Hold it, Mrs. Smith!" Joe called. "May we have that cup for a moment?"

She handed it to the boy. At the bottom were the crusted remains of the cocoa Hammerley had drunk the night before.

"I'll get the kit," Joe offered and went upstairs to the room where they had left their bags. Soon he returned with a small detective box the boys always carried with them on their trips. He set it on the kitchen table and removed an eyedropper with a chemical in it. He added a few drops of water from the faucet, then squeezed the solution onto the caked remains of the cup. Transparent crystals formed at the bottom.

"That's chloral hydrate!" Joe declared. "Mr. Hammerley, you *were* drugged!"

"Seems like a strong dose," Frank added. "Who made your cocoa last night?"

"Mrs. Smith, as usual," Hammerley replied.

The housekeeper's face went ashen. "I didn't put

anything in Mr. Hammerley's cocoa!" she cried out.

Chet put an arm around the excited woman's shoulder. "No one's accusing you," he said, trying to calm her.

"Let's test the can of cocoa," Frank suggested. He tried the same experiment and discovered there were knockout drops in the can, too. "That means anyone who had access to the can during the day could have done it," he concluded.

"It must have been yesterday," Hammerley stated. "I had cocoa from that can the night before last, and it was perfectly all right then."

"Can you remember who came to your house yesterday?" Joe prodded.

Hammerley frowned. "The usual tradesmen, some grain dealers from Lancaster, and a couple of politicians who want me to run for the town council in the next election."

"Crow Morven was here," Chet pointed out.

"Yes, but only in the front room," Hammerley replied. "He wasn't in the kitchen."

"He could have sneaked in while no one was looking," Joe suggested.

"Morven wouldn't do a thing like that!" Hammerley defended his foreman. "I trust him."

"He sneaked into the barn last night," Joe reminded the farmer. "And he was hiding in the bushes after the helicopter took off."

Hammerley shrugged. "He thought he left his

jacket. And later he told you he was on his way home. He stays up until that time quite often, checking around the property to see that everything is all right."

Frank signaled Joe not to press the matter any further. Apparently Hammerley trusted his foreman, and they would need proof to convince him of any wrongdoing on Morven's part.

Just then the foreman walked into the house. When he heard what had happened, he jeered at the boys. "You guys are a great bunch of detectives! Fooled by a copter."

He urged Hammerley to fire the young sleuths, since they had not been able to prevent the theft.

"After all," he insisted, "the weather vane was safe while I was on guard in the barn!"

"Maybe you know more about the chopper than we do!" Chet challenged him.

Morven glared at Frank. "I was on the ground when the chopper came overhead. You saw me. Remember?"

"Correct," Frank admitted.

Hammerley intervened in the dispute. "The question is, what to do now?"

"We lost the *Flashing Arrow*," Joe stated. "But we're determined to find it and bring it back!"

"Where will you begin?" Hammerley asked doubtfully.

"We have a clue. I saw the license number on the

chopper—JF333. Have you any idea what that could mean?"

"It probably means the helicopter came from Juniper Field," Hammerley said. "That's a small airport five miles from here. Why don't you drive over there and check it out?"

"No use driving," Morven advised. "The bridge up the road was washed out by the last flood. Hasn't been repaired yet. The detour will take you fifty miles around the hills. It's five miles to walk."

"Which direction?" Joe inquired.

"Across the pasture to the big maple tree on the other side. Follow the footpath between two big boulders and it'll lead you to Juniper Field." Saying he had some farm chores to look after, the foreman left the house.

"We'll walk, then," Joe decided. "Okay with you fellows?"

Frank agreed at once, but Chet hesitated. The idea of a five-mile hike did not appeal to him. But he did not want to be left out of the investigation, so he set out with Frank and Joe for Juniper Field.

As they passed the barn, they saw Morven looking at them from the skylight. He had a grim smile on his face and he shook his fist at them.

"That guy knows more than he lets on," Frank thought to himself. "We'll have to watch him very closely."

The three boys crossed the Hammerley farm between plowed fields and reached a barbed wire fence where the pasture began. Next to the gate stood a pen made of heavy boards. A gigantic bull in the pen glared furiously at them, pawed the earth, bellowed loudly, and rattled the boards by banging its horns against them.

"I'm glad he's not loose," Chet said fervently.

"So am I," Joe agreed.

The boys walked through the gate into the pasture. The big maple on the other side gave them their bearings, and they walked toward it at a rapid pace. Beyond it, the broad expanse of fields and meadows was broken only by an occasional tree or shrub.

Chet brought up the subject of Crow Morven. "We're not his favorite people," he observed. "Maybe he gave us a bum steer about walking to Juniper Field. You think we should go back and take the car?"

"No way." Frank grinned at the hopeful tone in Chet's voice. "We go by leg-mobile."

"Morven has no reason to give us a bum steer," Joe affirmed. "We'd find out how to get there anyway, and we'd know he was lying. He wouldn't want that to happen. Not if he's up to something."

"I sure wish somebody would come along and give us a lift." Chet sighed.

They were about in the middle of the pasture when suddenly the earth seemed to shake behind them. They heard the pounding of hooves in their direction.

Whirling around, they were appalled to see that the bull was out of its pen and dashing toward them. Its eyes were fiery with rage, and steam spouted from its nostrils. It shook its horns savagely as it hurtled forward at terrific speed!

Chet had moved a little to one side during the walk. The bull singled him out and headed straight toward him. Chet turned to run but stumbled and fell. The bull, lowering its horns, lunged forward to gore him!

8

Disguise and Alias?

In a flash, Frank took off his rust-colored shirt and draped it to one side like a bullfighter's cape. He caught the attention of the enraged beast, and it charged the shirt, stomping past Chet, missing him by a hairsbreadth. Frank moved the shirt farther away from his friend, and again the bull went for it in a violent attack.

As the Hardy boy maneuvered the bull into following the shirt, Chet scrambled to his feet. He ran to a nearby tree, climbed into it, and peered frantically through the branches.

Frank continued to play the role of matador with a cape. Stepping backward, he shifted the shirt from one position to another, each time goading the bull into another charge. Slowly but surely the boy guided the animal back to its pen. Its final charge sent it careening through the gate. Joe, who had followed his brother, locked the bull in with a shout of relief.

"You should have been a bullfighter, Frank," he said.

"No thanks. I don't want to be anywhere around if that brute escapes again."

Joe tried to secure the lock of the pen but found that the latch refused to stay in place. "The screw's loose!" he exclaimed. "Won't hold the gate closed properly. Somebody did it deliberately. I wonder if Crow Morven's responsible for the bull getting out?"

"He might have set us up when he told us to go through the pasture," Frank said. "Then he unscrewed the latch after he left the house. But we have no proof."

Joe took a small, multipurpose screwdriver out of his pocket and tightened the screw on the latch, while Frank examined his shirt. Finding nothing worse than a tear at the bottom where the bull had gored it, he put the shirt back on and they rejoined Chet, who was still up in the tree.

"Is it safe to come down?" he asked apprehensively.

"Sure it is," Frank said, and the three resumed their walk across the pasture. Near the tall maple

462

they found a gate, went through, and saw the path leading into the woods. Recognizing the two boulders Morven had mentioned, they continued on. A small plane zoomed low overhead and vanished beyond the treetops. They heard the sound of motors revving up, and when they reached the end of the woods, they were on the outskirts of the airport.

The plane they had seen was taxiing to a stop in front of the control tower. Another one was swinging around for a thrust down the runway into take-off. A number of small craft were parked around the perimeter of the airfield.

A single helicopter stood behind the control tower. It bore the painted legend JF333 on its side.

"That's our chopper," Joe said. "The one we saw grab the *Flashing Arrow!*"

"Let's check it out," Chet suggested, walking toward the helicopter.

Frank restrained him. "Not yet. We'll have to get an okay at the office first. Otherwise it might be the lockup for us if the owner blows the whistle."

At the office, Frank asked the clerk who owned the helicopter.

"We do," was the answer. "Juniper Field. The chopper's for hire."

"Was it rented recently?"

"Just last night. Why the questions?"

To avert suspicion, Frank said, "We might want

463

to take it out. Mind if we have a look?"

"Be my guest," the clerk offered.

"Can you tell us who hired the helicopter last night?" Joe queried casually.

"A tall man wearing a black beard and dark glasses." The clerk consulted his register. "His name is John Jones according to his flying license. He landed back here, paid his fee, and left."

When the boys were outside the office again, Frank remarked, "Sounds like a disguise, and the name has to be an alias, too!"

"Well, he couldn't have been Crow Morven," Chet pointed out. "Morven was on the ground when the chopper came over."

The helicopter was a small model with a single set of rotary blades. The cockpit, protected by wraparound unbreakable glass that allowed a view from side to side as well as in front, had seats at the instrument panel for pilot and copilot. A compartment in the rear permitted a passenger to be squeezed in.

The rear compartment also held the winch, a spinning drum worked by hydraulic controls. The tail of the helicopter formed a mesh of metal struts, designed to give balance in the air. The landing gear terminate in three wheels, two up ahead and one behind.

The craft showed signs of use the previous night. There were oil stains on the fuselage beneath the blades and the wheels were caked with mud.

"There must have been two guys last night," Frank observed. "The pilot and a man to work the winch."

Chet climbed into the back seat and began to spin the winch. "No cable or grappling iron in here," he informed Frank and Joe, who had gotten into the front. "They must have taken them away."

"Along with the *Flashing Arrow*," Joe said morosely.

The Hardys, who were experienced pilots, examined the instrument panel. "I wish we could go for a spin," Frank said. "I'll bet this whirlybird works like a charm."

"We saw that last night," Joe reminded him. "The pilot could have landed in our laps if he'd wanted to. I hope he left his calling card in here."

They spent half an hour searching the craft for a clue, but all they found were pamphlets on such things as flying rules, airport regulations, and maintenance instructions for the helicopter.

"No luck," Frank said disgustedly. "Let's get out of here." As he turned, he brushed against the front seats, sweeping a folded piece of paper onto the floor of the cockpit. A flash of red caught Joe's eye. He picked up the paper and was astounded to see a hex sign!

Someone had drawn in colored ink the red pentagram in a white square inside a black circle. The three boys looked in fascination at the mystic symbol.

"That's Mr. Hammerley's hex!" Chet burst out.

"Is there anything on the other side?" Frank asked.

Joe turned the paper over. It said in large printed letters: CHESAPEAKE CROSSING. Apart from that, the paper was blank.

Chet scratched his head. "I never heard of Chesapeake Crossing. Is it a town?"

"Yes, on Chesapeake Bay," Joe replied.

The boys descended from the helicopter, and, returning to the office, they told the clerk they were not going to hire the helicopter after all. Then they headed for the police station of the nearby town to ask about the stolen weather vanes.

The sergeant on duty said, "We haven't had a break in the case yet."

"Are there no clues at all?" Frank asked.

"The only thing we heard from an informer is that there's a fence for stolen weather vanes in the Chesapeake area of Maryland."

The boys stared in amazement but did not reveal their clue.

"Our informer doesn't know where the fence is," the sergeant went on, "but the Maryland police are checking on it. That's all I can tell you."

Outside headquarters, Joe commented, "Looks

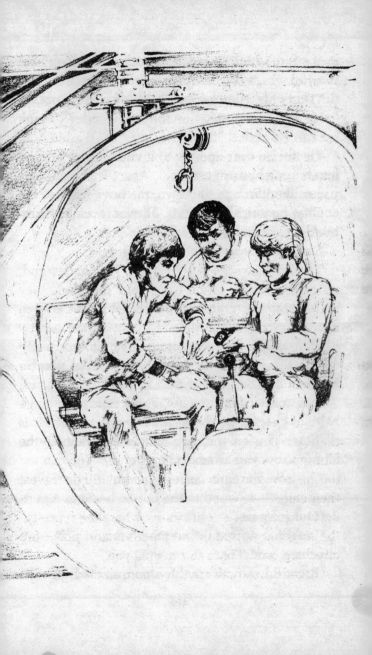

as if we'd better go to Chesapeake Crossing. That may be where the *Flashing Arrow* is, along with all the other weather vanes that disappeared around here."

Frank nodded. "Besides, Dad's in Washington. We'll still be near enough to give him a hand if he needs us on his spy case."

Strolling through the town, the boys came to the county historical museum. It was a single-story building with wings on either side.

A sign on the front door proclaimed:

WEATHER VANE EXHIBITION

"Let's go in," Frank proposed. "It might give us an idea."

They were the only visitors. The curator came out of his office. He was a plump, jolly man in white ducks, white shirt, and horn-rimmed glasses, who introduced himself as Gaspard Clay. He had a habit of clearing his throat as he spoke.

"Since you are the only ones here today, ahem, let me show you around," he offered. "You can see the whole museum, except, ahem, for the west wing, which is closed to the public because it's undergoing repairs."

"We'd like to see the weather vane exhibit," Joe informed him.

"Right this way. It's in the, ahem, east wing."

About a hundred weather vanes lined the walls of a large room or stood mounted on a long table. There were all sizes and shapes, some of wood, others of metal. Many portrayed animals, others formed stars, crescent moons, or sunbursts.

Clay bustled around discoursing volubly on the importance of weather vanes. "In the days before radio and television, ahem, farmers depended on them to tell which way the wind was blowing. Then they could judge whether rain was coming. Of course," he added with a smile, "weather vanes could not make long-range forecasts. But they were useful in foretelling the day's weather."

Before the boys left the exhibit, Joe mentioned their robbery case. "Mr. Clay, do you know anything about the stolen weather vanes?"

"Of course I know. I keep track of every weather vane in the county. Some of the pieces I remember best are gone."

"But you have no idea who took them?"

"None. I suppose you have heard about, ahem, the *Galloping Rider?* It's terrible to think of it being stolen."

"Yes," Frank agreed. "We're investigating that theft and the others."

"We saw the *Galloping Rider* at an auction!" Chet piped up and told about the incident.

"Well, I hope you have better luck the next time,"

said Gaspard Clay. "The man who took it ought to be in jail. If anyone tries to palm the *Galloping Rider* off on the museum, ahem, I'll let you know."

"You can reach us at the Hammerley farm," Joe said.

"Ah yes, the barn with the *Flashing Arrow*. It's a beautiful and very valuable antique."

"It was heisted last night!" Chet blurted.

Clay shook his head in dismay. "That's too bad. It was the masterpiece of all weather vanes in the county."

"Does Chesapeake Crossing mean anything to you?" Joe spoke up.

The curator smiled. "It sure does!" he boomed.

9

The Suspect

Startled, the boys stared at him. They wondered if this was the breakthrough they were waiting for.

"It means the very best crabbing there is," Clay went on jovially. "I go down to Chesapeake Crossing whenever I can. From there, you have two hundred miles of bay loaded with crab."

Again the Hardys felt disappointed. Only Chet was pleased by the curator's remarks. The word *crab* gave him delicious visions of steamed crustaceans served for dinner.

"There's a marina at Chesapeake Crossing," Clay continued. "You can rent a boat and head for the coves and inlets where the crabs are. All you need is a net, ahem, to make a big catch. I usually steam some of them on the shore and bring the rest home. I have a wonderful recipe for crab if you'd like to hear it."

Chet's eyes lit up, but Frank said hastily, "Not now, Mr. Clay. We have to get back to the Hammerley farm."

Clay shook hands with the boys in a friendly fashion. "If there's anything I can do to help you solve the weather vane mystery, please let me know," he offered.

The young detectives promised to do so, then left the museum and returned to Juniper Field. From there they began the long trek back to the farm. Chet was puffing when they arrived. His face was red and his feet felt sore.

Mrs. Smith told the boys that the farmer was out in the pasture. She added that he had phoned the police about the stolen weather vane and the drugged cocoa. Two officers in a patrol car had arrived and searched the farm but left without finding any clue.

Noting that the boys were hot and tired, the housekeeper brought them a pitcher of lemonade and a plate of cookies. Gratefully the trio dug into the refreshments, when the phone rang. It was Fenton Hardy.

"What have you been doing since we talked?" Mr. Hardy asked. "Any developments in the weather vane case?"

Frank described the theft of the *Flashing Arrow* while the boys had been guarding the loft.

"Those crooks are clever," Mr. Hardy noted. "Have you been able to trace the helicopter?"

Joe explained the discovery of the chopper at Juniper Field and the paper bearing the Hammerley hex sign along with the reference to Chesapeake Crossing.

"Chesapeake Crossing!" Mr. Hardy exclaimed. "Why, that's the place where Clifford Hunter was last seen!"

"His sailboat has not been found?" Frank asked.

"No. The navy has been watching not only Chesapeake Crossing, but the entire eastern coast very closely ever since he vanished, but he has not been sighted."

"I take it the owner of the marina where he kept his boat has been questioned?" Frank suggested.

"Yes. But he could shed no light on the matter. At first nobody thought anything about Hunter's failing to return, because every now and then he made runs down Chesapeake Bay that lasted for a few days. Besides, they knew the weather was good, so there was no reason to fear he sank in a storm."

"Maybe Hunter got stranded on an island in the bay," Joe said.

"Unlikely," Mr. Hardy replied. "Hunter's an expert sailor who knows every mile of the bay. Still, the navy sent out scouting planes to look for him. They didn't find a thing. I'm on my way to Chesapeake Crossing now to investigate."

"We're on our way there, too," Frank revealed. "Let's meet and compare notes."

Their father chuckled. "Not so fast. You've got another assignment first. I want you to go to Washington. I've arranged a briefing for you at the Pentagon. Be sure you've got your I.D. cards with you."

"What do we do when we get there?" Joe questioned.

"Ask for Joseph Wickerson. He's the head of the navy department where Clifford Hunter worked. He'll give you the details about the missing document. After the briefing, go on to Chesapeake Crossing. We'll meet and see if we can crack the spy case. Maybe we'll get lucky and solve the weather vane mystery at the same time. I'll be at the Sunset Motel."

After a little more conversation, Fenton Hardy hung up. Frank and Joe started back to rejoin Chet. Through the kitchen door they spotted Mrs. Smith standing at the sink. She was holding a cocoa can in her hand.

Frank nudged Joe. "I heard Mr. Hammerley say he's keeping the cocoa locked in the pantry so no one can spike it with knockout drops," he said in an undertone.

"Mrs. Smith must have a key to the pantry he doesn't know about," Joe whispered. "Let's watch her."

Mrs. Smith turned away from the sink and walked out of the kitchen. The Hardys followed her upstairs, where she went into one of the bedrooms.

"That must be Mr. Hammerley's room," Frank murmured. "She's making his cocoa for tonight. Maybe with knockout drops in it!"

"That means Mrs. Smith is a member of the gang and that they're planning something else!"

Frank nodded soberly. Together they tiptoed up to the door and cautiously peered into the bedroom. Mrs. Smith was standing at a bedside table with her back to them. She still held the cocoa can in her hand. Breathlessly they waited for her next move, hoping to catch her red-handed in the act of spiking Hammerley's nighttime drink.

As they watched, the housekeeper leaned toward a shelf on the wall near the bed and poured water from the cocoa can into the pot of a large philodendron.

Ruefully the Hardys grinned at one another. They were about to retreat silently when Mrs. Smith turned around and saw them.

"I want to talk to you boys," she declared.

"Uh-oh," Frank thought. "Here's where we get it for spying on her."

"It's about last night," Mrs. Smith continued.

"What about it?" Joe asked.

"Well, when I brought Mr. Hammerley's cocoa here to the bedroom, I heard footsteps downstairs. They surprised me because Mr. Hammerley was in bed and the rest of the workers were gone for the night. I thought I must be hearing things, except for what I saw when I got back to the kitchen."

"What was that, Mrs. Smith?" Frank inquired eagerly.

"One of the kitchen windows was unlocked. I always lock all of them before I serve the cocoa and leave. Someone was in the kitchen while I was upstairs! I didn't think of it this morning, with all the excitement, but now I remember."

"What did you do then?" Joe asked.

"I locked the window again, checked that the house was empty, and went home."

"Well, whoever unlocked the window couldn't have drugged the cocoa, because you were already serving it," Frank pointed out.

Joe snapped his fingers. "I've got it! The person who drugged the cocoa sneaked back and unlocked the window so he could get in during the night and destroy the evidence. You sure foxed him, Mrs. Smith. He must have been ready to blow his top when he came back later and tried to get in! You saved vital evidence without knowing it!"

The housekeeper seemed pleased as she accompanied the Hardys downstairs, excited that she was taking part in one of their cases.

When Mr. Hammerley came in, he listened to their plan to go to Chesapeake Crossing. "I don't know anything about the place," he admitted. "But I don't mind where you go, as long as you get the *Flashing Arrow* back. When are you leaving?"

"Tomorrow morning," Frank replied, without adding that the boys would stop in Washington before proceeding to their destination. The young detective did not want to upset Hammerley by revealing that they were working on the spy case as well as his weather vane mystery.

"Is there anything else you'd like to know about before you go?" Hammerley inquired.

"Do you suspect anybody here at the farm as a possible accomplice of the thieves?" Frank asked.

"I don't suspect anyone working for me at the moment," Hammerley replied. "But I fired a man two weeks ago because he was loitering around the house and I caught him stealing food. I never thought he might steal my weather vane, though. His name is Ed Bryle."

"Where can we find him?" Joe wanted to know.

"I have no idea. I paid him and he left without telling me where he was going."

"Do you happen to have a photograph of him?" Frank inquired.

Hammerley nodded. He went to a desk and

withdrew a picture from a drawer, then handed it to Frank, who examined it while Joe and Chet were looking over his shoulder. Bryle was a short, wizened man dressed in farm overalls.

"That's the man we saw at the auction!" Frank gasped. "The one who grabbed the *Galloping Rider* from Joe and ran off with it!"

Just then the telephone rang. Mrs. Smith said it was another call for the Hardys.

"Must be Dad again," Frank guessed and took the receiver while Joe stood close enough to listen in.

A weird, squeaky voice warned, "Hardys, beware of the hex!"

10

Danger in the Driveway

The phone clicked off. Frank held it in his hand for a moment, puzzled. Then he hung up and turned to Joe. "Did you recognize the voice?"

Joe shook his head. "Sounded like a real weirdo. I never heard anything like it."

"Neither have I. But it seems as if the weather vane gang will stop at nothing to get rid of us!"

"Which means we'd better keep our eyes open from here on out. They might send a hit man to take us off the case—permanently."

When the boys reported the warning to Chet and Hammerley, the two were perplexed.

"I don't know anyone with the kind of voice you describe," Hammerley said. "Could it be a hoax?"

Frank shrugged. "We'll have to solve the case before we can answer that."

Next morning, Chet received a phone call from Iola. She informed him that he had been chosen to represent Bayport High in a state archery competition. Knowing how badly he wanted to compete, Frank and Joe persuaded their friend to participate.

"We'll be meeting Dad," Joe pointed out. "He'll back us up."

"Just win the honors for good old Bayport," Frank added. "You can come to Washington with us and then catch a plane home."

After breakfast, the boys went outside to their rented car, which a farmhand had brought around the driveway and parked in front of the house. They were standing beside the car talking to Hammerley, when Crow Morven drove a pickup truck to the top of an incline leading into the driveway. The foreman jumped out of the vehicle and approached the group.

Suddenly the pickup began to move. Gathering speed, it hurtled down the slope directly toward the boys!

Frank saw it and barely had time to shout a warning. Chet and Hammerley dived into the bushes bordering the driveway, while Joe, who stood closest to the pickup's path, leaped onto the vehicle and wrenched the door open. He slid behind the wheel and managed to put on the brakes.

Morven had run behind the truck and was shouting excitedly. When he reached the group, Frank glared at him. "You aimed that pickup at us!"

"I forgot to put the brake on. It wasn't intentional, believe me!" the foreman insisted. But he grinned evilly as he spoke.

Chet waved a fist under his nose. "Next time, it'll be intentional. And I mean a collision of your nose and my fist!"

Hammerley watched the heated exchange with a worried frown. "Crow, I'm sure you didn't mean to hurt anybody, but you must be more careful in the future."

"Sure, Mr. Hammerley," Morven replied and walked away.

Joe parked the vehicle, then returned to his friends. They got into their car, said good-bye to the farmer, and drove off with Joe behind the wheel. About three miles down the road they saw a horse and carriage racing toward them. Afraid of an accident, Joe pulled to the right and stopped, letting the engine idle. The horse came to a halt in a cloud of dust as the driver tugged hard on its reins. It was the same wild-eyed woman with unkempt hair blowing in the wind, who had spoken to them previously!

"It's Mad Maggie!" Frank exclaimed.

"*Ja*, Mad Maggie!" she shouted. "And my friend is with me, see?"

She lifted a birdcage from the seat beside her and held it up. A large horned owl stared at the boys from between the bars.

"Is that a witch's owl?" Joe wanted to know.

"*Ja*, it is."

"Does it talk?"

"*Ja*, it talks. Listen." Leaning over the cage, she urged the owl. "All right, my pretty one. What do you say to these boys from Bayport who have come to the Pennsylvania Dutch country?"

The owl fluttered its wings and hooted.

Chet felt an eerie sensation, as if a clammy hand gripped his shoulder. He gulped as the sound grated on his ears. "Wh-what did your friend say?" he asked.

"It said the hex is working. Ye should have gone home when Mad Maggie warned ye."

Chet glanced at Joe. "I wish he'd start the car and get us out of here before she rides off on a broomstick!" he thought to himself.

The owl gave another low hoot that choked off suddenly.

"Do ye know what that means?" Mad Maggie demanded. "It means—when the weather is stormy, your search is in vain!"

Joe was dumbfounded. Could the words *weather* and *vain* be a code referring to the weather vane mystery?

"The rider gallops, the arrow flashes!" Mad Maggie went on.

Frank stared at her. "Are you talking about the *Galloping Rider* and the *Flashing Arrow?*" he inquired.

"*Ja*, that I do. They have flown away from here. My owl says so."

"Where have they flown to? Can your owl tell us?"

Maggie leaned over and whispered something in the owl's ear, all the while keeping her eyes fixed on the boys. This time the bird made no sound. It closed its eyes and appeared to be asleep.

"The place is secret!" Mad Maggie hissed. With that, she pulled the reins of her horse and drove off.

Joe headed in the opposite direction. "You think she really knows something?" he asked.

Frank shrugged. "Apparently she's heard of the thefts. But so has everybody in the county."

"She could be the squeaky voice you heard over the phone," Chet suggested.

"It's possible," Frank conceded. "The crooks might have hired her to scare us away."

"She succeeded, as far as I'm concerned," Chet declared. "I'm glad we're getting out of here!"

They came to the place where they had seen the auction. A couple of men were folding the tent and stacking the pegs. A third was loading unsold objects into a truck.

Joshua Korbo was showing his auctioneer's license to a county official who towered a good three inches over him.

"How was business?" Joe greeted Korbo after pulling up alongside the two men.

The auctioneer pushed his steel-rimmed glasses from his nose up onto his forehead. "Very good," he snapped, "in spite of what your fat friend did to my tent!"

Insulted, Chet was about to snap back when Frank spoke up. "Have you found any sign of the weather vane, the *Galloping Rider*?"

"None. I doubt it was ever here."

"We saw it!" Chet insisted.

"That's what *you* say." Korbo shrugged, then turned to talk to one of his assistants.

"I get the feeling he doesn't want to tell us anything," Joe said and drove on.

Frank chuckled. "He's still mad at Chet for knocking over his tent."

They continued in silence for a while. Then a big black car zoomed past them. The driver was a man in a black beard and dark glasses. He fitted the description of the individual who had hired the helicopter that snatched the *Flashing Arrow!*

"This could be our suspect!" Frank cried out. "Don't lose him, Joe!"

His brother trod hard on the accelerator, and the speedometer rose to the legal limit as they sped after him. Seeing he was being followed, the black-bearded man suddenly turned onto a side road. Joe reacted just in time to make the turn himself. He had to grip the steering wheel firmly to keep it from being torn from his grasp as he jounced over rocks and potholes.

The wild pursuit led far out into the country, where the man ahead tried to shake the boys by driving down country lanes and across open fields. He kept glancing over his shoulder to see how close they were. At one point they got near enough to see sunlight glinting off his dark glasses.

"He's our man all right," Chet said. "If he had nothing to hide, why would he try to get away from us?"

Joe stuck grimly to the trail, narrowing the gap whenever he could. But another turn by the fugitive made him lose ground on a cow path. Then he had to slow down because an Amish farmer in a buggy came between the two cars. The boys saw the black beard shoot along a bumpy dirt road into the woods and disappear among the trees. Joe followed as fast as he could, whipping past country lanes and down more cow paths.

"I hope this is the right road," he grated. "If you see that big black car, tell me."

"Will do," Frank said, shading his eyes with his hand and gazing into the distance.

"I wish that guy would stick to the freeway," Chet protested. Their rotund companion was sore from being bounced up and down in the back seat.

A moment later they rounded a curve at top speed. A large black car stood in the middle of the road, blocking their passage, and they were hurtling toward it!

Twisting the steering wheel violently to one side, Joe narrowly avoided a collision. His car flipped up on two wheels, as if it were going to turn over, righted itself at the last moment, and halted joltingly in a ditch.

The next moment the door on Joe's side was wrenched open and a harsh voice snarled, "Okay, you punks! The chase is over. This is the end of the road for you!"

11

Boys in Trouble

"Get out!" the voice commanded. "Resistance will get you nowhere!"

Frank, Joe, and Chet emerged from the car and found themselves confronted by two state police officers.

"Is this your car?" the older one demanded in a stern tone.

"No, it isn't," Joe replied.

"So you stole it!" the officer accused them. "We had a tip you guys were operating in this area. Figured you'd be coming down this road and set up our block in just the right place."

"Where have you stashed the other stolen cars?" the policeman demanded. "Of course you don't have to answer. You have a right to remain silent."

"That won't be necessary," Frank said evenly. "You've got it all wrong."

"No, we've got it dead right! You're the gang that's been stealing cars all over the county. We're taking you in. The charge is grand larceny."

Interrupted by the radio in the unmarked patrol car, the policeman walked over and answered the call, while his partner kept the boys covered. When the officer returned to the group, he shook his head.

"The stolen-car gang was arrested a few minutes ago up the road," he revealed.

"Then who are these guys?" his partner wanted to know.

The boys quickly identified themselves, and the officers were impressed to learn that Frank and Joe were the sons of Fenton Hardy, who was known to lawmen throughout the nation.

"We're sorry about mistaking you for the thieves," the older officer said. "But you did come down the road lickety-split, as if you were trying to get away as fast as possible."

"Actually, we were following a suspect," Frank said. "That's why we were going at such speed."

"Are you on a case?"

Frank mentioned the stolen weather vane mystery and inquired if the officers had seen a tall man in a black beard and dark glasses driving a big black car. But the policemen had not seen the suspect.

"He must have turned off this road onto a side lane before he reached our roadblock," the younger one said. "He could be in the next county by now." He promised to let the Hardys know if they encountered the suspect, then the three boys continued their drive to Washington. They managed to pick up Route 222, which took them past Pennsylvania's Brandywine Battlefield Park and across the Susquehanna River to Route 95. When they crossed an arm of Chesapeake Bay near Baltimore, they were set on a direct course toward the Potomac River.

After driving through Maryland and down the long Baltimore-Washington Parkway, they reached their destination.

"I could use some chow," Chet suggested.

"So could I," Frank admitted.

"That makes it unanimous," Joe said with a grin and wheeled into the parking lot of a diner.

The boys went inside and sat at a table by the window, where they could watch the flow of traffic outside. After a quick meal, Frank decided to call Joseph Wickerson's office. A secretary informed him that Wickerson could see them in about two hours. Then Chet telephoned the airport and made reservations on a flight from Washington to Bayport later in the afternoon.

The three agreed to kill time by doing some sight-seeing on their way to the Pentagon. They paid the cashier and were walking toward the exit with Chet in the lead, when a glint of dark glasses reflected momentarily in the plate-glass window and then vanished.

"That's the guy we're after!" Chet exclaimed. "I'm sure of it! Come on!" He wedged himself through the revolving door, helped by pressure from Frank and Joe who were behind him. They caught a fleeting glimpse of a figure turning the corner of the diner, then a car door slammed shut in the parking area.

"I'll stop him!" Chet declared and hurried to the strip of drive leading to the street. He raised his hand as a large black car approached. The Hardys ran up to him. They had not seen the person Chet was after but assumed that he knew what he was doing.

The black car stopped in front of Chet and the driver rolled down the window. She was a pretty brunette, who now pushed her sunglasses up on her head. "Why are you stopping me?" she asked curiously.

Chet turned beet red. "I'm sorry," he stammered. "I mistook you for someone else."

He stepped aside and let the car pass. "Don't kid me," he begged the Hardys.

Frank suppressed a smile. "We won't kid you, Chet. A detective has to move fast sometimes, and mistakes do happen."

Chet recovered from his embarrassment and they returned to their car. Soon they were driving up Capitol Hill to the juncture of Pennslyvania Avenue and Independence Avenue. They passed the Library of Congress and swung around the Capitol building.

"That's where Congress holds its meetings," Chet pointed out. "I'll bet they're helping the Hardys in there right now."

"They are?" Frank raised his eyebrows.

"Crime laws!" Chet explained. "Making it easier for you to nab the bad guys."

"Thanks a lot for the compliment, Chet." Frank laughed. "But I think Congress is more interested in helping the FBI than in helping us."

"Well, there's the FBI," Joe said and pointed toward the Justice Department. "Boy, what a crime lab they have!"

The Hardys had visited the FBI lab while working for their father. They had checked fingerprints in the FBI files, tested firearms in the ballistics department, and consulted the bureau's cryptographers on the best methods of breaking codes.

"Too bad we don't have time to drop in and say

hello," Frank commented. "Maybe we will on our next trip to Washington."

"I'd like to drop in on the president," Chet declared. "I'd tell him a thing or two on how to run the country."

"Like bows and arrows for the infantry," Joe joked. "Well, we'd better be getting to the Pentagon." He swerved onto Seventeenth Street, swung around the Washington Monument, and drove down Fifteenth Street past the Tidal Basin and the Jefferson Memorial across the Potomac to the south parking area of the Pentagon.

He pulled into a public parking lot, and the boys could see the famous military building beyond hundreds of parked cars lined up in double rows. An open space with grass, trees, and driving lanes led up to the broad facade of the Pentagon on their side. They got out and the Hardys escorted Chet to a bus stop.

Their friend was downcast. "I wish I could go with you," he lamented. "I'd like to stay on the case."

"You're still on the case," Joe reassured him. "You're just taking time out to shoot some arrows in Bayport."

"And if we haven't solved the mystery by the time the archery contest is over, we'll send you an SOS," Frank added.

Chet cheered up as he climbed into the bus. He grinned at them from the window, then the vehicle pulled away to go to the airport.

Frank and Joe gazed up at the enormous five-sided building from which the secretary of defense and the Joint Chiefs of Staff ran the United States Armed Forces.

"Come on, Joe. Let's go in," Frank said.

Joe chuckled. "Maybe if we stay long enough, we'll come out three-star generals!"

12

Pentagon Briefing

From South Parking, the Hardys entered the Pentagon through the river entrance and asked for Joseph Wickerson at the information desk. The receptionist put through a call and handed the phone to Frank.

"Wickerson here," Frank heard. "I'm finishing a report for the chief of naval operations. Come up in forty-five minutes. The room is 5E600. See you then." Wickerson hung up.

Frank asked the receptionist how to get to room 5E600.

"It's on the fifth floor of ring E," she explained. "The Pentagon has five floors, and there are five rings on each floor, lettered outward from the center from A to E. For instance, 1A means the first ring of the first floor, 2B means the second ring of the second floor, and so on. So, 5E means the fifth ring of the fifth floor. When you get there, look for room 600."

With time to kill before their appointment, the Hardys strolled around the Pentagon. Joe bought a guidebook to the building at a newsstand and flipped through it.

"Each of the five sides of the Pentagon is over nine hundred feet long. That's three times the length of a football field," he told Frank.

"I'd rather carry the ball on Bayport High field," Frank responded. "You'd need a lot more blockers here to score a touchdown."

He was referring to the crowds moving through the building. Civilian employees hurried in all directions. Men and women in military uniforms were reporting for their daily assignments. The Hardys noticed high-ranking officers of the army, navy, and air force walking by rapidly and saying little.

"The big brass seem bothered by something," Joe observed.

"I'll bet they're worried about Clifford Hunter and the missing document," Frank replied. "From what Dad said, if the submarine plan is gone for good, our whole military establishment is in big trouble."

The Hardys went up to the second floor, noticing that only the stairs and escalators were available to them. The elevators were restricted to freight and other heavy cargo.

They walked along corridors decorated with pictures of military history from the Trojan War to the Thor Missile. When they passed the office of the Joint Chiefs of Staff, they saw a sign warning, "Admittance by Authorized Credentials Only."

Frank remarked, "Our I.D. cards won't get us in there. We'd be stopped by the guard." Then he looked at his wristwatch. "Our forty-five minutes are nearly up. Let's go upstairs."

Continuing to the top floor, the boys reached ring 5E. They showed their identification and were allowed to pass. When they found room 600, Frank knocked, and a moment later the door swung open.

Joseph Wickerson, a burly man with a genial smile, welcomed them into his office. A desk stood at the window, with two chairs facing it, and there was a sofa in one corner. Maps of American naval installations and pictures of naval warfare lined the walls. One picture showed the first nuclear submarine, the *Nautilus*, about to dive.

Motioning the boys into the two chairs, Wickerson sat behind his desk. He clasped his hands and looked at them with a serious expression.

"How much has your father told you about the navy's spy mystery?" he asked.

"We know a classified document belonging to the navy is missing," Joe replied.

"Also, a civilian employee has disappeared," Frank added. "A man named Clifford Hunter."

Wickerson thumped his fist on the desk. "We've got to find Cliff Hunter. That's why we want you two on the case with your father. I'll explain the spy problem in a moment. But first I'd better give you the facts about the missing document."

Wickerson pushed a button and ordered, "Tell Archie Olson to bring the MASUB plan."

While they were waiting, Wickerson gave the boys a brief explanation of MASUB. "It stands for maser submarine. My department is perfecting a new device that uses maser beams for deep-water navigation. Cliff Hunter had responsibility for the scientific research, and Archie Olson drew up the blueprints. Both worked under my supervision. Do you know the meaning of *maser?*"

Frank replied, "Microwave amplification by stimulated emission of radiation. We've been studying masers in our high-school physics lab."

"Masers are stronger radio waves," Joe recalled. "You trap atomic energy in crystals and increase the energy by hitting the crystals with atomic particles. A wave shoots out that's longer and stronger than a radio wave."

"You've stated the science in a nutshell," Wickerson complimented them. "Well, the U.S. Navy has added a wrinkle that nobody else knows about. I hope!" he added in an obvious reference to Hunter's disappearance.

"Who made the breakthrough?" Frank inquired.

"Cliff Hunter!" Wickerson boomed. "That's why we have to find him quickly. He has not only the document but also a lot of advanced nautical science in his head. A foreign power could use his knowledge of laboratory research to endanger the U.S.A."

A knock on the door brought Archie Olson on the scene. A tall, thin man with a faraway look in his eyes, he spread the blueprint of MASUB on the desk. Taking a slide rule from his pocket, he pointed to its most important features.

"The key to our breakthrough," he revealed, "is that we can link masers end on end indefinitely— around the world if we want to. It's done by a computer that tells the atomic propulsion device of a nuclear sub when to release the next maser and in what direction. The captain and crew can go to sleep for the voyage. The masers will take them to their destination automatically."

Olson showed sketches of maser-producing crystals and demonstrated the relationship between the computer and the crystals. Then he explained how a computer could be programmed to keep the masers lined up.

"Can't the masers be detected?" Joe asked.

Olson shook his head. "They're protected by a nuclear shield. Here's the blueprint for the shield. Cliff Hunter worked out the formula."

Olson paused and looked at Wickerson, clearly wondering whether he should have mentioned Hunter.

"It's all right," Wickerson advised him. "Frank and Joe know about Hunter. In fact, they're in on the search for him."

After more discussion of maser and nuclear subs, Olson left, taking the blueprint with him.

Wickerson said thoughtfully, "The missing document is the original blueprint of the maser-producing crystals and their linkage to the computer. It's marked **MASUB TOP-SECRET**. When you see those words, you'll know you've found the plan Hunter took."

"Did you suspect he was a spy?" Frank queried.

Wickerson shrugged. "No, otherwise I'd have turned him in to the Pentagon security forces. But I thought there was something fishy about him after the Cosmo Rocket episode."

"What was that?"

"The navy has a classified project on a revolutionary new type of missile for our surface fleet. It's being developed by another department, and the members of my department have to get special clearance to look at the Cosmo Rocket files. Two weeks ago I needed to examine those files, so I got clearance and went in.

"I was surprised to see Hunter at the files. I asked what he was doing there, and he said he had clearance for some work concerning the connection between the navigational systems of subs and rockets.

"Since he was one of my trusted assistants, I didn't pursue the matter—unfortunately, because I know now that his clearance was forged!"

"Did he do anything else to make you suspect him?" Joe inquired.

"Well, he seemed to be always sneaking around and poking into things that weren't his business. Looking through the papers of other scientists, things like that. But I must confess it didn't occur to me that he might be a spy."

"Do you think he stole anything else?"

Wickerson tapped his fingers on the desk. "As far as I know, nothing else is gone. I run a tight ship, and only the MASUB document is missing from my files. I daresay Hunter fled because he knew he couldn't play the same trick on me twice.

"Of course, he got away with an immensely valuable blueprint. So, perhaps he figured one theft was enough. He'll be wealthy if he sells it to a foreign power."

The Hardys inquired about the discovery that the MASUB document was missing.

Wickerson frowned. "I summoned Hunter into this office the day before the discovery to discuss some bugs in MASUB. We went over the problems and ironed them out. At the end, I put the blueprint in this desk drawer, and we agreed to carry on the discussion the following day. We left the office and I locked the door and went home.

"When I got here in the morning, the blueprint was gone. I called the lab to have Hunter report to me at once. He wasn't there. So I asked them to send Archie Olson, who told me he saw Hunter leaving my office after hours the night before. Archie thought I was in the office at the time. Actually, I was out of the building."

"Hunter must have had a key to the office, since he came back after you left," Joe inferred.

Wickerson nodded. "He wasn't supposed to, but I imagine he contrived in some underhanded way to have a duplicate made. I wouldn't put it past him. He's a clever fellow. That's why he's so dangerous."

"What did he do after leaving your office?" Joe wondered.

Wickerson slammed the table in disgust. "He simply walked out of the building as he did every evening. Only this time he was carrying the MASUB document with him. At first it didn't hit me that anything was really wrong. I thought he'd come in with a good explanation. When I couldn't find him anywhere, I realized he had fled. Then came word that he was last seen at Chelski's Marina in Chesapeake Crossing. And now you know as much as I do."

"We're going from here to Chesapeake Crossing," Frank said. "We'll try to pick up his trail from there."

"Well, I'm glad I have you boys on the case," Wickerson assured them. "After all, you're sons of Fenton Hardy, who has done vital undercover work for the Pentagon in the past. You'll do your country a great service if you find Hunter and retrieve the sub blueprint he took."

Promising they would do their best, the Hardys left Wickerson's office and descended to the concourse of the Pentagon. They passed an exhibition of navy exploration in the waters around the Antarctic continent.

Joe paused for a look. "Frank, they've got a lot of mysteries to solve down there," he said with a smile.

"Yes, but no one can waltz off with the evidence. It would be a long swim home."

They went to South Parking, where Frank started the car and headed for an exit. He was nearly there when a car flashed out of a parking slot and cut in front of him. Frank hit the brakes in an effort to prevent a collision!

13

Surprise Encounter

The car stopped with a jolt that threw Joe heavily against the dashboard. The speeding car flew out the exit and roared off toward the Potomac.

Frank stared after it. "Joe, did you see who that driver was?"

Joe flopped back in his seat and rubbed his twisted shoulder. "No. Did you?"

"I sure did. He was Archie Olson!"

Joe winced in pain. "Olson may be a whiz of a scientist, but he's a lousy driver! He nearly racked us up!"

"Maybe he did it deliberately."

Joe stared at his brother. "But why would he do a thing like that? If you hadn't hit the brakes so fast, he'd have been knocked out in the collision, too!"

"Not if he expected me to panic and pile us up against one of the parked cars," Frank pointed out. "He'd have escaped, but we'd be in the hospital."

"And off the spy case!" Joe followed his brother's theory. "In other words, he may be a suspect!"

"Sure. He might be in cahoots with Hunter! We'd better let Mr. Wickerson know about this!"

Frank went back into the Pentagon and called from a pay phone. When Wickerson answered, the young detective described the near accident in South Parking and explained why he and Joe suspected Olson.

"Archie!" Wickerson exclaimed. "I would never have thought it of him. But you can bet I'll keep an eye on him from now on. Thanks for the tip."

Frank rejoined Joe, and they drove through Washington into Maryland. Heading due east, they came to Chesapeake Crossing down Chesapeake Bay from Annapolis.

The Sunset Motel was a medium-sized establishment made up of an office and a series of cabins along the shore. The Hardys registered and received the key to the last cabin of the group. They were stashing their belongings in the closet, when the phone rang.

Fenton Hardy's voice came over urgently, "I'll see you tomorrow!" Then he hung up abruptly.

"Uh-oh," Frank said. "Dad must be in a tight spot. He couldn't talk!"

"Do you know where he called from?"

"I have no idea."

"What do you think we should do?"

Frank shrugged. "He said he'd see us tomorrow. There's no point for us to stay here now. Let's have dinner and case the town."

"Okay."

The boys stopped at the motel diner for a quick meal, then went into Chesapeake Crossing. It was a typical town on the bay, with a long dock from which they could see boats bobbing up and down in the distance beneath a blue sky and fleecy white clouds overhead. Two headlands, on either side, protected a fishing fleet riding the gentle swell of the bay. Small craft were tied to the dock or anchored just out from it—rowboats, sailboats, motorboats, and houseboats.

Chelski's Marina occupied one end of the dock. Here boats were drawn up on land for scraping, painting, and repairs. Cars and barrels of bait lined the walls of the marina. Fishing boots, tackle, and crab nets were visible through the window.

"This is where Clifford Hunter was last seen," Frank commented. "Let's check it out."

The owner of the marina was a man named Herb Chelski. As the bell on the door announced the entry of the Hardys, he looked up from a crab net he was inspecting on the counter.

"What kind of boat do you want?" he inquired. "I have boats for the bay and the deep sea, and any kind of fishing boat you can mention. Except whale fishing," he added with a laugh. "If you're after Moby Dick, forget it."

"We're not after Moby Dick," Frank told him. "We're after Clifford Hunter."

Chelski stopped laughing. "Oh, the navy guy who disappeared. I told the FBI everything I know."

"We're cooperating with the FBI," Joe stated. "We're working for the Pentagon."

The Hardys produced their credentials, which Chelski scrutinized carefully. "Okay," he said finally. "I'll tell you how it was. Hunter owns a sailboat that he keeps docked here. He rents the space by the month. I got to know him pretty well. I thought he was a nice guy. What's he done?"

"I wish we could tell you," Frank replied. "But we can't. It's top-secret navy stuff."

"I understand. Well, I was here when Cliff came for his sailboat. He surprised me because it was a weekday and he usually takes his boat out on weekends. Besides, there was something funny about him this time."

"In what way?" Joe inquired.

"He didn't seem to be himself—acted nervous, if you know what I mean. But it didn't affect his sailing. He handled the boat as expertly as ever."

"And that was the last you saw of him?" Frank wanted to know.

"Yes. When he didn't come back, I figured he was on one of his longer trips down the bay. But when the FBI started asking questions, I realized Cliff was in some kind of trouble."

"Can you give us a description of Hunter's sailboat?"

"Sure. A thirty-three footer with a sail, and a motor for emergencies. The name *Bay Queen* is painted in green letters on the stern."

"I'd like to write down his address, too," Joe said. Chelski gave it to him, then the boys left the marina and strolled down the dock.

"I can understand why Hunter was nervous," Joe commented. "I'd be nervous too if I had just stolen a top-secret document from the navy."

Frank suddenly gripped Joe's arm. "Look there!" He pointed to a small, wizened figure walking along the dock ahead of them.

"Ed Bryle!" Joe marveled. "Where did he come from?"

"He doesn't know we're here. Let's brace him."

The Hardys applied their detective training to capturing their suspect. Joe stayed on Bryle's trail to make sure they would not lose him. Frank slipped around the dock and stepped out in front of the former farmhand. Joe at the same time closed in from the rear.

Bryle started when he saw Frank. He turned as if to run, but Joe was too near for him to get away.

"Hello, Bryle!" Frank said.

"Long time no see," Joe added.

Bryle flushed red and blinked his eyes. His voice shook. "What do you guys want?"

"A few answers," Frank replied. "What are you doing in Chesapeake Crossing?"

Bryle looked sullen. "I work at the marina. You got any complaints?"

"We heard you left the Hammerley farm," Joe stated.

"So? I got a better job here. Any objections?"

"Not as long as you return the *Galloping Rider*. Remember? The weather vane you snatched at Joshua Korbo's auction."

"You must be nuts!" Bryle snarled. "I wasn't at no auction."

"Come on, Bryle, we saw you!" Frank said. "You probably stole the *Galloping Rider* and hid it at the auction when Korbo wasn't looking. Then you came back to sneak it out during the bidding."

"And you only got away with it because the tent collapsed," Joe noted. "Otherwise we'd have collared you and returned the *Galloping Rider* to its owner. What have you done with it?"

"You can't prove a thing!" Bryle jeered. "Now let me go!"

Realizing he was right, the Hardys shrugged and Bryle smirked as he ambled down the dock.

"Too bad we can't blow the whistle on him," Frank said. "But we can always find him at the marina if we get any evidence against him that'll stand up."

The boys wandered around some more, then decided to take a boat out into the bay. Retracing their steps to the marina, they rented an outboard from Herb Chelski. They questioned him about Ed Bryle, and he said that Bryle was responsible for cleaning boats that had been rented and returned.

"Ed also brings boats to the dock when they're called for. He left one outboard tied to the dock. You can have it. Here are the keys."

Joe took the tiller as he and Frank chugged away from the dock and gained speed into Chesapeake Bay. Both were experienced sailors. They had their own motorboat back in Bayport called the *Sleuth*, which they cruised on Barmet Bay.

When they reached open water, they heard a roaring sound in the distance. The sound grew louder as it approached. A line of boats raced past, circled around a buoy, and zoomed up the other side.

"It's a race!" Frank shouted over the roar of

the motors. "I wish we had the *Sleuth* here to participate."

The last boat in the competition cut out too wide from the course and headed directly at them. Its propellers were low in the water, and its hull slapped the waves as it came. A youth about their age clung to the tiller, struggling to keep his boat on course. A couple of girls were perched on the seat watching him.

"I hope he has his boat under control!" said Joe.

"He doesn't," Frank warned. "Get ready for a maneuver to port!"

The other craft was almost upon them. Joe threw his weight against the tiller in a violent swing to the right. His outboard barely cleared the other boat as the girls giggled and waved at the Hardys. Spray deluged Frank and Joe, who heard the boy yell, "Sorry!" as he careened past them toward the buoy.

"Why don't you learn how to handle a boat!" Frank muttered, wiping the water from his eyes.

As dusk was falling, the brothers returned their boat to the marina and went back to their motel cabin. Half an hour later they heard a series of soft taps on the door. Frank positioned himself next to it against the wall, while Joe reluctantly turned the lock.

A man in ragged clothing, a scraggly beard, and bright red hair pushed past him into the room!

14

The Time Bomb

Frank grabbed the strange intruder around the shoulders as Joe kicked the door shut.

"Hold it!" said a familiar voice. "No need to be physical. But you could offer me a chair instead!"

"Dad!" the boys exclaimed in unison.

"Sh! Keep your voices down."

Frank looked puzzled. "You said you'd be here tomorrow."

"I had to say that in case the phone in this cabin is tapped. If someone listened in, he'll try to trap me tomorrow, and by that time I'll be gone."

"What's up?" Joe inquired.

"Joseph Wickerson relayed a warning from the FBI that foreign agents are on my trail. That's why I'm using this disguise and barged in on you without warning. Now fill me in on the Hammerley weather vane case."

The boys described their experiences at the farm, at Juniper Field, and in the town. They mentioned the weird, squeaky voice that threatened them over the phone, and told about encountering Ed Bryle, first at the auction, then in Chesapeake Crossing.

Frank concluded, "We haven't found a clue to connect Chesapeake Crossing and the paper with the Hammerley hex sign we discovered in the chopper at Juniper Field."

"Perhaps you should put the weather vanes on the back burner for the time being," Mr. Hardy said thoughtfully. "I could use you on the Pentagon spy mystery. I suppose Wickerson brought you up to date on the facts?"

"Yes," Frank said and told his father about their suspicion of Archie Olson.

Mr. Hardy stroked his chin quizzically. "I checked Olson out," he said, "and he came up clean. Of course, I may have missed a piece of incriminating evidence. Anyway, if Wickerson has him under surveillance, he won't be able to do any more damage."

He stood up and paced about the room. "Clifford Hunter is our real problem. To begin with, he hasn't left the country with the navy document. The CIA is quite certain, because if the foreign power involved had received the sub plan, it would have taken certain measures, like jamming our maser beams, for instance. Our monitoring devices show this hasn't been done.

"The danger is that Hunter might get out of the country at any time. The airports and shipping lines are being watched, and our government has special patrols on duty along the borders. So Hunter is probably lying low until the heat's off."

Frank spoke up. "Since he was last seen in Chesapeake Crossing, perhaps he's hiding not far from here. The bay's a great place to disappear. Lots of coves and inlets where a crook could hole up and nobody'd be the wiser."

Fenton Hardy nodded. "My thoughts exactly. Chesapeake Bay is so big, even the navy and the FBI haven't been able to look everywhere between Baltimore in the north and Norfolk in the south. My hunch is that Hunter hasn't gone any farther."

"So what's our next step?" Joe asked.

"I'll investigate by land to the south of Chesapeake Crossing while you two cruise in a power-boat along the shore. If we don't see any sign of Hunter or his sailboat, we'll try the north side."

"Good idea. When do we start?"

"Tomorrow morning. You know what the sail-boat looks like. Here's a picture of Hunter."

He handed over a photograph. It portrayed a youngish man with brown hair and eyes and a moody expression. Frank and Joe examined it closely, then Frank slipped it into his pocket.

"We got Hunter's address from Mr. Chelski," Joe said. "Do you think it would be worthwhile to question the neighbors?"

"I've done that already. And the government has searched his apartment thoroughly and contacted practically everyone he knew. All we came up with is that he was known to be a nice guy, who liked to read and sail. No suspicious traits or acquaintances. That's what makes this case so difficult."

Mr. Hardy stood up. "I'll keep in touch with you through this motel. And now I'd better leave, but I don't want to use the door. Someone may be watching it."

He went to an open window at the back of the room, climbed quickly and silently over the sill, and dropped to the ground. Seconds later he had vanished amid the shrubbery into the darkness of the night.

Early the next morning, Frank and Joe walked back to Chelski's Marina, where they found Herb Chelski going over his list of customers for the day.

"We'd like to hire a powerboat," Frank said.

"I've got just what you want," Chelski replied and went to the door. "Ed, bring the small cabin cruiser up to the landing. It's for Frank and Joe

Hardy." He turned back to the boys. "Go on down. I'll be there in a few minutes."

At the landing the boys saw a sleek powerboat approaching. Ed Bryle was at the wheel. Putting the motor in idle, he jumped onto the dock with a rope in his hand.

"Okay, fellows," he said in a friendly manner. "The boat's all yours."

Frank and Joe got in and Bryle tossed the rope onto the deck. Then he pushed the hull away from the landing. Frank shifted into gear and the boat moved off.

"What's come over Bryle?" he wondered. "He's so friendly all of a sudden."

"Probably didn't want his boss to know that we've met before and under what circumstances," Joe guessed.

They rounded one of the Chesapeake Crossing headlands and cruised along the shore, which was indented by coves and inlets, some small enough to be inspected from deep water, others requiring a closer approach.

Joe sighed. "This is like looking for a needle in a haystack," he said, trying to shield his eyes from the burning sun.

"Or a flounder in Chesapeake Bay," Frank added. "Boy, it's getting hot!"

They came to an inlet so protected by underbrush and overhanging trees that the interior could not be viewed from their boat. "That would be a good place to hide," Frank observed. "Let's go in."

He steered his craft into the inlet. Birds rose in raucous protest at the sound of their engine, but otherwise there was no sign of life. The inlet extended for a few hundred yards, then, reaching the end, Frank turned back for the open bay.

They scouted inlet after inlet, eating the sandwiches Joe had brought in lieu of breakfast without ever taking their eyes off the coastline. Finally something caught Joe's eye on the way out of a small cove. Leaning over the side of their boat, he plucked a life preserver from the water, inspected it, and cried out, "Frank! Look at this!" He pointed at the faded words on the side of the life preserver: *Bay Queen*. "This is from Hunter's sailboat. He's been here, and maybe he still is!"

They scouted all around the small cove but found no trace of the fugitive.

"The life preserver might have floated in here from somewhere else," Frank noted. "Let's go on farther down the bay."

Leaving the cove, they continued south. A sailboat moved across their bow in the distance. It was about thirty feet long, with a red band along the waterline. As it turned, Joe saw the word *Queen* in green letters on the stern.

"It's the *Bay Queen!*" he shouted.

Frank swerved toward the sailboat and gained speed. They closed in rapidly. A man glared at them from the deck. "What are you trying to do," he shouted, "cause an accident?"

"I'll call the Coast Guard," Joe offered.

"Wait a minute," Frank said. They had reached the stern of the craft and shot beyond it. He looked back and read the full name of the sailboat: *Chesapeake Queen*.

"I don't think the Coast Guard would have been interested in her," he pointed out with a chuckle. Crestfallen, his brother agreed.

After another hour, the boys began to feel hungry again. Joe took a fishing rod from a closet in the cabin, dropped a line in the water, and within minutes landed a mess of Chesapeake Bay perch. A stove in the small galley enabled him to fry his catch, and they found fresh bottled water to drink with their fish.

Then Joe took the wheel while Frank cleaned up the galley. They paused for an inspection of an inlet whenever the possibilities appeared good. But their quest was in vain. Glumly, Frank stared at their wake as they chugged along doggedly. Suddenly he called out, "Hey, Joe! I think we missed a cove. The entrance is almost hidden, but I just caught a glimpse of it."

Joe went into reverse and they came to a deep sandy cove with a mouth almost too narrow for their motorboat to pass through. Shrubs and large rocks all but hid the inlet from view.

"Better shut the engine off and drift in," Frank advised. "Otherwise we might hit those rocks."

Joe cut the motor and both boys grabbed paddles. Slowly and carefully they made their way through the narrow mouth of the cove. On the other side, amid the surrounding foliage, they could make out the dim shape of a sailboat rocking in the waves some distance away.

"That could be the *Bay Queen!*" Frank said excitedly. "Joe, get the binoculars!"

The younger Hardy produced a pair from a locker and focused on the sailboat. "We'll have to go in for a close-up," he decided. "I can't read anything from here."

He handed the glasses to Frank, who took a quick look and confirmed Joe's opinion. "But I don't want to pile us up on those rocks," he said. "The whole cove is full of them."

They were discussing the best way of maneuvering their powerboat, when the silence of the inlet was broken by an intermittent sound like that of a clock. Immersed in their problem of navigating into the cove, the boys at first had not noticed the ticking.

"Frank—what *is* that?" Joe stared at his brother in puzzlement. "Sounds like a clock. With the engine running, we didn't hear it before."

He stared at the dashboard, but the sound came from the engine compartment. Suddenly the truth hit both boys at the same time.

"There's a time bomb on board!" Frank yelled. "And it may go off any second!"

15

The Bay Queen

The Hardys dived over the side of the cabin cruiser simultaneously. Plunging into the water, they swam beneath the surface for several yards, then rose as their lungs began to pound for air. They moved away from the powerboat as fast as they could.

Only seconds later, the time bomb exploded! With a deafening sound, it tore their craft apart. Fragments arched high into the air and fell back into the water. Heavy bits of wood and metal splashed near Frank and Joe, who turned to see the results of the shattering explosion.

Soon there was only an oil slick where the powerboat had been. Life jackets and seat cushions floated on the surface next to fishing rods, floppy straw hats, and splinters from the hull.

Unharmed by the flying debris, Frank began to tread water. "Are you okay?" he called to Joe.

"I banged my knee when I went over the side, but it's just a bruise."

Together they swam to the rocks and clambered out of the water. They lay there, panting heavily, until their strength returned.

"Good thing we switched the engine off," Joe said. "Otherwise we wouldn't have heard the ticking of the clock!"

"Ed Bryle must have planted that time bomb," Frank said grimly. "He's the only one with a motive. He could have done it when he was getting the boat ready for us!"

"That's why he was so friendly," Joe added. "He thought we were headed for the bottom of the bay. We'll fix his wagon when we get back to Chesapeake Crossing!"

They sat up and looked around the cove. The sailboat was clearly visible now. It had swung around in the tide, and the words *Bay Queen* were written in large letters on the stern. However, there was no sign of anyone aboard.

Frank and Joe rose to their feet and stepped carefully toward the shore from rock to rock. Jumping into the sand, they circled around the cove through the underbrush, maneuvering as silently as possible because they could not be sure Hunter was not around. On the edge of the beach, they parted the tall grass and peered through at the *Bay Queen*.

The sailboat rode freely in the water. It was neither anchored nor tied to a tree to keep it from drifting off. Its sail was still up, and a wind off Chesapeake Bay made the craft rock from side to side.

"She wasn't sailed in here," Frank whispered. "I'll bet she drifted in from the bay!"

"Let's split up and approach from different directions anyway," Joe cautioned. "We don't want to take any chances."

Frank nooded and they cautiously moved out of the underbrush across the sand and waded through the water to opposite ends of the sailboat.

Frank climbed aboard at the bow, Joe at the stern. Quietly they descended the steps into the cabin. Both were ready for action if Hunter happened to be there, but they found the cabin empty.

Searching for clues, they discovered the ownership papers in a drawer under the front window. They were made out in the name of Clifford Hunter.

"That makes it official," Joe said.

"But it doesn't tell us where Hunter is," Frank replied. "Keep going!"

A few minutes later, the younger Hardy pointed to a wooden seat under a side porthole. "Look at this!" he said. Scratched in crude, scrawling letters in the paint of the seat were the words "Barren Island."

"Any idea what it means?" Frank asked.

"No. Maybe it's an island in Chesapeake Bay."

"We'd better check. But first we'll have to get this sailboat back to town so the FBI can go over it."

"Right. But how about drying out a little first? I feel clammy."

Frank and Joe went up on deck and sat in the sun until their clothes felt comfortable, when suddenly they heard the putt-putting of a motorboat beyond the trees. Then the boat stopped and an anchor splashed into the water.

The Hardys could not see who was in the craft, but they prepared to conceal themselves in case it was Clifford Hunter returning for his sailboat. Before they could move, they heard a loud splashing not far from the rocks. A tenor voice began to sing a rousing sea chantey.

"That can't be Hunter," Joe murmured. "Wherever he is, he'd hardly draw attention to himself."

"Right. But let's see who it is, anyway."

They jumped from the sailboat onto the sand and retraced their steps stealthily through the woods back to the rocks. A large boulder gave them cover from which to look down into the water. They saw the anchored motorboat with a man wading near it.

"Gaspard Clay!" Frank exclaimed in astonishment. The curator of the county historical museum, dressed in white nautical garb, wore a broad straw hat that flopped down over his ears. Protected by hip boots, he stepped through the water with a crab net drawn back across his shoulder like a baseball bat. He sang so loudly that it seemed deafening to the Hardys at such close range.

Every so often Clay swung his net down and drew it up leaking water and sand. If he had caught a crab, he dumped it into a large pot in his motorboat. Frank and Joe could not help laughing at the sight of Gaspard Clay out after crab.

"No point in hiding from him," Joe said.

Frank nodded. "But let's not tell him anything. He'll talk, and everyone in Chesapeake Crossing will know we're on the spy case. I'd prefer he not see the *Bay Queen*, either."

"Right."

The boys left the cover of the boulder and walked down onto the beach. Clay smiled when he saw them.

"This is quite a surprise," he declared. "How, ahem, do you boys happen to be here?"

"We took your advice," Joe said. "Went sailing on the bay. How's the crabbing?"

"Excellent! As I told you, best there is! I had a day off at the museum, so I came down here." As he spoke, he produced two more crab nets from his boat. "Will you boys join me?"

The Hardys exchanged glances. It would be one way to keep Clay from discovering the *Bay Queen*. Besides, they enjoyed crabbing, something they often did at home in Barmet Bay.

Taking off their shoes and socks and rolling up their pants legs, they each took a net from Clay and accompanied him through the water along the shoreline. They made sure to take a direction away from the cove where the sailboat lay. Clay offered no objection because the crabs were abundant everywhere.

"Ouch!" Frank exclaimed suddenly.

"Is something, ahem, the matter?" Clay inquired.

In reply, Frank lifted his foot clear of the water and revealed a crab clinging to his big toe. Gingerly he released his toe and tossed the offending crustacean into the pot.

"That's a smart way to catch a crab!" Joe kidded his brother.

Frank grimaced. "All right, wise guy. I didn't expect any sympathy!"

Clay finally decided their catch was big enough. "You boys caught some of the crabs," he said. "How about helping me, ahem, dispose of some? Eat them, I mean."

"That sounds great!" Joe said. "Too bad Chet isn't here."

They started for shore and Clay transferred a number of crabs from his big pot to a smaller one. Then he led the way to the beach. Frank and Joe gathered driftwood for a fire, and soon the water in the pot began to boil. Clay cooked the crabs, and the three had a hearty dinner sitting on the sand.

Afterward, Clay told them he had to return to Chesapeake Crossing. "I'm due, ahem, in the museum tomorrow. Want a ride to the marina? There's room for three in my motorboat."

"No thanks," Frank said casually. "We're moored farther south."

Clay nodded, caroled another chantey, and chugged off with a smile and a wave of his hand.

Frank and Joe returned to the *Bay Queen*. After thoroughly inspecting it, they decided it was seaworthy. Using the motor, Frank backed the sailboat away from the sand, turned it around, and guided it between the rocks out into Chesapeake Bay. A wind was rising.

"Let's try the sail," Joe suggested. "This wind'll give us as much speed as the motor."

Frank cut off the power while Joe took control of the sail, and they swiftly scudded over the waves. Later they changed places, with Frank guiding the sailboat through the wind and spray of the bay.

At last Chesapeake Crossing appeared over their bow. Frank edged the *Bay Queen* up to the landing of Chelski's Marina, and Joe leaped ashore with one end of a rope, which he looped around a stanchion to hold the boat in place.

Then they went to find Herb Chelski. He was in his office.

"I'm afraid your powerboat is gone," Frank said.

"If you hit a rock and the boat sank, you'll have to pay for it!" Chelski growled.

"It didn't sink. It went up in the air."

"Come again?"

"It had a time bomb aboard and almost killed us!" Joe declared. "We escaped just before it went off."

"What!" Chelski stared at him in disbelief.

"We think Ed Bryle planted the bomb," Frank added. "You see, we know he stole a valuable antique in Pennsylvania Dutch country and he wanted us out of the way."

"We'd like to talk to him," Joe added.

"Ed isn't here anymore!" Chelski exploded. "He quit his job just after you two left this morning." He looked greatly disturbed and ran his fingers through his hair in agitation. "Look, fellows, I'm awfully sorry. I'll have Ed Bryle prosecuted for attempted murder if he turns up again. But I hope you realize I had nothing to do with it—"

"Don't worry, Mr. Chelski," Frank assured him. "We know you didn't. But you must understand that we can't be responsible for the boat under the circumstances, either."

"Of course." Chelski seemed relieved.

"We found Clifford Hunter's sailboat," Joe said, changing the subject. "It was in a cove down Chesapeake Bay."

"You're kidding! You mean Cliff came back with you?"

Joe shook his head. "No. We have no idea where he is. The boat was abandoned. We tied it to your dock. Can you make sure it's kept as is until the FBI checks it out?"

"Sure," Chelski promised. "I won't let anyone touch it."

The Hardys said good-bye to the marina owner and returned to the Sunset Motel, where the desk clerk handed them a small package, about four by six inches and rather flat.

"I don't know who delivered it," he said. "I was away from the desk showing a guest to his room. When I got back, this package was here with your names on it."

Joe picked it up. It was lightweight. "Thanks," he said, and the boys went to their cabin. Frank immediately called the FBI in Washington. When he mentioned Clifford Hunter's name, he was shifted by intercom to the office of the director, who listened with intense interest to the story of the *Bay Queen*.

"You boys have done great work," he praised

them. "This is the first real break we've had on the case. An FBI agent will leave Washington for Chesapeake Crossing at once."

While Frank was making the phone call, Joe unwrapped the package. It was a cassette!

"There's a player in the lobby," Frank said after he hung up. "Let's try it."

The boys went to the machine that stood in one corner of the room. No one was there. Frank turned the player on after slipping the cassette into place.

Seconds went by, and they heard nothing but the slight rustling of the spool revolving.

"Nothing on it," Joe said finally.

"Must be a hoax," Frank agreed. He was about to remove the cassette when the silence was broken.

"Hardys, the hex is on you!" squealed the strange voice that had threatened them before. "Get off the case or you'll be playing tag with the crabs at the bottom of the bay!"

16

Barren Island Hideout

Startled, the boys let the tape continue in case there was more to the threat. However, the tape finished playing in silence. Frank turned the cassette over. The other side was blank, too. He took the tape out of the player and put it in his pocket. "Whoever this weirdo is," he said, "he's warning us off the case. I just wonder which one he means, the Pentagon spy case or the weather vane mystery?"

"Must be the weather vane investigation," Joe said. " He threatened us once before when we were still at Hammerley's to beware of the hex. At that time we weren't even working on the Pentagon spy mystery."

"Which means he trailed us here all the way from Pennsylvania Dutch country," Frank concluded. "We'd better make sure he doesn't follow us to Barren Island, or he might interfere with our work for Dad!"

"Right. That's our next project. Let's get a map and see if we can find the place."

Frank bought a nautical chart of Chesapeake Bay, then they went to their cabin. The phone rang as they walked in the door. The caller was their father, who asked them to go to a public booth and call him back so they could talk without being overheard by a potential wiretapper.

Frank and Joe went to the nearest diner and were soon speaking to the detective, telling him the news. When he heard about their discovery of Clifford Hunter's sailboat, he was elated.

"This gives us something to go on!" he exclaimed. "And it shows my theory was right about Hunter staying in this area. I'll keep looking for him on land; you follow up the Barren Island angle. It's near the Eastern Shore of Maryland."

Then he hung up and the boys returned to their room. They consulted their chart of Chesapeake Bay. Finding that Barren Island lay nearly opposite the mouth of the Potomac River, they plotted the best course from Chesapeake Crossing.

In the morning they rented another powerboat from Herb Chelski at the marina. They made sure no one was following them, then cruised to Barren Island. Edging up to the beach, they tied their boat to a small bush half hidden in the sand and went ashore.

The island was about a mile across. Sand and scrub vegetation met their eyes wherever they looked.

"Barren Island is the right name for this place. Who'd want to live here?" Joe said.

Frank pointed to a building on the opposite shore. "Somebody does. Even though it's hidden by those bushes, it looks like a big house. Let's check it out."

The boys rounded the island and pulled into a derelict wharf. The pilings that once formed steps leading up from the water had slipped into a jumbled heap. Climbing to the top, the Hardys found a walk made up of broken flagstones with weeds growing between them.

The house was in ramshackle condition. The windows were boarded up and shingles from the roof littered the ground. Most of the porch railings were broken, and birds nested in the chimney.

"I guess I was wrong," Frank said. "Nobody lives here. Looks as if the owners just sailed away and left the house to fall down."

Joe tried the front door. "It's locked," he said. Circling the house they found the back door locked as well. Joe scratched his head. "What do we do now? Break a window?"

"Let's check the cellar door first," Frank suggested, and they went to the wooden doors covering the entrance to the basement. Frank lifted one. It rose on creaking hinges and hung partway open. "It's too rusty to lie flat," he said. Descending the stone steps, he tried the handle to the cellar door. "It's open," he called in a muted tone to his brother. "Come on."

The boys went into the basement. It was clothed in semidarkness because the boarded windows let in only a few rays of light. A musty smell greeted them, the result of the house being boarded up for years. Water oozed through cracks in the foundation and lay in puddles on the flagstones of the floor.

"Nice home for rats!" Joe muttered as a rodent scurried out from underfoot.

The boys scouted through the cellar, poking around piles of torn fishnet, broken oars, and clamshells. "Look at this!" Frank said with a low chuckle. He held up a bow and arrow. "Chet should be here."

Joe grinned. "He'd try crabbing with it!"

Frank tossed the bow and arrow aside, and they went deeper into the cellar until they came to a second room in the back, where a flight of stairs led to the first floor. They could make out a number of barrels in the semidarkness.

Joe squatted on his heels. "Flour, sugar, salt," he read in large letters on the barrels. "This must have been the storage room. The other—"

A loud noise at the cellar door brought him to his feet. "Somebody's at the rear door!" he cried.

In a flash, both boys raced back through the basement toward the steps leading outside. The wooden doors were back in place over their heads!

"We're locked in!" Joe gasped.

Frank pressed his hand against one door and breathed a sigh of relief. "It's open," he said. "The wind must have closed it."

"Thank goodness!" Joe blurted out. "I really got scared for a minute."

"Me too!"

They returned to the cellar and Joe stopped at the stack of fishing rods. "Hey, Frank! I don't see the bow and arrow anymore. You think someone took them?"

Frank shook his head. "I tossed them aside and they probably got stuck in those nets. It's too dark to look for them. We've got to go through the rest of the house, so let's not waste time."

Passing through the cellar, they reached the stairs and went up to the first floor. The kitchen was large with an old-fashioned wood-burning stove. Kindling protruded from the top of a barrel next to it, and there were fragments of broken dishes on the counter.

"Do you figure anyone's been cooking on the stove lately?" Frank asked.

Joe drew a line through the dust between two burners. "Not since the year one." He lifted a heavy lid and looked inside. "Nothing but old ashes," he announced.

The dining room was empty except for a chair with a broken leg. They went into a hall flanking the living room, which was equally bare. A board had fallen from the picture window in front, admitting a broad shaft of sunlight. The fireplace was boarded up, and dust covered everything.

"Nothing in there," Joe said, after peering in from the hall. "Let's go upstairs."

The bedrooms on the second floor contained no furniture, either, and the boys drew a blank on possible clues. They proceeded to the attic, a low-ceilinged room up against the roof. Eight-by-fours formed two catwalks across the beams on opposite ends, which slanted down so sharply from the peak of the roof that the boys had to move part of the way on their hands and knees.

Frank took one catwalk and Joe the other. The ceiling was stained in many places by rain leaking through holes in the roof. A bird fled from its nest on one windowsill as Joe approached. They saw nothing except pieces of tar paper strewn about.

"Nothing here but the pigeons," Frank said, coughing from the dust. "They can have it. I'm getting out!"

"I'll race you to the door," Joe said with a grin.

They crawled along the catwalks to the attic door, emerged, and stretched their cramped muscles. Then they descended the stairs to the ground floor.

In the hallway, Joe expressed his disappointment. "We bombed again! Took that long trip over here for nothing!"

Frank had been staring at the floor. "Wait a minute!" he exclaimed suddenly. "Look here!"

He pointed to marks in the dust at the front door. "Here's a footprint. A lot of footprints!"

Joe was galvanized by the sight. "You're right! Let's see where they go."

The Hardys followed the trail through the hall into the living room and up to the fireplace. The prints became indistinct there in front of the boards covering the opening, as if someone had moved about in that particular area of the room.

"Somebody's been here!" Frank declared. "And there's a trail leading back to the front door!"

Joe dropped onto one knee and inspected the marks more closely. "There are *four* sets of prints coming in, but only *three* going out!" he declared.

Frank nodded grimly. "Something peculiar's been going on here. We'll have to—"

Wham! Something zipped across the room and slammed into one of the boards covering the fireplace. Looking up, the boys saw an arrow quivering in the wood just above their heads!

17

The Captive

Whirling around, the Hardys spotted a shadow flitting past outside the picture window.

"Let's get him!" Joe shouted.

They ran to the window and peered through the opening where the board had fallen down. On the ground outside lay the bow Frank had discovered in the cellar. They saw a tall man wearing a black beard and dark glasses running toward the beach!

"That's our suspect!" Joe cried. "The guy who rented the chopper from Juniper Field!"

Without another word, the Hardys hurled themselves against the remaining boards in the window, which gave way and clattered to the ground. Frank and Joe vaulted through the opening, landed in the sand, and ran after him.

They rapidly closed the gap between themselves

and the fugitive, who was running toward an outboard motorboat pulled up on the beach. Frank leaped through the air and hit the man with a flying tackle just before he reached the water's edge. They went down in a heap and rolled over and over in the sand, struggling furiously.

Frank was about to pin his antagonist as in a wrestling match, when suddenly the man reached into his pocket, pulled out a blackjack, and struck the boy on the side of his head. Dizzily, Frank fell into the sand.

Joe had rushed up and grappled with the fugitive, but he too suffered a blow from the blackjack that broke his grip. In a flash, the man dashed away.

Momentarily stunned, the Hardys pulled themselves up on their hands and knees, shaking their heads to clear the cobwebs. They heard the putt-putt of the motorboat racing away from the island. Quickly they rose and dashed to the beach, but now the boat was safely out of their reach.

"No use trying to catch him," Joe said in disgust. "He could be in Baltimore by the time we get our boat. Say, are you okay, Frank?"

"Just a bruise," his brother replied, feeling a tender spot where the blackjack had struck. "I'll live. How about you?"

"Same. He only hit me a glancing blow. Anyhow, we know he followed us into the cellar and took the bow and arrow. When he fired the arrow from the window, he was trying to frighten us away from the house—"

"Which means something's in there he doesn't want us to see!" Frank inferred excitedly. "Maybe Hammerley's weather vane's hidden in the place. We'll have to find out. Come on!"

The boys climbed back into the house through the picture window and retraced their steps to the fireplace. Just then they heard a low groan from behind the boards covering the opening!

"Someone's in there!" Frank cried out. He attacked one of the boards, wrenching it loose. Joe took another. Within seconds they had the fireplace cleared.

A man lay in a crumpled heap inside!

The Hardys lifted him into the living room and peered curiously at his face.

"He looks familiar," Frank muttered, trying to recognize the man through the stubble of his beard. He pulled the photograph of Clifford Hunter out of his pocket and studied it, comparing it with the man in front of them.

"That's him!" he gasped. "Joe, we've found the Pentagon spy!"

"He's been drugged," Joe said. "I'll see if I can bring him around." He took a small vial of smelling salts from his pocket detective kit and held it under Hunter's nose. The stricken man began to move convulsively. Gradually, however, his heavy breathing subsided to its normal rate. He opened his eyes and focused them on the Hardys. "Who are you?" he asked weakly.

"We'll tell you later," Frank promised. "First you need some fresh air."

He and Joe carried the man through the front door and set him down in the sand, leaning him against a rock. A breeze blowing off Chesapeake Bay cleared the captive's head. Then the boys introduced themselves.

"We've been looking for you," Frank informed him.

Hunter was puzzled. "Why? I don't even know you."

"The Pentagon wants us to get back the navy plan you stole," Joe explained.

"I didn't steal it," Hunter protested. "I took the document, but I didn't steal it."

"What do you mean?" Joe queried.

"Joe Wickerson told me to take it. Later I realized that he had slipped me a mind-altering drug—"

"Wickerson!" Frank exploded. "You mean to say your boss in the navy is the real Pentagon spy?"

Hunter nodded. "I'll explain. But first tell me what you know. It'll make it easier." He was very weak, and speaking was an effort for him.

Quickly the Hardys told about their visit to the

Pentagon and their interview with Joseph Wickerson. They added their suspicion of Archie Olson, who had almost run them over in the parking lot.

"Olson had nothing to do with the theft," Hunter said. "But he's a terrible driver."

The boys grinned. "He sure is," Frank said.

Hunter took a deep breath. "Wickerson didn't catch me in the files of the Cosmo Rocket. I caught him. I had clearance, and he didn't. That made me suspicious of him, and he knew it.

"Shortly afterward, I saw him pouring a white powder into my coffee. He said it was sugar, but since then I've learned that it wasn't. I'm not a spy, but I took the MASUB plan because Wickerson had me in his power!"

"He told you to remove the plan from the files?" Frank asked.

"Yes. He gave me instructions to take it to Chesapeake Crossing, where I kept my sailboat. He knew about that because he's been aboard on some of my cruises."

Hunter paused a few moments to rest, then went on: "Joe laid a trap for me. I got only a few miles out into the bay when a powerboat cut across my bow and made me heave to. Three men with guns came aboard the *Bay Queen*. Apparently Wickerson had told them where I would be."

"Did you recognize the men?" Joe inquired.

"No, I never saw them before. One was a short,

wizened fellow who dressed like a farmhand."

"Ed Bryle!" Joe exclaimed. "The guy Hammerley fired!"

"Who's Hammerley?" Hunter asked, puzzled.

"A farmer from Pennsylvania. Ed Bryle went to work at Chelski's Marina afterward and blew our boat up with a time bomb. Can you tell us more about the other two men who held you up?"

Hunter tapped his thumb against his chin. "Well, one of them was called Crow by the other two."

Frank gasped. "That must be Crow Morven, the foreman at Hammerley's farm who also tried to get us out of the way!"

"Your life must have been in great danger," Hunter said worriedly.

"That's part of detective work," Frank said. "Can you tell us anything about the third man?"

"He was tall, had a black beard, and wore dark glasses."

"That's the guy who just tried to hit us with an arrow!" Joe declared. "I wish you could identify him by name."

Hunter shook his head. "Sorry, but I can't help you with that. I'd recognize his voice; and the only other thing I noticed was that his beard looked, well, sort of plastic."

"It must be phony," Joe commented. "Part of his disguise. The dark glasses are, too."

"What did the men do after they boarded your sailboat?" Frank asked.

"Blackbeard took the MASUB blueprint from me. Then he ordered the others to lock me in the cabin. I could hear them talk about their plans up on deck."

"Good! What did they say?" Frank urged.

"I discovered Wickerson is a spy scheming to sell the MASUB document to a foreign power. They laughed about the way he had used his mind-altering drug on me and made me steal the plan. I was scheduled to be the fall guy," Hunter added bitterly.

"Did you scratch the words 'Barren Island' into the bench of your sailboat?" Frank asked.

Hunter nodded. "My captors mentioned that they were bringing me here, where they intended to hold me and make me tell them everything I knew about the navy's nuclear submarine program. If I wouldn't cooperate they said they would sink me into the bay."

The exhausted scientist fell silent for a moment, and the Hardys mulled over his story. Finally Joe asked whether Hunter had heard the men say anything else.

"Yes, strangely enough they mentioned weather vanes!"

18

The Horse Thieves

Frank jumped up excitedly. "So there's a connection between our two cases after all!" he exclaimed.

"What do you mean?" Hunter asked, baffled.

Frank told him about their investigation of the stolen antiques. "What exactly did your captors say about weather vanes?" he inquired.

"That they had a lucrative business going with them. They had a code system based on hex signs," Hunter explained. "The weather vanes they picked out were identified by the hex sign on the building from which each one was to be lifted. I also heard the men mentioning a weather vane called the *Galloping Rider* and that it was going to the Korbo auction."

Frank nodded. "We saw it there. But we thought the fence was in Chesapeake Crossing."

"It is," Hunter replied. "But they routed the antiques through different channels. For instance, they said that the *Flashing Arrow* was not sent directly to the fence, either, because those boys from Bayport had poked their noses into the business."

Hunter shifted weakly in the sand. "That's all I can tell you. I heard nothing more. Do you have any idea where my sailboat is?"

Frank told him that the boys had found it and returned it to Chelski's Marina.

"Oh, I'm glad," Hunter said. "She's a fine boat. I'd hate to lose her."

"What happened when your captors brought you to Barren Island?" Joe queried.

"They gave me another dose of the drug, but this time it was weaker, and when they tried to pump me about navy secrets I was able to remain quiet. So they boarded me up in the fireplace. Told me I'd have plenty of time to think things over in solitary. Who knows, they might have let me die if you boys hadn't come along!"

Joe stood up. "You know, the man in the black glasses who shot an arrow at us before he took off in his motorboat—maybe he went to round up his buddies. We'd better get out of here. Will you be able to walk down to the beach, Mr. Hunter?"

"I think so." Hunter stood up but teetered dizzily. He leaned on the boys and they hurried to their powerboat as fast as they could. Minutes later they skimmed across Chesapeake Bay.

Night was falling when they returned to the marina. Herb Chelski had gone home, and the watchman who took the boat did not know Clifford Hunter. The boys were relieved, because they felt it would be best if Hunter had a chance to rest in their cabin before the FBI was notified.

When they arrived at the motel and walked into their room, Mr. Hardy was sitting in an easy chair. He stared at the trio in utter surprise.

"You found Clifford Hunter!" he called out and jumped up in excitement.

"Yes, Dad," Frank replied. "Mr. Hunter, this is our father. He was asked by the government to head the search for you."

Hunter smiled wearily and sank into a chair. He could hardly speak. While Joe went out to get some food for him, Frank quickly told his father what had happened.

"This matches with what I found out," Mr. Hardy said. "I had become suspicious of Wickerson because he seemed to hamper my investigation with false clues. But I needed to find Mr. Hunter to prove that Wickerson was the real Pentagon spy!"

He turned to the scientist. "I'm sorry you had to go through all this. I'll phone Washington right away and have your boss arrested."

Mr. Hardy made the call, and after he hung up, he smiled. "Joseph Wickerson was taken into custody an hour ago," he reported. "He was caught stealing a document from the Cosmo Rocket file."

Joe returned with a plate of food and hot coffee, and the scientist ate hungrily while the boys told their father about the weather vane connection.

"I'd like to call Mr. Hammerley and tell him what we learned," Frank said and went to the telephone. When he reached Hammerley, their friend was greatly alarmed.

"I saw Ed Bryle here today, and shortly afterward he and Morven rode off on two of my horses!" he sputtered. "Can you come back here and find them?"

"We'll be there in the morning, Mr. Hammerley," Frank promised. "We have an idea who the weather vane thieves are. They're tied in with a spy case our father's been investigating."

"Have you caught the gang?" the farmer asked hopefully.

"Not yet. But we will!"

The following morning, the boys drove to Pennsylvania, while Mr. Hardy and Clifford Hunter took an early flight to Washington. When the boys arrived at the Hammerley farm, their host told them what had happened.

"I found out that Morven had hidden Ed Bryle

on the farm overnight," he told the boys. "So I fired him on the spot. About an hour later they both rode off on my horses!"

"Bryle must have come here after he tried to blow us to smithereens with a time bomb on Chesapeake Bay," Frank said and reported their adventures to the farmer. When he repeated the conversation he had overheard taking place between Bryle, Morven, and the black-bearded man, Hammerley was stupefied.

"You mean Morven was plotting to steal my weather vane while I thought he was guarding it from the thieves?"

"That's right," Frank said. "And that's why he tried to get us off the case by playing mean and dangerous tricks on us."

"I wonder where he and Bryle went," Joe spoke up. "Do you have any idea, Mr. Hammerley?"

"The police asked the same thing when I phoned them about the horses. I told them I didn't know where the scoundrels had gone. I still don't know."

"Let's check the stable," Frank suggested. "We might find a clue there."

The Hardys left the house and walked past the barn. They looked up at the roof, which seemed bare now that the *Flashing Arrow* was not there any longer, turning in the wind.

The stable stood about one hundred yards from the barn in the direction of the pasture. It was made up of a series of stalls, from which horses stared through half-doors marked with their names. Two empty stalls with "Star" and "Bronco" on them showed where Morven and Bryle had obtained their mounts.

The boys entered the stable and walked along a wall hung with equestrian equipment. As expert riders who often cantered along bridle trails near Bayport, they eagerly examined saddles, boots, and horseshoes.

But the search was in vain. "I didn't expect them to leave a road map," Frank grumbled, "but after we found the paper in the chopper ..." his voice trailed off.

"I know what you mean," Joe said. "Too bad we weren't in luck this time."

After they reported their failure to Hammerley, Frank raised a question. "Why did Morven and Bryle take horses, not one of the cars? They could have made much better time in a car."

"Not if they were headed for town!" Joe exclaimed, seeing his brother's reasoning. "They went the shortest way—across the pasture and through the woods. A car couldn't get through, and they didn't want to lose time driving around the detour where the bridge is out!"

"That makes sense, young man," Hammerley agreed. "I'll call the police right away and tell them to look for those two crooks!"

He went to the phone and tried to get a connection. Then he replaced the instrument in its cradle with a despairing gesture. "The phone is dead!" he declared.

"Morven and Bryle must have cut the line," Joe guessed. "I just wish we knew where they went. They could be anywhere in town or even at one of the farms around it!"

The boys sat in glum silence trying to plan their next move. Suddenly Frank had an idea. "Mr. Hammerley, do you have a cassette player?"

"Sure I do. I record messages for the grain dealers all the time. Why do you ask?"

"I'd like to try something." Frank told Hammerley about the tape they had received at the Sunset Motel. "Mind if I play it again?" he asked.

"Of course not. Follow me."

When Hammerley heard the weird voice, he was puzzled. "Who in the world would talk like that?" he wondered.

"Is there a speed control on this machine?" Frank asked.

Hammerley showed him where it was, and the young detective turned it down. He replayed the tape, adjusting the speed even further. The voice diminished from the weird squeak to a normal range, and everyone gasped.

The speaker was Gaspard Clay!

19

Caught by the Enemy!

Frank and Joe stared at one another and Hammerley stood staring, his mouth open, as the cassette spun on to the end of its message.

"Gaspard Clay!" he gulped. "How did you know his voice was on the tape?"

"I didn't," Frank replied. "It just occurred to me suddenly that whoever made the recording might have changed the frequency to disguise his voice. When Joe and I experimented with tape recordings in our lab, we did that once."

"That's right," Joe added. "Lucky you thought of that, Frank. Say, I'll bet Clay made this recording right after we talked to him at the museum. When we asked him about Chesapeake Crossing, he must have figured we were headed there. So he warned us over the phone first, then took the cassette down there to try to scare us away."

"As long as Clay is one of the weather vane gang," Frank mused, "he's probably involved with the Pentagon spy, too."

"This is all very confusing," Hammerley said. "Why don't you bring me up to date on your investigation?"

Frank explained the connection of the two cases. "Morven and Bryle also worked for Wickerson," he said. "Since they went into town, they probably have joined Clay."

The light dawned on Joe. "The stolen weather vanes might be at the museum!" he exclaimed. "We'd better get over there fast before the gang moves the stuff out!"

"May we borrow two of your horses, Mr. Hammerley?" Frank asked.

"Sure. Take Red and King. They're the best saddle mounts I own."

The Hardys raced to the stable, took down bridles and saddles of burnished leather from pegs on the wall, and hurried into the stalls. Frank took Red, while Joe saddled King. Then they led the animals out of their stalls. The horses champed at the bit and pawed the ground as the boys mounted them.

Frank patted Red on the shoulder and tugged on the bridle. "Come on," he coaxed. "Let's see what you can do!"

The horse cantered a few steps then broke into a fast gallop. Joe was right behind his brother as they neared the pasture and urged their horses forward at top speed. They took the fence in flying leaps. When they came to the boulders the boys had passed on their way to Juniper Field before, they fell into single file and rode along the narrow path through the woods. Arriving at Juniper Field, they circled the airport then slowed their horses to a canter in the town.

Night was falling when they drew rein within sight of the county historical museum. Frank maneuvered close to Joe. "The gang might hear us coming," he warned. "We'd better go the rest of the way on foot."

They dismounted and tied the horses to a tree, then they sneaked through to the edge of the woods. The museum was dark except for a light in one room.

"That's the west wing," Joe noted. "The one Clay said was closed for repairs."

"Well, something's going on in there now," Frank pointed out.

Reaching the museum grounds, they climbed a picket fence and crawled toward the building on their hands and knees. They moved along cautiously in case a member of the gang was standing guard. Judging that the coast was clear, they rose to their feet and flattened themselves against the wall on either side of the lighted window. Gingerly they peered around the frame into the room.

It was filled with weather vanes!

"There's the *Flashing Arrow!*" Joe whispered, "and the *Galloping Rider* is right next to it!"

Crow Morven and Ed Bryle were shifting the weather vanes and stacking them near the door. "We can load these up in a hurry," Bryle declared as he placed the *Flashing Arrow* at the end of one stack.

"We sure fooled the Hardys," Morven gloated with an evil grin. "They never caught on when I cut the phone line from the barn to the house. And they didn't figure out that I sneaked into the house and doped Hammerley's cocoa. Too bad I couldn't get into the kitchen and destroy the evidence. But that dratted Mrs. Smith locked the window after I unlocked it."

"Those nosy kids!" Bryle complained. "I'd feel better if my time bomb had gone off sooner and done away with them. As long as they're around, there's no telling where they'll turn up next!"

Morven nodded. "That's true. But there's nothing we can do about it now."

Having finished shifting the weather vanes over

to the door, the men returned to the center of the room where there was a table flanked by a number of chairs. They sat down. Morven tilted his chair onto its back legs and placed his feet on a corner of the table. "Wanna play a game of poker while we're waiting?" he asked.

"Why not?"

Frank nudged Joe. "We've got enough evidence to blow the whistle on them. Let's get the police before they clear out of here!"

The Hardys were about to move when Frank pulled Joe back against the wall. A beam of light flashed past them. Instinctively, they froze to avoid being seen.

"It's a headlight," Frank whispered. "A truck's coming."

The vehicle eased up to the museum through the darkness and stopped at the door of the west wing. The driver got out. He was the tall man wearing a black beard and dark glasses!

Climbing the stone steps, he knocked on the door; first three slow knocks, then two rapid ones, and finally three slow ones again.

"That must be the gang's signal," Joe thought to himself.

A chair scraped on the floor inside. Footsteps approached the door. When it opened, Morven was standing there.

"Hi, boss," he said.

The newcomer went into the museum. The Hardys returned to their post at the window and watched him sitting down. Unlacing his heavy shoes, he took them off and pushed them under the table, revealing as he did so that they were specially built with soles about three inches thick.

He drew a regular pair from beside the chair, put them on, and stood up. Now he was of medium height. He grabbed hold of his black beard on one side and stripped it off with a single motion. Then he removed his dark glasses and replaced them with steel-rimmed spectacles, which he pushed up on his forehead.

"Joshua Korbo!" Frank and Joe gasped the name as they recognized the auctioneer.

Korbo tossed his beard and dark glasses aside. "I won't need these anymore," he said. "Our weather vane caper in this county is over. I'll use a different disguise the next time. We go into action again a hundred miles from here after the heat's off."

"Good idea," Morven said. "I could use a little vacation in between."

"We'll use the same system," Korbo went on. "Each time, I'll prepare a paper with a hex sign identifying the weather vane and the place to hide it. Then we truck it on to Chesapeake Crossing."

He took a list from his pocket, went over to the weather vanes, and checked them off with a pencil.

Morven and Bryle watched him in silence. They seemed afraid of an explosion if Korbo found any of the stolen items missing.

"All here," he said with satisfaction after a moment or so. "I'll bring in my fence now so we can move our goods."

He went to the door and called out, "Bucky! Come in and have a look!"

A man got out of the truck, walked up the stairs, and entered the room. He was the desk clerk from the Sunset Motel!

Clay didn't have to sneak into the motel with the cassette, Joe now realized. All he had to do was walk in and hand it to Bucky! Some motel clerk—he's an international smuggler!

Bucky looked over the stacked weather vanes. "This is a good haul. The *Flashing Arrow* and the *Galloping Rider* will go for about twenty grand apiece. The rest are nearly as valuable. I'll be able to fence them abroad. My contacts will buy every American weather vane I can send them. And all the classified Pentagon documents from Washington!" Bucky added with a grin.

"No more documents from now on," Korbo said.

"What are you talking about?"

"Wickerson got caught and arrested last night. Not only that, the Hardys were at Barren Island and freed Clifford Hunter!"

"What!" Morven and Bryle were flabbergasted.

"If you hadn't failed with your bomb plot," Korbo said to Bryle, "we'd be in better shape. Wickerson is a real threat to us now if he talks, and so is Hunter, not to mention those nosy detectives!"

Bucky became nervous. "Let's load up as fast as we can. I have a cabin on the beach at Chesapeake Crossing where we can store the goods safely until we see the midnight signal out on the bay. Then I'll deliver them by powerboat."

Korbo turned to Morven and Bryle. "Okay, start moving the stuff out to the truck."

Frank and Joe put their heads together underneath the window. "You go for the police," Frank said in a low tone to his brother. "I'll watch the crooks."

"Oh no!" boomed a voice behind them. "You're both going, ahem, inside!"

20

The Flashing Arrow *Clue*

Whirling around, the Hardys were confronted by Gaspard Clay and two other men brandishing ax handles at them.

"Up the steps!" Clay commanded. "And no tricks or we'll use these on you!"

Frank and Joe, seeing they had no alternative, entered the west wing of the museum, closely followed by their captors.

"The Hardys!" Korbo exploded. "Where'd you find them?"

Clay explained how he had caught the boys listening outside the window.

"Then they must have heard everything we said!" Korbo grated.

"Doesn't matter, boss," Morven rasped. "Now we can get rid of them for good."

Bryle scowled at the boys. "The time bomb I planted on your powerboat should'a done you guys in a couple of days ago!"

"You made the mechanism too loud," Frank told him. "We heard it when we cut the engine."

"Well, you only postponed your fate," Clay smirked. "I tried to warn you off the weather vane case and told you the hex was on you, but you wouldn't take the hint. Now you'll pay for it!" He turned to Morven. "Tie 'em up. We'll drop them into the Chesapeake Bay!"

Morven produced a rope and shoved the boys against the far wall next to the door to the main building. He tied their ankles and bound their hands behind their backs.

"Can't we at least sit down?" Joe spoke up. "It's not our intention to make you comfortable," Korbo replied sarcastically. "Not only are you going to stand up, you're going to shut up!" He turned to Morven. "Gag 'em, Crow!"

Morven tied handkerchiefs across the boys' mouths. Then he drew a four-pronged grappling iron from under a table. "This is what we used the night we snatched the *Flashing Arrow*," he said with an evil grin. "It'll sink you in the bay when we get there!" He looped the rope with which he had tied their ankles around the prongs of the grappling hook so it served as an anchor holding them in place.

"Now we'd better start loading the truck," he suggested. "We don't want to waste any more—"

A police siren in the distance interrupted Morven's sentence.

"The cops!" Korbo exploded as the sound grew louder. "They're coming this way. Everybody duck!" He ran to the door and locked it, then snapped off the light, plunging the room into darkness. Seconds later several squad cars roared up and surrounded the museum.

"You cannot escape!" Mr. Hardy announced through a bullhorn. "Throw down your weapons and come out with your hands up!"

There was a moment of stunned silence, then Korbo recovered his wits. "We have Frank and Joe Hardy in here, and we'll blow their heads off unless you let us go to our truck and get out of here!"

"You want a murder rap against you in addition to all the other charges?" Mr. Hardy demanded.

"I want to get out of here and I have enough bullets for all of you!" Korbo screamed in rage.

"What if your bluff doesn't work?" Morven hissed. "Maybe we should try to escape through the east wing!"

"Shut up!" Korbo grated. "Don't you realize they've surrounded the whole place?"

Frank tugged on his bonds in frustration. If only he could tell his father that the gang was unarmed! As he moved, he felt something scraping his back. "Feels like a light switch," he thought. He remembered a signal he had once worked out with his father when they were staking out a hut in the woods. "The coast is clear" was transmitted by turning his flashlight on, off, and on again in equal intervals. His heart pounded as he manipulated the switch behind him. Would it work?

Suddenly the room was bathed in light. Before the gang could figure out what had happened, Frank turned the light off, then on again. Mr. Hardy instantly recognized the message, and moments later the police broke through the door. "Hands over your heads!" they commanded. Stunned and dazed, the criminals obeyed.

Mr. Hardy and John Hammerley had followed the officers, and the Bayport sleuth untied his sons.

"After dropping Clifford Hunter off in Washington, I flew out to Lancaster and called Mr. Hammerley," their father explained while he took off their gags. "He told me you had ridden into town and he asked me to meet him at police headquarters. Then we decided to check on the museum."

"Good thing you did," Frank said with a sigh of relief. "We were to be dropped into the bay after the crooks got away."

The police chief was amazed when he recognized the members of the gang. "Joshua Korbo and Gaspard Clay were two of the most respected men in the county!" he exclaimed.

"That's how they got away with it," Joe pointed out. "Nobody suspected them, including us."

An idea struck Frank. "Clay," he addressed the curator, "I bet you followed us that day we found you crabbing."

Clay looked sullen. "Why should I tell you anything?"

"Because if you cooperate, things will go easier for you," Mr. Hardy said. "However, I want you to understand that you don't have to answer without consulting with your attorney first."

Clay realized he was defeated. With a helpless shrug, he looked at Frank. "Yes, I followed you. I saw your powerboat explode and realized you swam ashore. So I stopped to crab, ahem, where I thought you'd hear me and come down for a look. If you had ridden back with me to the marina, I might have disposed of you on the way. Unfortunately, you refused."

"Not so unfortunate for Clifford Hunter," Frank said pointedly.

Clay glared at the boys. "You knew about Chesapeake Crossing from the paper Bryle dropped in the helicopter. But how did you know enough to come to the museum tonight?"

"Easy," Joe replied. "You told us."

"What do you mean?"

Joe described how Frank had discovered that the squeaky voice on the cassette was Clay's. "So," he added, "we thought something must be up at the museum."

Korbo seethed. "You guys know everything, don't you!"

"We know that you had a perfect cover," Frank replied. "As an auctioneer, you could travel around the county and list the weather vanes. Then you sent your hoods to steal the best ones."

"Also," Joe added, "your auction gave you a good place to hide the antiques. They looked like items you intended to sell. By the way, how did you get involved with Bucky?"

"We were in the rackets together," Korbo admitted. "Then he set up a fence in Chesapeake Crossing. One day he told me he could handle the coming thing in stolen goods—valuable weather vanes. So I went into heisting weather vanes for him."

"And since Clay was a member of your gang," Joe spoke up, "you could use the museum as a warehouse."

"Right. And everything was terrific," Korbo snarled, "until you came snooping around. I had to switch to the helicopter because you were in the barn loft and Morven couldn't get at the *Flashing*

Arrow that night. I piloted the chopper and Bryle snatched the weather vane with his grappling hook right from under your noses!"

Bryle guffawed. "I can still see you two climbing over the roof. But we got there first. We didn't even need Crow's signal."

The light dawned on Frank. "So that's what you were doing," he accused Morven, "when we jumped you in the barn."

Morven scowled. "I thought you would be asleep. I was supposed to give the exact location of the place with a flashlight. When you caught me, I told you I was looking for my jacket."

"Anyhow, we got away with the *Flashing Arrow*," Korbo continued, "and landed at Juniper Field. My plan was for Bryle to drive it to Chesapeake Crossing, but he couldn't find the paper with the hex sign. I realized he must have lost it in the chopper while operating the winch. So I told him to take the weather vane to the museum instead."

"Then you went back to the auction where we saw you the next day, packing up," Joe continued.

Korbo nodded. "I put on my disguise when you left and drove to Chesapeake Crossing to confer with Bucky."

"We know," Frank said. "We saw you in that big black car and chased you."

Joe changed the subject. "Why did Wickerson get into the spy business?"

"He needed money," Korbo replied. "He lost a lot at the racetrack, so he sold his valuables. He had a good collection of antiques, and I auctioned them off for him. Eventually they were all gone, but he was still hard up.

"One day he told me he had access to classified Pentagon documents relating to navy research and asked me if I could sell them. Naturally I checked with Bucky. He has a lot of foreign contacts. Bucky said yes, and Wickerson forced Hunter into taking the MASUB plan from the Pentagon files."

"Where is the document now?" Frank asked.

Bucky, who was frightened to the point of panic when Korbo revealed his past, pointed a finger at the auctioneer. "He has it!"

"Hand it over, Korbo!" Mr. Hardy ordered.

"I don't have it. You can search me if you like."

The police went through his pockets, but they were empty, and a search of the other gang members failed to produce the Pentagon plan.

"Maybe he hid it somewhere in the museum," Frank suggested.

The officers searched the building thoroughly without finding the blueprint, however, and further questioning of Korbo netted no answer. Suddenly Joe had an idea.

"Wait a minute!" He lifted the *Flashing Arrow* and placed it on the table. Then he unscrewed the arrowhead and pulled it off. He inserted his finger into the hollow tube and maneuvered it upward until the end of a paper began to show. Smiling, he withdrew it with his thumb and forefinger. He unrolled it and held it up. It was the MASUB blueprint!

"How did you know?" Frank asked his brother.

"I remember unscrewing the hollow arrowhead when we were on the barn roof, and it hit me that a document could be rolled up and hidden in there!"

"Excellent deduction!" Mr. Hardy praised his son. "You've done the U.S. Navy a great service!"

The police took the gang to headquarters, and Mr. Hardy and John Hammerley accompanied them. Frank and Joe, meanwhile, went back to their horses.

"Do you think we'll ever get another good case to work on?" Frank asked his brother on the way.

"I sure hope so!" Joe replied. "Life would be dull without mysteries."

Frank nodded. He had no idea that soon they'd be called upon to solve *The Apeman's Secret*.

When they climbed onto their horses, Joe suddenly grinned. "One thing I could do without, though."

"What's that?"

"The hex!"

The Hardy Boys®
Ghost Stories

by Franklin W. Dixon

Six chilling mysteries

The Hardy Boys are experts at solving mysteries that have the police baffled. But the adversaries they tackle now are no mere mortals. Ghostly spirits from another world haunt Frank and Joe with blood-freezing fear . . .

The ghastly scarecrow that stalks the night . . . A haunted castle, cursed by witches . . . The phantom ship that sails to doom . . .

Dare you face them?

Armada

SUPERSLEUTHS

by FRANKLIN W. DIXON and CAROLYN KEENE

A feast of reading for all mystery fans!

At last, the Hardy Boys and Nancy Drew have joined forces to become the world's most brilliant detective team!

Together, the daredevil sleuths investigate seven spine-chilling mysteries: a deadly roller-coaster that hurtles to disaster, a sinister bell that tolls in a city of skeletons, a haunted opera house with a sinister curse — and many more terrifying situations.

Nancy Drew and the Hardy Boys — *dynamite!*

Armada

BLACK HARVEST

by Ann Cheetham

A chilling story of terror and suspense…

The west coast of Ireland seems a perfect place for a family holiday — until everything begins to go horribly wrong…

Colin becomes aware of a ghastly stench from the land — a smell of death and decay… Prill is haunted by a fearsome skeleton-woman, who crawls through her dreams in hideous tormnt… Baby Alison falls sick with a sinister illness…

And their cousin Oliver? In those stiflingly hot summer days, as some nameless evil from the past closes in on them, Oliver remains unnaturally, unnervingly calm…

Armada

The Beggar's Curse

by Ann Cheetham

Is there no escape from the village of evil?

When Colin, Oliver and Prill arrive in Stang they realize at once that something is wrong with the village. Up on the surrounding hills spring is blossoming, but in this dark little valley no flowers bloom and birds never sing.

Prill knows there is something sinister about the age-old rituals of the village play. Colin knows the gruesome incidents that keep happening are no accidents. But Oliver alone knows the awful secret of Stang and sees the ancient evil rising from the black waters of Blake's Pit. He feels the terrible power of the beggarman's curse . . .

The Beggar's Curse is a chilling sequel to *Black Harvest*, which was chosen in a special selection by British children as one of their favourite books in 1984. One reader said of it: "It was like opening a fridge door . . ."

Armada

Armadas are chosen first by children all over the world. They're pocket-sized and pocket money-sized — and they make terrific presents for friends. They're colourful and exciting and there are hundreds of titles to choose from — baffling mysteries, daring adventures, spine-chilling horror stories, rib-tickling joke books, thrilling stories about schools and ponies — and lots more. Armada has something for everyone.